We must hold high the banner of the great unity of the Chinese nation and promote all ethnic groups to embrace each other tightly like pomegranate seeds in the big family of the Chinese nation.

— Excerpt from Comrade Xi Jinping's speech at the Central Work Conference on Ethnic Affairs held on August 27-28, 2021

Left / Jorma Grassland in early summer

Upper right / Kazakh herdsmen who are good at singing and dancing

Lower right / Hospitable Mongolian herders presenting a pure white hada to guests from afar

In Baomuba,

Winter is as warm as spring, and summer is as cool as autumn.

A lonely man comes here, he would have more children;

A poor man comes here, he would become prosperous.

...

-Mongolian heroic epic *Dzhangar*

Hoboksar, where the Mongolian heroic epic *Dzhangar* originated,

With the first Dzhangar Palace in the world,

Just like Baomuba,

Makes the people of all ethnic groups living there happy and healthy.

Pomegranate Flowers Bloom

STORIES OF ETHNIC UNITY IN XINJIANG

New Classic Press

2024

NEW CLASSIC PRESS

Published by New Classic Press (UK) ★

5th Floor, 99 Mansell Street, London, E1 8AX, UK,

Great Britain ★ Established in the year 2008 ★

Seeking business opportunities worldwide

Pomegranate Flowers Bloom: Stories of Ethnic Unity in Xinjiang

Written by He Jianming

Translated from the Chinese by Yang Jie, Bian Xiyuan, Chen Kaixian and Fu Ya.

First published in Liaoning People's Publishing House Co. Ltd. in 2023

This English Edition Published in the United Kingdom of Great Britain and

Northern Ireland

by New Classic Press Limited in 2024

ISBN 978-1-917143-09-7

First printed in the United Kingdom of Great Britain and Northern Ireland

10 9 8 7 6 5 4 3 2 1

DESIGNED BY SRA BERKS

The publisher's policy is to use paper manufactured from sustainable forests.

As for Xinjiang, a beautiful and mysterious place, if you only imagine it in your mind, but you have never been there at all, or just took a cursory journey through it, you may never truly understand or know its beauty, its people, and what happened there ...

I have been there. Having visited the streets, communities, and homes of ordinary people in a lot of villages as well as in many cities, I could say that I began to understand it. Its beauty is more than we can see! The true beauty of Xinjiang lies in our hearts, the sincere hearts embracing each other like pomegranate seeds!

Inscription

In a place far away,
pomegranate flowers are in full bloom ...

There is a kind of fruit flower called the pomegranate flower. When in full bloom, it is like a flaming fire, which is extremely gorgeous. Its fruits are like stars in the sky, shining like glass ... so intoxicating!

When the pomegranates are planted in a place, the beautiful and auspicious wings will surround the land tightly in their happy and warm embrace ...

Yes, then we have a strong yearning for that place —

When you arrive there, you may want to sing, expressing your pride and love thoroughly and completely ...

You may wish to dance, releasing the sorrow and delight in the beating melody heartily...

You may wish to open your arms and shout aloud:

I am eager to hug you and kiss you deeply ...

This place is Xinjiang and here is Tacheng City.

Now, I came to Tacheng, Xinjiang. So I want to sing, dance, stretch my arms, raise the wings of thoughts and emotions ... even stay there eternally, and love it forever.

There is no doubt that you are the incarnation of beauty. The grassland extends thousands of miles away, linking the sky and earth, where horses, cattle, and sheep can roam uninhibitedly;

You are a symbol of strength. The wind and snow in the air are the carving knives waved by Heaven to reshape the earth, each of whose impassioned roaring is a note of strength;

You are the psychical shrine of seeing and hearing. The distinctive red houses and thousands of accordions that can play beautiful melodies decorate the whole urban and rural areas into a beautiful paradise that time seems to stop once in a while.

The frequent wars in the old days were incited by your beauty, the one that can not be replaced, and your important geographical position, where every invader wanted to have a finger in the pie ...

But you were born as a part of the Chinese territory, no matter how fierce the wars had been, your belonging and blood ties would never be changed.

You are what you are, solid, upright, and firm like a tower. The shape and the spirit of the tower have forged out a city, which is called "Tacheng"!

Yes, Tacheng, your uniqueness makes you a Northwest pearl and a treasure land of the motherland.

Tacheng's uniqueness constitutes its characteristics with a kind of physical and spatial legendary trait that Tacheng has its wonderful connections with each orientation, which is full of philosophical, natural, and humanistic meanings. It demonstrates the connections between history and reality, frontier and mainland, the sky and earth... It also shows the organic connections between love, beauty, and happiness.

Therefore, converging and merging here are compatriots from nearly 30 ethnic groups of Han, Kazakh, Hui, Uyghur, Mongolian, Dongxiang, Daur, Russian, Xibo, Kirghiz, Tatar, Uzbek, Manchu, Zhuang, Tibet, Miao, Buyi, Korean, Dong, Yao, Bai, Tujia, Tu, Qiang, Salar, Evenki, and Yugu.

Due to the connections, the rivers and mountains on the earth extend reasonably and freely in the ups and downs, while man and nature coexist in prosperity, love and gratitude remain unshakable and become even firmer as time goes by under the burning of thoughts and emotions, with souls and actions resonating in strength and warmth ...

This is Tacheng where there is not only the common beauty of Xinjiang but also the elegance and harmony never found elsewhere.

What you can see most in Tacheng are smiling faces, whether in the countryside or the city, people are enthusiastic and warm-hearted. No matter where you come from or which nationality you are, a kind smile can dispel all your wariness and estrangement. Laughing makes people more beautiful and handsome, more energetic and younger.

Moreover, Tacheng people have strong self-confidence. They believe that only by following the great Communist Party of China and trusting in the mother country wholeheartedly will people from the outside world show more respect and love to their homeland. Therefore, in Tacheng, if someone asks, "What's your nationality?" Tacheng people will confidently say, "Here, we all belong to 'Tacheng Ethnic People'!"

"Tacheng Ethnic People?" Is there a name like this among fifty-six ethnic groups?

No, there isn't.

But Tacheng people would still tell you firmly and confidently: There are no ethnic minorities in Tacheng, only the "Tacheng Ethnic People", because we have always been close to each other regardless of people's nationalities, so over time, Tacheng people have merged into a united "ethnic group", which is the intimate "Tacheng Ethnic People"!

Ha! "Tacheng Ethnic People", How confident you are! It's so meaningful.

My story will also begin with making acquaintance of the "Tacheng Ethnic People", and thereby I understand why the pomegranate flowers here are in such full bloom and why the pomegranate seeds are always held so tightly ...

The first impression to all those who have been to Tacheng may be the red houses here. The red color of these red houses is different from that of the red walls of the Forbidden City in Beijing, which is more gorgeous and blazing. It is a kind of burning red color, which makes people feel an upsurge of emotion, like certain desire and impulse of youth, particularly tempting.

佳 超 市

The snow of Mt. Tianshan connects the earth and the sky.

After spring comes, it melts into trickles,

Flowing over the vast land of Xinjiang,

Thus, plants begin to sprout and turn green;

Thus, the grapes in Turpan are ripe, the apples in Aksu get sweet, and the dates in Hotan turn red;

Thus, the girls on the pasture become much more beautiful, and the young men more handsome and doughty;

Thus, thousands of miles of border areas and frontier become more prosperous and impregnable.

the words to me, "Thank you for calling on me from Beijing," she meant.

"What does 'Manreyamu' mean in Uygur?" I asked her.

"Mary," she pronounced the word very clearly.

"Virgin Mary?!" I couldn't help but exclaim in surprise, then held her hands again.

A sudden big smile brightened her wrinkled face. At that moment, on the cupboard right behind her, I noticed a photo — a pretty, dignified, and graceful Uygur female — taken in the old mother's youth time. In the photo, she was so charming that even movie stars would be eclipsed by her admirable beauty.

"My teacher Seypidin was the vice Chairman of the First People's Government of Xinjiang. When he was at school, he drummed it into our mind that 'Xinjiang was, is, and will be an integral part of China's territory!' It is his words that have motivated me to dedicate myself to this border city in my whole life ..." Raising her hands, she enthused in Uygur, then patted her son on his arm, urging him to translate for me.

What a lovely old mother! I could see an irrepressible gleam of excitement burning in her eyes as if she would like to pour all her "secrets" out to me, a visitor from Beijing. Thanks to this occasion, I had a chance to personally touch the most gorgeous blossom in the garden of ethnic unity in Xinjiang.

Her story began at the age of three when she sat in the rocking chair on the back of the horse placed by her father ...

In that year, her parents drove a donkey cart with the family and fled from the south to north.

"I was three years old and my sister was only one year old. We just marched to the north, and further ...parents would take us to wherever no one settled. Then we arrived and settled in Dabancheng, a picturesque northern town with seven springs and seven rivers," she said.

"It was an otherworldly place, but when fighting broke out among the warlords at that time, the town was inevitably involved from time to time. In addition, father has just started his own business. Consequently, we moved farther north and arrived in Tacheng at the end of the 1930s.

Then father was busy expanding his business, while mother, a female of ingenuity, made some daily necessities for the family and for sale. At that time, we just lived an austere life like that. A common Uygur family with three sons and three daughters, how could we have wild wishes?" She spoke slowly.

One day, little Manreyamu followed her father to the street. The pretty girl felt nervous and was at a loss.

"Who are the parents of this little girl?"

A Han gentleman met little Manreyamu and became fond of her. Then he asked her, "Would you like to go to school?" Little Manreyamu shook her head silently. She didn't know what to say but her eyes said everything. Although she had a strong thirst for school, the poverty of her family would hold her back. Her parents would not agree.

"I will see your parents ..." Then the man shouted out loud in the street.

"I am her father." For the convenience of doing business, her father could speak simple Mandarin.

"You should take her to school for education. I can see that she is a smart girl," the man suggested.

"Schooling is for the rich but not for us. We are even worried about our next dinner," her father said in disappointment.

"If it is free of charge, would you allow her to go to school?" the man continued, pressing her father to give an answer.

Taken aback, her father stared at the man and then shook his head with a long sigh, "We can never expect that a free crusty pancake would fall down from the sky, even it is sunny and fine ..."

"Now a free crusty pancake did fall on your daughter's head. It all depends on you to catch it!" the man laughed and said.

"May I ask who you are, sir?" the father asked urgently.

"I am the headmaster of a school here and I can let your daughter study in the school for free." The man turned out to be Liu Haiyan, a well-known headmaster of the only school in Tacheng.

"Oh, Mr. Liu! Pardon me." the father took little Manreyamu to make several bows to the headmaster.

That's how little Manreyamu became one of the three children who could study for free in that school.

Clever and quick-witted, she performed so excellently in study that both the teachers and classmates liked her very much. One year, she won a scholarship worth 3 yuan. When she told her mother the good news, her mother praised her with great joy, "That's great! You are our future!"

These words had left an enormous impact on Manreyamu. From then on, she began to realize how important it was to offer support and love to family members and other people. As what Mr. Liu always taught her, "How to beautify the world? It requires deep love from the heart of each person. Love makes the world gorgeous ..."

Thenceforth, "love" is engraved in her belief, filling her heart completely.

But gradually, she realized that in the days of endless turmoil and war, love given by an individual person was negligible if the border area were still suffered from tribulation. Only when more people understood the meaning of love for the motherland, could the love in their hearts shine brightly, inspiring people to make the country better.

"One can never understand history and reality without knowledge, and accordingly he would fail to love his country. If one shows no love for his country, how would he cherish his family and loved ones?"

She came to contemplate and understand that those who cherished selfless love were no one but sensible and historically knowledgeable people. Only those with knowledge and skills could be able to bring the border area with peace, stable homeland, progressive society and happy life for the people here.

That's why she made up her mind to dedicate herself to educating people.

At first, she taught in a primary school. Although the classrooms were shabby, she highly valued her work. She regarded every lecture and every chance of educating children as a divine mission, considering her words as delivery of love, for she could see an uncontaminated world from children's eyes of innocence and sheer curiosity.

"It would be sinful to cultivate the tender buds without pure and nourishing water ...Since I stood at the podium for the first time, I have thought and always done in this way."

The 97-year-old mother required her son to translate her above words in particular to me completely.She wasn't satisfied enough until I took them down in my notebook and correctly checked with her.This made me more respectful to her.

She has learned Uyghur and Tatar languages in school, but didn't have the chance to study Mandarin well. For this reason, she thought that she should take the responsibility to offer unconditional love to more children in the non-Mandarin schools, just as what Mr.Liu, the benevolent man offering her the opportunity to school, had done.

After the founding of the People's Republic of China in 1949, numerous people who had suffered from hunger and homelessness have lived a steady and happy life, while all the children have access to school. Seeing that, she smiled more brightly.

When her teacher Seypidin became leader of the People's Government of Xinjiang, she was more confident that her work could play an integral role.

Since entire Xinjiang, including her beautiful hometown Tacheng, was on the path of development, talents were in need everywhere. As what she did was to cultivate more talents for the border area and the nation, she dedicated more energy and time in her work.

In the early days when New China was founded, experienced and educated Uygur women teachers like her were scarce in middle schools in Tacheng.

In addition, she ardently loved the career. Therefore, she became one of the most popular teachers, with students following her to ask for answers and advice even after class. In the school, she was the teacher who spent the most time at the podium every day.

"My dear, how jealous I am of these children. I wish I could be with you all the time like them, watching you, listening to you ..."

A young and handsome military officer sighed emotionally every time when he was standing before Manreyamu, and then held her tightly in his arms ardently.

He was her beloved one, an excellent legal officer of a military institution at the border, handling diplomatic and military affairs with neighbouring countries on behalf of Chinese government.

His tasks were all linked to the country. Each time he talked about the cases he met in his work, she would deepen her understanding of the meaning of "the country" and what it meant to love our own nation.

"I defend our national dignity through maintaining principles, while you brighten our country's future through education. We have both given our great love to this land ..."

Well-educated, gifted with words, and rigorous in legal reasoning, the man often evoked upsurge of emotion in her heart.

Her tenderness and beauty were also nourishing him like trickles flowing through the land ...

Their love fused together, integrated with each other, blazing and subliming to a higher level.

Finally, their love and marriage had brought them fruits of life — their children coming to this world one after another. Nurturing babies increased her burden, yet she felt happier and more satisfied.

"Dear teacher, my parents don't allowed me to go to school ...I can't see you again from tomorrow!" One day, a student called Maolida said in sadness, lowering her head with tears dripping down.

"why? Take your time and tell me in detail ..." Manreyamu started to be anxious.

"My parents said that I am old enough to ...to ..." she couldn't continue.

"What did they say?"

"They said that I should get ready to marry, instead of going to school ..." hadn't finished her words, she crouched down and began to cry bitterly.

"No! No way!" With anger and anxiety, she rushed to the student's home.

She had discussed with the girl's parents all day long. Finally, they were persuaded to allow Maolida to return to school.

But Maolida was not the only case in the class. It was a traditional custom that girls should get married as early as possible after they were old enough. Another 29 girls were facing the same problem.

Manreyamu had to persuade their parents one by one, ensuing that all the girls could continue to study in school.

Maolida is now75 years old this year and has become a professor at a famous foreign university. In her recollection of her growth, she said gratefully, "Wherever we are, we will never forget my dear teacher, Manreyamu, who has changed our destiny. We are always her students. She expressed her sincere love to us, making us feel warm all our life. Because of her, we will love our motherland and our hometown forever."

Manreyamu has dedicated herself to the cause of education for 42 years. when I asked her how many students she has taught so far, she laughed at me with her hands open, and said, "They are as many as birds flying in the sky."

Hearing that, we all burst into laughter.

She was not exaggerating. At the beginning, she was a subject teacher, then a homeroom teacher, and finally a headmaster. So many students educated by her have graduated over several decades. Aren't they as many as flocks of flying birds in the sky?

With happiness,she told me a story which she was most proud of. It was about her meeting with Comrade Xi Zhongxun and correspondence with President Xi Jinping, a unique story you would not hear elsewhere in China.

In 1950, shortly after the liberation of Xinjiang, one day, Manreyamu was having a class when a cadre from Tacheng told her, "Get your baggage quickly for a meeting in Xi'an, some leaders would like to meet you!"

A meeting? In Xi'an city? Meet with the leaders? It was such a novelty to her.

"Where is Xi'an? Why do we have to go there?"

"The Northwest Bureau of the Central Committee of the Communist Party locates there, about 3,000 kilometers away from Tacheng at linear distance or 5,000 kilometers away along the roads!"

What? 5,000 kilometers? Startled, she felt apprehensive, for she had never left Tacheng so far and Xi'an was such a faraway place for her. However, she was also particularly excited, for she was going to meet the "leaders" — officials like her respected teacher Seypidin.

But how could they get there? Since the PRC was just established, from Tacheng to Dihua (now called Urumqi), there were only dirt tracks for horses and camels, let alone the difficulties with plodding across the Gobi desert and plateaus, trudging eastward and then southward along the Hexi Corridor to Shannxi province by way of Gansu. Not to mention the difficulties and hardship along the trip, the time spent on the journey could frighten all: nearly thirty to forty days.

"Good Heavens! Which means of transportation will we take? Horse or camel?" Manreyamu asked carefully, regarding the journey as an impossible task.

"Ha ha ha! Whose horse or donkey could keep running for dozens of days? You will get there by four- wheeled motor vehicle!" The cadre told her.

That's great! Going to Xi'an by motor vehicle!

She rejoiced with wild excitement, for she finally had a chance to travel by motor vehicle the first time in her life!

At that time, only officials or technicians and engineers from mines and factories could travel by motor vehicle. Now it would be her turn to travel by motor vehicle, moreover, she would spending dozens of days in the vehicle!

Just thinking of that could make her laugh in dreams.

But she never expected she would encounter numerous difficulties on this journey ...

True! It is a motor vehicle. However, it was not that type of comfortable and safe coach or sedan car, but a truck.

Everyone was given a dinner pail and a towel to wash their face and body. No water supplied, they had to drink any water they saw along the way.

What about meals? Neither could they cook in the wild, nor could they stop to eat at each town station they passed by.

What's more, they might not pass by a town even after driving for one to two days, let alone inns or hotels. The truck served as their "temporary accommodation" …

Such were their conditions on the journey.

One day after another, they traveled eastward without knowing when they would arrive — a destination Manreyamu and other young delegates from Xinjiang were longing for …

A bumpy journey. The truck kept jolting without an end.

Carsickness! They were suffering from repeated dizziness and barfing …

They slept under the stars with wolves roaring in the distance. But in their dreams, Chairman Mao greeted them at Tian'anmen Square. They had no fear in mind but sang in high spirits all the way …

> The grassland was dried yellow in the old days,
> Only because there is no red sun.
> Uygurs were all in poverty,
> Landlords rode on their necks.
> Chairman Mao sent the people's Liberation Army,
> Uygur people were free.
> This remote land takes on a new look,
> Poor slaves broaden their big smiles.
> They play musical instruments while singing songs,
> To eulogize the Communist Party of China …

"Sounds fantastic!" "Encore!" Manreyamu sang like a lark, attracting other people.

"Yeah, yeah, Manreyamu. Sing out loud!"

At the same time, some young delegates couldn't help dancing on the truck carriage. Their enthusiasm encouraged Manreyamu to sing to her heart's content:

> How sweet the apricots are in the garden!
> How mouthwatering the barbecue is on the grill,
> A girl blinks her black eyes,
> To warm the heart of a young soldier in PLA,
> A romance since then begins ...

Travelling on one road after another, they sang one song after another. The journey to Xi'an seemed endless, they could sing forever.

Along the way, the dust "made them up" into another look. However, their love and expectations for the future, life, and motherland still remained the same ...

"The trip was so long. We sang, danced, and told jokes merrily in the daytime. When it came to night, we slept on the bumpy truck. Extremely excited and longing for the future, I immersed myself in innumerable dreams, some of which I could recall till now ..." When reminiscing about the old days, the old mother was so energetic that she was not like an elder aged 97 at all.

On the truck, she had no idea about when and where it would stop. But she remembered that every night, her dream was all about her children and the students in the school.

She could still recollect that in a dream, she went to Beijing with her children to present flowers to Chairman Mao, who told her that to see if a person have love or not, we should find if he could dedicate his whole life selflessly to the work he loved, for this kind of love would be the greatest emotion to his motherland.

" Following Chairman Mao's instructions, I have stayed in Tacheng to work hard in education sector for the rest of my life!" She was delighted to share this "secret" with me that she never told others before.

In more than a month, they arrived in Xi'an. When they got off the truck, they were even unused to walking on the ground, tottering as if treading on air. Not until they were informed that the leaders would receive them immediately could they recover and walk steadily.

It turned out that Secretary Xi Zhongxun, head of the Northwest Bureau of the Central Committee of the Communist Party, would meet the youth representatives from Xinjiang. It was the first time that Manreyamu had a meeting with a high ranking official. At the meeting, she found Secretary Xi was young and approachable, kept smiling while talking.

During the meeting, he came up to these young people and said amiably, "As the first generation of youth representatives of ethnic minorities in Xinjiang, you have great potential and embrace a bright future. Would you like to stay here? Whoever wants to stay will be sent to Beijing for training."

"Would you like to stay, Comrade Manreyamu?" the secretary asked with great expectation in his eyes.

As her heart was pounding with excitement, she recalled the words of Chairman Mao in her dream in a sudden. Who would teach those children in the school if I left Tacheng or Xinjiang? And who would take the responsibility of developing Xinjiang and guarding the border?

"Sorry, Secretary Xi, I can't stay. I have to go back to my hometown, to Tacheng, Xinjiang." She replied.

She could read the surprise from her fellows' eyes: what a bright future it is to stay and study in Beijing! Although she understood their regards, she shook her head and reaffirmed her determination to return.

"Good! It is an admirable choice to go back and dedicate your youth and enthusiasm to the hometown. Best wishes for you and hope to see you again." With a great smile, Secretary Xi extended his hand to Manreyamu.

"Thank you so much, Secretary Xi. I will bear your words in my mind for good ..." She shook hands tightly with Secretary Xi, feeling her blood boiling.

This marked the most glorious moment in her life. With this honour, she returned home and didn't leave for the rest of her life.

Over the following decades, she never wavered her determination to dedicate herself to education in her hometown even for a second, no matter what temptation she faced.

As she was excellent, some people advised her to get a more significant job in other cities, such as Beijing or Urumqi. But she always refused politely, explaining her love for her students, Tacheng and border areas. She decided to give all her love to the children so that she would never let down what Chairman Mao and Secretary Xi had expected of her.

Her intense love for the motherland, determined belief and wholehearted dedication to the work portrayed her as a respectable and awe-inspiring woman, just like a birch standing tall and erect in the desert.

Tacheng was located in the border area and was targeted by foreign separatists in an attempt to sabotage the unity of China. As a headmaster of the middle school in Tacheng, Manreyamu was repeatedly instigated to leave there, to be headmaster of a larger school. But she rejected resolutely. Even threats or intimidation failed to weaken her resolve and belief.

She told those with ulterior motives sternly many times, "I will never leave my motherland. I do believe that the land under my feet, which is more valuable than my life, will belong to our country forever. I was born on this land where I will spend my whole life. Never attempt in vain to instigate me nor separate me with my children!"

"She is so tough!" The separatists felt disappointed and returned home empty-handed.

"She is a great mother as well as an honourable teacher ..." Her colleagues and those who used to be her students gave such a comment on her.

She gave an evaluation about herself, "As a teacher in the border area where ethnic minorities live, I feel most delighted and satisfied that my students are growing up like verdant saplings in a desert, making the area more beautiful, prosperous and peaceful."

At the podium in school, she has proved what she had stated. She is truly a loving teacher who has students all over the country.

Many of her colleagues and friends left Tacheng and afterwards became officials or eminent persons, and so did her students. Only Manreyamu held fast to her work in her beloved middle school, at a little podium.

The year 1985 marked her retirement from the position as dean of No.2 Middle School of Tacheng.

Over the past decades, she has toiled and moiled and cultivated numerous talents. People thought that since her retirement, she would live in comfort for the rest of her life. However, she was unwilling to waste time doing nothing.

She has learned one thing from her lifelong education work that: apart from school, the society and family also play important roles in children's growth and development. For this reason, all-round management and caring services are needed, especially for the children who are poverty-stricken and lack parental care, requiring warm help from the society.

This belief encouraged her to launch another important initiative in her life — a public welfare activity named "Caring Mother" which lasts to this day, leaving a tremendous impact on Xinjiang and even the entire nation.

"As we provide social welfare services, we all have a mother-like heart, aiming to do everything we can to take care of every child in need and let them grow up in warmth and happiness ..."

Initially, she gathered dozens of retired teachers she knew well to her house, revealing her aspiration which she has been pondered over but has not yet materialized. When she gained unanimous support from her fellows, she stated the words mentioned above to members of the "Caring Mother" team.

Other members echoed her statement one by one, "I agree. When we were teachers, our duty was to teach students. Now as we retired, we choose to help children in need. We will devote our unconditional love and care to them ..."

"I appreciate what you said! From now on, we have to publicize our activity, making us widely known among children in need and their families. In addition, we need to understand that as vulnerable members of the society, they may be reluctant to let their difficulties known. For this reason, we must be more active to offer our hands ..." Manreyamu said.

Then they started with investigative visits to each community, making thorough analysis and verification of every family's status. In accordance with the results, they schemed to bail out those struggling families.

But how would they raise enough money?

"It is only natural we chip in for the fund." Each one of us donated a certain amount of money — some took out 10 yuan, others 20 or 30. Manreyamu contributed 1,000 yuan from her pension for the first donation.

"The first child we supported was heavily poverty-stricken. Her parents were both disabled persons who couldn't afford the fees for her school. We donated 1,500 yuan to her, allowing her back to school. She achieved very good scores in school and was finally admitted to a university.

Her success made us — the 'caring mothers' very excited with a sense of fulfillment. Accordingly, all became more active and energetic in public welfare activities later ..." The old mother smiled with glee when she recollected the feelings then three decades ago.

As retirees, if they would like to do something, apart from taking money out of their own pockets, whether their families would understand and support them was another challenge. Some "caring mothers" may particularly be confronted with family conflicts when their children need them to take care of the grandchildren.

Manreyamu told them seriously, "We do need to help other children, but it doesn't mean we should place them before our own children. Instead, we must make whatever efforts to care for them. Under such precondition, could we do our best to help children of the others. That is what I have to emphasize. If we fail to take good care of our own children, how could we love the others?"

Her words have relieved the mental burdens of those "caring mothers". Finally, it turned out that they could orderly handle the household affairs while spending spare time to help the others as well, which was perfectly done to their heart's content.

In Tacheng and also other cities in Xinjiang, quite a few girls were forced to drop out of school after or even before graduating from junior high school, because their parents insisted that girls at that age should get married rather than waste time in school. They need help from the "caring mothers".

"No, we must help them back to school!" Manreyamu made up her mind, for she quite understood that illiterate girls would have an utterly different future from the well-educated. So would the boys.

More than ten days before school opened on summer vacation were the busiest time for those "caring mothers".

Even each one of them would take responsibility for several families, require one,two or even more home visits in order to persuade their parents.

"When one of our members failed to persuade, we would call other members together to support her. We never give up until parents agreed to send their children back to school," Manreyamu said.

"There was a challenging case. Since the parents had gone to work in another city, we could only repeatedly communicate with them over the phone.Distance had made it more difficult with persuasion. Only when we sent one member of our team to meet the parents in their workplace and patiently persuade them to sign a letter, allowing their daughter to continue her study, did we finish the task ..."

Aged 97, she is still able to recall every important occasion in detail, which is so impressing.

Later, she paid more attention to recruiting more members so as to make their service available to a larger number of children and families.

She believed that each member of the"caring mothers" must be a person cherishing a mother-like heart, dedicating herself to public service, in her words, just like a flower full of aroma.

That's right. People adore aromatic flowers, because they are not only affectionate and fascinating, but also bringing a sense of security, spiritual sustenance,love and strength.

The aroma of the "caring mothers" is their loving care for others.

Such love is the most beautiful "spiritual fragrance" in the world, the power for the people in trouble to overcome adversity, the confidence of the poor to overcome their sense of inferiority, and the motivation for the downhearted to go forward ...

Manreyamu has taken the lead, inspiring other members to become close friends, "good mothers" to all those who need help.

"'Caring mothers' are loving mothers. As a song puts it: Mom is the best in the world, all because she is the most caring one. Thus, the 'caring mothers' must be responsible and considerate!"

Manreyamu has always reiterated that. Although she is at the age of a grandmother, she tries not to be treated as a "grandma" while taking part in the work to help children in need.

"Because being a 'grandma' usually means family members would give you proper care and tolerance. But we are 'caring mothers',which means we should bear misunderstanding and grievance and devote ourselves heart and soul ...."

Over the years, the team of "caring mothers" has expanded from several members to a large group including female retirees from the Party and government offices as well as enterprises, even from self-employment businesses.

In 2002, under the promotion of Manreyamu, the team was officially registered as a public welfare organization in the Department of Civil Affairs. Since then, the team has organized various activities in an open and legal manner. Additionally, the team does not only offer financial aid for students in need, but also care of other vulnerable people such as lonely seniors,organizing them to play sports and join entertainment activities. Sometimes they would even assist government and the communities in the work for popularization of education and civilization.

"How many 'caring mothers' are there?dozens or several hundred ...What is the exact figure in Tacheng at present?" Hearing my question, she laughed and said, "It is as innumerable as flowers blooming in spring. Everyone regards the membership as an honour, striving to do good deeds."

Her words have been proved exactly right. Wherever you go in Tacheng, you can find "caring mothers" in each street, community, rural farm, factory, enterprise, and even barrack and school. "Caring mothers" have become a splendid scenery not only in urban areas but also in each county and village ...

"We have members in Urumqi, Xi'an, Lanzhou, Beijing and Nanjing. My friends living in Shenzhen told me 'caring mothers' are there as well," she introduced in an excited tone.

Not long before I first visited Manreyamu, now an honorary chairman of the organization, a meeting had been held to change the leadership and a "young" middle school principal who had just retired succeeded her as the new executive chairman. When I came to Manreyamu's home, I saw the new chairman was reporting to her, asking for advice.

The chairman told me that these years have seen numerous branches of the organization sprout throughout Xinjiang under the leadership of Manreyamu, with more than 300 Tacheng members and at least 1000 members from other cities in Xinjiang.

"I am not sure all over China, but members in Xinjiang all know well about our dear old mother, Manreyamu as the founder of the organization. As a prestigious role model, she has always inspired and encouraged all 'caring mothers' in Xinjiang ..." the chairman said.

"I would like to show you a precious thing," the old mother smiled at me and gave her son a hint.

"Got it!" Then her son stood up immediately and took out a large envelope from the bedroom after a while.

Manreyamu unsealed it, took out a letter imprinted "The Central Committee of the Communist Party of China" as the letter head, then showed it to me with great care ...

"Goodness, it was written by Comrade Xi Jinping!" I was surprised at the very sight of the letter, even though I had heard about it before.

At that moment, her eyes were full of the light of happiness. "Yes, he wrote to me ..." she said.

It was exactly written by Comrade Xi Jinping.

In the letter, he praised Manreyamu of the dedication she had made to the cause of education, fostering large numbers of ethnic students in all walks of life for the people and the country, while she still kept engaged in charity at old age, which was really admirable.

It was his hope for her to continue to play an active role, to influence and mobilize more people of ethnic groups, promoting national solidarity, working for shared development, making more contributions for the people and the country.

Comrade Xi Jinping wrote to her on May 4th, 2013.

Talking about what happened nine years ago when she wrote to Comrade Xi Jinping and later heard from him, she was extremely excited as if she had returned to the days 70 years ago:

"After the18th National Congress of the Communist Party, I heard that Comrade Xi Jinping was elected as the general secretary. Later, I was informed that he was the son of Secretary Xi Zhongxun, who had received me in Xi'an. I am exceptionally delighted by the news. I will have a look at the photo of Secretary Xi Zhongxun and us whenever I am at leisure.

In 2013, when I heard Comrade Xi Jinping was elected as the president of the nation, I was so delighted that I wrote to him. In the letter, I described the occasion his father had received us. Besides, I reported to him how I had dedicated in education during the following decades, following the instructions of Secretary Xi Zhongxun.

I wrote in the letter to Comrade Xi Jinping: I am a senior teacher from Tacheng, Xinjiang. It is a beautiful and richly endowed small town inhabited by united ethnic groups in a harmonious community. Years have witnessed great changes here.

We live together in unity just like a big family, without the concept of 'distinction between each other among ethnic groups'. Now we have enjoyed great development, under the leadership of the Party, we celebrate one festival after another. People are jubilant and life is thriving day by day. Tacheng is developing, where people are living a stable and happy life ...

My letter was sent to Comrade Xi Jinping in care of a leader in Xinjiang. I never expected that I would hear from him in a couple of days.

That day, I was too excited to sleep, asking my son to read the letter out loud again and again, then I read it myself again and again ...especially when I read about his recognition of what I had done, I felt I was on the top of the world!"

As the recollection brought great pleasure to her, she began to dance, gorgeously and elegantly. Her good mood has infected her children and they started a "Xinjiang-style" party with dance and songs —

Even though you came from afar, you would be impressed by the enthusiasm of the free-spirited locals in Xinjiang ...

"When you come back to Beijing, please give my bests regards to Comrade Xi Jinping. Tell him that I am fine. Tacheng has been better than previous years, where people of various ethnic groups live in particular unity and the city is also becoming more and more beautiful ..." Before I left, she held my hands tightly and repeatedly reminded me not to forget what she said.

"Well, Mother Manreyamu, I will surely pass on your words!" I had to say so, facing an elder aged nearly a hundred years old.

Although the old mother has never been to Beijing, her heart was very close to there. I could feel deeply about that in her words as well as during the visit to her home.

When I just stepped out of her house, I saw a procession of "caring mothers" in colourful ethnic attires approaching.

They were dancing and singing in the streets to encourage the public to join the efforts of developing a civilized Tacheng.

The new chairman of the "Caring Mothers"organization told me: apart from voluntary assistance for those in need, "caring mothers" will also participate in various social activities organized by the government, street communities, and schools.

"In many occasions, 'caring mothers' may do better than any other people, especially things relating to national unity. Therefore, there is a consensus in Tacheng: 'caring mothers' can handle everything, no matter how tough it is. It is indeed the case in Tacheng, that's why you may see 'caring mothers' everywhere and every day ..." the chairman said in great pride.,

It is the most attractive scenery I have seen in Tacheng — Amiable mothers of various ethnic groups team up to devote their love to the others. They are mothers and grandmothers of children as well as wives of men, they constitute half of the world.

People from half of the world are devoting love, how about people from the other half? We may learn the answer from Tacheng, a city where people make no distinction between each other among ethnic groups.

Through this visit, the name of "Manreyamu" is deeply engraved in my heart. In my mind, she is the synonym for "mother" and an incarnation of "love".

Hence, grapes of Turpan turn ripe, apples of Aksu sweet, and dates of Hotan ruddy ...

Hence, girls in the meadows become more beautiful, shepherd boys more handsome and masculine ...

Hence, thousands of miles of border and territories become more prosperous and stable.

On the first night, the first day in Tacheng, I saw the pomegranate seeds, plump and mellow ...

Chapter 2

The Legend in Yuliu Lane

The country is its people; the people are the country.

Every inch of the country,

Has been forged by people of all ethnic groups who have supported and helped each other for thousands of years.

They are songs of heroes and songs of life.

It is true in history as well as at present.

The "Love at Yuliu" between a man from Shandong and his Uyghur brother,

Inherits the truly unbreakable blood ties in the territory of China for thousands of years,

Which is the route we must take to create beauty and richness ...

The wind of seasons pleases people's minds and eyes; the wind of history enlightens the wise. The day when I stepped into Yuliu Lane in Taserhai Village, Emin County, my heart began to surge with passion ...

The man sitting in front of me was Lin Zhongdong, who was a capable and intelligent man at first glance. He must be a tough and strong handsome boy when he was young.

"People from Tianjin Wei are all like this ..." he said.

"Are you from Tianjin?" I was a little surprised.

He looked casually. "Yes. There are a lot of people from Tianjin to Xinjiang, especially those from Yangliuqing. Because we are 'catching up with the big Camp', so they are all at least as hefty as me ..."

"Yangliuqing", people"catching up with the big Camp" ... These words really stunned me.

He laughed at me amicably, "Then you have to learn something about history."

"Every time you come to Xinjiang, lots of historical and realistic knowledge need to be replenished. In fact, we are here to learn." I think that meeting everyone in Xinjiang, you'd better not pretend to know something you don't, because we are here to "make up missed lessons" about science, social truth, and emotion, not to mention nature and beautiful scenery.

"I have heard of 'Zuogong Willows'(Zuogong is the honorific title of Zuo Zongtang, a famous statesman, strategist and national hero in late Qing Dynasty)," I said.

"Yes, the journey which we, the people from Yangliuqing in Tianjin, took to here is almost the same as that the 'Zuogong Willows' took ..."

His words reminded me of some residues of memory in my mind—a little knowledge about "Zuogong Willows".

For composing another piece of work, I have just read the article *History of Opium Trade* written by Karl Marx in 1858, in which China was analyzed as follows, "An vast empire with a population of almost one-third of mankind is still content with the status quo regardless of the current situation. It is isolated due to being forcefully excluded from the rest of the world, and therefore strives to deceive itself with the illusion of its perfection. Such an empire is destined to be defeated in a desperate duel. " Marx's predictions were actually proved to be true after he made this argument.

The decadent Qing Government implemented the policy of secluding the country from the outside world with the pride as a "Celestial Empire", which was doom to fail as Marx predicted. However, in this large and populous eastern country, there were some sober patriots, and Zuo Zongtang was one of the most prominent.

In 1879, on the long march from Hunan Province to the west was a vast and mighty troop, wearing typical clothes in southern China, speaking a southern dialect that northerners couldn't understand, and advancing hard amid yellow wind and dust. On a tall steed in front of the troop was an elder with bright eyes and white hair, who was Zuo Zongtang. Curiously, behind him, more than a dozen soldiers carried a pitch-black coffin, which was so eye-catching among weapons and military flags.

"If we can't recover Xinjiang, then lay me in this coffin!" Zuo Zongtang said to the soldiers before they started the expedition. That year, as a general, he was 68 years old. His determination and volition inspired all the brave soldiers following him. Thus, General Zuo and his army opened a magnificent and great chapter in the history of Xinjiang.

During the long and arduous Westward Expedition, especially after leaving Gansu Province, Zuo Zongtang was deeply impressed by the desolation and severe environment of the Gobi Desert. Realizing that without planting trees, the survival of soldiers and recovery of the territory would not last long, he mobilized the soldiers following him from Hunan Province to plant trees along the way and chose willow trees which were the easiest to take root and grow. In this way, the Westward Expedition Army turned into a tree-planting army who implemented the policy of one battalion in charge of planting trees and another in charge of managing. Thus, willows were planted everywhere along the way. At the same time, local inhabitants were called up to take care of the trees. By doing so, there appeared a spectacle with patches of trees in the Gobi Desert reaching for thousands of miles ...

> The general has not returned from the borderland,
> Soldiers from Hunan Province are stationed at Mt. Tianshan.
> Willows are planted along three thousand miles away,
> Attracting the vernal breeze to blow beyond Pass of Jade.

This famous poem, written by Yang Changjun, a subordinate of Zuo Zongtang, was inspired by the wonders made by the tree-planting army at that time. It was said that the soldiers led by General Zuo were all carrying willow saplings. As long as they stopped, the first thing to do was to plant willow trees. Whether in front of or behind the barracks, or along the roadside, they planted willow saplings everywhere ... In the coming year, the snow melted and there were plenty of water, people would see willows in rows with the vernal breeze blowing gently, and the look of the desolate place changed drastically. In order to show gratitude to General Zuo, people respectfully called these trees "Zuogong Willows".

"The willow trees we see in Xinjiang today were left by Zuogong and his army ..." Lin Zhongdong said so with admiration and gratitude, so did several old Uyghurs sitting around him.

"Did you people from Tianjin Wei come to Xinjiang to carry on the cause of General Zuo?" My question did make Lin start talking.

"Sure. Without Zuo Zongtang's great cause of regaining Xinjiang, I'm afraid few people from Tianjin could have been here until this day!" Lin suddenly straightened up and his eyes glowed.

He began to tell me the stories—

"It could be dated back to the years when my great grandfather lived ..." His first words took us back to the 1870s. "My grandfather told me, at that time, in Yangliuqing, a grand ceremony would be held on the local dock on the third day of the third lunar month every year, which was called 'catching up with the big Camp', that is, everyone gathered in groups on the dock to prepare for a spectacular expedition, which would last for several months travelling thousands of kilometers ... What for? They were going to follow Zuo Zongtang and his Westward Expedition army!"

Lin Zhongdong's accent revealed his identity as a Tianjin Wei local.

Tianjin is a hundred miles away from Beijing, and the Grand Canal between them passes through Yangliuqing. The dock there was very important in the old days, so it was also well known.

In the second half of the 19th century, Yangliuqing area was constantly affected by war, coupled with drought, floods, and locust plagues, which made people suffer. Yangliuqing people who were good at doing business started a great journey to build bonds with Xinjiang, which is the widely circulated and legendary feat of "catching up with the big

Camp".

The generation of Lin's grandfather "caught up with the big Camp". This made these poor people who risked their lives and left their families change from the ones suffering from hunger and coldness to wealthy businessmen along with Zuo Zongtang's recovering, pacifying Xinjiang, and making Xinjiang prosper, thus making their own brilliant achievements here.

You can think of it this way: Xinjiang is an area with multi-ethnic population. Many ethnic groups moved here because of war, migration, garrison, or being attracted by the beauty and richness of Xinjiang. Only people from Tianjin (Yangliuqing) chose to settle here owing to a specific business model created in the process of following Zuo Zongtang. That was the history of three and four generations of Tianjin Wei people before Lin Zhongdong's.

We may start from the Tongzhi Period of the late Qing Dynasty. In 1865, with the support of Britain, Mohammad Yaqub Beg, a commander of the Khanate of Kokand in Central Asia, led an army to invade Xinjiang when the place was in turmoil. He occupied Kashgar (now Kashi) in southern Xinjiang and then Aksu. Heading north, he attacked and occupied Urumqi and most of northern Xinjiang in 1870. The next year, Russia took the opportunity to send troops from the north and occupied Ili in northern Xinjiang. At that time, Tacheng belonged to the Ili Prefecture. It was clear that the aggressors wanted to separate Xinjiang from China's territory.

The Chinese nation once again was in danger of destruction and partition by foreign powers. Dealing with the crisis, the Qing Government eventually had to take military actions to pacify the northwest region, and General Zuo Zongtang was entrusted with this great mission. As early as more than 20 years ago before the Westward Expedition, he had a famous "Night Talk Along Xiang River" in Hunan Province with Lin Zexu, who had guarded the border of Xinjiang for three years. At that time, Lin talked to Zuo in detail about the significance of northwest defense, and encouraged him, "I shall dedicate myself to the interests of the country in life and death irrespective of personal weal and woe". Zuo and Lin were both patriotic ministers, and Zuo also believed that "even if we abandon the garrison in Xinjiang, we could not succeed in autarchy", and "we retreat an inch, the enemies move forward a mile". However, for many years, his proposition of recovering Xinjiang had encountered great obstruction, which mainly came from Minister Li Hongzhang who advocated that "maritime defense" was more important than "land frontier defense". He thought,"If Xinjiang was lost, it wouldn't hurt a lot; but if the coasts were not defended, the country would be in more serious danger." Therefore, it was better to abandon Xinjiang and spend the limited military expenditure on the southeast coastal defense.

Thanks to Zuo Zongtang's effort, having argued for half a year, Zuo's perspective of paying equal attention to both "land frontier defense" and "maritime defense" was eventually adopted by the Qing Court.

It was not until 1875 when the situation in Xinjiang became increasingly critical, that Zuo, the Governor of Shaan-Gan, was appointed as an imperial envoy to supervise the military affairs in Xinjiang.Thus the curtains opened for the war defeating Mohammad Yaqub Beg and recovering Xinjiang.

Coincidentally, before the war started, as the soldiers were sharpening their swords, one person did something exerting a great influence on the situation. He was An Wenzhong from Yangliuqing, Tianjin, an authentic "fellow villager" to Lin Zhongdong. He provided logistical support for Zuo Zongtang's army while creating opportunities for the Yangliuqing people to make a living in Xinjiang.

The term"catching up with the big Camp" was created by An Wenzhong.

He was a child of a ordinary family in Yangliuqing. His father was a boatman who had four sons, and An Wenzhong was the eldest. Having been in school for only one year, he became a boatman with his father at the age of 14.

In 1876, preparing for the "Westward Expedition", Zuo Zongtang began to transport military supplies from Baoding Camp to Shaanxi, in need of hiring a group of boatmen urgently.

"I want to go. Why don't we leave this good business undone?" An Wenzhong, who spoke the Tianjin dialect, answered back to his father. He was 17 years old and had suffered enough of towing boats on the canal, so he decided to find a way to "make a living" by himself. As the saying goes, if you want to get rich, you'd better be next to the barracks.The young man understood the truth in the saying,so he applied for the job with determination.

"Golly, there is gold everywhere!" When An arrived in Xi'an with a transport team, he found a "secret"— selling goods to the army was profitable. The army was short of daily necessities, yet compared with civilians during the war, the officers and soldiers were richer and could afford the goods.

An Wenzhong began to make a bulk purchase of some petty commodities such as threads, needles, towels, and soaps, and then became a "hawker".

"Xiao An Zi, give me a pack of cigarettes!"

"Xiao An Zi, get us some towels! Our crotches are bleeding ..."

"All right, man!" While one shouted "Xiao An Zi", the other responded "OK" with the exchange of goods and money ... Before long, "Xiao An Zi" became a well-known "cargo maker" in the barracks and had become a big shot in business who earned a lot of money!

"You want to be rich too? Then come with me! If you follow me, I'll make sure you earn enough! Why don't you go!" An Wenzhong returned to his hometown triumphantly, and people in Yangliuqing treated him like a god. When he called on, nobody could stay still except the dumb, stupid, or disabled ones.All the others followed him to the West. For the first time,groups of Yangliuqing people travelled far away towards the direction of their dreams ...

However, An Wenzhong's trip to "catch up with the big Camp" was not always plain sailing. After Zuo Zongtang's Westward Expedition troops entered the northwest region, they encountered great difficulties-the dual test of the natural environment and the war. Whether they won or failed, in good or bad conditions,they could not live without eating or drinking, especially daily necessities. No matter how frugal they were, the soldiers would have to take a bath and change their clothes every a few days. An was so smart to figure out that the farther the army went westward, the more daily necessities soldiers would need, and the more hopefully his"small business" would become a big one.

"Do you dare to go to Suzhou(now Jiuquan in Gansu Province)?" An asked his fellow villagers. "How many days will it take to get there from Xi'an?" Someone asked.

"I don't know either." An shook his head.

"Then can we carry the goods there?"

"If everyone knows that it can be done, then the business would have been done by others ..." An answered.

"If you can't guarantee that we make it, we might lose money!"

"If you don't want to go, then forget about it. Don't say these negative words! If all know there is already a pile of gold , why bother to dig for it!"An was a little upset.

As others were hesitant and doubtful, he picked up the load and started off.

"Wait, wait for us!" Later, those fellow villagers followed him one after another.

This expedition was really rough and thrilling. But when they arrived in Suzhou, An and his partners did earn a lot of money, because the soldiers who had not changed their clothes and taken baths for almost a month snapped up the daily necessities when they saw them. Regardless of price, as long as the goods were available, they might spend all their money on them.

"How about the trip? Have you left for nothing in these 40 days?" At night, An asked his fellows who were counting money.

"Not for nothing! I'll go with you next time! "

"That's right. I'd be a fool not to go with you!"

"Well, since there are still a few days for the army to take a break, we should waste no time in stocking ... It is said that it will take at least two months to arrive in Xinjiang, and I heard that the subordinates of General Zuo will issue us a certificate!" An revealed an important piece of information.

In order to prepare for the war, in 1876, Zuo Zongtang ordered his right-hand man Liu Jintang in charge of military supplies. General Liu then decided to recruit vendors to sell goods to the army, granting a license to each merchant, and incorporating these vendors into the army's logistics units for unified management.

A massive army entering Xinjiang was nothing trivial, and the military supply was also a big issue which could not be solved only by An and his small team of peddlers. Therefore, General Liu sent a official to negotiate with An, "Can you mobilize five hundred vendors to go with us? If not, we would hire someone else."

"Yes, I can make it! Not to mention 500 men, even recruiting 5,000 men would not be a problem for the Yangliuqing people!" At this time, An not only built up an unusual relationship with the soldiers, but more importantly, he shouldered more responsibilities for the country—"Xinjiang is also our homeland and must be taken back from the bandits!"

"Ok. A deal is a deal. After this has been done, I'll report to the Imperial Court to grant you a reward!" General Liu was very happy to hear that An had taken his order.

In April 1876, An led hundreds of Yangliuqing vendors to follow the army into Xinjiang, who searched for sources of goods during the military operations, and sent daily necessities, vegetables, and medicines to the barracks continuously, thus satiating the urgent needs of the army.

In 1877, Zuo Zongtang defeated the invaders.

In 1881, Ili was recovered and Xinjiang returned to the embrace of China. At the suggestion of Zuo Zongtang, in 1884, the Qing Government officially decided to set up a province in Xinjiang, and called the Western Regions "Xinjiang", meaning "a newly recovered inherent territory", and its capital was set in Dihua (now Urumqi).

The first provincial governor of Xinjiang was General Liu Jintang, who had made great contributions to the recovering of Xinjiang. As soon as he laid a solid foundation in Dihua, he gave "Xiao An Zi" a task of coordinating military provisions, and disbursed a large sum of money to buy goods locally and transport them to Xinjiang for sale, aiming at restoring and rebuilding Xinjiang's economy. An lived up to Liu's expectations, accomplished the task remarkably, and handed in the profits to General Liu. His selfless dedication was appreciated by the Qing Court who then awarded him the official title of "Head of the Government Finance Bureau".

It was a long-term and arduous task to restore Xinjiang's economy. To this end, An started his business in Xinjiang and founded the Wenfengtai Store of Beijing Goods. Within a few years, due to his good management, he soon became rich as "Mr. Big in Tianjin Gang" who dominated the business sector.

After entering Xinjiang for more than 20 years, An had built a road to success as "Tianjin Silk Road" for people in Tianjin, especially for those in Yangliuqing. By such a special way, Yangliuqing people entered Xinjiang one after another, either by oneself, a household, a family or a village, marrying local people to gain their influence increasingly, who turned to be "new Xinjiang people" to enrich Xinjiang till the time of Lin Zhongdong's father.

I need to make clear An Wenzhong's final fate. In 1909, he returned to Tianjin, handed over the stores in Xinjiang to his younger brother An Wenxi, instructing him to shrink the business. Soon after, while doing business with the Russians, An Wenxi died of depression due to the loss of 80 containers of fine black tea in transit. A year later, fighting broke out in Dihua, most of the Tianjin stores were looted. Only Wenfengtai of An's family survived, thanks to its suspension. After returning to Tianjin, An Wenzhong founded a gunny bag shop and a bank. Although the business was not as good as that in Xinjiang, his prestige was still there. Therefore, after the fighting, under his guidance, people continued to go to Xinjiang and formed a "Tianjin business network" and life circles all over Xinjiang. Especially in border cities like Tacheng, Tianjin people have left countless descendants, who have been deeply integrated into the local life.Not a few of them married local people. Their pioneer, An Wenzhong, died of illness at home in Tianjin in 1942 at the age of 91. On the floor tiles of his yard at Yangliuqing, engraved were four characters meaning"I only wish to be content with my lot".

With wisdom, courage, and tenacity, this great businessman who came out of Yangliuqing Wharf in Tianjin firmly grasped the business opportunities of "catching up with the big Camp" in the midst of war and turmoil, with an insight into the situation, handling all the things properly,whose doctrine, behavior, and morality worth praising. Under his influence and guidance, the legendary story of "3,000 peddlers in Mt. Tianshan" has been circulated everywhere in Xinjiang, as an impressive chapter on the great integration of all ethnic groups there.

After having read the story of Zuo Zongtang's Westward Expedition and the legend of An Wenzhong, and listening to the "story of Yuliu Lane" in Taserhai Village, I seem to have found the root of cultural bloodlines engraved on this land.

Before I interviewed Lin Zhongdong, a local cadre first guided me to Yuliu Lane which was being renovated ... The construction was on a large scale. With the help of cadres assisting Xinjiang from Liaoning Province, the local people renovated the main lane through an original natural village and officially named it "Yuliu Lane". Green shades and flowers are on both sides of the neat and wide lane, and walls of the houses have been freshly painted. The ink and wash murals on the walls are bright-colored and eye-catching, in an ethnic minority style, making people pleasant and comfortable.

"Look, this tree is very special, isn't it? A willow stalk grows on an elm tree, a sign of vigor and vitality ... The elm and willow are combined into one, lush, straight, tall, and strong!" The village cadre led me to the middle of the lane, pointing to a Yuliu tree, and said to me.

It is miraculous. A wicker grows from the root of an elm, and the longer the wicker grows, the more flourishing it is. Now as we have seen,the elm and willow grow vigorously together reaching to the sky ...

"Amazing!" I couldn't help marveling at it. The symbiosis between elms and willows in nature seems to have existed since ancient times. At that moment, I suddenly recalled a poem written by Tao Yuanming, "The elms and willows screen the backside eaves, white peach and plum trees shade my yard with leaves. The distant village dimly looms somewhere, with smoke from chimneys drifting in the air." It seems that elms and willows really grow together in harmony in the world.

Elms are deciduous trees, which implies nobility, bravery, and the spirit of defying difficulties and challenges. Willows are also deciduous trees with strong adaptability to the environment. Ancient people believed that wickers could exorcise evil and ghosts and had the connotation of affection and love. The elms are unyielding and willows are gentle, so their combination means the unity of heaven and earth in love, thus there has been sayings about elms and willows growing together in harmony since ancient times.

On the first day of my interview in Emin County, I was moved by the story of "harmonious Yuliu family" here. The protagonists are Lin Zhongdong and his brother Kurrusi Usman. One of them is Han and the other is Uyghur; one is an "outsider", and the other is a native in Xinjiang. However, the two of them and their families live together as a "combination of elm and willow", interpreting a touching and heartwarming "story of Yuliu Lane" in the small border village-

As a descendant of Yangliuqing people, Lin Zhongdong knew little about how his father came to Xinjiang, because he was just a common person. However, the year 1964 might naturally remind us of the historical background at that time. Just after going through a three-year-long famine, the whole country was eager to develop, especially the development of Xinjiang which once again became a hot spot. In a word, more people were needed there.

Many mainlanders who had suffered from natural disasters or been affected by some ultra-left trends took the "running to Xinjiang" as the best choice to change their destiny at that time.

Lin's father was one of them. He used to work as a postal worker in Tianjin. In 1961, he was labeled as a "rightist (someone who was politically conservative and traditional)" due to "historical stains" and "neglecting political taboos". Then he was sent to the countryside.

"In Xinjiang, as long as you work honestly, no one would treat you as a bad guy again." Father told Lin since he was a child. Therefore, when his father made the decision to take the whole family to Xinjiang, the family of nine did not object.

"I am the fourth son in my family with six more brothers and sisters, so there are totally nine people, including my parents. Later, several relatives went with us after knowing that we were going to Xinjiang ..." More than a dozen members from Lin's family travelled thousands of miles to Emin County, Tacheng in Xinjiang, where they knew nothing and nobody there.

"If we go further west, we will go out of the country, so we have to stop ..." Lin Zhongdong said.

Lin Zhongdong's father, Lin Mingen, was a man with knowledge and status in his hometown. However, because he was a "rightist", even when he worked in the countryside, no one wanted to be with him and talk to him. Those who spoke to him were the supervisory cadres who came to teach him a lesson and would never be kind to him.

"But after arriving in Xinjiang, my father often told the whole family: At that time, the vast majority in Taserhai Village was Uyghur. On the first day when we came here, the local Uyghurs enthusiastically helped us settle down, and slaughtered sheep and cattle to receive us with the best wine while we held a party all night long without any discrimination ..." Lin's first "Xinjiang memory" was also that "he was brought to their home by a group of children who looked different from him", where "they gave him food and shared good toys with him."

Lin Zhongdong said that although he was a little afraid of strangers at that time, he could see that those who spoke an unknown language were always smiling and kind.

"We were being loved." Lin said this was how he felt during his childhood in Xinjiang. "It was just like dry saplings being moistened by rain …" Lin's family took root in this small village with a majority of Uyghurs in Emin County, Tacheng.

"When I first came here, there were less than 60 households in the village, but now there are 202 …" He said. "At that time, there were only two Han households, but now there are 50. In addition to Uyghur and Han, there are people from six more ethnic groups living here, including Kazakh, Russian, and Mongolian." Lin Zhongdong said that here is a typical multi-ethnic village.

The situation Lin's father's generation were facing in Xinjiang was quite different from that Yangliuqing predecessors faced "catching up with the big Camp". The former needed to settle down here, and there was no way returning to hometown, but the latter went home after finishing their business. "Although we were still young at that time, we felt the pressure on our parents who took their whole family thousands of miles away to a strange and completely different living environment and couldn't even understand the language of the locals. At first, they could only communicate with each other by hand gestures, which led to some inevitable misunderstandings. In addition, the Han people were absolutely a minority at that time. How to work, how to get food, and where to see a doctor, the simplest things in their hometown became something so difficult here …" Lin Zhongdong didn't mention anything specific, but I heard there have been some misunderstandings and even disputes because some Han people who came to Xinjiang for the first time didn't understand the living habits of ethnic minorities.

"Our family has been in Taserhai Village for 60 years, and there has never been any dispute with compatriots of other ethnic groups, thanks to Uncle Usman Akemba, the father of Kurrusi ..." When I visited him for an interview, Lin Zhongdong first led me to Kurrusi's home which was right in front of his.

Yuliu Lane used to be a narrow dirt lane, but now it has been transformed into a wide asphalt one under the construction of rural revitalization. "I'm too attached to it, which binds the deep relationship between our two families, so it is seen as a lane binding our blood and affection. With this, the blood and family ties have been promoted among multiple ethnic groups in the village."

What he said triggered the "seven mouths and eight tongues" of the elderly uncles and aunts in Yuliu Lane—

"In the first few years after Lin's family came here, because of the language barrier and unfamiliarity with the place, there had inevitably been some estrangement between the family and other villagers. Later, our old village head, Usman, father of Kurrusi, had looked for an opportunity to let the commune members listen to the broadcast from the Central government on the radio.Lin's father,Lin Mingen, being literate, had been asked to translate the messages to Usman, who then conveyed them to the commune members(villagers) so that all of us could hear the voice of Chairman Mao and the CPC Central Committee in Beijing as quickly as possible ..."

"Lin's father was literate, good at reading newspapers and keeping accounts. With Usman's support, he gradually became an accountant and was respected and loved by all the villagers. His diligence and sincere dedication made the villagers particularly tolerant and receptive to 'outsiders'. Since Lin's family settled down, the village has accepted dozens of 'outsiders' who came to the village for various reasons. They made this village, once with a small population, become a vibrant and advanced one. In the early 1980s, when order was brought out of chaos, Usman heard that unjust cases could be rehabilitated. He went to the town and county many times hoping to clear up the false charge against Lin Mingen. He even appealed to government units in Tianjin. As a result, the "rightist" label weighing on Lin Mingen's head for so many years was removed, several months earlier than other wronged people!"

"Lin's father was pulled from the mud pit to a bright road by Usman whose son's dream of getting rich comes true with help from Lin, hand in hand ..."

On account of their parents' close brotherhood, Lin Zhongdong and Kurlusi have been a pair of intimate brothers since childhood. Lin learned a lot of Uyghur vocabularies from Kurrusi, and Kurrusi could read Chinese books and newspapers gradually ... These simple things should not be underestimated, which were necessary for "outsiders" like Lin and enabled them to willingly put their "roots" deeply in the strange frontier region, building in the new "land"an unabridged home for the rest of their lives. Every season they passed and every sunrise and sunset they watched here were completely different from that in the past. This would make them feel distressed. Sometimes, their emotions could affect their instantaneous choice. Lin was not a well-educated man, and he did not seem to be good at expressing such delicate emotions and feelings, but what he inadvertently said was really shocking. He said, "Sometimes if things went wrong, I would be extremely resentful of my father's choice at that time, and I would also complain about why it was so unfair to people, but at times like this, my good brother Kurrusi would say to me in the simplest and purest words: 'Don't think about anything, as long as I am here, my home is here, your home will never fall down in Tacheng ...'"

Lin's eyes were wet as he said so. He said, "With such a good brother, what am I not satisfied with? We are common people,what we want is just peace and a little wealth. The rest does not belong to us."

"When I was a child, my father wore the hat of 'rightist'. If we stayed in my hometown,the whole family would be despised. But in this new hometown, we have hardly encountered setbacks in this respect. In fact, after I became a brother of Kurrusi who was older and stronger than me, I always walked with my chin up and back straight on any occasion." Lin said proudly.

Kurrusi is not as active and resourceful as Lin, but his simple and honest character is a kind of perseverance and a sense of trust that can be relied on. "His ideas are gold. If you walk behind him, you won't lose out ..." Kurrusi praised Lin in such way.

It is this pair of Uyghur and Han brothers who walk together to interpret the past and present life of Yuliu Lane with true love ...

There had been no Yuliu Lane in Taserhai Village before. Since ancient times, elms and willows have grown on their favorite land with their own habits, but the national kinship has prompted the birth of a supernatural phenomenon, which is indeed a miracle.

After the reform and opening up, with the care and help of Kurrusi's father, Usman, the old village head, and due to his father's rehabilitation, Lin Zhongdong had transformed from a farmer into a winery worker "paid by the government" overnight. However, things soon changed, the "iron rice bowl" didn't last long before Lin became a laid-off worker.

"Annoying! It's really annoying!" Those days, Lin, a seven-foot man,unable to relieve the sorrow, closed himself indoors, drank in silence, and sighed to the sky.

"Come on, I'll drink with you ... let's relieve the sorrow together!" Kurrusi brought a bottle of nice wine, filled a cup for Lin, and said seriously, "My dad told me,at the time you first came to Xinjiang, it was really suffering. Compared to that time,the present difficulties would be noting!Ever since I was a child, in my eyes, nothing can beat you,brother. Losing iron rice bowl is nothing good, but you are a brain, I believe you'll get rich earlier than anyone else… I'd like to get rich with you!" Kurrusi patted Lin on his shoulder and encouraged him.

"Brother, do you really think that highly of me?" Light flickered in Lin's eyes.

"What are you talking about? from a child to a grownup, when didn't I think highly of you?" Kurrusi's eyes widened.

Lin picked up the cup, glugged down most of the wine, and then said, "From tomorrow on, I will try to find the right way to make a fortune for us …"

Perhaps Lin was born to have the talent of Yangliuqing people: good at business, familiar with commercial activities, intimate with merchants. Soon, he found that from Tacheng to Emin, people raised a lot of cattle and sheep, but they know nothing about meat processing, let alone making money out of it. With his sensitivity to business, Lin began to prepare the business of slaughtering cattle for beef. The usual way of business is to buy cattle from herders, slaughter them, and then process beef. But Lin considered that cattle raised by the herders, including those bought from pastures, were usually very thin with low meat yield. So he decided to go another way: buy cattle first,fatten them, and then slaughter them after they were fed up …

Having done field work for a couple of days, Lin told Kurrusi about his thoughts as he went back home. "That's a good idea!" Kurrusi, who knew more about cattle farming than Lin Zhongdong, immediately agreed with him.

"But it will take a lot of money to buy cattle!" Kurrusi was a little worried.

At this time, Lin took out 60,000 yuan from his bag with a smile on his face and said, "I have raised this sum of money. We may get going!"

"I know you can make it, bro!" exclaimed Kurrusi with great excitement.

From then on, the pair of door-to-door Uyghur and Han brothers has started a decades-long" history of striving to get rich together"—

"First, it is pivotal to bring the cattle back in winter. Because at that time, herders are more likely to sell their cattle, who need money at the end of the year, so the selling price is relatively lower. Second, after winter, when spring arrives with booming flowers, and the pastures become lush and fertile, the cattle will grow faster. In order to bring cattle back in the first winter, I remembered that I had almost run through all the dozens of pastures around Emin County until our cattle pens were full ..." Lin recounted.

"My brother, we may divide the jobs like this: you go out and I stay at home; You are in charge of buying and selling, and I am responsible for raising and fattening the cattle," Kurrusi said to Lin.

"Agreed! That is a deal." That night, they drank a lot.

"In the first winter and following spring, my brother Kurrusi made remarkable achievements. He meticulously prepared hays for winter, and once the snow melted, he drove the cattle to find the best pasture in spring. Kurrusi was very familiar with every luxuriant grazing land in Emin and Tacheng, which resulted in our first herd of fattened cattle growing faster and plumper than those in common pastures. When we slaughtered the cattle, the meat yield was 10%-20% higher than that of common farmers and pastures! In addition, coupled with our shortened feeding period, over the course of three to four years, our meat production has gained one more cycle than the others. With a shorter cycle, our payment would be more timely, giving us a competitive edge in the business. The surrounding pastures and farmers were more willing to collaborate with us. Kurrusi and I became very busy ..." The early stage of their business was still fresh in Lin Zhongdong's memory.

"Later on, our slaughtering business gained increasing fame, and the cattle raised by ourselves could not meet the demand, so we ran around every afternoon to find out if there were beef cattle available for sale and then brought them back. What we did from night to dawn was slaughtering cattle and handling beef, delivering them to the market for sale early in the morning, while some of them were directly wholesaled to vendors ..." Lin introduced beef processing and production vividly, making people feel as if they were there.

"How many cows can you slaughter and sell in a day?" I inquired.

"Initially, it was one or two, then three or four, and the most could be up to six or seven,even a dozen ..."

That was a pretty large amount!

Lin nodded and explained, "Our business can't be compared to the meat processing factory in the city. They were all mechanized and operated automatically in an assembly line, but we relied only on manual labor. Except for recruiting dozens of people from our village and neighboring villages for the process of slaughtering, buying cattle and selling beef were mainly the job of Kurrusi and me at the beginning ..."

Lin shared with me that what impressed him most was the process of buying cattle. "From our village to pastures and the neighboring villages, there used to be no roads, even no narrow trails, only gullies and hills. Sometimes, when driving a herd of cows back, we had to turn over the hills and ditches hundreds of times, the cows were so exhausted that they frothed at the mouth, not to mention how tired we were, but Kurlusi and I made it through. How many times we had stumbled and starved during the journey, only God knows!" By one look at the deep wrinkles on Lin's dark and weathered face, you may feel the hardship they have experienced.

"Once when I was crossing a ditch, I fell down and got so hurt that I couldn't walk. My good brother Lin carried me home laboriously, and he had to drive cattle at the same time ..." Kurrusi said with eyes wet.

"My brother has done more for me!" Lin patted Kurrusi on his shoulder and said affectionately.

In this way, the brothers embarked on their entrepreneurial journey step by step, which was hard but brilliant. Their beef slaughtering business has thrived. Each year the profits are shared equally between Lin's and Kurrusi's family, after deducting workers' salaries and necessary expenses.

"They share the profits equally?!" Upon hearing the news, someone quietly came over and asked Lin Zhongdong, "You originally invested 60,000 yuan, while Kurrusi only contributed 8,000 yuan. According to the investment ratio, you should get a larger share ..."

Lin shook his head and replied, "We are brothers. I never heard of brothers sharing things unequally."

When Kurrusi's family heard about it, they were all moved to tears.

The brotherly relationship between the two families has become deeper with the passage of time. While the cause of getting rich together has become more and more prosperous, the relationship between members of the two families has become closer.

Tang Suyun, Lin's wife, worked for the Family Planning Commission in Emin County. More than 30 years ago, she had a car accident on her way to the countryside. Suffering from a comminuted fracture of her left kneecap, she was hospitalized. At that time, Lin's daughter was only 3 years old and his wife needed care, but he had to work. "I, I can't deal with these on my own!" After seeing Kurrusi, Lin was about to cry.

"Don't worry, don't worry. I talked with my wife over this matter. She would go to the hospital to accompany your wife during the day and you can switch with her at night. You may bring your daughter to my house and then do what you have to do! What do you think?" Kurrusi said to Lin.

"You have arranged so well, bro. I have nothing to say!" Lin was happy instantly.

For the next three months, Adaleti Mamuti, Kurrusi's wife, stayed with Lin's wife and daughter to look after them until Lin's wife was discharged from the hospital.

Lin and Kurrusi's families are so close that they have won praise all over the village. From the early 1960s to the present, for decades, the two families have lived better and better together harmoniously, just like the vernal breeze blowing over every cropland and lane in Taserhai Village, warming this small village composed of multiple ethnic groups ...

"Ah, come and have a look! — there is an elm and a willow growing together here, and they are so luxuriant!" One day,someone found a lush and thriving Yuliu tree in the middle of the lane, near Lin's and Kurusi's houses. In a deeply rooted elm's knot, a willow grows like magic and their branches are twined together,stretching up to the sky. The two trees were united naturally, which was wonderful and heartwarming. What a wonder!

Yuliu tree, a wonderful phenomenon, immediately caused a sensation over the nearby villages and even made Taserhai Village in Emin County more famous. People spread the news like this: the elm and willow have souls, so they integrated with each other because they were moved by the 50 more-year-long fraternity between Lin's and Kurrusi's families ...

Hence, the story about Yuliu tree and friendship between Lin's and Kurrusi's families in Taserhai Village has spread farther and farther, moved countless people who came to learn from them. At first, came the people from nearby villages and Emin County, then from Tacheng and Xinjiang, at last from other provinces. Groups came to listen to the stories of the two families united as one for more than half a century.

More people come to the lane, visitors to the Yuliu tree line up. Family members of Lin and Kurrusi are often crowded round to stand by the tree to be photographed, being asked to "tell their stories in person"… The lane in Taserhai Village is getting increasingly crowed, and the beautiful story about the Yuliu tree has been spread far away. Then one day, Lin and Kurrusi went to the villagers' committee and expressed their common wish to the village cadres: The brotherhood between their two families is just the epitome of Taserhai Village, and the Yuliu tree is a symbol of ethnic unity here. They suggested changing the name of this lane to "Yuliu Lane".

"Good suggestion! Yuliu Lane is the symbol of the unity among all ethnic groups in Taserhai Village. Wonderful! Do you agree to name it 'Yuliu Lane'?" At the villagers' meeting, the cadres solicited opinions.

"Agreed!" the villagers agreed unanimously. They said, "We should learn from Lin Zhongdong and Kurrusi, let the spirit of the Yuliu tree be passed down from generation to generation!"

The construction of Yuliu Lane has now been completed. The clean, tidy, brand-new, and spacious lane is entertaining to the eyes, showing a vibrant scene of the new socialist countryside everywhere …

At the end of the interview, I couldn't help but come to the magical Yuliu tree again, looking at it lovingly with an uncontrollable emotion surging in my heart. I recited the following words out of my mind on the spot:

The elm and willow grow from the same root, better than twin lotus flowers on one stalk.

We are inseparable.

Neighbors are united as one family, filling the lane with warmth;

A good story becomes a classic, and the small village becomes well-known.

...

After bidding farewell to Yuliu Lane in Taserhai Village, on my way to another interviewee's home in Emin County, I saw an exciting scene: a forest of elms and willows stretching for several kilometers seemed to be greeting us ...

Although an elm may not be as tall, straight, and formidable as a birch, its down-to-earth image possesses a simple beauty that resonates with the spirit of the commoners. Especially in northwest China, where winter lasts long and spring arrives late, autumn comes before people are prepared to embrace the scorching summer heat, Tacheng in this season shows its rare beauty of nature and spirit.On clear and cool autumn days, the elm leaves turn into beautiful yellow butterflies freely dancing and leaping in the air, before passionately returning to the embrace of the earth, nourishing the growth of new plants. Meanwhile, the willow branches are preparing for the test and baptism of the cold wind, until the warmth of coming spring awakens the dormant hanging leaves, sprouting new green buds ...

This is the life history of elms, recurring year after year. My friends from Xinjiang told me that they are fond of elms because elms are just like people in Xinjiang. Generations of Xinjiang people, like elms, never loathe the desolation and barrenness of the Gobi desert, nor do they detest persons living a hard life. They always coexist and grow in harmony, embellishing the rivers and mountains. In particular, farmers here like to plant elms in front and behind their houses, for the name of the elm sounds like "a surplus" in Chinese. "Planting elms" means "having extra money". Although the elm flower is not as delicate and charming as the peony and rose, when it blooms, its flower seeds are like copper coins strung together, both good-looking and auspicious, so even city dwellers love it too. From a natural biological point of view, elms also have the effect of dispelling unhealthiness and promoting health. Therefore, in Xinjiang, where cold days are more common, elms have been favored since ancient times. In traditional Chinese culture, there are many poems praising them, because they are endowed with the meaning of homesickness, so ancient poets particularly liked to use elms as a metaphor for missing relatives and friends, such as "What is there in heaven? Rows of white elms only", "If the elms and mulberry trees were the receiver, I'd like to send a letter of love-sickness", and so on.

Willows, on the other hand, have a different life history: when they appeared in Xinjiang, they came with a mission and responsibility, along with the storm and smoke of war ... The process was tragic and tearful, like the poems said, "Lonely as usual, the love-sick soul is thin as a green wicker." "Apricot petals fall like a drizzle, which almost moisten my cassock. A breeze blows to my face through the willows, I don't feel cold." " The Qiang flute player doesn't need to complain that no willows grow. Beyond the Gate of Jade, no vernal wind will blow."

Willows have tenacious vitality, able to take root and thrive no matter where they are. They never care about fertility or infertility of its environment; as long as they have a little living space, they will strive to be your windshield and beautiful clothes, and let you miss your distant loved ones and friends beneath the swaying wickers. They have affection and faith, capable of transforming barren lands into tender shades and fertile fields, offering poetic tranquility through restless and troubled times. Therefore, since the "Zuogong Willows" appeared, Xinjiang, once regarded as "wilderness", has been no longer wild. The once lonely faraway place has become romantic, tempting and poetic.

Rows of elms and willows stand in front of me, made me fall into reverie and be sentimental ... At the end of the road, there were other villages and towns. I suddenly discovered that there was a larger Yuliu forest in front, where the elms and willows coexisted and flourished together. It is extremely harmonious.

"Do you want to hear another story of 'Love of Yuliu?" Chen, Secretary of the Tacheng Federation of Literary and Art Circles asked me.

"Of course! How can I miss such stories!" I responded.

"Ha-ha ..." He smiled and said, "In this place, the Love of Yuliu among people of all ethnic groups can be seen and heard everywhere ..."

Therefore, I had another story.

It happened in Yumin County, near Emin County. Yumin and Emin are the two closest counties to the regional capital Tacheng .

When I came to Yumin County, what impressed me the most was that the natural scenery here was captivating, especially the green hills nestled in the embrace of Baerluke Mountain, with continuous undulations and graceful postures that evoke my imagination. When you looked around, you may feel relaxed and happy. Because the grassland here was particularly lush, there were many "Mujiale" tourist sites run by nomads, which made people feel that the entire Yumin County was a hospitable place, and it was indeed so. The point was that people here were not only nice to business people, but also maintained a natural kindness to all visitors in daily life. Upon hearing about the "Love of Yuliu" between Lin Zhongdong and Kurrusi in Emin County, a friend in Yumin County immediately told me that there was a same story in their Muye New Village in Jiangges Township.

They told the story about Fan Bochang, a Han cadre, and Muhetar, a Uyghur villager ...

Fan and Muhetar were neither relatives nor friends, and one of them lived in the town while the other in the village, but they were well-known and enviable "in-laws". It was destiny that brought them together, and now they are so close that they can no longer be separated.

When did it begin? It had been too long that now Muhetar, who has a bulging pocket, can hardly remember it. He often told people about his story with Fan Bochang cheerfully.

One day, Muhetar attended a wedding in the village and met Fan, a labor union cadre of the County People's Hospital who went to the wedding feast as well. Attending a wedding banquet was supposed to be a happy thing, but Muhetar, who had an empty pocket all the time, was not happy and wore a sad face. Fan, sitting at the same table with him, saw it and said, "Come on, come on, let's have a drink! What makes you unhappy? Tell me later ... Let's have a drink first! "Fan filled Muhetar's glass and invited him to drink. Unexpectedly, after drinking, Muhetar not only failed to relieve his worries but also began to complain and curse for a while. In the end, he made the host of the wedding party extremely upset.

"Brother, what's your difficulties? Tell me ..." Later, Fan asked Muhetar.

After a long sigh, Muhetar shook his head and said, "One word: poor!"

Fan smiled and asked him, "Do you think you have fewer arms or legs than others?"

Muhetar stretched his arms and legs and said, "They are all here and my strength is not inferior to anyone."

"That's it. Build up your confidence and strive to become a 'little rich man' within three years!" Fan held Muhetar's hand and said.

"Me?" Muhetar shook his head repeatedly and asserted, "I never dare to be a 'rich man', all I want is to make a living so that my family could be satisfied with their living condition ..."

Fan deliberately kept a poker face, "This is not like what a man says. As long as you have confidence, I will help you make the dream come true!"

"You? Willing to help me?" Muhetar stared blankly at Fan Bochang in disbelief.

"I'll give you an idea to make money— if you made it, the profit will be yours, and if you failed, I'll help you pay back the money ..." Fan Bochang said.

Muhetar stared at Fan Bochang for a while, then suddenly burst into laughter and asked, "Aren't you drunk today?"

Fan blew a sigh at Muhetar and said, "I'm not drunk.I mean what I said."

"Really?"

"Really."

Muhetar was stunned for a while and then asked seriously, "Then, tell me how to make money and what should I do?"

Fan began to talk formally, "Do you remember the wedding banquet we attended together last time?"

Muhetar said warily, "Stop mocking me!"

Fan hastily waved his hand and said, "I'm serious. Have you ever noticed how far away the eating house where the wedding banquet was held is from your village? And wasn't the place small and crowded? Wasn't it in bad enough condition?"

Muhetar nodded and said, "It was really disappointing, and they charged a rather high price ..."

Fan then asked, "Have you ever thought about why their business is still so prosperous?"

Muhetar answered, "They took the advantage of no competition from a second one."

"Yes, what if there is a second one that is better than it? And with cheaper price ..." Fan Bochang asked.

"Yes!By doing so,he would make a fortune! If there was one in our village, it would be convenient for the neighboring villages!" Muhetar suddenly understood. "Do you want to help me run a business like this?"

"That's it. Do you want to do it?" Fan said with a smile and then fixed his eyes on Muhetar.

Muhetar was embarrassed. "Stop staring at me ... I'd love to do it. But can I?"

"Why not? You don't lack arms or legs."

"But I'm sh ...short of money!" Muhetar blushed and said.

"Go to the bank for a loan!"

"A loan has to be guaranteed. My ...my family doesn't have much money. Who would be willing to bear this risk for me!" Muhetar's face darkened.

Fan patted his shoulder and said, "I will vouch for you. Let's go tomorrow."

Muhetar couldn't believe it and shook his head repeatedly, "Why should you help me like this? What if I failed? What if I can't pay it back, I would be so sorry for you. No, no, I can't do that ..."

"Man! Who told you to pay it back?" Fan Bochang was a little angry, "Besides, how do you know you would fail?"

"It's just 'in case'!" Muhetar argued.

"There is no 'in case'. You'll definitely make money." Fan suddenly became obstinate and added, "Even if there is 'in case', I will take it, and it has nothing to do with you, all right?"

Muhetar was astonished. He didn't understand and asked, "Why did you do this? Why do you take the risk for me? "

Fan heaved a deep sigh and said, "My family used to be poor, but later, I went to work and had a fixed income, then my family lived fairly well. After seeing you get drunk and say those sentimental words, I wondered if I could help you find a way out of poverty. So, I did some field work for you on opening a new type of 'Mujiale' eating house these days. It shows that there is no 'Mujiale' around your village able to hold comprehensive events such as weddings. I consulted many experienced people to help make a plan.We concluded that running a 'Mujiale' eating house would be completely viable and profitable.That's why I encourage you to do it! How dare I push you forward without being sure? Am I so stupid to pour my money down the drain? I told you this because I am totally sure ... What do you think I do for a living? I am a labor union cadre who have helped lots of laid-off workers become successful in self-employment."

"I see! I see! Brother, my good brother ..." Muhetar hugged Fan with gratitude and burst into tears.

"That's right, we are brothers, good brothers!" Fan was also a bit excited.

To build a "Mujiale" eating house, Muhetar had a shortage of 200,000 yuan, in need of a bank loan. As expected, when a guarantor was needed, Fan, who was standing behind Muhetar, came to the loan manager, patted his own chest and said, "I am the guarantor, I will sign."

The fund for building a "Mujiale" eating house was ready. The foundation was located on the vacant land near Muhetar's house. After several months of construction and decoration, the "Mujiale" eating house opened. Soon after its opening, several fellow villagers' wedding banquets were held in its wedding hall. The new eating house has good facilities and delicious food. Besides, Muhetar was very familiar with the local ethnic wedding custom, so the business proved to be successful. Due to the perfect wedding venue and equipment, together with his sense of responsibility, attentive service, and reasonable pricing, he was not only invited to preside over and arrange wedding banquets by his own fellow villagers, but also appointed by customers from neighboring villages and nearby towns ... In a word, the business is booming.

"Good brother, I have earned a bit of money this year. This is your share of profit, and you must accept it ..." Before the Spring Festival of the coming year, Muhetar came to Fan's house and insisted on giving a wad of money to him.

"What are you doing? Do you think you are really rich now? Even if you did get rich, I would never take your money! If you do this, then our brotherhood ends today!" Unexpectedly, Fan became angry, almost pushing Muhetar out of the door with his money.

On that day, Muhetar shed tears, it was tears of gratitude and emotion. "Brother, you have treated me better than my own brother ..."

Fan invited Muhetar to the sofa in his living room and said, "We are good brothers! It's just the right time for you to come today. Let's see how you can expand the business to attract more people from the town to spend weekends and holidays here ..."

"Ah!" That was exactly what Muhetar thought. On that day, the pair of Uyghur and Han brothers discussed and planned until midnight.

After all, Muhetar's "Mujiale"was a small business, far from reaching professional operation and all-weather business volume, so his family members still had to do farm work and raise sheep as usual. Muhetar had to make purchases in the county, but he didn't have a car yet. "Just make a phone call, I will go to settle it for you!" When Fan knew this, he told Muhetar without hesitation, "If you want to buy something in the county, just call me or send me a message. I will deal with it. I could buy it during my lunch break or after work!"

It was really convenient for Muhetar, but Fan became the one running a voluntary errand for him. "I'd like to do it, and I am happy. Seeing my brother's business booming, I would be more enthusiastic to run the errand!"Fan Bochang said this as many people talked about it.

Life can be tedious, sometimes, even troublesome, which takes your time and affects your emotions. However, it is the space in which everyone lives. Some of its contents can be designed by themselves, while others one cannot foresee. You may have some control over your life, but there are always things which one cannot control or predict. Under such circumstances, it's not easy for man to maintain seamless friendship with another one. The relationship between two people, even the dearest and closest friends or blood relatives, is easy to be closer for a period of time, but difficult to last for several years, several decades, or a lifetime, not to mention that Fan has no blood ties with Muhetar but offers help to him all along. Many people didn't believe Muhetar could carry on the business to the end, let alone make money, for the acquaintances of him all knew he was not good at business. Besides, many of them thought that running a "Mujiale" in the countryside, with wedding events as its main business, was not an easy way to make a fortune, At most, it may be merely maintained or become slightly profitable. Therefore, when Muhetar's little business started, many were worried about him. What they didn't say was: If Fan the urban man could help Muhetar to the end, he might get rich, otherwise he could hardly take his capital back ...

"Ha, you think too much! My Han brother is even closer than my own brother. We are the best friends! What you're worried about won't happen!" Muhetar said firmly.

As expected, after several years, Muhetar's business has been getting more and more prosperous, like sesame blooming. He not only offers the well-known wedding events, but also introduces other entertainment items in "Mujiale" one by one. His customers are not only from Yumin County and other places in Tacheng area but also from Urumqi, even Shanghai and Beijing. Muhetar's good Han brother Fan Bochang takes care about his business, even including his family affairs. Muhetar's 90-year-old mother has weak legs and feet and often goes to town for medical treatment. When Muhetar is busy and has no time to take care of her, Fan will drive her to town. He said to a thankful Muhetar, "Your mother is also mine, what are you sorry for?" It made Muhetar feel that he had treated Fan as an outsider.

"My eldest son didn't find a suitable job after graduation. It was also my good brother who helped him land one in the county. My son's problem seemed to be his. And he arranged it better than me!" Muhetar was extremely grateful for Fan's sincere assistance.

"Don't keep saying that. In fact, you have given me and my family a lot of help! Over these years, my family has never been in want of milk and vegetables!" Fan said.

This is what we call brothers-to treat each other unselfishly. I will try my best to assist you when you need backup. I will help you out when you are in trouble. Knowing you are happy, I would be more delighted than I am happy myself. And we never care about gains or losses, just seek to help each other achieve success and work together on a path of happiness ...

In Yumin and Tacheng, the brotherhood between Fan Bochang and Muhetar has influenced and impressed many people, and changed many families who had not interacted with each other before. Now, "Love of Yuliu" like them, as well as Lin Zhongdong and Kurrusi, can be found everywhere.

During my interviews all the way in Tacheng, elms and willows born from the same root can be seen everywhere. This kind of intimacy, dependence, co-prosperity, and symbiosis... are so impressive and touching. These are blood ties between brothers and sisters of all ethnic groups in Xinjiang! That night, with sweet feelings in my heart, I fell into a rarely comfortable and wonderful dream.

Chapter 3

The Story on the Rocking Bed

The reason why pomegranate seeds embrace each other tightly is that the riper the fruit is, the closer they are,

Which shows the power of love and unity.

With that, one can withstand any invasion from formidable adversaries.

A small wooden rocking bed from Hayrat's family, with the love of three generations,

Held up the hopes of dozens of lives.

Illustrating the reason why pomegranate seeds are huddling so tightly together.

Here is Xinjiang, a land so vast that if you throw a whip away, you could hardly get it back ... Getting off the horse, you would find your campsite, a new beginning of your life, or maybe it's the birthplace of another life.

The vast and boundless land, along with the long and intricate border is significant features of Xinjiang. The distinctive and legendary courier station culture that emerged within this context was documented in the 14th- century *Geographical Records* in *History of the Yuan Dynasty*. At that time, the courier stations were scattered throughout Xinjiang, bustling with a dense population, facilitating economic and cultural exchanges between Xinjiang and the mainland. Marco Polo, a renowned Italian traveler, expressed his admiration with words such as "indescribable" and "extraordinarily marvelous system" after observing the courier station culture in Xinjiang at that time. In his travel notes, he wrote:

There were roads connecting Khanbaliq(now Beijing) with all provinces in all directions. On each road, specifically the main ones, based on the location of the town at intervals of approximately forty or fifty kilometers, there were courier stations and hotels built to receive the business travelers. These places, also known as courier stations or post offices, were grand and magnificent, with ornate rooms adorned with satin curtains and portieres for the use of high-ranking officials and noble lords. Even if princes and marquises were to stay in such a place, their dignity would not be compromised as all necessary items could be obtained from nearby towns, and the imperial court also regularly supplied for some of the stations.

On the north slope of Mt. Tianshan lies a well-known "Golden Triangle", which now includes Usu City, Kuytun City, and Dushanzi District of Karamay City, one of the areas where the ancient courier station culture is particularly well-developed.

Usu, located in the hinterland of northern Xinjiang and the southwest margin of Junggar Basin, has a total area of 20,700 square kilometers.

Due to the presence of valuable resources both on the ground and underground, as well as its unique terrain with the Kuytun River, Sikeshu River, and Gurtu River traversing the whole territory where Mt. Irenhabirga and Mt. Bharakonu reach the altitudes of more than 5,000 meters, Usu has been a "strategic place of the west-frontiers" since ancient times, where passes could be set everywhere so that it was a natural barrier against the enemies and bandits, an ancient battlefield of feudal lords fighting for supremacy. If one has a chance to explore the land of Usu, he will find remnants of ancient battlefields everywhere, with ruins, fortresses, old trenches, as well as helmets, armor, arrows, and shells unearthed later, all of which make people think of the ancient war and tragic historical events ...

During the reign of Emperor Qianlong (1736-1796) in the Qing Dynasty, it was recorded in the history books that Zhao Hui, the General to stabilize the borders, commanded an army to put down the rebellion led by Dash Tseren. Despite the long distance and limited troops, General Zhao won the battle with a smaller force and annihilated the rebels, relying on the unique terrain of the Usu Mountains where many strongholds were established to serve the army as courier stations. When the good news was sent to the capital, Emperor Qianlong was overjoyed and even composed a poem to congratulate him, leaving behind a deed praised far and wide in history.

Just from the meaning of the Mongolian word "Usu", we can also tell the uniqueness of this land. It used to be called "Kurkarawusu", which means "black water of the snowy land" in Mongolian, implying that this region has both snow and black water. In the old days, people were unaware that the black water was oil, but they knew it could be burned for heating. Usu was referred to as the "west lake" in the languages of local ethnic minorities such as the Kazakhs, indicating that it was considered a beautiful lake due to its abundant water sources. However, this beautiful land was also a key place which military strategists had fought for and a place coveted by people with ulterior motives through all the dynasties. Before Zhang Qian visited the Western Regions, only a few Han people made a living here. After the Tang Dynasty, most of the Han people who stayed in Usu were soldiers. By the time of Emperor Qianlong in the Qing Dynasty, the court sent more soldiers to set up garrisons for defense and farming. Since then, there had been relatively more Han people who had made contributions to the harmonious social and cultural traditions of this land with their descendants. Later, after General Zuo Zongtang and General Liu Jintang led troops to defeat Mohammad Yaqub Beg's invasion in Xinjiang, some soldiers from Hunan, Hubei, and Guangdong provinces chose to settle down and engage in farming. In addition, when civilians and criminals who were exiled here began to farm and Jingu(Tianjin) vendors who "caught up with the big camp" came here to open shops, the number of Han people gradually increased. Many places gradually developed from courier stations to the settlements of people who came here to reclaim wasteland. Like the famous "Eighty-Four Households" in Usu, which used to be a courier station with only one or two households but later developed into a gathering place with eighty-four Han households living and doing business there, hence it was called "Eighty-Four Households", which is now a township in Usu.

In most local villages developing around the courier stations like these, men largely outnumbered women at first. Later, as people started to settle down and cultivate the land, women and children followed over. Gradually, some of them married the local ethnic minorities such as Kazakhs, Mongols, and Uyghurs, which made contributions to the great integration of ethnic groups here.

After the founding of the People's Republic of China, along with the discovery of Karamay Oilfield, Usu became one of the important transportation hubs in the western region, where materials and people frequently flowed. Therefore population grew rapidly and the function of the ancient courier stations were brought into full play, marking the beginning of a new era.

"No need for the courier officer to report here is Shatou, by seeing the courier station, one could expect it is an ancient town." Usu's history and culture are intertwined with the courier stations, giving birth to new life and influenced the fate of the region. Perhaps only those who truly understand the courier station culture that runs through the veins of Usu can comprehend the following story that took place in the folk naturally —

There is an interesting place called "Jiujianlou". I have a habit of being particularly sensitive to place names wherever I go, because I often find that numerous fascinating pieces of information left by our ancestors are hidden in those seemingly random names. You can often understand the beauty of a new world by unlocking their meanings ...

Hayrat, sitting in front of me, is an ordinary 44-year-old native, who grew up in Zhanjia Village, Jiujianlou Township, Usu.

How did the name of "Jiujianlou" come about? I was quite interested in it.

This question sparked a lively discussion among Hayrat and the villagers, who were eager to share their stories proudly. I was so happy to see that —

Hayrat's elder brother, Jurat, took pride in knowing the origin of a "treasure" in his family — the rocking bed.

The Hayrat family is Kazakh, and their ancestors came to Usu with their tribe about one or two hundred years ago. Their grandfather, Khaybal Hayrat, was very respectable in Usu. The name structure of a Kazakh typically consists of their given name, such as "Khaybal", followed by their father's name, in this case, "Hayrat". Khaybal lived for 96 years, who was long-lived among Kazakhs. It is evident that his grandson Hayrat has carried on his name, reflecting the significance of familial heritage within this ethnic group.

After hearing the story of Hayrat's Grandfather Khaybal, we learned that he originally lived in another nearby township, which was Imperial Palace Township, and then moved to Jiujianlou.

To my surprise, in Usu, thousands of miles away from the capital, there was name like "Imperial Palace", which revealed the historical changes that had taken place in this region. This uninhabited place of Usu later became military settlements. The military forces here had different composition, with some sent by the imperial court, some belonging to local tribe chiefs, and some fleeing from the chaos of war to make temporary garrison. After arriving here, they had to reclaim the wasteland for a living. It is said that when an army sent by the court came here, they planted a large number of aspen trees, which grew tall and big, attracting a lot of attention. As a result, coveting the dense aspen forest, many wanted to occupy the place. The soldiers who planted these trees were very angry, therefore, someone carved two large characters on the tallest aspen tree, "Imperial Palace", indicating that these trees were planted by the imperial army, which were forbidden to cut down. It also implied that this area was stationed by the imperial army, and anyone who dared to encroach would face severe consequences. Upon seeing these two characters on the tree, most people were scared away. Occasionally, those who dared to offend were defeated in the end.

That is how this place got the name "Imperial Palace".

Hayrat's home, Jiujianlou, was different. The natural environment in that area was not as favorable as the "Imperial Palace", but as more and more people coming and going, every now and then, many of them needed to find a place to rest temporarily and stay overnight. Therefore, some kind-hearted people built a storied house near the river valley,with the ground floor served as a place for guests to have a meal, drink tea or have alcoholic beverages, while the upper floors were for accommodations. Nine such storied houses had been built successively, hence the name "Jiujianlou", meaning "nine storied houses".

"My grandfather had been well-known in the vicinity of Jiujianlou and called the 'Kind-hearted Uncle'." Speaking of grandfather's past, Hayrat almost danced with excitement. "Throughout his life as a nomad, my grandfather had done countless good deeds, and the people here still remember his name. He was benevolent, leaving behind not only legends passed down through generations, but also an extremely precious item for us, which was a rocking bed ..."

A rocking bed? I didn't understand.

"It is a little cradle for babies to sleep in ... we call it a rocking bed." I understood as he explained.

Nomadic people like Kazakhs have lived a pastoral life since ancient times, and constant migration was usual in their daily lives. It is common for women to give birth while on the move. Although their children were so young, they could do nothing but move on with their families without stopping. But when they are traveling or pasturing, how can they do with their babies? Unlike the Han people, who often put their babies in cradles and sing lullabies to them, the nomads can't use fixed cribs. Some clever adult came up with a wonderful idea: to make a small rocking bed that the infant could lie in. When the nomads packed up their tents and rode for a long journey, they would hang the rocking beds on horseback with the babies sleeping in it. Even if they travelled to the ends of the Earth, the babies would lie in the cozy beds and enjoy their carefree childhood with the bumps of horses ...

The rocking bed holds a significant cultural meaning for nomadic people, as it represents the cradle of their life. It has nurtured countless dreams and aspirations of people towards the grasslands and distant homeland and also awakened their yearning for a peaceful life and fertile land.

On my first day in Tacheng, someone mentioned the "story of the rocking bed", which piqued my curiosity and made me eager to know more about it. A rocking bed is quite simple in design, with a wooden pole, about the thickness of an arm, serving as the main beam. On both ends of it, a frame made of several wooden strips is attached, forming a rectangular shelf, which is the bedstead for babies. In the middle of the frame, a soft blanket cloth is hanging there, on which the baby could lie. By gently pushing the bed, it would start to sway back and forth, so it is called a "rocking bed". Babies can peacefully enjoy the soothing motion provided by their loved ones. The bed has the same function as a traditional cradle but with a simpler structure, making it more suitable for hanging on horseback to ensure a secure sleeping environment for babies.

Slumber, slumber, O my darling baby,
You are a gift from Heaven.
When you were born,
Grandma gaily scattered candies,
Grandpa gave you a precious name.
Wishing you to grow up quickly,
To be a happy and brave Kazakh.

Slumber, slumber, O my darling baby,
Put you in the holy bed,
Tell you many stories.
Praying for your healthy growth,
To become the continuation of our dreams,
May Heaven shower you with light,
Full of wisdom and strength.

Slumber, slumber, O my darling baby,
When will you slumber,
Hoping you will slumber soon.
Slumber, slumber, O my darling baby,
Slumber, slumber, O my darling baby ...

This Kazakh *Lullaby*, widely circulated in Tacheng, Xinjiang, especially in the Usu area, is deeply ingrained in the hearts of young mothers, who may improvise it, infusing their maternal love into their children's dreams.

"My father told me that my grandmother was just such a mother ..." Hayrat said affectionately, and then added, "My mother is also such a person."

Slumber, slumber, O my darling baby,
Mom is rocking gently in your dream.
Softly rest and safely slumber,
Slumbering in the cradle, warm and cozy.
Slumber, slumber, how warm it is.
Slumber, slumber, O my darling baby,
Guarded by thy father's arms.
All the blessings of happiness in the world,
All the warmth belongs to you.

...

Franz Schubert's *Lullaby* is well-known all over the world, while in China, almost every ethnic group has their own version of lullaby. Here is one of them:

My baby, sleep tight,
In your dreams, I will be by your side,
Laughing with you and accompanying you when you are tired,
I will always be by your side.
My baby, sleep tight,
How many times will you dream of me,
With me around, dreams will be satisfactory.
Waking up in comfort.

...

The lullabies from different cultures in both China and foreign countries share similar content and rhythms, conveying the love of parents and loved ones to a newborn life.

Hayrat's grandfather passed away in the 1960s, his grandmother departed even earlier, and his parents who brought up six children also died later. Now, Hayrat's child is already 13 years old. He still holds deep affection for the rocking bed left by his grandfather.

"My mother told me that to greet the upcoming baby, my grandfather went to find a Populus log specially and hired the best local carpenter to make a rocking bed, which nurtured three generations of my family. What's even more unexpected is that this custom-made bed has now become an unbreakable bond of kinship between my family and the neighboring villagers ..." What Hayrat said was the key point of my interview.

The rocking bed left by his grandfather is now placed in a public place in Jiujianlou Township, where villagers can study and participate in cultural activities, serving as a precious cultural relic representing the unity among tens of thousands of villagers from different ethnic groups, for everyone to visit.

Although the paint on the colorful main beam of the bed has faded over time, the colors are still bright. It can be seen that Hayrat's grandfather made it with exquisite workmanship. The main beam had been ground with a mechanical lathe, which feels particularly smooth. On the back of the main beam, I found some knife marks ...

"Why were these marks carved?" I asked.

Hayrat counted the marks and said, "There are twenty-seven knife marks, which means that in addition to my brothers, sisters and me, twenty-seven more babies have been nurtured in this bed ..."

"Twenty-seven?!" It was amazing! I was surprised and asked, "What is their relationship with you and your family?"

With a proud smile on his face, Haiyrat replied, "Although we are not from the same family, they are also my brothers and sisters, some of whom even rank as my junior in the clan ..."

The following is the story of "Ethnic Legend on the Rocking Bed" —

"I am the fourth child of six siblings. I can't remember when my younger brother and I used the rocking bed. When my brother Hayrat was born, I was already 6 years old. Our father and grandfather were busy at work and my mother had to do housework and take care of us. I remember that I often helped to take care of my younger brother by the rocking bed ..." Hayrat's brother Jurat said so. He is now the director of the Natural Resources Institute in the Township. After hearing my arrival, he went back home from work specially. Being a few years older than Hayrat, Jurat seemed to know more about the rocking bed than his brother.

"My little brother used the bed for less than a year when Zhou Haiyang, the son of our neighbor Wang Juzhen, was born. Wang came to borrow the rocking bed, but I was not willing to lend it. My mother told me, 'Your brother is learning to walk, he doesn't need the bed very much. How about lending it to her?' So, I agreed. I was just over 7 years old at that time and didn't quite understand," Jurat said. "It didn't take long for the rocking bed to be given back, coming along with it was Zhou Haiyang, who was one year younger than my brother. I heard that his family was busy at work and didn't have time to look after him, thus my mother decided to take care of him. My brother and I were both very happy. My little brother who was still wearing diapers rocked the bed which Zhou was lying in like I did. Later on, they grew up together, Zhou Haiyang became my mother's adopted son, and my brother Hayrat likewise became his mother's adopted son ..."

"Excuse me, please slow down, I'm a bit confused ..." I interrupted Jurat and asked Hayrat, who was sitting beside me, what happened.

Despite being in his forties, Hayrat was still very shy. After hearing my question, his eyes turned red unexpectedly, and said, "My mother passed away early. Zhou Haiyang and I grew up together. He has two younger brothers, who also used my rocking bed. When they were very little, I often went to their house to accompany them in the rocking bed, or to play with Zhou. His brothers gradually became mine, and I have such a close bond with their family as if we were real siblings ... So, their mother is also like my own mother."

On that day, there were many villagers around, talking to me about Hayrat and Zhou's family.

Zhou's family are all Han people, but Hayrat, a Kazakh, always felt at home when he visited the Zhous, and Zhou Haiyang's mother, Wang Juzhen, never regarded him as an outsider. As Hayrat and Zhou Haiyang grew up a little older, she took them to graze animals, mow grass, and ride horses together.

"One summer, it was very hot. At that time, Hayrat, who was in his teens, was wearing a pair of army green sneakers, which made his feet overheated. I happened to be at Zhou's house that day and saw Wang pulled Hayrat to sit down, taking out a pair of new black cloth shoes, and said to Hayrat, 'Put on these shoes. Don't make your feet overheated on such a hot day!' She helped Hayrat take off his sneakers and put on the new shoes. Hayrat burst into tears and knelt in front of her with three kowtows, and said, 'Thank you, auntie. Now that I'm wearing the shoes you made, I will be your son. May I call you mom?' Wang stunned for a moment but responded immediately to hold Hayrat in her arms. She said, 'Alright, good, golly good, I will be your mom, I will be your mom!' I witnessed all these and was moved to tears ..." An aunt of Hui nationality in the same village continued to tell me the following story vividly.

"Afterwards, Wang often said that she gave birth to five sons, and now with Hayrat, she has six of them, and the number symbolizes good luck in tradition! Sister Wang also gave him a distinctive name that is Halang."

The aunt's voice was like singing, she told this captivating story with great enthusiasm, and the audience were all infected.

In the name"Halang", "Ha" stands for Kazakh, while "Lang" means "waves". As Zhou's children all have "Hai" in their names, so "Lang" indicates that Hayrat is a son of the Zhous.

"My elder brother is very simple and honest. In our family, my brothers call him Halang at my mother's request, because all of our names have the word "Hai(namely the sea)". Do you like this name?" said Zhou Haiyang who came out of nowhere, patting Hayrat on the shoulder. They were like real brothers.

"They have been close to the point of being inseparable since they were young, even closer than their own brothers!" Jurat said with a hint of jealousy, which made people burst into laughter.

"It was the rocking bed that has brought us together and made Hayrat my good brother!" Zhou Haiyang said that his two younger brothers also spent a wonderful babyhood in the rocking bed. For those two or three years, Hayrat and Zhou had became "bed rocking boys", soothing and comforting the two little brothers by rocking the bed. Thanks to such emotional links, Zhou said, they became as dear to each other as members of one family.

"Mom was so kind to me!" Hayrat, a sentimental Kazakh man, became teary-eyed when he talked about Zhou Haiyang's mother. He recalled, "From the age of ten, I had been wearing shoes made by my mom for ten years. At that time, as a growing up boy who liked playing sports, I wore out at least 20 pairs of black cloth shoes. In 1999, my own mother died of a sudden cerebral hemorrhage. At the end of that year, when I was enlisted in the army and left my hometown, Zhou Haiyang's mom, who was also my mom, particularly bid me farewell. She put two pairs of brand-new black cloth shoes in my baggage and handed me 100 yuan wrapped in a handkerchief, while repeatedly reminding me to obey the command of the Party and my superiors. My comrades-in-arms were envious when they saw this, saying how nice my mom was. Little did they know that she was not my real mom, but she treated me as her own son ..." When Hayrat talked about Wang Juzhen, he couldn't restrain his emotions to weep.

Zhou Haiyang continued, "My brother Halang is awesome. He served in the army for 5 years and received 6 commendations, being recognized as an outstanding soldier twice. Moreover, he proudly joined the Communist Party of China in his third year of service. He's really great!"

Everyone might envy this pair of Kazakh-Han brothers.

"All thanks to my mom's encouragement," Hayrat said. After serving in the army for five years, he was demobilized from troops and went home for work. As time went by, he was still single even at the age of 25, but most of his peers had got married, which made Wang Juzhen so anxious that she became busy looking for a girlfriend for him.

After some arrangements, Hayrat began to date a beautiful Kazakh girl named Aminah Askelbek. The couple soon got married. On the wedding day, Wang Juzhen, acting as Hayrat's mother, helped to entertain relatives and friends of the bride at the head table warmly and considerately. Hayrat said, in a choked voice, "My own mother died early and failed to see the lively scene of my wedding, but my Han mother has given me the most complete and beautiful wedding blessings ..."

"The emotional links between our two families began with the rocking bed." Zhou Haiyang said. In 2010, Hayrat's son, Yedly Hayrat, was born, the rocking bed was given back to Hayrat. "Two years later, my son came into the world, the bed was taken to my house again ... And now, my son and Hayrat's son became companions who were together every day!"

The brotherhood of younger generation made Hayrat happy. He said, "The brotherhood of the two little ones is even closer than ours, beyond description!"

The relationship between three generations of Hayrat's Kazakh family and Zhou Haiyang's Han family originated from the rocking bed, which is stronger than blood ties.

In Zhanjia Village where Hayrat's family is located as well as several nearby villages in Jiujianlou Township, you may hear so many stories about the rocking bed that they could not finish in a few days. Jura uttered, "From my father to me, and now to my son, the three generations have been linked by this rocking bed, which bound us closely with our neighbors of different ethnic groups like pomegranate seeds. So many times when I met a stranger, he would suddenly hold my hands and invite me to have a meal at his house. I asked, 'Why?' He would reply, 'Because we are relatives!' After meticulous inquiry, it turned out that he had also slept in our rocking bed when he was a baby!"

"What my brother mentioned is one circumstance. I often encounter another ..." Hayrat said. As the heir of the old house, he often came across things like this. A stranger would suddenly come to his house, and call him "brother" or "uncle". Hayrat, who was puzzled, could only respond with a smile. When he asked, they said that they had once slept in that rocking bed!

"Great! Since you are back home, let's have a meal together!" Hayrat and his wife are warm-hearted people, always entertaining guests with fine food and wine.

Last autumn, Hayrat met with another "big brother" from Shandong who said that he had left Jiujianlou for more than 20 years. He worked as a manager in a Shandong construction company and earned some money. This time he came back to visit his Kazakh "mother", namely Hayrat's mother. "I haven't seen nor heard of him, but he came all the way to find us from thousands of miles away through many twists and turns. How can I refuse him? He said that when he was a child, he came to jiujianlou with his parents who was totally unfamiliar with the local condition. He had been fostered in my family, spending his first two years in our rocking bed. Consequently, he had deep and unforgettable feelings with my family, my mother, and the rocking bed. Later, I accompanied him who came from afar to pay respects at my parents' tombs, and took him around for several days in my hometown which looked completely new. He lived in my house for several days, saying that he seemed to have returned to his happy childhood ..." Hayrat said.

"His family, just as at the time his mother was alive, is always bustling. At that time, we were busy at work, having no time to look after our children, then we brought them to Hayrat's mother. Thus her house had become a voluntary nursery ... There had been more than a dozen children at most, and Hayrat's mother became a ' Queen of Children'! The younger ones would sleep in the rocking bed, while the older ones would play with her. For decades, Hayrat's family had always been a bustling and big happy one. From Hayrat's grandfather on, the entire family has been exceptionally hospitable and kind-hearted. Hayrat's family with the rocking bed has united the people of all ethnic groups in several neighboring villages as close as one family." said an aunt named Zhang Yuxiu. At that time, she had a daughter aged three and a son aged one. She was not able to take care of her own children because of work, so she left her children in the care of Hayrat's mother on the way to work every day and then went to work without any worries.

"Hayrat's mother had looked after my children for at least two years." Aunt Zhang said gratefully.

The cadres in Jiujianlou Township who accompanied me to Hayrat's home told me: There are more than 10 ethnic groups in their township, including Han, Kazakh, Mongolian, Hui, and Uyghur. The rocking bed has been used by at least 27 children from different ethnic groups, generating numerous "stories beyond stories".

Cai Zhongfu, aged 57, and his neighbor Wang Zhenghai, a Hui villager, who was 10 years younger than Cai, have another "brotherly bond" because of the rocking bed. The story started with Cai Zhongfu, who was born in early March of the lunar calendar in 1963 —

Cai Zhongfu was born at the time when spring sowing was going on in Usu. Cai's family was busy doing farm work and had no time to look after him. They borrowed the rocking bed, and Cai's elder brother and sister were assigned to rock the bed.

> Baby brother, go to sleep,
> Sleep tight, have a dream,
> When you awake, you'll see Papa and Mama
> Coming home …
> Go to sleep, baby brother,
> Papa and Mama praise you for being
> A good baby at home
>
> …

In front of the rocking bed, Cai's sister hummed a *Rocking Bed Song* composed by herself. Later, his brother followed her. Cai was lying comfortably and happily in the rocking bed, entering his childhood dreamland while they were singing.

"A person's memory of childhood, especially those of infancy, are actually very few, but my memory of the rocking bed is so clear as if it was my best time in life. Whenever I opened my eyes, I could always see smiling faces ..." Cai said.

After Cai had spent a happy infancy in the rocking bed, his parents returned it back to Hayrat's family.

On May 19th, 1973, Wang Zhenghai, Cai's Hui neighbor, was born. The situation of the Wangs was similar to that of the Cais. When his parents were busy working in the fields, little Wang Zhenghai was left in the care of his brothers and sisters.

Wang Haiying,Wang Zhenghai's grown-up sister, talked about the days when she took care of her little brother, she covered her face and became a little embarrassed:"At that time, my parents went to work in the fields, sometimes we had to help them when we were not in school. My brother and I were still young. Hoping to slack off, we would rush to look after baby brother at home. However, we were not able to hold him, so our parents borrowed the rocking bed from Hayrat's family. My elder brother and I were both very delighted to take care of the baby brother who was lying in the bed tamely. That was how we watched him grow up in the bed day by day ..."

When he grew up, Wang Zhenghai began to herd cattle, mow grass and play hide-and-seek with the children in the village. During this process, he learned that Cai Zhongfu, who was 10 years older than him, had also once slept in the same rocking bed. It was by this link that the two boys gradually became inseparable good partners and brothers.

"Maybe it's because we grew up in the same rocking bed, although I am 10 years older than Zhenghai and we are from different ethnic groups, I feel as if he were my own brother ..." Cai said.

In the 1980s and 1990s, Cai Zhongfu and Wang Zhenghai successively got married and had children. In 2012, a new district was built in Huangqu Village where they lived. Coincidentally, Cai and Wang both moved in and became door-to-door neighbors.

"Big brother —"

"Little brother —"

From then on, the two brothers live together harmoniously, which is so admirable.

In the summer of 2012, Wang's mother suffered from acute cholangitis. Upon hearing the news, Cai immediately drove her to the hospital. Afterward, seeing that his mother was safe and sound, Wang was so moved that he went to Cai's house to express his gratitude with kowtows to his brother.

"At that time, I had just started my business. I spent all my money on cattle and sheep with little money left. It was Zhongfu who sent my mother to the hospital and paid for all the expenses. He not only saved my mother but also my whole family." Wang said.

In 2014, Wang opened an agritainment inn. When Wang was short of hands, Cai's wife would become a free part-time employee.

Ma Jinhua, Wang Zhenghai's wife, said, "When my husband and I were overwhelmed with receiving the guests, Mrs. Cai would come to help, all we need to do is just a call of 'Sister Juhua'. We are a family!"

In 2016, Cai was elected as the director of the village committee. His family has a larger farming area, so he was extremely busy during the farming season and couldn't manage everything on his own. Wang would give him a hand. "He never says 'No' to me!" Cai said.

Time flies by and they have been neighbors for 10 years. When Wang Zhenghai and Cai Zhongfu met me, they warmly told me, "We have never quarreled or argued with each other. We make dumplings at the Spring Festival and fried sanzi at the Corban Festival together ... We are family and brothers!"

"The affection originates from the rocking bed of Hayrat's family ..." Wang, holding Cai's hands, came to Jurat and Hayrat, respectfully saying,

"My brothers, thank you so much!"

Scenes like this can be seen almost every day in Hayrat's house.

"Do sit down. We are family. No need for courtesies." By this time, Hayrat would hand out beers, while his pretty wife would bring out watermelons, inviting their "brothers" and "sisters" to taste the most delicious food in Usu.

"Very nice ... Have another drink! Drink your fill! The Usu beer does not intoxicate us but our hearts; Our watermelons are so sweet, sweetening our hearts!" Hayrat, who was usually shy, became eloquent and enthusiastic.

"You are all my brothers and sisters. I am extremely happy to see you come back and visit us again ... Come on! Bottoms up !" Hayrat's face gradually turned red ...

"Drunk? I'm not drunk ... I'm happy and proud. Because we have slept in the same rocking bed, our lives are linked by this bond to make us one family, which is so beautiful, just as at the time we were young, lying in the rocking bed. Rocking and rocking, it lulled us into beautiful dreamland ..." Everyone thought Heyrat was drunk,but he said, "I am certainly not drunk, the Usu beer does not intoxicate people, only my heart is intoxicated ..."

While he spoke, he made the gesture of rocking the bed affectionately, then his "brothers" and "sisters" all stood up and followed him ...

Hayrat's yard soon became a joyful place. Later, more and more people joined them, making the gesture of rocking the bed while singing the beautiful and charming *lullaby* —

> ...
> Slumber, slumber, O my darling baby,
> When will you slumber,

Hope you slumber quickly.
Slumber, slumber, O my darling baby,
Slumber, slumber, O my darling baby,

...

On the evening when we left Jiujianlou, this beautiful Kazakh *lullaby* kept echoing in my ears.

Chapter 4

The Story about the "National Flag Bearer"

The most symbolic representation of a nation's territory is where its national flag flies.

A national flag declares the national sovereignty.

Li Guanying, the flag bearer at the Founding Ceremony of People's Republic of China,

And Shalekjiang, who raises the national flag at his own small yard for decades,

With the persistence and faith of a citizen,

Declare the dignity and sovereignty of the country.

What impressed me most in Xinjiang, especially in Tacheng, was that the people and government here paid special attention to the significance of the national flag. This kind of national consciousness, with profound historical and practical significance, was unparalleled compared to anywhere else.

Far from the frontier, we enjoy the warmth of our country every day, but our national consciousness may not be so strong. However, it is quite different for the people in Tacheng, who live in the frontier. Their national consciousness is manifested in every aspect of their lives, which is truly admirable.

This may be related to its history or distance from the "heart(capital Beijing)" of the country.

It would be a long story if historical problems are involved. We may write another book to describe it. But what does it have to do with the distance from the "heart" of the country?

We have lived in Beijing for a long time. Taking Tiananmen Square as an example, Beijingers may not have deeper impression or feelings towards it compared to people from other places. It doesn't mean that we do not have deep feelings for it. We are just "used to it", and it becomes not that special. However, when I first went to work in Beijing, I had so strong feelings towards Tiananmen, Tiananmen Square, the Great Hall of the People, the Monument to the People's Heroes, and the flag-raising ceremony that I couldn't even sleep well. Being a new Beijinger, the first thing one should do is to go to Tiananmen Square to watch the flag-raising ceremony, and then enter the Great Hall of the People to attend a meeting, all these are nice ideas. But when all have been done, I'm afraid most people are reluctant to go to Tiananmen Square again, especially to get up so early to watch the flag-raising ceremony. It has nothing to do with our loyalty to the country. We are just too familiar with these things.

Afterward, I found, for example, if you went abroad to a totally strange place, suddenly you saw the Five-Starred Red Flag(the national flag of the PRC) before you, it would make you feel pleasantly surprised and homey,with a strong sense of security welling up in my heart.

Having seen the national flag in different places, we gradually come to understand the meaning of it. The Five-Starred Red Flag raised at Tiananmen Square makes me feel the heartbeat of my motherland, with a healthy, sunny, vibrant, progressive and invincible force. The national flag seen overseas makes me realize that Chinese people are important members of the global village, deserving of respect and admiration, and we can do what we are willing to do and should do safely and freely.

After arriving in Tacheng, I especially noticed that Five-Starred Red Flags fluttering in the wind could be seen everywhere here. It suddenly dawned on me that here was the frontier, and wherever the red flags was planted, it was our land — the territory of the People's Republic of China!

Tacheng is undeniably far away from the capital Beijing, the eastern city Shanghai, and the southern city Guangzhou. However, it is too close to the border. If you step across it, you will be in the neighboring country.

In Xinjiang, especially in border cities like Tacheng, the national flag stands a silent oath — Here is our territory and the people here are our people.

Thus, when talking about the nation here, there must be many "stories about the national flag", which are particularly appealing and intriguing ...

Mongolian Autonomous County of Hoboksar is the farthest county from the central urban districts of Tacheng, a particularly vast area having the longest border line with Kazakhstan. On the edge of the county, beside the Provincial Highway 318, there is a very conspicuous and spectacular cemetery. A high marble tombstone stands in its center, engraved on it are seven Chinese characters — "Tomb of Comrade Li Guanying". It is absolutely rare to see such a grand scale cemetery in the vast Gobi and grassland. Even the tombs of ancient princes were not often comparable in magnificence and size. In summer, standing in front of it, one can catch sight of the lush grasslands at the northern foot of Mt. Tianshan and its snow-capped top. This graveyard evokes respect from all the visitors.

Who was Li Guanying? A martyr or a hero? People in Hoboksar shook their heads and said, "He had been a veteran stationed in the border area."

"Why was he different?" I was confused.

"Because he was the flag bearer who walked in front of the parade at the Founding Ceremony, that is, the first flag bearer of New China ..."

"Oh, I see!" I couldn't help feeling surprised. But why had he come to this remote border area? And why was he much respected by people here?

What was his story?

This "secret" remained sealed for more than 40 years. It was amazing to know that the flag bearer at the Founding Ceremony had left an unimaginable legendary story in Xinjiang —

Li Guanying was actually an ordinary man, but what he had experienced was extraordinary. If calculated by the date of his birth, he would be 100 years old if he were alive this year.

Li Guanying was born on April 9, 1923, in Gushi, Henan Province. His father served as a senior officer in the Northeast Army under General Zhang Xueliang's command. After the July 7th Incident, their family moved to Lanzhou, Gansu Province, due to being wanted by the Japanese army.

In Lanzhou, Li Guanying, young and handsome, was admitted to the Northwest Repertory Theatre. Later, in 1944, the theatre was dissolved due to the war. Unwilling to give up the ideal of becoming a successful man, Li went to Chongqing, the "alternate capital" at that time, for a job. With his father's assistance, he joined a training program for naval personnel sponsored by the National Government of China to study in the United Kingdom. During his stay in Britain, he was greatly influenced by European industrial civilization and socialist thoughts, which led him to contemplate his life and the destiny of his country, and gradually learned about communist theory. At that time, something happened, which had altered his life. In order to compensate for the loss of six harbor patrol boats that were entrusted to the British authorities in Hong Kong but went missing, the British government decided to transfer their cruiser, HMS Aurora, which was later renamed as "RCS Chung King", to the National Government of China. In 1947, Li Guanying returned to China as a naval specialist after completing his study in the UK, and then was assigned the mission of bringing the "RCS Chung King" back to China. This ship had became the most powerful main warship in the Kuomintang military forces led by Chiang Kai-shek, who himself had even presided over a military conference of senior Kuomintang generals in the Northeastern Theater Command on board the ship.

On February 25, 1949, before the "RCS Chung King" Uprising, Captain Deng Zhaoxiang assigned Li Guanying with the important task of uniting his fellow sailors for the Uprising. On the day of the Uprising, facing the rising sun, Li Guanying put on a new uniform of the Chinese navy, stripping off the emblem of the Kuomintang army, together with his shipmates, sailed the "RCS Chung King" slowly into Yantai Port in Shandong Province, to report to the upcoming New China.

People who participated in the "RCS Chung King" Uprising had made indelible contributions to the founding of the People's Liberation Army(PLA) Navy. Chairman Mao Zedong sent a special commendation telegram for their action. For the first time, Li Guanying felt a sense of glory to be the master of the country.

On the February of 1949, a grand ceremony was held in Dandong Liberated Area in Northeast China to celebrate the establishment of the first People's Naval School of New China. Deng Zhaoxiang, who led the "RCS Chung King" Uprising, was appointed as the principal of the school and most of the cadets and instructors of the school were also participants in the Uprising. Li Guanying became one of the first instructors there due to his experience, but at the same time he was also a cadet.

"On behalf of the superiors, I hereby order 50 cadets to undertake a classified military mission … And you'll depart this afternoon!" On that day, Li Guanying, like other instructors and cadets, attended the morning exercise. However, what made it different was that he and the other 49 cadets were summoned by the school authority to another location. Li looked around at the group and noticed that all members were handsome men.

"Sir, what task are we carrying out? Are we going to the south to support the battle for liberating Southwest China?" Veteran Li quietly asked his superior and got the answer, "The task is confidential, and even I am not aware of it!"

"Set off —" With the command given, 50 naval cadets boarded the southbound train, passed through Shenyang(in Liaoning Province), and arrived at Beijing Qianmen Station late at night.

"We've arrived in Beijing!"

"Are we coming to Beijing to protect Chairman Mao and Commander-in-Chief Zhu?"

"That would be incredible if it's true …"

As they waited for their next order at the train station, everyone began whispering and speculating.

"All comrades of the People's Naval School, attention! Towards the trucks, march off!" Suddenly, the commander gave the order. Li Guanying and his counterparts quickly boarded two trucks parked beside the station, passing through several streets in Xicheng District, Beijing, then entered the Huangsi Barracks, now the former dormitory compound of the PLA's General Political Department on Huangsi Street, Beijing.

After getting off the trucks, a senior officer came out to receive them and issued an order, "Your mission today is to head to the assigned dormitories immediately and get some sleep!"

That night — in fact, there was only a few hours left to dawn, Li Guanying and his 49 schoolmates were so excited that they didn't get much sleep. When the reveille sounded at dawn, they were informed that they were going to participate in the grand military parade for Founding Ceremony of the New China!

"Hurrah —"

"We are going to witness the establishment of New China!"

This was something Li Guanying could never have imagined, he felt so lucky. Since that day, Li Guanying and his comrades had been filled with joy and excitement, as if they were living in a sweet dream. But what surprised him even more was that, because he was good-looking with standard height of 1.76 meters, precise military postures and skilled parade drill movements, he was chosen to be the flag bearer for the Navy Square Formation, leading the way at the front of the parade.

"Sir, what do our military flag and national flag look like?"

"Sir, when will be our turn?"

"Sir, what is the sequence for us to pass through Tiananmen Square and receive inspection by Chairman Mao and Commander-in-Chief

Zhu?"

"Sir ..."

"Li Guanying! Now listen to me: Don't think about anything else, just focus on the flag bearer movements drill , or you will be dismissed!" The commander was bored and scolded him.

"Yes, sir! I will practice well!" Li Guanying answered loudly.

In the following three months, Li didn't dare to be careless, and trained every movement rigorously until he performed flawlessly. Anyone who had participated in a military parade would know that although the moment in front of Tiananmen drawn attention from millions of people, not everyone could withstand the rigorous training for months. Li and his fellow soldiers, as participants in the first parade of New China, not only had tight training schedules but also carried out a military mission — prepared to fight any enemies attempting to disrupt the parade at any time.

The wheels of history were irreversible, and everything was advancing according to the will of the Communist Party of China and the combat paces of the People's Liberation Army ...

The long-awaited and momentous moment had finally arrived: At 3 pm on October 1, 1949, sounds of jubilation reverberated throughout Tiananmen Square, overwhelming entire Beijing in celebration of the birth of New China. Mao Zedong, Zhu De and other leaders of the Party and the State ascended the Tiananmen Rostrum with vigorous steps.

"The Central People's government of the People's Republic of China is founded today!" Chairman Mao Zedong made a solemn announcement, which resounded through the sky, while audience of three hundred thousand people cheered together.

"The march-past begins —" That was the first military parade of New China. Taking the lead was the square formation that Li Guanying marched in, while Li was the most prominent member at the forefront of the 16,000 soldiers. During the Ceremony, the first parade adopted a formation with a navy representative serving as the flag bearer of the entire troops. Li Guanying happened to be the one who held the flag among the three flag guards, with the other two holding rifles on either side of him. As the flag bearer, Li naturally stood out, drawing attention from hundreds of thousands of people. He and two comrades had the honor to follow General Nie Rongzhen's convertible, which meant that he was the first soldier to be reviewed by Mao Zedong and Zhu De!

Li, with a majestic and powerful demeanor, marched towards Tiananmen Square with firm and proud steps, who was ready to be reviewed by the great leaders ... As Li took a goose step, he swiftly tilted the flag at a 45-degree angle, and the fluttering flag led the way forward, paying tribute to all the soldiers of our army since Nanchang Uprising, and saluting the New China and her supreme commander!

His eyes were a little wet, but bright and shining .

His steps were a little quivering, but firm and powerful.

His heart was pounding, but it must always be calm ...

It was the image of the flag bearer at the Founding Ceremony of New China, and this sort of parade arrangement was also unique in our history. Since then, more than a dozen military parades at Tiananmen Square have been organized in the sequence of the army, navy and air force. Only in the Founding Ceremony, the navy took the lead, and Li Guanying became the flag bearer in this "unique" event, recorded in the history of the PRC.

However, Li, the flag bearer in the Founding Ceremony, was only an ordinary citizen who couldn't take control of his own destiny amidst the turbulent history ...

After attending the Ceremony, Li returned to the Naval School, and then was assigned as an instructor at the Naval Academy of People's

Liberation Army in Dalian for four years.

However, in 1954, Li Guanying received an inexplicable notice of transfer, assigning him to work at the Dalian Shipyard. At a time when our naval defense forces were being strengthened, it was rather peculiar for someone with a background in naval military studies to be suddenly transferred. There was certainly some "political reasons" behind it, although no one informed Li at the time, or perhaps it was not convenient to disclose the "internal" details. In this way, Li took off his uniform and came to his new position. However, Dalian was unfamiliar to him, and he had no relatives or friends there apart from the troops. Considering that his mother was in Lanzhou, he applied to return to Gansu Province and was granted approval.

As a demobilized cadre who had participated in a uprising, Li should have been properly resettled. However, during the time of the ultra-Left, "historical issues" weighed heavily on him, being brought up from time to time. Shortly after, there was a nationwide "anti-rightist" movement, and his background as the son of a senior officer in the Kuomintang and his own "historical issues" were brought up again. At that time, dealing with such issues required one to return to one's hometown. He had traveled back and forth across the country, returned to his hometown in Henan Province for help. However, when he took great pains arriving in Henan, he was told with regret, "Your hometown is a small county, now under the jurisdiction of Anhui Province. We have no authority over it."

When Li wearily arrived in Anhui, the functionaries there told him that they didn't have time to deal with these irrelevancies which happened before liberation.

"At least I am a demobilized officer from the army. You should assign me a job, right?" Li, who hadn't had a decent meal for several days, pleaded with the officials from the Anhui Civil Affairs Department.

"We need to discuss this ..." Such a response kept him staying in the guest house of the Department for two years, but he still couldn't secure a job.

"How did you manage to get by during those two years?" Later, someone asked him.

"I ... I ... I don't even know how I got through it myself." Being a veteran, Li had never experienced such frustration before, but this time he truly felt a deep sense of injustice: Being young and strong, yet he was unable to work. Despite his rich knowledge in the naval field, he had to beg someone for help in finding a job on land.

"At that time, if a capable person didn't have a job, people would think that something might be wrong with you or you're not a good guy." Li later recalled his days living in the guest house in Hefei(the capital of Anhui Province) and said, "When you were staying at someone else's place and eating their food, you naturally couldn't just take advantage of them. So, in order to avoid being kicked out, I served as a handy man to do what others didn't want to do and take on the responsibilities that others were afraid of ... In short, I had to adapt and compromise while being dependent on others."

Aged thirty-five or thirty-six, Li Guanying, a former revolutionary soldier, an instructor of People's Navy Academy, and a flag bearer at the Founding Ceremony of the PRC, found that he had neither a home nor a formal job. After two years, he felt that he couldn't wait any longer in Hefei, so he decided to go to Beijing, where he had once been honored with the highest recognition, to make an appeal ...

"How could such a thing happen?!" The leader from the Ministry of Internal Affairs who received him was very angry after hearing Li's account, and then he asked, "So where would you like to work? Please choose for yourself, and we will try our best to meet your requirements."

Li Guanying, with a sincere expression, tears welling up in his eyes, lips trembling and said, "Sir, I am alone, free of constraints and concerns ... I will follow your arrangements."

"That's great! Comrades from the army have a higher level of consciousness!" The leader was pleased to hear that and said, "Currently, the place where talents are in great need is Xinjiang. Are you willing to go there?"

"Yes, I am! I would like to go anywhere as long as I am needed by the Country!" Li agreed without hesitation.

Making a choice was simple, but the distance from Beijing to Xinjiang was so far away. His choice would thoroughly change his life, but he didn't think too much or had any better options. Having a job with a salary to sustain his life was enough. After arriving in Xinjiang, Li was assigned to the Red Flag Farm of the Six Division in Xinjiang Production and Construction Corps.

"Ah, well, all the formal positions have already been occupied, you may only work as a farming worker, with the monthly salary of 39.38 yuan ... What do you think?" The personnel cadre said to him.

"Okay!" Li nodded. "Getting paid proves that I have a job." That was what he said to himself. It was true. A few years before, he didn't have a job, which made him anxious.Now things were different. He got a work unit and would get paid, he work the country!

Li Guanying didn't even think about what unit would he work at or whether the work was hard to do or not.

To work in the Xinjiang Production and Construction Corps was actually nothing easier than that of farmers. Li's work unit was located on the edge of the Gurbantunggut Desert in the northern foothill of Mt. Tianshan. What he needed to do was to reclaim farmland, as well as build reservoirs. During that time, the reclamation projects were not only arduous but also required tremendous effort. He once dug 8.5 cubic meters of earth in a single day, setting the highest record in the farm. As a result, the comrades in the Corps called him a "workaholic" and he was honored with the title of "Model Worker."

It was in this environment that Li Guanying realized the value and honor of labor for New China, thus he developed a special affection for frontier construction, and transformed the prestigious honor of being the flag bearer at the Founding Ceremony into a belief in supporting frontier development and promoting unity among different ethnic groups.

While many people use phrases like "displaced" or "wandering across the country" in times of hardship, few have experienced a life as turbulent as Li Guanying's …

In 1960, after working for a year in the Xinjiang Production and Construction Corps, Li's farm was transferred to the road maintenance section in Transport Department of Xinjiang Uygur Autonomous Region,so he became a road maintenance worker.

In October 1961, workers of the road maintenance section were collectively sent to serve the needs of agriculture. Without hesitation, Li was the first to sign up, and from then on, he dedicated his life to the vast land of Hoboksar Mongolian Autonomous County …

Initially, he worked as a shepherd in Red Flag Commune (now Chagankule Township). From a distance, the local Mongolian masses watched this single man who loved to sing on the grasslands, guessing that he might be an offender under labor reform. Upon hearing that he was a model worker and an intellectual who could write and sing, they began to get close to him.

"Can you help me write a letter to my child studying in Xi'an?"

"Sure."

"Can you help the production team issue a blackboard newspaper?"

"Definitely."

"Can you teach the herders to sing?"

"Of course."

"Can ... can you give a general knowledge class to all cadres in the township every week?"

"Absolutely! I am a single man with no concerns or burdens. As long as I am needed, feel free to assign me any tasks!"

"Mr. Li - We sincerely appreciate what you did ..." His neighbors, the village Party secretary, and commune officials said to him warmly, "You are like a family member to all of us. If you are wronged or have any trouble, just speak up, and we will help you work it out together!"

"Thank you, thank you so much ... You are surely my family ..." On Li's 40th birthday, herdsmen of a dozen households who pastured together in the grassland, held a grand Mongolian-style birthday party for him in a tent. Li Guanying, who rarely drank wine, got drunk that day, with immense happiness, tears streaming down his face."

We have traveled a long and arduous journey,
Crossing the mountains, rivers, and the Gobi Desert.
Leaving behind our loved ones and fellow countrymen,
Our tears never dry while we weep,
My beloved hometown, it is only when we are displaced that we truly appreciate your preciousness.
When we yearn for you, we look up at the rising sun ...

After experiencing countless hardships in life,
My tears have dried up, only a single heart left.
Leaving behind distracting thoughts and boundless worries,

Settle down in Xinjiang for farm work, finding solace in
the frontier.

Here is my home, where the wanderers no longer roam
and struggle.

When I miss you, I cast my eyes on the moon in the
sky …

The first half of this song was a folk song passed down from the
ancient garrison camp in Tacheng, describing their life in exile, and the
second half was a self-composed song reflecting Li's feelings.

"Mr, Li, you're not young anymore. Many Mongolian girls are fond
of you. It's time for you to get married!"Many a time, people came to
persuade him.

But Li always smiled indifferently and said, "My heart belongs to this
land, and my emotions are left to the drifting clouds …"

Many people didn't understand him. Was it the language of a poet or
the lament of a long-suffering person who were disappointed in love ? This
had been a mystery for a long time.

It was not until in the spring of 1997 when someone walked into Li
Guanying's extremely crude bachelor dormitory for only 8 square meters
and found a small mourning hall inside, was the mystery finally solved …

When he was young, Li Guanying, a fine-looking man, had a beloved
girlfriend. However, due to his drifting and unstable life, his sincere love
faded away like the passing time, deeply hurting his heart.

This story began in 1942 when Li was admitted to the Northwest
Repertory Theatre. At that time, he played the role of Zhou Puyuan's
youngest son Zhou Chong in the play *Thunderstorm*, and Miss Chen,
who played the role of Si Feng, was his girlfriend. In 1944, the theatre
disbanded due to the war, and the young couple went to Chongqing,

Miss Chen's hometown, after a series of hardships. It was here that Li Guanying got the opportunity to study in the UK for three years. They kept correspondence constantly and looked forward to the future. In 1949, before Li Guanying could contact his girlfriend, he headed to the liberated areas with his comrades in the Uprising. Then he participated in the Founding Ceremony. Chongqing was liberated rather late. He tried every means to contact his girlfriend but failed …

In 1950, Li was transferred to teach at the Naval Academy of PLA in Dalian, and he finally got into contact with his girlfriend in Chongqing after continuous efforts. "Come to Chongqing. Let's get married!" His girlfriend wrote to him. Li was overjoyed but faced a dilemma. As the Korean War broke out, the troops had just been ordered to get ready to go to the front line, and they should keep the information about wartime mobilization confidential. "What's going on? If you have other thoughts, then we break up!" Frustrated by his repeated delay, his girlfriend demanded an explanation.

In 1954, after leaving the army and returning to Lanzhou, Li learned that his girlfriend had already married an army officer and accompanied him to Lanzhou, and she had once paid a special visit to his mother.

Everything had gone. Li made an appointment with his ex-girlfriend at the Baita Mountain Park, where they used to date 10 years ago. As they reunited, the scenery remained the same, but everything else had changed. She came to meet him with a child over one year old in her arm. Li could only offer his sincere blessings for their happiness and found himself unable to say anything else.

The brief encounter, lasting less than half an hour, made his heart broken …Watching his ex-girlfriend walking away, Li turned back with tears coursing down his cheeks.

Two years later, Li, who was looking for a job, learned that his mother had died of illness, but he couldn't get back to Lanzhou, so he asked his ex-girlfriend to help handle his mother's funeral. She did so with great care and thoughtfulness.

Li was both grateful and regretful: How nice it would have been if she were his mother's daughter-in-law! He cried. Such crying of him often echoed on the long and lonely nights ... It was still the same even when he was in Xinjiang.

Outsiders had been unaware of all these.

They only knew that "Mr.Li", who lived alone in a small house of seven or eight square meters, was an optimistic and open-minded old farmer.

He has spent 41 years in Xinjiang reclaiming land and 38 years as a herdsman. During that time, someone often asked him, "Have you never thought about returning to Beijing or Lanzhou? Have you never regretted or complained?"

"No. I really haven't!" Li Guanying replied affirmatively, "Since the day when the authority informed me about my assignment in Xinjiang, I have never felt regretful or lost. In Xinjiang and Tacheng, my life is tough but enriched. I have a sense of honor here because I am a man with a job, and I am respected. Especially I have built up close bond with the people of various ethnic groups here while I would make a small contribution to the development of the border regions. It makes my life worthwhile!"

When he said so, there was no trace of pretense. His sincerity was so touching and poignant ...

1999 marked the 50th anniversary of the founding of the People's Republic of China. In May, the camera crew of CCTV's *Great Parade* found Li Guanying, after taking a long journey. They couldn't help shedding tears when they came to the small earthen house of 7-8 square meters and saw the living conditions of the flag bearer at the Founding

Ceremony of PRC.

"Oh, my senior comrade, why didn't you tell people about your glorious past? At least the government could solve your difficulties in life!" One crew member said.

Li's hands trembled as he held the hands of the journalists from Beijing, as if putting out all his strength. He said, "I'm fine and content with the status quo. I've done something for the people of various ethnic groups here, and I am happy that they recognized my efforts ..."

The "mystery" about Li was finally unraveled.

On December 31, 2000, the flag bearer of military parade at the Founding Ceremony, who had been through trials and tribulations but was still tenacious, passed away quietly at the age of 78.

As he was quietly buried in the westernmost land of his country, there was no noise or controversy. He had no personal property or descendants, but only a bright-colored Five-Starred Red Flag hidden beneath his pillow, along with a warm heart accompanying Tacheng, where people of all ethnic groups united.

On the day of the burial, hundreds of people from various ethnic groups and his close friends came to pay their respects to this old comrade, offering flowers and wine ...

I arrived in Tacheng in June 2022, the 100th anniversary of Li Guanying's birth. Learning that his story had been widely spread among the people of Tacheng, I decided to go to his cemetery and pay tribute to this flag bearer of the Founding Ceremony, who had dedicated his entire life to the development of border areas and the promotion of national unity and prosperity.

His grave was magnificent. Above the 30 steps, stood a marble tombstone engraved with the words "Tomb of Comrade Li Guanying". It bestowed the most honorable dignity upon the lonely veteran, who had been unknown to the public before his death, and whose life was hard but full of passion for striving. At that moment, I believed that Li Guanying, resting in peace, must have been happy and content.

At that moment, I seemed to see a Five-Starred Red Flag fluttering in front of me, which was the same flag that Li Guanying and his comrades once held high as they marched through Tiananmen Square ...

Ah, the Five-Starred Red Flag! In the years when it was made as our national flag, numerous revolutionary martyrs have dyed it red with their selfless spirit of sacrifice. And in the peaceful years when it is protected as a symbol of the PRC, there are also countless common people like Li Guanying, who have offered their hard work and even bitter tears to ensure that it never fades and flutters highly forever!

Ah! In Tacheng, there are many stories about the national flag, like "the story about Li Guanying",which are so attracting that I am eager to know them.

Haldun is a residential community in downtown Tacheng where lived an old Uyghur man named Shalekjiang Yiming, who is now 75 years old. People told me that on the eve of the centenary of the founding of the Communist Party of China in 2021, the residents of the community had cheerfully celebrated two joyful events for Shalekjiang. One was that he gloriously joined the Communist Party of China, the other was that he had attended a flag-raising ceremony at Tiananmen Square in Beijing.

"Shalekjiang is so fortunate and glorious!" Before I walked into Shalekjiang's courtyard, several Uyghur uncles and aunts of the community told me in languages that I barely understood.

Some atmospheres are truly created. Human consciousness is the product of spirit, which is probably the case for any ethnic group.

Shalekjiang's small yard is a solemn and sacred place because a national flag of the PRC is fluttering highly there which is like a lighthouse that brought the residents of Haldun community together.

Does a national flag really have such charm? Can it really gather a group of scattered people together like pomegranate seeds? Actually, when I heard that I was going to interview Shalekjiang, there were some "doubts" lingering in my mind, although they were not easy to express. However, when I walked into his yard, looking up at the national flag fluttering highly above his roof and the wooden pole supporting it, a sense of sacredness suddenly emerged and flowed through my veins, all the way to my brain ... I stood still, gazing at the flagpole, which was about 14 to 15 meters tall, simple yet sturdy. The flag here surely couldn't be compared to that at Tiananmen Square, despite sharing the same meaning, but could the flag in an ordinary household really have the same effect and sacred power to people?

At that moment when I was approaching the flag, I realized that the feeling was the same.

I was very curious about how the national flag at his yard was raised ...

Shalekjiang can speak Mandarin, though not very fluent, could be understood in a slower speed. "Now my small yard has been expanded with the help of the government. The old house used to be a bungalow. The two buildings on the right side are built as a national flag education exhibition room ..." Shalekjiang pointed to the red house next to the flagpole and said.

I see. I had a look at the small yard,which was about fifty to sixty square meters and quite neat ... "Is the flag-raising ceremony held here?" I asked.

"Yes," Shalekjiang nodded. Probably he understood what I meant to ask and further explained, "Usually, about fifty to sixty, or seventy to eighty people came here. But on festivals, there would be so many people who even stood outside the yard ..."

"Do you raise the flag and hold a ceremony everyday?"

"Definitely."

"Do you sing the national anthem or play the music of it?"

"We have a small device for playing music ..." Shalekjiang made haste to take out his fixed music player. "We used to use cassette tapes. Now we have this special music player for the national anthem!" He played a segment of the national anthem to me, which sounded magnificent.

"Do you hoist the flag by hand pulling?" I walked to the flagpole and noticed that there was no special device on the wooden pole. What they had was just a hemp rope and probably an iron pulley at the top of the flagpole.

"Yes ..." He replied.

"Can you match with the music?"

"It takes practice, over and over again ..." He said, at the beginning, either the music played too fast or he pulled the rope too quickly. After practicing for more than ten days, he mastered the timing and rhythm. "Now I'm very skilled, punctual to the minute!" Shalekjiang told me proudly.

"Who else can do it so accurately?" I wondered when Shalekjiang was not at home or had other things to do, who else could replace him?

"Wang Fulin will do, and my sons ... Now my grandson can also help me raise the flag!" Shalekjiang immediately listed a series of names loudly. It seems that his flag-raising ceremony was already very mature and complete.

"But when we started, there were indeed many troubles, some of which were unimaginable ..." as he explained, I realized that what seemed like a simple task actually was very difficult. It was highly necessary for him to raise this national flag!

The story should start with the severe violent crimes committed during the Urumqi "July 5th" Incident in 2009.

"During that time, influenced by hostile forces from abroad, there was a rare turmoil in Xinjiang, which made people panic and at a loss because ordinary people generally didn't know the truth. So, it was better to avoid unnecessary trouble, and the most chose to keep a low profile. As a result, the separatists and bad guys who were influenced by foreign forces became more engaged. The overall condition in Tacheng prefecture was relatively better than that in other regions, but the psychological turmoil of the residents was severe. People like us who loved our country and the Communist Party of China were very worried. We all wished to do something for our country and the unity of the Chinese nation. But given the situation and people's mentality, we couldn't come up with a better and more effective solution. I was extremely anxious! I am 75 years old this year. Although I was born in the old society, most of the time I grew up with New China and knew what kind of regime was good. Particularly as my parents told me: In the border cities like Tacheng, we knew how important the country was to us! Only when the country became strong could our lives be happy and stable; otherwise, we would be in trouble every day ... Thinking about these things, I couldn't sit still, I should do something for the country and the borderland ..." Shalekjiang couldn't stop talking when he mentioned why he raised the flag at his yard.

I could tell that Shalekjiang was an extraordinary old man who loved thinking, had a way and strong will. Moreover, he had a firm stance and clear-cut attitude.

"It has something to do with the influence of the PLA when I was a child ..." Shalekjiang became particularly nice to me when he heard that I had been served in the military for over ten years. "I have always been fond of PLA soldiers since I was a child and I would always remember what they had done. They had once raised a small national flag at my yard.

Small but impressive, the flag made me understand the concept of the country and the significance it had to the people."

It turned out that in 1950, when Shalekjiang had already cut his wisdom teeth, the PLA started to take control of the western border after they stationed in Xinjiang. Lack of military facilities or camps in the Tacheng prefecture, the troops had to stay with the local inhabitants. Shalekjiang's parents also vacated their own house for the soldiers to live in. "At that time, we made four rooms available for the troops, and they had stayed for eight years ..." Thus, Shalekjiang has cherished a deep affection for the PLA soldiers from an early age.

These fatherly PLA soldiers often held him in the arm, taught him how to count and write his name in Chinese, sang *The East is Red for him*, and gave him a shining red five-star badge.

"These were all vivid memories in my childhood," Shalekjiang said, "but what impressed me most was the moment the soldiers raised the Five-Starred Red Flag in front of my house, which made our family special and proud."

Shalekjiang said that not until he grew up did he realize the Five-Starred Red Flag was the national flag of China. "So, ever since I began to know better, I have understood what the country meant to us, and we must protect the land in Xinjiang for our country ... Here not only is our homeland but also the territory of our country!" This "national consciousness" that Shalekjiang spoke of was thus rooted in his heart when he was a little boy.

"I often thought that Xinjiang has always been the territory of China since ancient times, so it is no use spreading false rumors here! I decided to come out and tell my neighbors and fellow villagers not to be deceived by bad people! Just as the PLA had done, I would raise the national flag highly ..." Shalekjiang told me his original aspiration.

No in-depth argument, just a clear declaration: Here is China, we are all Chinese, no one is allowed to distort or manipulate this unshakable truth, and any conspiracy or destructive activities are destined to fail! This was what Shalekjiang thought in his mind, he believed that was also what it meant when the PLA raised the national flag at his yard.

"Decades ago, on behalf of our country, the PLA did so. Today, I will take the same action to prove again that Xinjiang is a part of China, and nobody is allowed to do anything harmful!" On that night, Shalikjiang gathered his whole family together and told them what he thought. He knew that to raise the national flag at home every day, he should get the support of the whole family.

"Dad, you're so great, and I'm on your side!" His daughter, who was a teacher at school, was the first to speak. She nestled against her father's shoulder and said with great happiness, "Starting from my grandpa our family have loved China and Xinjiang, uniting compatriots of all ethnic groups.Dad has learned from grandpa and inherited the good tradition from him."

She enlivened the otherwise dull family meeting, everyone started to talk about what they knew about their grandpa.Talking about grandpa, Salaydin, Shalekjiang's son who was a doctor at the People's Hospital in Tacheng, became excited. Besides his parents, he knew most about his grandpa's stories, so he was eager to speak first as always.

"We have a great dad today, first and foremost, because we have a great and caring grandpa ... Dad, was it in 1962 that my grandfather helped the Meng Guangzhi's family?" Salaydin's question brought Shalekjiang's mind back to his younger years —

Yes, it was in 1962.

What kind of age was that? It remained fresh in Shalekjiang's memory. At that time, the whole country was going through the three-year famine, thousands of people rushed to Xinjiang. Meng Guangzhi from Shandong Province was one of them. In a place with vast territory and rich resources, even if it was difficult, one could still dig up a handful of wild vegetables to eat in the field. .

He traveled westward alone, first to Lanzhou, then to Urumqi. Whether he could have enough to eat became his first standard to measure the living and working quality of a place. Hearing that there were "endless white flour steamed buns"in Tacheng, he came here with the last glimmer of hope.

Luckily, Meng Guangzhi, who had graduated from high school, found a job as a worker in a construction company in Tacheng, earning enough to feed himself and his family.

What's more, Meng Guangzhi, with no relatives here, met many kind-hearted Uyghur fellow villagers when he was looking for a place to live in the Haldun community. They entertained him with hot tea and meals, making the Han lad, a newcomer, feel the warmth of spring.

"Grandpa and dad couldn't speak Mandarin, so they had to use hand gestures to communicate with Meng Guangzhi. Eventually they provided the house next to ours for free to Uncle Meng's family." Salaydin, a graduate of Xinjiang Medical University, could tell the story of his grandfather and father in fluent Mandarin.

"It was unlike the time now, if a stranger came to the village, especially in the border areas, people could be very sensitive because capturing criminals and 'wanderers' was an important political task." Shalekjiang said. To protect Meng Guangzhi, Shalekjiang's father spared no effort, telling the whole family to keep the "secret". "Later, someone came and tried to take Meng away by force. Your grandpa patted his chest and told them that Meng was a good man, an intellectual who knew building technology well. He could guarantee Meng's innocence with his life. In this way, your grandpa saved him …"

With everything settled, Meng took his whole family to Tacheng and became good neighbors with Shalekjiang's family. A short mud wall witnessed the interactions between the two families, which has become a much told story of "Uighur-Han uniting as one family". If one cooked Xinjiang pulled noodles, and the other made Shandong pancakes, they would always send the food to their neighbor to taste first.

"Later, our two families truly united as one," Shalekjiang said. "That should be in 1964, Meng Zhaoyuan, Meng Guangzhi's eldest son, was 8 years old. There were many children in Meng's family so they had a large family expense, which solely relied on Meng's salary. Accordingly, I found every way to give his children delicious food until Meng Zhaoyuan went to college …"

In 1985, Meng moved into the flat assigned by his work unit with his family, but they still kept contact with Shalekjiang's family. They would gather together on every festival.

"My Chinese was learned from Meng's family when I got together with them," Uncle Shalekjiang told me proudly. There was a 30-square-meter patriotic educational base exhibition room on the second floor of a house to the right of the small yard, which was filled with national flags and various local folk musical instruments collected by Shalekjiang. He said that over the past twenty years, he has used many musical instruments and music players during the flag-raising process.

On the wall was a brief introduction to Shalekjiang's "Flag-Raising History" decorated by the community. "This is Meng Zhaoyuan, who told me that to be grateful to our family, when he applied to college, he would choose Uyghur language as major at Xinjiang University. And he did what he said. After graduating from university, he went to southern Xinjiang as a journalist and later transferred to the children's channel of CCTV … He's retired now." Shalekjiang pointed to a black-and-white photo on the wall, which was an old photo taken together with the two families in front of the yard.

The photo should have been taken forty years ago. The two families of Uyghur and Han having no blood relationship have merged into one, which was like what Shalekjiang's children referred to — their grandparents and parents were all guardians for patriotism and the promotion of national unity.

"Dad, no matter what you do, we will always support you!" The family meeting made Shalekjiang excited.

"Good! I am the head of the family, although at this special time, to raise the national flag at our own home takes risk, requiring courage, I think it is worthwhile. Xinjiang has always been a part of China since ancient times, and all ethnic groups here have always been united together. We will never allow anyone to undermine it! We are common people with limited abilities, but our determination to defend the dignity of the country and the unity of all ethnic groups is noble and sacred." Shalekjiang briefed me that during the family meeting, everyone became more determined when they recalled the decades-long close relationship with Meng Guangzhi's family.

Shalekejiang told me, "Before Meng Guangzhi passed away, I paid him a visit, which was the last time I saw him. At his funeral, I borrowed a video recorder from a friend to record the whole process, leaving precious materials and memories for his family ... A few years ago, when the Mengs heard that my wife suffered from uremia, they kept urging us to go to Beijing for treatment. As it was too far away, we didn't go, but Meng Zhaoyuan sent us money several times. At that time, my salary was only five to six hundred yuan, but Meng's family sent us 20,000 yuan at a time, and later sent another 10,000. They have done more than our own siblings could have done. So in our family, as soon as everyone heard that I decided to raise the national flag at our own yard to declare the unity of all ethnic groups in Xinjiang and our refusal to the attempts to split the country, all family members supported me at once, which made me particularly gratified."

I learned from the neighbors of Shalekjiang: Meng Guangzhi came to Tacheng alone and settled down with the help of local people. Later, his children were born here, and now his grandchildren are working in Tacheng. As for Shalekjiang, his action of raising the national flag has been a declaration of national unity and patriotism, actually in hope of the same "national unity and family bond" as his and Meng's families flourishing throughout Xinjiang like blooming flowers.

What Shalekjiang didn't expect was that although his decision of raising the national flag at his small yard was unanimously approved at the family meeting, he encountered difficulties in actual operation. "I believe raising the national flag is a very serious matter. Although it is at my own home, what I wish is to strengthen a sense of national consciousness and unity among the people around, so I hope the relevant departments would support my action. But when I applied for their approval, they were unable to provide an immediate answer because they had never met such a situation before. In the past, raising the national flag usually took place in one's work unit or the spacious squares. They were not sure whether my idea and practice of raising the national flag at my own home everyday would meet the relevant requirements," Shalekjiang explained, feeling at a loss.

What should he do? Without official approval, raising the national flag might not produce the results that he wished!

Shalekjiang was worried, stomping his feet: What could I do?

"Ask the Tacheng Federation of Trade Unions for help." Suddenly,

Shalekjiang got an idea: He could get help form his old patron. He used to work in a public-owned food company. Customers had often complaint about getting short measure when they bought meat at the company, but Shalekjiang could do nothing. After his children all found jobs in 2009, to serve the customers better, he quit his formal job at the food company and contracted to run a meat shop.

To ensure that the customers could buy quality-assured meat, Shalekjiang opened his own "Trusted Meat Shop". Firstly, all the meat sold were quarantined. Secondly, he put a scale in the shop available for any customer. If anyone found that the meat they bought from his shop was short in weight, they could complain to him and receive twice the money they had paid as compensation. This enhanced the reputation of his meat shop in Tacheng. Later, Shalekjiang improved the service further. He noticed that "office workers" didn't have time to queue up to buy meat, so he installed a telephone in the shop. Those "office workers" who needed to buy meat could simply give him a call, and then he would prepare the meat as requested, getting ready for them to pick up on their way home from work. Xinjiang people enjoy eating meat, so buying meat is a daily routine for many residents. He found that the elderly, the sick, pregnant women, and other vulnerable individuals were inconvenient to wait in line. In order to help these disadvantaged groups buy fresh and satisfactory meat, he wrote down a long list of their names and home addresses in the shop. During lunch break or after the shop was closed, he would deliver the meat to these people who found it difficult to shop on their own. The reputation of "Good Person Shalekjiang" and the "Trusted Meat Shop" gradually spread in Tacheng. The Municipal Federation of Trade Unions learned about his deeds and decided to commend him.

Since then, Trade Unions had become his patron. When he encountered difficulties in raising the national flag, he thought of the

Federation again.

"To raise the national flag at your home?! What a brilliant idea! Now, we really need people like you who can boldly express their views and stance on key issues about what is right or wrong. Raising the national flag is a patriotic action and a declaration of the unity of the Chinese nation. We firmly support you!" Upon hearing Shalekjiang's idea, the leaders of the Municipal Federation of Trade Unions immediately expressed their support.

"When I came back from the Federation, I felt as if I got a piece of gold. Two days later, they officially approved me to raise the national flag at my own yard." Shalekjiang said, and he immediately called for a second family meeting.

"Don't underestimate flag-raising, it's actually quite complicated!" Shalekjiang said, "When I invited the neighbors to attend the ceremony, some were very supportive while some were not that enthusiastic. There were even a few people said that I should beware of someone who might stab me in the back. Facing the severe situation, I called a second family meeting to reconcile the thoughts of the whole family first and then assign tasks to them to encourage villagers to attend our ceremony. Specifically, for the first time, we must have no fewer than 20 participants, which meant each of us must invite at least 5 people."

At that family meeting, Shalekjiang spoke very seriously, "This is not just our affair. The flag-raising ceremony is related to whether the upright force could dominate our community or not. That is to say our ceremony must be a success. Apart from our family, our neighbors in the community must also participate!"

The meeting then became serious. Shalekjiang looked at his family members solemnly ... He was waiting for their resolute response and unwavering support.

"Dad, don't worry, we will complete the mission!" His children assured him.

"Grandpa, I will also bring 5 classmates to join!" Subira, his granddaughter, said.

"Good, thank you! Thank you so much, my Subira!" Shalekjiang was thrilled. Then he said, "As for me, I will go to invite the Imam. His participation is crucial."

Through the efforts of the whole family, as they had expected, more than 20 people agreed to join them, including the Imam, retired cadres, community workers, students and neighbors.

"But we had to make a careful plan to ensure that we could succeed with the flag-raising ceremony and the participants would be happy, willing to follow the entire procedure and come again next time." Shalekjiang was taking pains to make the ceremony go smoothly.

There would be children and elderly people coming to his house. According to the normal procedure of the ceremony, everyone would share their views on patriotism and national unity, which would take at least an hour. So, he needed to prepare walking sticks for the elderly and toys for the children, as well as provide breakfast and souvenirs for those who came. If it rained, raincoats would be essential for the day. Most importantly, a national flag and a tape recorder should be ready.

"Money is needed to prepare all of these!" Shalekjiang was once again in a dilemma. What should he do?

The family meeting was held again.

"This activity is initiated by us, so we can't ask the government or work units for help. We have to find a way out by ourselves ...Let's take out as much money as we could!" Shalekjiang said.

"At that time, a few of us were at work, but the wages were low so we didn't have much savings." Shalekjiang said. In the end, the whole family managed to pool 3,800 yuan.

Everything was ready. And they exercised flag-raising countless times.

"Dad, a big problem must be solved!" A day or two before the flag-raising ceremony on National Day, Shalekjiang's son Salaydin, reported to him, sweating profusely.

"What's wrong?" Salaydin's words startled him.

"Look, we have raised the flag, but it's not fluttering! It looks unsightly!" His son pointed to the national flag at the top of the flagpole.

"This won't do!" Shalekjiang looked up and also became anxious. He asked, "Isn't the blower windy enough?"

"No, it isn't. The wind is too weak ..."

Shalekjiang broke into a sweat in an instant.

Their neighbor, a mastermind, Wang Fulin, spoke up, "There is a large blower at school that has been unused for years. How about borrow it!"

"Go, hurry up!" Shalekjiang ordered his son immediately.

"Okay!"

"Use it for raising the national flag at your home?" The principal was puzzled at first, but once he understood, he did not hesitate and said. "Take it!"

"Thank you!"

All the problems were solved, and then all they needed to do was to wait for the morning of National Day on October 1st this year ...

"Probably the closer it got, the more nervous I became. On the evening before October 1st, my son and I had rehearsed the details of the ceremony repeatedly and we had thought of every possible cases, so my son urged me to rest early. But I was too excited and nervous to fall asleep and afraid of any loopholes occurring, which was something that must not happen. It seemed that raising the national flag at home may not be a big deal. However, I felt it was not just an ordinary household matter but a big event relating to our country, which was significant. Raising the flag meant to declare the integrity of the country's territory and the unity of all ethnic groups in Xinjiang. So it should not be affected by any flaws in the process. It was a big deal because the national flag bore the attitudes and emotions of our people from all ethnic groups towards our country. The more I thought about it, the more afraid I was of something going wrong. I couldn't sleep, so I quietly got up from the kang(a heatable brick bed in North China), put on my clothes, and pushed open the door to look into the yard. I found that it was drizzling outside ... Oh no, this was not good! If the national flag got wet, it won't be able to be raised on the ceremony tomorrow, and even if it was raised, it won't look good! I quickly woke up my son and asked him to roll up the national flag!"

By the time they finished packing up the flag with plastic paper, their clothes were soaked.

"Dad, now you can finally get a good sleep, right?" Salaydin said.

"Okay, I see." But how could he sleep tight when the national flag hadn't been raised yet.

On the early morning of October 1st, 7 o'clock was the time arranged for the flag-raising ceremony, but before 6 o'clock, Shalekjiang woke up the whole family. "Take your job according to the assignments last night!Be quick with the job, double-check everything. Especially for those who were responsible for breakfast, make sure there is enough food. Be sure the food is not too cold or hot. Remember to prepare the umbrellas in advance ..."Shalekjiang was trying to get everything done perfectly, but he was still afraid that he hadn't given enough instructions for something, so he urged everyone to check their assigned tasks again and again until he was convinced that everything was foolproof. Then, he nodded his head and went to the door ...

What Shalekjiang was most worried about as well as anticipated were things like these: Who would come? Who would be the first to arrive?who should have come but didn't? and who came unexpectedly? ... "What did it mean to be anxious and restless, I experienced it that morning!" Shalekjiang said so when recalling the first flag-raising ceremony.

"Good morning, Shalekjiang, my good brother!" The first person to arrive was Wang Fulin, an friend who was several years older than him. They were good buddies who lived in the same community. Hearing that Shalekjiang was going to raise the national flag at his home, Wang was the most staunch supporter. "Today is the first time for you to raise the national flag, so I had to be the first one to come!" Wang Fulin said.

"That's great, my old brother!" Shalekjiang took Wang Fulin's hand to walk into the yard.

Later, several community cadres arrived. They came early with a double mission: to see how was the flag raised as well as to assess the results.

"Uncle Shalekjiang, we have reported what you have done to our leaders. They all said you did it right, and they asked us to give you our full support!" one community cadre said.

"Thank you, thank you so much! Without your support, I wouldn't be able to do it. And I would like to be guided by you ..." Shalekejiang spoke from his heart.

"Good morning, Grandpa!" A few pupils wearing red scarves ran to Shalekjiang like cheerful flying swallows.

"Good morning. I have prepared various toys for you. You can play first and then join the flag-raising ceremony ..." Shalekjiang took out the prepared toys for the children.

It suddenly became lively at the yard.

"Here we come!"

"Welcome. Come inside and take a seat ..."

"Ah, with your presence, the sun will shine my small yard soon after the rain!" When Shalekjiang saw the Imam coming, he went forward in haste to support him with his hand into the courtyard ... At this moment, the freshly arranged yard was bustling with people, who were very happy.

"My son, play the music—" As at least twice as many people as expected, namely more than 50, attended, Shalekjiang excitedly asked his son, Salaydin, to turn on the recorder to play music as a prelude to the ceremony. With the music and songs, Xinjiang people, who loved to sing and dance, joyfully started to dance, no matter they were young or old, men or women.

"Great, today is our National Day, and everyone should dance and enjoy!" Even the Imam gaily encouraged everyone to dance. And all of this was exactly what Shalekjiang had hoped for.

"Now, everyone, tidy up your clothes and get ready for the flag-raising ceremony ..." When there were four to five minutes left for the ceremony, Shalekjiang announced.

"Okay!" "We are ready!" Everyone tidied their clothes and stood up.

"It is the time for the national flag raising ceremony —" Shalekjiang stood up straight and solemnly announced.

At that moment, although everyone in the yard were common folks, there were old people, children, men, and women, among them were villagers from dozens of ethnic groups like Han, Uyghur, Kazakh, Mongolian, Hui, Daur, which made the ceremony very typical.

"Please be quiet. Now play the national anthem of the People's Republic of China and raise the national flag ..." It seemed like Shalekjiang put all his strength to shout. Immediately, the majestic national anthem of the People's Republic of China resounded over the small yard.

Arise! ye who refuse to be slaves!
With our very flesh and blood,
Let us build our new Great Wall!
As the Chinese people have arrived at their most
perilous time,
Everyone is forced to expel his very last cry.
Arise!
Arise!
Arise!
Millions of hearts with one mind,
Brave the enemy's gunfire, march on!
Brave the enemy's gunfire, march on!
March on!
March on!
On!

As the song finished, the national flag reached the top of the flagpole precisely!

We did it! We had successfully raised the flag! At the moment when the song and music stopped, Shalekjiang gazed at the fluttering Five-Starred Red Flag, with tears of joy filling his cheeks ...

Many people at the yard were moved to tears.

"Congratulations, Shalekjiang!"

"Uncle, congratulations to you!"

"Yakexi(Bravo in Uygur language)!"

"You have done so well!"

People clustered around Shalekjiang and his family, speaking with great excitement.

"This is my my first time ..."

"Me too!"

"This flag-raising ceremony is so educational!"

"Xinjiang has long been an inseparable part of China. China is the motherland of all ethnic groups in Xinjiang. We love China and Xinjiang ..."

People were so excited to share their views on attending the first flag-raising ceremony. The originally scheduled one-hour event actually lasted for more than two hours. Reluctantly, people left Shalekjiang's small yard, asking about the time of the next flag-raising ceremony.

"Shalekjiang, you have to tell us in advance because I must attend. I wish my family and colleagues will come together. This ceremony is so instructive ..." When saying goodbye, everyone expressed their wishes to Shalekjiang.

"Definitely! You can rest assured, from today on, this flag will always flutter in the sky above my yard!" Shalekjiang announced excitedly.

"Long live the motherland!" "Xinjiang Yakexi!"

From then on, like a vernal breeze, the news of flag-raising at Shalekjiang's yard spread rapidly throughout the Haldun community, Xincheng Sub district in Techeng, and even farther places ... Ever since October 1st, 2009, the flag-raising ceremony has never stopped for 13 years!

"Uncle Shalekjiang, there will be two Party branches from different units holding a flag-raising and oath-taking ceremony here this morning and they also wish you to guide them. Can you arrange it?" During my interview, a community worker came to ask Shalekjiang.

"Why not? Let them come over, and I'll prepare soon ..." Shalekjiang told me that the place had become an education base for Party members of the community and many institutions as well as a patriotic education base for schools, more than a dozen signs hung. He has not only kept raising the flag every day but also voluntarily provided flag-raising and revolutionary tradition education for institutions, troops, schools, sub districts, and enterprises. "I got so busy! For the last few years, there was no media coverage. Now people from not only other areas in Xinjiang but also from all over the country have come here. I am now a full-time national flag instructor and publicist for patriotic education .... I am very proud and honored. I never expected that I would do something that everyone supported after retirement."

In the exhibition room of the education base, Shalekjiang pointed at his certificates and told me that what he felt most honored was to be recognized as a national model for ethnic unity because of the flag-raising activity, received by the Party and state leaders.

"A national flag has united people from different ethnic groups in this region, which I feel honored about for my whole life ..." Shalekjiang said. After the national flag raising, some of the misled crowd now had enhanced their understanding of the Communist Party of China and the country, who then believed in the Party and became patriotic. "No one can mislead or deceive them again!" Shalekjiang firmly stated. "Since the first flag-raising ceremony in 2009, there has not been a single incident of betraying the country or undermining ethnic unity in our community. Everyone thinks and acts in unison, and the community construction and people's ideological consciousness have reached an unprecedented height!"

During the interview, although I didn't spend much time at his home, I could still feel the "National Flag Effect" that his family brought to this community and the city of Tacheng. It was definitely something that Shalekjiang hadn't expected before.

Many institutions constantly called or sent people to enquire about when he was available. They all wished to come to his yard for the flag-raising ceremony, ideological education, and patriotic education ...

Activities came one after another. Shalekjiang's family were busy, in addition, community officials, neighbors like Wang Fulin, and many old and young volunteers were also busy helping receive guests. There were visitors from Tacheng and other parts of Xinjiang, besides, several groups of visitors came from Shandong Province, Guangxi Zhuang Autonomous Region, and Jiangsu Province.

"How did you know about Shalekjiang's story?" The guests laughed at my question. "We read about it in the newspaper and on our phones! So we are here ."

"There are flag-raising ceremonies at Tiananmen Square, why did you come all the way here?" They answered my second question, "We just stop by. But we feel it truly commendable and exceptional for a Uyghur uncle in the border areas to persistently raise the national flag for the sake of our national stability and ethnic unity. So we came to learn and experience the distinct and valuable of it ..." That accounted for it.

"Why have you been raising the national flag together with Shalekjiang for over a decade?" I interviewed Wang Fulin, a former border veteran and close friend of Shalekjiang, at his home.

"As an old Party member and veteran, I often dealt with border diplomatic affairs with neighboring countries on behalf of China when I served in the border guards. At that time, our communication technology was relatively backward, so we used our respective national flags as signals for national contacts and negotiations. At each contact, national flags of both sides must be hung highly ... It was so sacred that I could never forget. Afterwards, during a meeting of the Political Consultative Conference Xinjiang Committee, I heard that Shalekjiang decided to raise the national flag at his own yard in the complicated situation at the time. I was touched and felt that I should support him. Knowing that his family were too busy, I said to him, 'Brother, from now on, I will raise this bright

Five-Starred Red Flag together with you!' And that's how it has been until now ..." Wang Fulin said proudly.

After meeting Wang Fulin in person, I felt that his name didn't quite match his appearance. Unlike what his Chinese name implied, he was very handsome.

It was astonishing to see someone in his 80s looking so handsome.

Upon further inquiry, I learned that Wang Fulin's father was a Hui and his mother a Kazakh.

"I attended a Mandarin school, so my parents gave me a name in Mandarin. At that time, there were few ethnic minority teachers in Tacheng, and most teachers came from all over the country. For convenience, I got a name just as my Han classmates ..." Wang Fulin's explanation cleared up my confusion.

Wang's wife, aged 80, who was also a member of an ethnic minority group, was very attractive. Therefore, as a couple, they were not only attractive and handsome, but also elegant. Such looks of people could only be found in multi-ethnic families in Xinjiang.

While I praised the couple for their stylish looks, they said, "We are actually both roots of the bitter beans(sophora alopecuroide) — loving dry land, being strong in vitality ..."

"Are you both natives?"

"Yes, we are. My ancestors including my parents were all farmers on this land," Wang Fulin added, "In fact, the agricultural technology in Tacheng has always been advanced, therefore the border trade has been prosperous and lively since ancient times ..."

It seems that the beauty of Tacheng indeed has its historical reasons, and the beauty of its people and agriculture is the most prominent.

Our conversation returned to the topic of the flag-raising ceremony. "He has persisted for more than a decade, and even at such old age, he still insists on doing that ... I have to wake him up every time for fear that we would delay the ceremony," his wife said.

"I am the one who fling up the national flag, and this action is very important in the process," said Wang Fulin, while he stood up from the sofa to demonstrate the action to me seriously — So impressive! His movements were extremely standard and powerful.

"I learned this from the soldiers on TV while they raised the flag at Tiananmen Square." Wang said with a smile.

I heard from Shalekjiang that Wang not only helped him raise the flag but also provided financial support multiple times. "As a common retired worker, life was not easy for Shalekjiang. At the beginning, it took lots of money to organize a decent flag-raising ceremony, and it was not organized by institutions or the country, he all paid for it himself. My wife and I have better conditions than his family, so we helped him several times ..." Wang told me that he and his wife joined the Party in 1980. "As party members, we should play an exemplary role in Xinjiang. Now that we are old, we may only do something as much as we can. Helping Shalekjiang raise the flag is an expression of consolidating our Party spirit in our old age. While we are still healthy, we will continue to do so as long as we can!"

The elderly man didn't make grand speeches, but I could imagine how elegant, dignified, and proud he must feel with each strong flag-raising motion.

This is the image of an old Party member and that of a Chinese veteran. Under the national flag, such elderly people are respectable and adorable.

When we returned to Shalekjiang's small yard, the busy-working man said that in the morning, he had already conducted explanations on national flag education and patriotic education for three groups of people and received two batches of visitors from other places. As we were leaving, we also saw several locals with watermelons and other food talk with him affectionately ...

"They are all my 'relatives'." Shalekjiang said.

"Actually, they are not Shalekjiang's blood relatives. These people are locals that Shalekjiang and his son have helped ... Their family is also a big united one of all ethnic groups," the community cadre said.

That explained the matter.

A national flag made Shalekjiang and his family well-known everywhere. According to a community cadre, Shalekjiang has so far received more than 60,000 people to participate in his flag-raising ceremonies and conducted over 500 patriotic education classes. Each person who came to participate in the ceremony and attend the class would receive a small national flag made by himself as a souvenir.

Shalekejiang had a couple of unforgettable experiences. On June 1, 2021, he attended a flag-raising ceremony at Tiananmen Square while had an exchange with the soldiers of the National Flag Squad. His presence also inspired them. Kong Dexi, a political instructor from the People's Liberation Army Honor Guard, said, "Uncle Shalekjiang's spirit is precious. His family, living in the faraway border areas, insist on raising the national flag every day, which demonstrates their deep love for the motherland. They have defended the sacredness and dignity of the border areas with practical actions, deserving the admiration of us all."

When his son, Salaydin, travelled to Russia, he fetched out the national flags of the PRC made by his father, at Red Square in Moscow many Russian friends cheered warmly and all wished to get a Five-Starred Red Flag, expressing their friendliness towards China.

"I wish to strengthen the unity among all ethnic groups through the flag-raising ceremony, and what makes me the happiest is that someone has passed this tradition ... Now, my son is doing good deeds as always, and my granddaughter has become a model of ethnic unity at school. I am even happier and more fulfilled than I did it myself," Shalekjiang said.

His granddaughter was recognized as an "Excellent Teenager For Ethnic Unity" in Xinjiang Uygur Autonomous Region in 2016.

Salaydin is a well-known local doctor who has taken care of a paralyzed Han aunt, Zhao Xiu'e for thirty years. His story, like his father's, has already spread throughout the Tacheng Prefecture ...

"There are five Party members in our family. Although my wife has passed away, she was a probationary Party member during her lifetime. We are all faithful guardians of the national flag, countless neighbors like Wang Fulin are also members of us. We have formed a strong fortress together. As long as we are here, this fortress will remain, and the land beneath our feet will always bear the name of China and belongs to China!" The 75-year-old Shalekjiang looked determined and convinced.

Now, the small yard, adorned with the fluttering national flag, is becoming more and more beautiful, attracting a growing number of people. And I know, as long as the Five-Starred Red Flag continues to fly highly at Shalekjiang's home, the story of his family will continue to unfold in a more exciting and vivid manner here. There will also be new stories, just like the beautiful and vibrant flowers on the grasslands of Tacheng, blooming one after another ...

Chapter 5

Passwords in the Names

One of the most important reasons that the Chinese nation has survived and thrived,

lies in that people of all ethnic groups are inseparable by blood ties.

Our ancestors have left us with nearly 6,000 surnames among 56 ethnic groups.

Sophisticated as the relations are,

it is not difficult to identify the forbears of each family or person.

That is why we always say, "The Chinese nation is one family."

There is a girl called "Han Lian Han Bing". Her name is just like a password,

deciphering the genetic code of the saying, "The Chinese nation is one family."

What a charming place Xinjiang really is? Only when you walk to the farthest reaches of this land and go deep into thousands of households can you find the answer.

With a fast tour, you can only get a sketchy glimpse of the natural landscape. Yet if you further savor it, you will be rewarded with amazement and surprise —

The beauty of Xinjiang permeates the vast nature, reflected in the lifetime of thousands of creatures on the earth, as well as at the wonderful moments of life.

Girls in each ethnic group who are beautiful, outgoing, tender and good at dancing are most attractive, always making people fall for them easily ...

Such pure love, together with a beautiful song, can easily affect every one. Unexceptionally, I am always immersed in the melody "Tacheng Girls."

> Eagles from Mt. Tianshan carry me here,
> Where my beloved girl lives.
> I stop and fold the wings,
> Only for touching your face, my love.
> Fragrance of flowers in Tarbagatay is the perfect foil for your aroma,
> Which makes me intoxicated and lie on the ground to enjoy the glowing sunset.
> But stars fail to be brighter than your eyes,

I would like to indulge in your eyes for good.
Your sweet dimples tell stories.
Your lips are soft, holding a lilac
As pure as the snow-white flowers,
Chanting in a low voice like a Bayan.
Even the spring of Chuhuchu cannot quench my love
for you,
My beautiful girl under the Weiren mountain.

...

One will become enthusiastic by the sight of a passionate scene in which handsome boys dance merrily to melodious songs sung by gorgeous girls.

If, as the dancing and singing subside, you follow the locals into their families and lives, you may really find something more fascinating and wonderful ...

"Is your name Han Lian Han Bing?"

"Yes, it is ..."

I was surprised at the girl's affirmative answer. Although I think I am close to a "very knowledgeable" person, I have no idea why her parents gave her such a name.

"Which ethnic group do you belong to?"

"I am Kazakh."

"But aren't the names of 'Akbar Majit' or 'Kurbat Uleiman' more common to Kazakh people?"

I have a Kazakh colleague called Akbar Majit. He once told me that Kazakh children would inherit their father's names, which followed their own names. Taking "Akbar Majit" as an example, "Akbar" is his name, while Majit is his father's. Uygurs also use this nomenclature.

People who are familiar with the ethnic minorities in Xinjiang can tell which ethnic group, Kazakh, Uygurs, or Mongolian, the name belongs to, because each name has its unique characteristics.

However, the name "Han Lian Han Bing" completely confused me — my question about her ethnic nationality was not only out of curiosity but also to prove my intuition that this name must come from certain interesting stories, especially those about national unity.

"I am Kazakh!" she laughed and said.

"Are your parents also Kazakh?"

"No, my father is Kazakh, while my mother is Hui."

"Does your name follow your father's?"

"Yes."

"And what's your father's name?"

"Han Bing."

Hearing this, I guessed that her grandparents were Han and Kazakh. "Is that the case?" I asked her.

"Yes, you are right," she nodded.

"Are there many intermarried couples between different ethnic groups here?" I asked carefully for fear that I had made a mistake.

She answered me frankly, "Yes, my family is typical. Including my grandparents, our big family is home to 83 members of four generations from seven ethnic groups: Han, Kazakh, Uyghur, Hui, Mongolian, Russian, and Tatar ..."

"What a wonder! Can I pay a visit to your house?" I asked.

"Of course! Welcome!" she hospitably invited me at once.

On that day, cadres from the Federation of Literary and Artistic Circles, the Publicity Department, and the street community in Tacheng accompanied me to the house of the fifth child of the Hans, who is the third aunt of Han Lian Han Bing.

"Welcome! Come in, please." we were greeted at arrival. It is an ethnically diverse family, being called the Lao Han family by the locals.

As we entered, we saw a large living room filled with people of all ages in colorful clothes ...

It was tempting to see two large tables with all kinds of fresh fruits and homemade delicacies. What a cozy and welcoming vibe!

"Come on, let's introduce the families to our distinguished guests ..." The hostess, Han Lian Han Bing's aunt, presented everyone in the room to me, including those who stood, sat, and even babies held in people's arms.

But I failed to remember all of them: Kazakh, Uyghurs, Mongolian, Hui people ...Each of them has a long name. It may take three days to match each member's ethnicity and name — what an interesting family!

After bursts of merry laughter, the hostess said, "I think it's better to start our family's history with the story of our parents. Without them, the great unity of nationalities in our family is out of the question".

"Yep, yep, especially for me. Even though you introduce the family to me very clearly, I may be confused ..."

I have been a professional interviewer for several decades, it was the first time I encountered such a complicated family. Therefore, my frankness was also a plea to some extent.

"Sure! Ok!" Ha-ha ...The laughter hadn't come to a stop since we entered the room. Despite my confusion about their names and identities, I felt more comfortable in this enjoyable family atmosphere.

The hostess, Dawulitihan Kamushafu, ranking third among the daughters in Lao Han Family, has two older sisters, two older brothers, and a younger brother and sister. The youngest boy, named Han Tao, passed away early, leaving a daughter.

"Let's begin with 'Lao Han'," I suggested.

"Yep, Granny is the person of authority in our family. Without her, our family would not exist ..." A child said. I was interested in their "Granny".

"This is her, our 'Queen Mother'!" Han Lian Han Bing went before her aunt and showed me a faded black-and-white photo of a young couple.

The man was apparently Kazakh, stalwart and handsome; the woman was a good-looking Han, yet her eyes and hair differed slightly from standard Han people.

"Granny has a little Russian blood ..." Han Lian Han Bing explained.

"It would be better to let me share the story of my parents with you!" Dawulietihan was apparently the leading role of this big family.

Then she started, "My mother, Han Guifen, originally came from Yangliuqing, Tianjin. ('Another person I have heard coming from that place. A thought even struck me that I could publish a book about people from Yangliuqing living in Xinjiang.')

Mother told us that she moved to Xinjiang with her older sister, possibly for the sake of the historical tradition of 'catching up with the big Camp.'

She didn't talk about her parents much, nor about whether my father's parents had been to Xinjiang. But she told us that her grandfather had Russian blood, as people from Yangliuqing had once arrived at the border between China and Russia, and even had been to czarist Russia when they followed General Zuo Zongtang to recover Xinjiang."

"The history of our family can be composed into a book," sitting around the table, Han Guifen's first and second daughters interposed.

"Mother first reached Altay, a prefecture north of Xinjiang, and stayed at Jeminay county. Later, she participated in the revolution led by the Communist Party as a nurse in the guerrillas. She followed the troops from Jeminay County to Hoboksar. Eventually, she became one of the residents here ..." the hostess continued,

"Our father, Jiamushapu Bahatel, was a heroic Kazakh soldier. In his early years, under the influence of the October Revolution in Russia, he participated in the revolution led by the Communist Party and devoted himself to countless fights. He was an officer of the troop for which my mother worked. He once got injured in the battle and was taken good care of by Mother. As time went by, they fell in love with each other ...

In 1950, they followed the armies to Hoboksar County and married here.

At that time, Father was the first director of the Public Security Bureau of the county. He was a standard Kazakh with nice looking and manly bearing.

Mother could also speak the Kazakh language fluently thanks to her early experience in Altay and her marriage with my father.

Before the founding of the People's Republic of China in 1949, ethnic minorities who intermarried with Han in Xinjiang were few. Therefore, the marriage of my parents, who were Han and Kazakh, respectively, served as an inspiring example for others in Xinjiang.

Later, people gradually called us the 'Lao Han Family' due to our parents' popularity in 1950 and our mother's capability — our mother did enjoy considerable prestige!"

Hearing that, all the children in this family laughed out loud in happiness and pride.

"Did your parents impose restrictions on your marriage, such as ethnicity?" I was most concerned with this question.

If families regardless of their ethnicity are better and better, should it be necessary to worry about any issues concerning national unity?

"Since our parents have taken part in the fights for peaceful liberation in Xinjiang, they were open-minded while they deeply realized how vital the intermarriage among different ethnic groups was for Xinjiang. Their marriage was an example for us and other people around them.

When we grew up, they supported us to choose spouses independently.

For example, I took the lead and married my husband, who is a Han coming from Hubei; my first younger sister and second younger brother married Hui people; my first younger brother, the oldest one among boys, married a Salar girl; my second younger sister married a Kazakh man ...

You can conclude that we advocate free love, regardless of ethnicity."

The eldest one pointed at Han Lian Han Bing and said, "As for these children, none of their parents disagree with them over the ethnicity of their partners or spouses."

"What about the difference in daily habits and languages? How do you handle that? Would that bring quarrels?" It was another question I took an interest in.

The second eldest one gave me an answer, "At the time when we dated, as working in the same organization or lived in a large community, lovers could naturally communicate, starting with the simplest words. After getting married, we could already speak each other's language.

The linguistic barrier was not a problem, let alone habits and custom. As we ate and lived together, what else could not be settled?

As for quarrels, they are inevitable in every family, even in those of the same ethnic group.

Guided by words and actions of our parents, we rarely saw quarrels in our family.

Even though there are one or two bickers, other family members will come together, and then the dispute will be settled ...it is true, isn't it?"

"Yes! Ha-ha ..." Again, everyone burst into laughter, with someone even starting to dance —

> What a surprise today.
> Why not wait for me?
> I come for you with ardour.
> The tent is absent. So are you.
> Gaoretai Gaoretai,
> My beloved,
> I linger over where you lived.
>
> ...

It is a well-known Kazakh folk song which several generations of the Lao Han family can sing together, irrespective of ethnicity. Only by this scene can we see what a harmonious and happy multi-ethnic family it is!

Such a delightful and multi-ethnic family, just like the primordial gene of society, serves as the most important factor of the stability of society and times.

So, what is its password? I especially want to decode it. The Lao Han family gave me an opportunity — the password is mysterious, grounded, and attractive.

Having chosen spouses who they truly fell in love with, irrespective of ethnicity, Han Guifen and Jiamushafu, grandparents in the Lao Han family, have set an example for other people of their generation. This kind of example is important and groundbreaking, impacting future generations tremendously.

The reason why Xinjiang has been stable for decades after the founding of the PRC while ethnic groups there have maintained cohesion and unity which is unshakable and undivided at any time is that thousands of "Lao Han families" are supporting and weaving a social network, showing national unity, people's patriotism, and love for the Party.

The "gene" of national integration in the Lao Han family has been combined not only in the form of a family but also through the "name chain" — a word I invent — which passes on from generation to generation in the future ... That is why I am particularly interested in the name "Han Lian Han Bing".

"Literally, a name just represents an identity of a person. Actually, it helps the generation of our parents express their expectations for descendants, hoping their children will always hold strong feelings for the motherland, the CPC, and Xinjiang ..."

Han Hong, Han Guifen's eldest daughter, told us a story about her name. She was born shortly after the founding of the PRC when Xinjiang was transformed into a brand-new socialist province.

Her mother firmly told her father, "I would like to name her Han Hong, taking my last name."

Jiamushafu, a Kazakh and director of the local public security bureau, agreed, "A nice name, Han Hong. As she is also Kazakh, she should carry my name as'Han Hong Jiamushafu.'"

Reaching an agreement, the young couple pursuing ethnic unity, laughed merrily.

Habitually called "Han Hong," their eldest child has officially used this short name in her personal profile and household register.

Although she married a man of Han, she reserved her national identity as a Kazakh.

She has a son named Li Gang Bieke. However, I found that "Bieke" is not the name of her husband. Then what does "Bieke" mean?

"It means 'handsome' in Kazakh!" As I didn't realize this point until I was writing this book, I asked Han Lian Han Bing on WeChat, and she gave me that answer.

Ha-ha ... There are many mysteries in the names of this family. So interesting!

The second child of the Lao Han family is also a girl, so she still takes the surname "Han" and is called Han Yaowu.

A girl is called "Yaowu ('Yao' means 'want' and 'wu' means'martial' in Chinese) "?

"Influenced by Chairman Mao's line of poetry 'Love military attire rather than red costumes' , my parents gave me such a name.

Yet I never 'swagger around' at home!" Han Yaowu explained to the people around her, which made the whole family laugh again.

In the Lao Han family, which is filled with laughter all the time, every "small branch of the family" has its own stories relating to national unity.

The eldest child said, "When my parents were in charge of the family, they seemed to have made a rule: the surname of daughters should be 'Han'. So two of the eldest daughters were called Han Hong and Han Yaowu.

However, the younger three sisters didn't follow the rule and were named Dawuleti Khan, Mailan, and Kulan ... Their names are of 'Kazakh-style'!"

"Why?" I asked.

"Mother said that as the country carried out reform and opening up policy, our family should keep pace with the times. That means the girls' names should be more attractive, ethnically more typical, and more meaningful. In Kazakh, 'Dawulettihan' means 'national prosperity' while 'Kulan' and 'Mailan' mean 'festive,'" she explained.

"As for my youngest uncle, though he was a boy, Granny named him Han Tao. Unfortunately, he died tragically young ..." Han Lian Han Bing added.

As she mentioned him, there was slightly an oppressive atmosphere in the room.

After a while, Han Hong went on, "Mother preserved our family's tradition. Taking my father's feelings into account, she followed Kazakh custom and named the first son, ranking third among all the siblings, Aybuick Jiamushafu.

As for the second son, Father suggested: As he needs to take care of us after we retire, he should take the surname of 'Han', called Han Bing.

Han Bing has a daughter, 'Han Lian Han Bing,' whom you are familiar with. She is an outstanding CPC member working for the Department of Organization. She makes our whole family proud."

So Han Lian Han Bing carries her father's name! Hearing that, members of the Lao Han family and I smiled at her, which made her blush.

Han Lian Han Bing's parents were sitting next to me.

The father Han Bing said that he and his wife, Mi Guilan, met while working in the corps. At that time, Miguilan had a crush on him, a handsome man fond of literature and arts and good at playing instruments. After a sweet romance, they got married.

As a Hui girl, Mi said that when being informed that Han Bing was Kazakh and his mother was Han, she worried that whether there would be frequent conflicts or troubles in such a family?

But the post-marriage life was out of her expectation. She said, "After I became a member of the Lao Han family, I found that there were no so-called ethnic problems. Everyone is particularly humble and considerate. It is truly a harmonious and united family."

So she quickly integrated into this extended family, where she has enjoyed extreme happiness for decades.

Her daughter, Han Lian Han Bing, has also grown up and got married with Su Wenqing, a young man of Hui. Naturally, Mi Guilan, of the same ethnicity, is very satisfied with her son-in-law.

"We have a happy and satisfactory nuclear family ..." Mi Guilan and

Han Bing's spirit and complexion might tell that what she said is true.

"This is my ID card ..." As Han Lian Han Bing showed me her card, I laughed, for I hadn't seen such a name among the Chinese citizens before.

It makes people curious. A name like "Han Lian Han Bing" consisting of "two" names is never used by Han people. What's more, it is rare to combine "Lian(means lotus)" with "Bing(means soldier)" as the name of a girl ...

Whenever I think of this exotic name, I would laugh heartily, because everything is possible in this vast world, wonderful things happen hither and thither in Xinjiang, and there is such an impressive name in the ethnically harmonious society!

The name "Han Lian Han Bing" and the meanings it carries are of great significance. The story of the Lao Han family just well demonstrates that Xinjiang will always be an integral part of the motherland — the People's Republic of China.

An interesting name even illustrates how the Chinese nation maintains unity and harmony.

"Grandma passed away in 1983, and Grandpa in 1997, at the age of 85 ..." Han Lian Han Bing said.

"From our childhood, parents have instructed us that we must love our country and care for everyone around us, even strangers. They particularly requested us to serve the people and dedicate ourselves to the development of Xinjiang when we grew up,"

Dawuliehan, the third child of the Lao Han family, recalled affectionately, "Although two elder brothers studied in the school teaching in Mandarin, they spoke Kazakh at home. Similarly, Mother spoke Mandarin at work, while Kazakh at home, for my father was not good at Mandarin. Under the influence of Mother, all our siblings can speak good Mandarin, very convenient for work outside while we can fulfil the role of people from ethnic minorities who speak different languages. All this is owed to family education by our parents ..."

Han Yaowu, the second child, continued, "Once my sisters and I walked on the way home from school, suddenly it rained heavily. After a while, the flood blocked our way.

Facing the rapid current in the river, Mother on the other side was extremely nervous but couldn't do anything to help us. As we struggled hand in hand to the other side, Mother cried, 'Watch out!' and then encouraged us to move forward bravely ...

The moment we crossed the river, Mother hugged us tightly and burst into tears.

As a young kid, I failed to understand why Mother began to cry when we were safe. Later, I learned that she was exceedingly anxious at that time ...

What she said back then still lingers in my mind, 'you must bear in mind that whatever we do, it is of great importance to unite and join hands.'

Her instruction is a lifelong benefit to me. After I grew up, especially when I faced ethnic issues, I still remember that unity and cooperation are the key solutions to problems.

Later, when we became parents, we passed on the teachings of our parents to our children."

We have stayed in this delightful and harmonious family for nearly half a day. It seems that there are still many interesting "passwords" to be solved ... and there appears to be endless secrets.

I have found another impressive "secret": In the Lao Han family, no matter which ethnic group the parents belong to, children have the right to choose their names and ethnic nationalities on their own.

For example, Han Yaowu followed her father to be a Kazakh and married Yu Qingming, a man of Hui. Their son Yu Zhongjun is Hui by his own choice and married a girl of Han named Gou Ling, with their son choosing Hui as his ethnic nationality.

While Yu Zhongxia, the eldest daughter of Han Yaowu, did not choose to be Hui as her brother but joined Kazakh as her mother did.

Her husband, Lu Xiang is Han. So their son chose to be Han.

When I asked the purpose of all these interesting yet irregular choices of ethnic identity, they all laughed, saying that it was completely subjected to the personal whims of the moment.

"We don't care which ethnic group we belong to, bearing in mind that we are of the Chinese nation!

In the household register and ID card, we casually fill in the section of the ethnic nationality without much consideration. If there is a reason, it may be attributed to the willingness to inherit parents' ethnic nationality."

A son-in-law or maybe a son of one of the nuclear families explained, and everyone all agreed.

Since I left the house of the Lao Han family, even till now, a thought of "the journey in Tacheng" would remind me of "Han Lian Han Bing" and the impressive scenes when I paid a visit to their home — what an emotional, delightful and instructive memory it is!

After being attracted by the name "Han Lian Han Bing", I came to pay attention to the "secrets in names" of similar Xinjiang people. I found that across Xinjiang, such kinds of names were common, and the characters varied at different times.

For example, in the early days after the founding of the PRC, there were names "Hongqi Maimanti(Hongqi means 'red flag' in Chinese)", and "Yuejin Jitimi(Yuejin means 'progress')". In the later years, children were named "Xiangyang(which means 'facing the sun')" and "Zili(which means 'independence')."

Later, much more interesting names appeared, such as "Xianghai(means 'facing the sea')Gurtu" and "Guocui (means 'national quintessence') Manzeya" ...

All such names are branded with the mark of the times. It is not comprehensive to understand them literally. Maybe for the Han people, a Chinese character is plain;

while for the ethnic minorities in Xinjiang, such words symbolize the greatness of the motherland, the development of the Chinese nation, and the fashion of the times. They can be recognized as the signpost of what people pursue now and in the future. They are the beliefs, willpower, and aspirations of the people.

As an official language of China, Chinese is sacred to people of all ethnic groups. That's why they use Chinese characters to be a symbol of themselves. Such a choice comes from their yearning and pursuit, even their hope from the bottom of their hearts, to tie their fate and whole life to the great development of the Chinese nation and the flourishing cause of socialism. They follow the tide of times and dedicate themselves, expecting to make their life glorious and bright.

Perhaps my friends in Tacheng thought that I was particularly interested in such names marked by the times, such as "Han Lian Han Bing" and "Xiangyang Hongqi", so before I left, they told me another story between two revolutionaries of Han and Kazakh.

The Han "revolutionary," Yang Zhaohui, is a veteran living in the downtown area of Tacheng.

When he was in the army, he became a member of the CPC. In 2012, he was seriously ill and treated in a hospital in Urumqi. For more than three months, he has fallen into unconsciousness.

Luckily, he was on the mend under the meticulous care of his wife, Ren Juqin, and the effective treatment at the hospital. After recovery, he exercised regularly to tone the body so as to better devote himself in his post. He was selected as an outstanding Party member due to his excellent performance in the work. People all recognized him as a "tough revolutionary."

Surprisingly, working in a new-funded company downtown, Yang Zhaohui has a good relationship with Yang Zhixue, a Kazakh who lives uptown in a self-governed village called Jiangmuerzha of the Asier Township.

Yang Zhixue told Yang Zhaohui that there was a Kazakh named "Geminghan" (male revolutionary) in his village. Born in 1967, the guy unfortunately died of illness two years ago, leaving his wife, Shartanati Azhubai, and three daughters. His daughters all took his name as their surnames. His second daughter is Nazalk Geminghan, and the third is Turguli Geminghan.

"Was their father really called 'Geminghan'? Sounds interesting," I laughed. This name is indeed more directly than "Han Lian Han Bing" to express the enthusiasm for revolution!

"Kazakhs were all keen for revolution; therefore, many boys born in the 1960s and 1970s were named 'Geminghan'.

Consequently, as daughters of one of these 'Geminghans', the three girls followed the tradition of Kazakh and were named 'Geminghan' as well ...."As the cadre of the Federation of Literary and Art Circles explained, I came to understand the stories behind these interesting names.

After Yang Zhaohui, a Han revolutionary, came to the Jiangmuerzha Village, a bond of friendship was forged between him and the Kazak people.

It was said that after Yang experienced the serious illness, he and his wife have a next-level understanding of the world.

Previously, he had practiced what he preached and took the lead in every work; after recovery from the disease, his realm of spirit ascended to a higher level: he enjoyed helping others.

Someone once asked him, "How did you come to such insight?"

He replied plainly, "When I was in critical condition, everyone came to help me. From then on, I have understood one thing:

It is important to live well, but if you regard caring and helping others as a pleasure, your life will be more worthy and meaningful. Thus you know how to conduct yourself in the society."

With such insight into the self-development, Yan has reached a new realm of life: doing his best to help others .

Before Yang arrived at Jiangmuerzha Village, he was told that the poor widow Shartanati was in a desperate plight as her two younger daughters fell seriously ill one after another. Fortunately, her eldest daughter got married, which could lighten her burden.

It is rare for a family to encounter successive misfortunes in a short time. We can easily imagine how difficult it would be for them.

Knowing the facts, Yang would like to help them out. When he told his wife Ren Juqin, a virtuous and warm-hearted woman, she comforted him, "Just do what you want, and I will always be here with you."

"Great!" Then, he and his wife came to the house of Shartanati with several large bags full of daily necessities. He told her, "From now on, you can regard us as your relatives. Whatever difficulty you are subjected to, we will stand with you ..." Then they left the things they brought and a stack of cash to Shartanati.

"It's ...it's so kind of you ... I even don't know what to say," she was too excited to express her gratitude.

"You don't have to say anything. We are family now!" Ren Juqin hugged her and said, "Sister, the most pressing matter for us now is to find a good hospital for Turguli and Nazalk. Otherwise, we would be sorry to

Geminghan ..."

"Mm-hmm!" Shartanati suddenly shed tears.

Thus, a Kazakh "Geminghan" had gone, but a Han "Geminghan" came to help. He spared no effort to contact hospitals that could treat the girls disease. After a period of treatment, the two girls were back to health and returned to their warm home.

On the day when Yang paid a visit to Shartanati's house again, the two girls merrily ran forward to hold his arms on either side, shouting with joy, "Our daddy 'Geminghan' is back ..." Yang Zhaohui laughed and replied, "Yep, I am the 'Geminghan', your daddy!"

"Daddy!" "Daddy!"

"Here!"

Like the names "Han Lian Han Bing" and "Xiangyang Hongqi" that I met before, the "passwords" behind the name"Geminghan" and its stories contain the heart-felt love, deep understanding, and sincere belief of Xinjiang people for the motherland, the Party and the Chinese nation with their actual deeds.

It must be exceedingly magnificent if these "passwords" can be arranged into a program, like fresh blood flowing inside the veins of each member of the Chinese nation, just as the mighty Yangtze River surging forward and the sturdy Great Wall guarding the frontiers firmly, as well as the most powerful life blood and triumphant songs of life!

The "passwords" in the names "Han Lian Han Bing","Xiangyang Hongqi" and "Geminghan" are the precious original genes of the Chinese nation ...

They interpret the code of eternal and valuable pomegranate-like gene cells of the Chinese nation.

Chapter 6

Veteran, You Make Me Cry

History warns every country with lessons paid for with blood:

Every inch of your land, your territorial integrity,

Was defended by heroic people and heroes of the people with their lives.

Therefore, showing respect and care for the border-defending heroes,

Is the duty and responsibility of every citizen.

The story of veteran Zhang Qiuliang sets a monumental example for us.

The Gobi at the northern foot of Mt. Tianshan is too big to see its edge. Sandstorms there are even more fierce, causing a running car to sway like a small boat in turbulent waves ...

That is Mt. Beiyang. Beside the bare rocks at its foot, we raised our right hands to salute each other, and then shook hands, which is how brother in arms greet each other.

And this is how I met with the legendary "Tianshan veteran" Zhang Qiuliang. In a village with a large number of ethnic minorities, it is rare to have a Han family living there. Zhang Qiuliang's arrival was even more extraordinary. His home is just across a road from the troops he once served in ... Being a former soldier who has interviewed countless military personnel, I think that Zhang Qiuliang's experience is probably the unique one in the entire army.

Thus, his story is particularly worth reading —

"Did you also join the army in 1976?"

"No, it was in 1977 ..."

"Ha ha ... that's close enough, so we are true comrades-in-arms. I joined the army one year later."

"But wait, you are several years younger than me. How could you join the army only one year after me?" I did the math and found it strange.

He smiled and said, "I'm from Shaanxi Province. My family was extremely poor when I was young. At that time, I grew up like a willow branch, tall enough but underweight ... During the physical examination, I ran to a well and gulped down cold water. Just then, the commanding officer receiving new recruits saw me and asked why I drank so much water. I stupidly replied, 'I'm not heavy enough.' He looked at me and circled around me, then patted my shoulder and asked, 'Do you really want to be a soldier?' I immediately answered, 'Yes, I do.' 'Why?' he asked again. I said, 'To defend my country and have enough food to eat.' His eyes suddenly filled with tears, and he nodded. After that, I was drafted into the army ..."

In 1977, Zhang Qiuliang traveled from Shaanxi to the place where his family now resides — the border town of Shawan in Xinjiang, and became a soldier in the army.

Six years later, in 1983, he left the army and returned to his hometown. In 1984, he married a local girl. Just after their honeymoon, he said to his newly-wedded wife, "I want to go back to Xinjiang."

"Why?" She asked.

He replied, "There is a childless elderly couple in a village near the military camp, who need to be taken care of. When I was in the army, I used to visit them with the 'learning from Lei Feng' group. Since I left there, I have been worried about them. And most importantly, there are seven martyrs' graves in the mountains that also need to tend ..."

"Well, you'd better go early and come back soon. I'll be waiting for you at home," his wife said.

He stood there dazed, staring at his wife without uttering a word.

"What's wrong? Do you plan to be away for a long time?" she assumed.

He shook his head but still remained silent.

"You man!" His wife couldn't hold back her laughter and said, "Can't bear to leave the warmth of our newlywed bed, huh? Then you set off early and come back as soon as possible."

He finally uttered, "I am not going alone, but taking you with me."

The new wife was stupefied.

He continued, "If we go together, we would settle down there and never come back …"

She was stunned, afraid of having misheard, "What? We will settle down there and never come back?"

He nodded, "Yes, that's true."

She suddenly sat down on the kang(a heatable brick bed in North China), tears streaming down her face like broken pearls. "Is there a paradise or a garden?"

"It is the Gobi Desert." He said.

"What's that?" She had never been far from home and had no idea what the Gobi Desert looked like. What she thought was that if she really went there, she should have her own yard and farmland to raise their children … She then asked, "Can we have a bigger piece of farmland?"

His replied excitedly, "Yes, I promise. It will be very big. However big you want it, I'll mark it out for you!"

She blushed, turned tears into smiles, and said. "Why didn't you say it earlier? I'll go with you then."

In this way, the young couple, carrying the wedding quilt and four sacks filled with their belongings, left their home in Shaanxi to Kaziwan Village in Shawan County, north of Mt. Tianshan. It was already dark when they arrived. Zhang Qiuliang took his wife to stop in front of a small yard surrounded by mud walls and said, "Here we are. Follow me to meet my parents."

"What? You have parents here too?" His wife was quite shocked and asked hastily.

He smiled and explained, "I didn't tell you earlier. Uncle You Peike and Aunt Zhang Xiuzhen don't have children. When I was in the army, I often led the 'learning from Lei Feng' group to help them do something on Sundays. They accepted me as their adopted son. Now that you have married me, then we should pay them a visit and call them 'Mom and Dad'!"

In a strange and remote place, being able to call someone "Mom and Dad" could also be considered as a taste of "comfortable home". On their first night, the young couple slept on the ground and felt quite cold. His wife pinched his arm under the covers and said, "What else have you concealed from me?"

"Ouch, gently, gently. I haven't hidden anything from you. I'll take you out to see the farmland you want at dawn ..." He tucked their quilt and whispered in her ear.

"Really? Then let's go to sleep earlier. I'm exhausted!" she said.

The next morning, as soon as she woke up, she tugged at his clothes and whispered, "Let's go to see our land ..."

"Okay." He led his wife into the back hill, going straight ahead.

"This mountain doesn't look like the yellow hillside back home. Why isn't there grass and trees in the field?" she wondered, kicking little stones tripping her on the ground.

"This is the Gobi Desert. When the wind blows hard, it can lift these stones into the air." He picked up a fist-sized stone and said.

"I don't believe it. That would be a ghostly wind!" She shook her head.

He said, "That's exactly what it is."

She stared at him, dubiously.

"Oh no, the ghostly wind is really coming!" He looked towards the sky and suddenly said.

Looking in the direction he pointed to, she saw a huge "cover" rising with yellow smoke from afar, pressing toward them ... She was frightened, screaming, "Oh my god!"

"Run!" He grabbed her hand and quickly took shelter in a hollow in the mountain.

Just as they hid away, the entire world turned into an overturned pot. The hurricane carried all the sand, stones, and debris on the ground, mercilessly ravaging the earth like a demon, testing the endurance of every inch of land.

This was the Gobi Desert, where the weather here was rather changeable.

"Why ... Why is it so terrifying ..." She trembled in his arms and was unable to speak clearly.

"It's okay, you'll get used to it." He reassured her.

"How ... How can I get used to it?" At that moment, a flying stone hit her foot, causing her to collapse on the ground in pain. She cried, with her tears like rushing rivers ...

"Alright, alright. Didn't you want to see how large our 'land' is? Get up and I'll show you." He coaxed her into getting her up, walking deeper into the calm Gobi.

He pointed to the boundless expanse of land, like a wealthy landlord, saying, "As long as you don't mind making your feet tired, wherever you could run to would be your farmland ..."

"You ... You run by yourself! I will never do that! I just want a piece of land big enough to grow vegetables and raise chickens!" she said, tears streaming down her face.

This time, his heart softened. He carried her on his back and said, "Alright, alright. After I visit my comrades-in-arms, I'll do anything as you wish!" He labored to climb the slope with her on his back and walked towards the other side of Mt. Beiyang ...

She wiped away her tears and asked him, "Where are your comrades? Why do you have to visit them?"

While gasping for breath, he explained in detail, "There are seven of them, all unmarried. Two of them had girlfriends before, but they broke up later. They have been 'lying' silently in this remote and barren Gobi Desert in solitude, hardly known even by their families. Only our comrades come to visit them. If we didn't come to see them anymore, no one in this world would know about them ..."

The more she listened, the more scared she felt, until she felt chilly all over. She asked, "How did they die?"

He said gravely, "They sacrificed themselves bravely to defend our homes, the country, and borders. Some died of accidents, but they are all revolutionary martyrs."

As they walked, he suddenly stopped and stared at a chaotic rocky area at the foot of the mountain ... He then put her down and sprinted towards the scattered "mounds" that were blown away by the storm.

She chased after him, seeing him desperately use his hands to rebuild the scattered "mounds" into neat piles of sand and stones. She felt that he was so sad as if he had lost his soul ... "I'm sorry, comrades! I ... I came too late! I'll criticize myself deeply! I promise, from now on, I will never leave you again! I promise not to make you suffer anymore ... I promise!"

He wept while piling, swore to them ... as if he wanted to stick his soul and body to the Gobi Desert, to merge himself with the seven martyrs lying underground.

"Are they all your comrades?"

"Yes."

"They all died?"

"Yes."

"None of their families know they're here?"

"No, they don't. It's too far for them to come here, so I want to accompany my comrades ..."

For the first time, she saw him burst into tears.

It seemed that she began to understand what he thought. She stood up and gazed at the boundless border of the motherland, seeming to understand why his comrades rest in peace here quietly ...

So she crouched down and began to scoop up rocks and sand just like her husband, building mounds of soil for the their graves, as if dressing them in neat and majestic military uniforms ...

Gradually, he smiled gratefully.

She smiled back with understanding and happiness.

In this way, they settled down in this Gobi Desert, staying by the side of their seven comrades ...

Now we should have known his name, Zhang Qiuliang, a demobilized soldier from Kaziwan Village in Shawan County and a veteran who has been guarding his comrades' graves for nearly 40 years.

When I saw him, except for the small restaurant called "Veterans' Station" at his doorstep and the old green military uniform he often wore, he was completely a local farmer, with a dark face and a visibly stooped back, speaking the pure "border language," who had become a true local inhabitant. Uncle You Peike and Aunt Zhang Xiuzhen, who treated him like their own son, also passed away after he had supported them for 9 and 13 years respectively, and they were properly buried.

"In the year when I came, there was a large-scale demobilization in the entire army, so the people from my original unit scattered. These martyr cemeteries also lost dedicated caretakers. I felt even more responsible for guarding my comrades and from then on, I became a voluntary guardian of the martyr cemeteries ..." Zhang Qiuliang said that for nearly 40 years, he never thought about anything else, he just felt that these comrades should be accompanied.

Needless to say, looking at the simple house where Zhang Qiuliang's family lived and the current state of this couple with silver hair, who were newlyweds back then, one could guess how they had managed over the decades.

"How did you injure your finger?" Because I sat close, I saw that Zhang Qiuliang's right little finger was broken.

He said, "This area is close to the border, and the condition of social security has always been complicated. I served as the village Director of Security for 14 years, dealing with countless crimes and criminals. My hand got injured while I was sending a hooligan to the police station ..." Zhang Qiuliang spoke lightly because such incidents were common to him.

It was not easy to settle down in the remote Gobi Desert, but it is even more difficult for Zhang's family to manage martyrs' tombs voluntarily.

"How did you overcome all these difficulties?" Naturally, this was the thing I was most concerned about.

Zhang Qiuliang stretched out his hands towards me and said, "With my hands. I haven't learned nothing but making adobe bricks, which are used to build walls ... When I was young, I could make around 1300 bricks a day, earning five or six yuan. Now that I'm old, I can still make around 1000 a day."

After hearing his words, an image of a young demobilized soldier sweating as he made adobe bricks immediately emerged in my sight. What he did must be very hard! However, for the sake of his comrades, this veteran silently carried out this unremarkable yet tear-jerking task, from youth to middle age, then to old age ...

Every snow-stormy New Year's Day and Spring Festival, stepping on knee deep snow, Zhang Qiuliang would bring cigarettes, alcohol, and food to stay with his comrades at their final resting place;

On every "the Party's Day (July 1st, anniversary of the founding of the Communist Party of China)" and "Army Day(August 1st, anniversary of the founding of the Chinese People's Liberation Army)", under the scorching summer sun, he would bring the Party and army flags to their buried place to sing *Without the Communist Party, There Would Be No New China* and military songs loudly for them;

And on every "Labor Day" and "National Day(October 1st)," he would come to their graves to offer them wine, cigarettes, and paper offerings, paying respect to the dead on behalf of their relatives ... At last, he would tidy up their graves.

These are the things that Zhang Qiuliang and his family must do every year and they have never failed to do them, regardless of fierce wind, heavy snow, or other adverse weather conditions. If he was not at home or couldn't walk , his wife and children would do it for him.

It takes quite a long journey over hills and desert sand dunes from Zhang Qiuliang's home to the martyrs' cemetery. How many times have Zhang Qiuliang and his wife fallen and stumbled on the way over the past few decades? How many cuts and scrapes have they suffered on their knees and arms? When Zhang Qiuliang and his wife showed me their arms and legs, I could only see rough fissures like that of old trees ... Some of the scars had already hardened. From that, we can imagine how painful it was.

"Once in a blizzard, on my halfway, I was buried in a snow pit which was higher than a man and I couldn't get out. If I stayed there for too long, I wouldn't survive, so I had to find a way to climb out. I almost crawled home on that day ... I can't remember how many times such things have happened over the decades. But this was not the most bitter thing. What was most painful was that the graves were 'relocated' after repeated sandstorms, and the mounds were leveled, at least dozens of times!" He said.

"Did you rebuild the mounds every time they were leveled?"

"Of course," Zhang said, "It was difficulty to shovel soil and stack stones on the Gobi desert. And it usually took half a day or even overnight to build a tomb, which was exhausting ..."

Zhang's wife curled her lips and said, "Once you almost buried yourself in the pit. If I didn't dig you out, would you have the chance to meet the writer today?"

"That never happened!" Zhang felt a bit uncomfortable as his wife exposed his embarrassing incidents.

"In fact, those things were nothing compared to the difficulty and hardship of finding relatives for the martyrs!" Zhang Qiuliang told me that because the cemetery in the border areas was too far away from the mainland, their relatives never came. What worried him even more was that he didn't know where their relatives were.

Who wouldn't miss their departed loved ones? Especially for the relatives of martyrs who were buried far away from home, on the one hand, they are deeply concerned about their loved ones who parted with their parents in younger days to join the army but sacrificed themselves on the frontier; on the other hand, due to frequent relocation of the army, their relatives cannot find the exact burial place of their fallen loved ones. Thus, even missing them so much, they can do nothing. This is the situation for the seven martyrs Zhang Qiuliang guards. Their connections with relatives were severed, even the enlistment records of their native places and home addresses were also lost after the disbandment of their original units.

"Our old military unit had been disbanded, and I didn't have the new contact address. That was the most overwhelming thing!" When Zhang Qiuliang was discharged from the army, he was an ordinary soldier and had very little contact with his comrades in the old unit, especially those who had information about the martyrs. In order to find their relatives, to give them a chance to come and visit the martyrs' graves, Zhang Qiuliang has dedicated himself to it for over a decade ...

"The martyrs I guard, who all sacrificed their lives during the time before and after I joined the army, all of them in their twenties and unmarried. They came from different provinces like Shaanxi, Sichuan, Jiangsu and Henan. Gu Kerang, not buried together with the other six comrades, during his lifetime was a squad leader who joined the army in 1976 and died at the age of 20. On an ordinary day in 1978, when a meeting was held at the army company headquarters, a criminal carrying a grenade rushed into the conference room. At this critical moment, Gu Kerang, who was on duty nearby, bravely rushed forward without any hesitation. He tightly held the criminal's hands and waist, using all his strength to drag him out of the room. Soon after, there was a loud explosion, Gu Kerang and the criminal died together. He protected the other eight comrades with his own life. I knew about Gu Kerang's story since I stepped into the military camp, and it deeply moved me. But at that time, the roads leading to the other six martyrs' graves were blocked by thick snow. Due to the limitations, Gu Kerang's bone was buried on a mountainside about 2 kilometers away from the other six martyrs' tombs. Over the years, I hoped that their relatives could come and see these who had defended our country with their lives and if possible, take them back to their hometowns ..." Zhang Qiuliang's conduct moved us all.

It was by chance when he went back home for a visit, Zhang Qiuliang found the home of martyr Hu Xianzhen through the address provided by a comrade, and met Hu's mother. At that time, Hu's mother was already in her 70s, and due to Hu's death, her eyes had been blinded by tears. As Zhang sat in front of her, the elderly woman, with trembling hands, held him in her arms, continuously stroking his head and face, and she kept saying in tears, "My son, you finally came back. I missed you so much!"

As she spoke, the old woman burst into tears.

"Mother, I am your son. Please treat me as your son!" Zhang Qiuliang knelt in front of Hu's mother and pleaded.

"My son! My good son ..." The blind mother gently helped Zhang Qiuliang up, wiping away her tears and nodding incessantly. She said to him, "My son, you are a few years younger than Xianzhen. Please visit your brother's grave and burn some paper offerings for him on his memorial day each year! That's all I want ..."

"Definitely! Mother, you can rest assured." Zhang Qiuliang promised.

After that, Zhang Qiuliang felt more urgent to find the relatives of his deceased comrades, and he experienced countless sleepless nights to this end.

In order to find the birthplaces of the martyrs and the departments handling their enlistment through multiple ways, Zhang Qiuliang had to invest a great deal of financial resources and energy. To this end, he contracted 200 acres of barren land from the village and started farming with his entire family. They sold the crops to fund their search for the families of the martyrs. Their efforts paid off, and one by one, Zhang Qiuliang found their relatives.

"Kerang, my son, I'm almost 90 years old now ... I finally have come to see you." On September 8, 2019, in the chilling autumn wind on the Gobi desert of the northwest border, the 89-year-old mother of Gu Kerang was carried by Zhang Qiuliang and several other Shawan locals to her son's grave. It was the first time that the elderly woman, with silver hair, appeared in front of Gu Kerang's tomb, together with her six other children. The scene has remained etched in Zhang's memory, "Seeing her face cling to her son's gravestone sadly, everyone present was in silence and didn't know what to do. Especially when we heard the elderly woman murmuring, 'When I died, I would come to accompany you', everyone there shed tears."

"41 years have passed. I count on my fingers every year after my son joined the army …It is you who helped me to fulfil my lifetime wish! Child, let me kowtow to you …" When Gu Kerang's mother came from the grave site to Zhang's house, she wiped her tears and gratefully held Zhang and his wife's hands, about to kneel down.

"No, no, we can't take it! Aunt, please get up … Kerang was not only my squad leader but also my brother. We are all family here, no need to stand on ceremony." Zhang Qiuliang quickly helped her up.

At that moment, he became a true family member with his comrade's mother and other relatives.

Today, Zhang Qiuliang's home has become a well-known "Veterans' Station". He not only voluntarily receives the relatives of the seven martyrs, but also welcomes comrades and young friends from all over the country, whether he knows them or not. And he is no longer the only one guarding the martyrs' grave site. His eldest son has become the second generation of "guardian of the border graves." Zhang Qiuliang has more things to do at his "Veterans' Station," such as finding relatives of unknown martyrs in other places and learning about their stories during their lifetime. These are all what Zhang is doing today …

"But on holidays and memorial days, I still have to go to sweep their graves." On the day of the interview, he gladly took me to the martyrs' grave site by walk. We offered flowers and bowed together to the martyrs who rest there.

I saw Zhang Qiuliang kneeling on the ground, devoutly burning paper offerings for each grave, and carefully tidying up each tombstone … Over 40 years, he has been doing that in an ordinary, respectful, and meticulous manner.

My eyes were spontaneously filled with tears again.

After returning to Beijing, I wrote an article about Zhang Qiuliang with the title of *The Eternal Watch* for the *PLA Daily*, which received a great response and was quickly republished as a cover story by *Duzhe*. Before I started to write this book, Zhang Qiuliang sent me a WeChat message saying that with the help of the local community and the county, he has already built a "Veterans' Station" at his home to specifically serve local veterans and help them embark on the path to prosperity.

"There are already dozens of people who have joined, and I plan to expand the functions of the 'Veterans Station' to the entire township and the county. I hope to unite the veterans who have worked and fought in the border areas through this platform and support frontier construction in a different way ..." Zhang Qiuliang's "Guardian Spirit" is spreading across the land where he perseveres.

I am looking forward to visiting this veteran's home and station again next spring when the flowers bloom. I believe it will be even more beautiful and touching.

Chapter 7

You Are the Ferghana Horse in People's Mind

As an ancient and unique breed,

Ferghana horses are well-known for their swiftness, stamina, wisdom, and distinctive hair.

Their metallic luster is similar to that of pomegranate juice.

Their colour spectrum in common reflects

"Benevolence","kindness","loyalty and righteousness", and "honesty",

Which are the basic background colour of traditional culture of the Chinese nation.

A disabled Han farmer, with his mettle and humanity,

Led people of all ethnic groups around him to prosperity.

His deed illustrates that people of all ethnic groups have a shared destiny.

When crossing the Mengbulak grassland, we were tremendously impressed by a herd of mighty horses whizzing past us. A local companion told me they are the Ferghana horses, also honored as "Kings of horses."

"No wonder they have an imposing manner!" I exclaimed admiringly. I learned that in European countries, Ferghana horses have a good name as "handsome guys" while they are a breed of choice in horse racing or equestrian competitions.

A striking contrast — After witnessing the powerful horses that day, I was going to visit a feeble man who suffered from polio due to illness and had been living on crutches. His name is Cao Zhenxin.

Before the interview, I had been expecting the appearance of this disabled person who is almost deified in Emin County and even the whole city of Tacheng. However, at first sight of him, I was highly disappointed, as if seeing Mount Tai collapse in half — a socially sophisticated man with less than 1.4 meters in height — Could he save a village with a majority of ethnic minorities?

But the villagers said, "Yes, indeed, he helped us get rich."

"Without him, we would still be employees who were bullied in other places!" A group of Uygur, Kazak, and Hui villagers gathered around, explaining to me in non-fluent Mandarin as if they were afraid that I would leave soon.

"Is he so marvelous?" I asked while pointing to Cao Zhenxin, who threw away his iron crutches and tried to reach the stool alone.

They nodded in smiles, "Absolutely, yes!"

Hearing that, I came to feel curious about Cao, the man who was not different from any other disabled people.

"How could I start my story?" Having been striving in business circles for a decade or two, he has become tactful, sophisticated, and socially experienced, without any sense of inferiority or shyness. You could not find any signs of timidity or discomfort in him when facing strangers, as if he was doing his business as usual.

"What about talking about your family and childhood at first?" I suggested.

His legs were bent and atrophied, while he had eagle eyes, with the power to see through the vicissitudes in this secular world.

"You are not from Xinjiang, are you?" He asked me. After I nodded, he continued, "Then I should explain the general background to you ..."

"The general background?"

"Yes, that's it."

He said that born in 1958, he was tremendously influenced by the situation of the times. "Especially for Xinjiang, it is quite necessary to learn the background if you want to understand the ethnic issues in the past as well as at present."

He is certainly out of the ordinary. What he said at first surprised me. More astonishingly, the story he told about the hardship his family had endured and that he had experienced after becoming disabled was utterly beyond what the common people could imagine.

He used to live in Miquan, Changji Hui Autonomous Prefecture (now Midong District, Urumqi).

"Grandpa was an intellectual, but he was labeled as a 'rightist' in the anti-rightist movement."

Father was a rich peasant, viewed as having bad family background at that time. So, he had to lead the family of eight to flee our hometown.

It was the time when Xinjiang, a vast land with abundant resources, started to develop its economy; labor was in urgent need. Back then, many people from the mainland were moving north of Xinjiang to find jobs. We also planned to escape from Miquan so that we would no longer be despised because of family background. That was why Father took our family of eight people, old and young, all the way west and then north. Finally, we arrived in Tacheng ..."

In the 1950s and 1960s, the border area around Tacheng had been very turbulent. Under the instigation of foreign separatists, several incidents had happened that many residents, especially those in rural and pastoral areas, had emigrated across the border, leaving many vacant houses and fields.

In 1962, 4-year-old Cao and his family settled in Xiajiele Agashi Village, Jiele Agashi Town, Emin County.

Being closer to the border, Tacheng posed more living challenges to the dwellers than Urumqi. However, they got freedom and could live in a relatively relaxed mood. His father built a house at an abandoned cattle pen and the family started a peasant life from then on.

"Back then, the village cadre was Hameithy, a Kazakh, who was very nice, never regarding our family as outsiders. It was his kindness that made us get the idea to settle here. And we did. We have lived here till now." There was a feeling of rejoicing and gratitude in his tone.

Having suffered a tragic childhood, he seemed to be unwilling to recall those miserable memories. That was why he often used the words commonly heard in business circles but he seldom described his personal life and inner thoughts. However, several old villagers sitting next to him couldn't help to tell stories about the childhood of "Boss Cao" and his family when they had just arrived in Xiajele Agashi Village:

"When they first came here, it was difficult for them to survive the frigid winter in the cattle pen. Therefore, our village committee lent them some cow dung, several straw mats, and some flour. To repay the kindness of villagers, his family sent elder sons to assist neighbors with some work and elder daughters to look after their children. Among many siblings, 'Boss Cao' ranked in the middle, who was always ignored by others when he was a child and even was despised, especially after he was crippled. At that time, everyone would bully him. What a poor boy!"

As the aged villagers narrated, I secretly observed "Boss Cao", seeing that his face was no longer as smiling and unrestrained as when I first met him. It seemed that the villagers' words evoked the pains hidden in the heart of this disabled yet self-reliant man.

"Among eight siblings, I ranked the fifth, who usually got less care, not to mention that afterward I got polio ..." Speaking of this, Cao grabbed a piece of watermelon, took a hard bite, then wiped his mouth. After that, he fell into silence.

"After I was crippled by polio, I lost the chance to go to school ...my parents wouldn't let me go to school. I also thought that attending school was not my business." His voice arose again, low and mournful.

It's easy to imagine what life would be like for this 6-year-old child who suddenly couldn't walk and live a normal life. He would become a burden to the whole family with ten people barely free from starving,

From the attitude of the adults, little Cao had envisioned his tragic future. However, what could he do as a child? Being free from hunger was the luckiest thing for him, and how could he even expect to attend school?

"I was once thirsty for attending school, but the reality broke my dream ..." Saying that Cao whispered in my ear, "Many times, I had secretly waited behind the mound on the ridge, trying to follow other village children to go to school. But I couldn't keep up with them. I would be left behind by them halfway!"

How could a disabled child catch up with healthy and energetic ones? This had frustrated the self-esteem of a proud boy, which made him gradually feel inferior to others. Many times, he cried himself hoarse on the cold grass, but no one came to care about him. From the age of six or seven when he fell half paralyzed, to the age of twelve or thirteen when he could live independently, he had experienced all kinds of hardship. Perhaps with too many siblings, Cao often felt that he was a burden, unimportant to his parents.

"Once, when I herded the sheep, a storm came so fast and violently that I had no time to drive the sheep to shelter from the wind, resulting in more than a dozen lost. I could foresee that when I broke the news to my parents, they would beat me seriously. I was too scared to go home, even till the night fell.

Even worse, it snowed. I found a shelter, but the snow soon blanketed the ground. Thinking that maybe it was my last day on earth, I began to cry for a long time. Then I thought, as a disabled child, death was not a big deal for me. I was just a burden to my family, despised by everyone. It would be better to get it over with and die.

I was really getting ready to die that day, but later I was saved by several good-hearted passers-by . They carried me to their home, gave me food, warmed me up, and let me sleep on a heated brick bed, spreading a leather blanket.

They are Kazakh. Although they couldn't speak Mandarin very well, their words and gestures made me feel extremely warm in my heart. Since then, I have sworn to live well and repay their kindness when I grew up ..." From that day on, Cao started his brand new life.

Next year, at 13, he began to learn to ride horses.

It would be a wild fantasy for him, a polio teenager with atrophied legs, to ride a horse. It was a fight against one's destiny. Cao said that he must win.

Unimaginable as it was, this super man's dream miraculously came true: Cao made up his mind to learn to ride a horse, for he wanted to be able to make a living. Herding for his family would be a good choice, and the skill of riding horses was a necessity. Yet how could a polio teenager ride a horse? Such an idea would sound "insane" in the eyes of ordinary people.

"What if I make it? Will you allow me to herd cattle and sheep?" The stubborn Cao stole a whip from his father and hobbled away from home to the distant pasture with a horse.

"You, can you do it?" His mother secretly wiped her tears behind him while his father shook his head angrily, "Let him go! It would be better he fell to death!" It was an angry remark, he didn't mean it.

Cao left home and soon disappeared in the prairie. Walking beside the tall horse, he was only as tall as the horse's leg, invisible soon as they went through a bush.

"Little cripple, can you ride a horse? Come on, just ride on my shoulders!"

"Ride a horse? Does the horse obey you?"

"Ha-ha ... do you take the horse as a mound for you to pee?"

The voices of those people in the pasture were all of sarcasm, forcing Cao to wait for others to leave and then start to practice alone.

"Kneel! Kneel!" he stood in front of the horse and shouted repeatedly.

"Hah, don't you listen to me?" The horse stayed still, even staring at him with its big eyes. It seemed to say: Look at your height! Do you want to ride on me? No way!

"Pop —" he wanted to whip the horse yet tripped over the whip.

"Hiss —" the horse screamed and kicked Cao off two or three meters away.

Angrily, he wanted to hold the horse's leg but failed to reach it. What to do? Seeing the horse refuse to kneel, he took its leg as a tree to climb! As he moved, the horse squealed again and turned around to throw him meters away.

"Ouch!" Cao felt painful as though his body were broken. But he didn't give up, picking himself up from the stones and attempting to conquer the robust horse, yet to no avail.

Covered in mud, Cao burst into tears, complaining about the unfairness of life. He couldn't go to school as his peers did nor ride the horse like other commanding herders.

He cried himself hoarse, and till the end, he couldn't talk.

Initially he was in a flood of tears and gradually he had no tears left to cry, only with his confused eyes gazing at the horse.

Suddenly, the horse knelt on his front legs, stretched out his back feet, leaned forward to lie on its stomach beside him, and then made a gentle sound, "hiss —."

Surprised, Cao asked, "What, you mean I can ride you? Did you let me ride you?"

The horse gave out "Hiss —" again.

"Ha-ha, yes, that's what you mean!" Excitedly, Cao gathered strength and jumped onto the horseback with his atrophied legs. "Ha-ha, I made it! I made it!"

The horse seemed to know Cao's feelings at that moment, carrying this disabled boy to ride in a few rounds.

"Horses have emotions like human beings. They know everything!" Cao said.

Nevertheless, horses were animals, bullying the weak and fearing the strong. To learn to ride a horse and herd the animals, Cao kept practicing getting on and off, saddling and whipping the horse. He couldn't remember how many times he had fallen off the horse, yet in his memory, he was thrown off the galloping horse at least five or six times, with his arms and thigh bones broken several times. "I was taken to the hospital with broken arms and legs. With plaster and gauze on and treated for several days, I returned to the pasture for training ..." Although Cao could make light of his bygone hardships now, in the past, whenever he struck the ground from horseback, he would think, "I am done for this time".

But he survived, and his father said he had more lives than a cat. "Once my ribs were broken, I just covered them with gauze for two days. Then, I began to herd the cattle and sheep on horseback. The horses seemed to take special care of me. Later, I could ride various kinds of horses. I can say that I am an excellent rider!"

Standing side by side with me, he doesn't even come up to my chest. Yet he can rein all kinds of wild and mettlesome horses. What a miracle! It is a pity that the interview was held in his factory office that day. If it was in the ranch, I could see his wonderful equestrianism on the spot. I wonder, with his atrophied legs, how he could ride, flying on the horseback,or making the horse listen to him ... Both sounds unbelievable.

"The horse will listen to me. Give it a signal, and it will know whether to squat or stand. It doesn't need too much effort!" Cao said that after three or four years, he could tame all kinds of horses as long as he had trained them for two months.

"In the wild grassland or the mountains, I can call horses a few miles away back to me with a whistle. A good horse is smarter than a man and reliable. I have reared many fine horses. I had pastured for the production team for more than 20 years, recognized as the master of riding horses. I could earn 13 work points back then, 30 percent higher than a strong laborer could do ..." Hearing this, I looked at him in a new light.

"Indeed, he earned the highest work points at that time," several old villagers nodded and scrambled to say, "He worked attentively and honestly, always did what was the most difficult."

"Healthy and strong, other villagers are able to do almost everything without worrying about work points. Except for me, I could only find some toilsome, grueling, and dirty work that no one would like to do so that I could earn more work points." Cao said. At that time, a work point was worth about ten RMB cents. He said that in 1983, when fields were contracted to households, he, a disabled youth with polio, became the richest farmer in the village. For to lighten the burden of his family, he had moved out to live alone at the age of 20.

"Since then, although I was disabled, no people in the whole village could look down on me any longer because I have more money than anyone else ... don't you believe it? I am telling the truth, and you can ask them —" Cao pointed to the villagers around our interview site and said proudly.

"He is the richest one! He had much money then, and now he has more!" As someone said, everyone laughed, so did Cao.

"During the eight years when I rode horses for herding, I learned Kazakh. Most of the herders in the village were Kazakhs. I was on good terms with them and thus my Kazakh became fluent. We were like family."

I came to admire this disabled man who was unattractive and having difficulty in movements.

"When the new policy implemented, I got a horse worth 170 yuan, a cow worth 90 yuan, a pickup worth 80 yuan, and more than 80 yuan in cash, higher than any other person in the production team. That was why I was called the richest villager." Cao was indeed a remarkable man. In those days, in the pastoral areas on the border, a single man with so much property really deserved the title.

Previously, Cao had the least status and dignity in the village, but now, he became the richest man. With the trend of reform and opening up, all the villagers of different ethnic groups wanted to emulate the great success of this disabled man. Gradually, no one called him "Crip Cao" any longer but addressed him as "Boss Cao."

"They've been calling me like that for decades!" It was obvious that Cao was used to and enjoyed being called "boss."

Self-reliant and hardworking relentlessly, this disabled man who was formerly despised by everyone has finally made a fortune and won others' trust and reverence.

Just at that time, a Han woman, Ren Huafu, a native of Qingdao, Shandong Province, came to the village.

The place was completely strange to this divorced woman. One day, when she came across Cao, she told him her story briefly in tears. "Brother, I would be grateful if your could offer me a place to live and some food to eat. I could do anything for you." After saying that, she knelt in front of him.

"Ouch, don't do this! Get up, please ..." He threw away his crutches in a hurry to help her up but didn't stand firmly and fell on his back.

"Did ...didn't you get hurt?" What a gentle and emotional voice of a woman! As Cao had never felt that tenderness before, he stared at the woman patting his clothes to remove the dust.

The woman settled down in Cao's home. Every day Cao returned from work, she would prepare delicious meal and his favorite wine for him. He hoped that if only life could keep like that forever!

"You are a cripple man! How can you dream of such a good thing?" Being sober and realistic, he immediately scolded himself: Do you want to marry an angel? Look at you in the mirror first!

"Boss..Cao, I want to stay here. what do you think?" One day, after dinner, the woman asked him coyly.

"Why not? You can stay here as long as you want. Anyway, I live alone, and the other rooms are vacant." Cao said.

"I, I want to live with you ..." The woman lifted her head, bolder than before.

"We are living together now! Just stay here; I will not drive you away." He said.

"I, I mean ..." She flushed with anxiety, "I want to live with you in the same room ..."

Cao's lips began to tremble, "Eh ...my ...my ..." He subconsciously looked at his withered legs and then stared at the woman with a sense of inferiority.

The woman stood up, stretched out her hands, gently picked him up, and then walked straight to his room, saying, "As long as you don't detest me, I won't be ashamed to live with you ..."

Later, they got married.

What a strange couple! The wife was tall and robust while the husband was thin and short. The man was the backbone of the family, revered as "Boss Cao" by other people. The woman could pick her husband up with both hands, while she was incredibly tender and considerate at home.Ren Huafu, who had fled from famine in her hometown to this village back then, was now a grandmother of a 5-year-old grandson. She said that her eldest son was 36 years old, and her youngest son was 32 years old.

I do not know how the couple has gone through the hardships over the past 30 years. But one thing is obvious: without Ren Huafu's effort, Cao, a polio patient who needs help for walking, would fail to support such a perfect and prosperous family. He would be merely a single old man of fortune. Similarly, without Cao's hard work, all other family members, including Ren Huafu, may not have enjoyed what they have now. It is Cao, a physically weak but mentally strong man, who has supported his family with unremitting efforts.

Cao Zhenxin is an admirable man.

Whoever strives for his future must be   marvellous and happy. I could draw such a conclusion when I saw Cao and his family, including children and grandchildren, live joyfully and happily.

However, more admirable is Cao Zhenxin's effort to lead the fellow villagers to get rich,despite his weak body — And I came here as an interviewer actually owing to this story.

What people could not dare to imagine often turns out to be objective facts.

"Having suffered a lot in my childhood while enjoyed assistance from so many people at the time of hardship, I have been eager to do something useful to repay my benefactors, neighbors — Uygur, Kazakh, and Hui people who are kind-hearted and ready to help others. However, due to my physical weakness and limited ability, I have been exploring a way to get wealthy over the past several decades.There have also been failures ..." Cao said.

In the early stage of the household contract system, he volunteered to drive the unattended livestock to the pasture to prove that he was not inferior to others in terms of personal ability and labor. During the following seven years, he started with grazing more than 300 heads of livestock for the village and finally earned 40,000 yuan for pasturing.

The first barrel of gold enlightened him: It turned out that contracting agriculture and animal husbandry on the grassland or desert could also make money! Then, he invested 40,000 yuan in 2,000 mu fruit fields in neighboring villages. Unfortunately, despite his hard work for nearly 1,500 days, as an inexperienced and unskilled orchard man, he failed and was in debt of 6000 yuan. Some one ridiculed Cao in private, saying that not only did he have atrophied legs, but now he broke one of his arms.

Heartbroken, Cao's wife shed tears while holding her husband in bed to massage his skinny body.

"Leave it alone. I'm used to failure now. It's not a big deal." He wiped away her tears and said, "Don't worry. You have to believe one thing: the difficulties that have fallen upon me will help me be more likely to succeed than others. Just wait and see!"

"I believe that! But I'm worrying about your health ..." She couldn't bear to see her husband get hurt physically and mentally.

Hearing that, Cao immediately made a "challenging move" again — jumping out of bed and then performing a set of "somersaults", which made his wife amused yet worried.

Later, Cao bounced back to embark on a new business journey: he and his wife planned to raise sheep. At first, they planted barley on their 56 mu of contracted land and then bartered the harvested 60 bags of wheat for 33 lambs. When he saw that the small-tailed Han sheep had high reproduction rates, he resold 33 sheep for small-tailed Han sheep.

Cao is an experienced herder. Yet raising ewes for reproduction was different from driving livestock out to pasture — moreover, the lambing process required expertise and much patience. As a novice in this industry, Cao spared no effort to learn the relative knowledge and skills. Generally speaking, an ewe can deliver several lambs one night. Due to his disability, Cao had to "take the sheepfold as his home" and stayed up all night to help the ewes during the delivery.

A few years later, with the number of sheep soaring from dozens to more than 400, Cao had earned some profits.

He has been on his way to wealth.

This time, he became slow and steady, doing business step by step: First, he reared four Xinjiang brown cows, reaping more than 30,000 yuan in profits that year. Then, encouraged by this success, he raised money to buy 10 Holstein-Friesian cows. Like rolling a ball of snow downhill, he has bred more than one hundred captive cows. Now, he is the most capable money-maker in the village, with an annual income topping 500,000 yuan.

"Crip Cao gets rich!"

"Even he can build wealth. Are we still waiting for nothing?"

Cao's success had an overwhelming effect, prompting the villagers to reexamine the gap between themselves and him and followed him to raise cows.

But after a few days, some villagers had troubles: their cows were not so "obedient," either sick or giving less milk.

"You must calm down. If there are any difficulties, I will help you out." Knowing what bothered the villagers, Cao volunteered to open a dairy farming training class for everyone.

As the problems about raising remained unsolved, more thorny issues stood out: some villagers couldn't afford cows. Besides, they worried about the risks of losing money.

The villagers gathered around Cao's dairy farm to ask for experience and even a "promise."

After considering for a while, Cao threw away his crutches and then jumped hard to sit on the table, shouting out loud, "I feel flattered at being trusted by all of you. I assure you that people with disabilities in the village can buy cows on credit from me, or entrust me with breeding the cows for you, I can assure you a satisfactory income; I will sell my cows at the lowest price to other villagers. I will take responsibility for settling all the troubles you will encounter for free. In a word, I will go all out to help you without any charge!"

"Great! Boss Cao, with your promise, we will go full steam ahead!" The villagers cheered.

Kurbanjiang is a disabled newcomer from southern Xinjiang who lived with his relatives. Not having much money, he was struggling to get by. In order to help Kurbanjiang survive during the most challenging period of his life, Cao gave him a fine cow worth 15,000 yuan for free. "Now I have three cows. I may earn seven or eight thousand yuan a year. My life is getting better!" Kurbanjiang "showed off" in public.

Mao Tai, a Kazakh villager, used to raise local cattle, lacking enough experience in dairy farming.On one hand, he would like to raise cows; on the other hand, he was worried about failure. Then, he asked Cao whether he could buy a cow on credit and sell the milk to Cao to pay the debt. Cao generously answered his request, "No problem. You have my support as long as you know how to make money!" Later, without any cost, Mao Tai earned thousands of yuan the following year.

Besides, Cao offered two cows on credit at cost price to another villager, Wang Zhishuang, who lived in a pinch. With these two cows, Wang Zhishuang develops his business gradually and now owns more than 20 cows. Last year, he earned nearly 100,000 yuan.

"Following Boss Cao, you can definitely make a buck. So he is the 'boon' of our village ..." All the folks came to sing Cao's praises, which greatly touched me.

As I looked at Cao, he was beaming with pride.

The most impressive part of the interview came from the officials in the town when they introduced the remarkable achievements made by Cao: In 2011, to help the villagers get rich, Cao registered a Dairy Farming Cooperative with another rich farmer, Liu Yue'er. They have recruited 115 members and registered the "Yue'er" milk trademark. Up to now, the cooperative has ensured an annual income of more than 100,000 yuan for each member, making the villagers truly embark on the road to wealth.

From the faces of Cao and other villagers, I could tell that the interview excited them all. Their reactions reminded me of Huang Dafa, the winner of the "July 1st Medal" and "Touching China" Award 2021. Five years ago, I first interviewed him in the mountainous area of Guizhou.

At that time, Huang Dafa was nobody with a small dream. "I want to go to Beijing and Tiananmen Square," he had told me several times before becoming well-known nationwide.

He has a touching personal story while I am an experienced storyteller, so I confidently assured him, "You will be invited to Beijing after the publication of this book about you."

I was not being boastful. Later, Huang's dream came true. What's more, he won a supreme honor unreachable to most people: General Secretary Xi Jinping gave him a seat when taking a group photo with the central leadership at the National Moral Models Commendation Conference. As the scene was broadcast on CCTV news, his deeds were soon spread in every corner of China.

On that day, the interview with Cao made me think of Huang naturally. In my mind, both of them have admirable qualities that can touch people the most. Humble and physically vulnerable, Cao has lived bitterly — he must use two crutches to support his body while walking, and if he wants to sit on a chair, he has to jump high with all his strength.

How does he usually do business with people? How did he jump on a horse to gallop? How did he establish livestock farms, dairy farms and formed the dairy farming cooperative for hundreds of households? Every day on his way to run a business, he must settle many issues.How did he, with atrophied legs, lead hundreds of villagers to a broad path of wealth and happiness?

Isn't it worth paying tribute to this determined and self-improving disabled person?

Yes, we must do so to this ordinary herdsman who has protected an ethnically harmonious and prosperous world in the border areas with his strength!

At the moment of departure, a poem *Ferghana Horse* written by Mr. Niu Han, a poet whom I am familiar with, suddenly rang in my ear —

Running a thousand miles through the Gobi Desert to reach the river,

Running a thousand miles through the desert to arrive at the grassland.

In windless July and August,
Gobi Desert is the fiefdom of fire.
Only galloping,
Galloping with four feet rising high in the air,
The wind can be felt in front of the chest,
Hundreds of miles of sultry floating dust can be passed through.
Sweat was licked by thirsty dust and sand,
Sweat crystallized into the white markings of horses.

The sweat ran out,
The bile drained away.
With eyes sprinting to the emptiness,
With broad pectorals vibrating.
Silently mobilize the inner parts,
From shoulders, feet, and buttocks,
Blood is oozing out bit by bit.
On the earth,
Only Ferghana horse,

Blood vessels interconnect with sweat glands.

There are no wings on the shoulders or feet,
Nor steam under the hooves.
Ferghana horse is not endowed with the power of
divine creatures,
It only gallops forward.
Sweating with steam all over the body like red clouds,
In order to climb over the snow-covered Daban,
and the frozen sky,
Life keeps burning.

Shedding the last drop of blood,
It can still run a thousand miles with bones and
muscles.

Ferghana horses,
Throws itself at the summit of life,
Incinerating into a flower,
A snow-white flower.

Yes, Cao Zhenxin, aren't you a Ferghana horse in our frontier? Your posture galloping forward transcends the beauty of all other things. Like an eagle, you have commanded the admiration and respect of all creatures while pursuing self-improvement!

Chapter 8

Ballads From the Horseback

Camel bells over the Gobi grassland,

With a deeply affectionate and melodious sound,

Ring for national prosperity and people's well-being.

Those who ring camel bells,

Are spreading the most precious nutrition in Chinese traditional culture — love and kindness.

History has repeatedly proven that wherever there is love and kindness

There is vigorous and vibrant development ...

In Xinjiang, there is a famous highway called Duku Highway, also known as the "Tianshan Highway". In 1976, at the beginning of my military service, I learned that a road was being built there because it was built by my comrades-in-arms, who were from the Infrastructure Engineering Corps of the Chinese People's Liberation Army. Later, during the 1983 Disarmament of a Million, the authority revoked the unit designation of the engineering corps, but the "Transportation Command(TRANSCOM)" in the unit was kept and incorporated into the newly established Armed Police Forces.

Years ago, *The Soldiers Deep in Mt. Tianshan* (a novel written by Li Binkui in 1980) spread the story of the road construction soldiers in Mt. Tianshan to the whole country ...

For many years, as a news officer who once served in the former headquarters of the engineering corps, I have often hoped to go back and see the road built by my comrades-in-arms in the depths of Mt. Tianshan and especially wanted to see the 168 martyrs who sacrificed their lives for building it. So many lives have lost for building a road, one could imagine how difficult and dangerous the "Tianshan Highway" is!

Unexpectedly, I have such an opportunity to come after several decades. On the day of the interview, we came to the most difficult section of the Duku Highway in the Haxilegen Glacier area of the Celicti Ranch in Usu, Tacheng Prefecture, a place where my deceased comrades-in-arms were buried ...

The Jorma Martyrs' Cemetery is located in Jorma, Nilka County, Yili Kazak Autonomous Prefecture. A 20-meter-high monument stands there, marked with the words "Comrades who sacrificed their lives for the construction of the Duku Highway are immortal forever" on its facade. On its back, there are inscriptions and the names of the martyrs in both Chinese and Uyghur languages. The youngest among them was only 16 years old, and the eldest was 31.But they have been buried here for several decades ...

> See my comrades off when they embark on a journey
> Silently shedding tears without a word
> The sound of camel bells is ringing in my ears
> The road is long, and the mist is thick
> Parting is common when we strive for revolution
> Bidding farewell as usual but with different feelings,
> My comrades, oh, my comrades,
> My beloved brothers,
>
> ...

The song *Camel's Bells* suddenly resounded in my mind, as if it had been echoing above the martyrs' graves incessantly.

It is self-evident that the Highway brings great convenience to the north-south transportation in Xinjiang. Before this highway was built, people in northern Xinjiang, especially in the grasslands and Gobi deserts of Junggar Basin, Tacheng Prefecture, had to ride horses to graze and travel. Even after the opening of the Duku Highway, in the grasslands and pastures of most areas, people still ride horses as the main means of transportation.

> The sun just climbs up from the sky

> A young herdsman walks out of his tent
> Mounting on my chestnut-colored horse
> With my Dongbula in tow, hey
> Driving my large herd of horses
> Comes to the foot of Mt. Tianshan
>
> ...

The horse gallops while he waves his whips. For decades, Dr. Wuhaas has been used to visiting his patients at their homes with his horse and medical box, which is far more plentiful than the usual ones because it is the "hospital" for the herdsmen who lived in the grasslands. And Wuhaas is the only doctor in this "hospital" ...

Perhaps many people do not understand what I mean. Then, you can imagine that in the desolate grasslands and vast Gobi deserts, on the ranches far away from cities and highways, or even in a hollow of the hill, if there is a herder who falls ill, and now the only person can help is Dr. Wuhaas. Upon hearing the news, carrying a medical box, Dr. Wuhaas goes to save the patient's life but finds that immediate surgery is necessary for him. Whether the doctor can treat the disease or not, he must start to handle, for the patient's life or death are matter of minutes,or even seconds, and he has no spare life to lose. Therefore, Wuhaas must have all the things that a hospital may be equipped — if he doesn't, he must try everything to create them! Otherwise, the patient may lose his life.

How many things can a medical box hold? It's simply impossible to put everything inside. Not to mention medical instruments, what else can it contain besides scissors, needles, and limited bottles and gauze? And according to the usual preparation, you can only fill the medical box with drugs and apparatus according to the ability of a barefoot doctor! However, in the vast Gobi desert and the mountain hollows in the grasslands,

Wuhaas's medical box shoulders the responsibility of a hospital, i.e. that of human lives!

This is the responsibility that a doctor should take on the pastures. And that is what Wuhaas does. Therefore, people call him the "Angel in the Grassland".

When I met this "Angel," he was already an elder with a weathered face and a slight hunch back. It was impossible not to get old — since he started to work in the grasslands and Gobi Deserts in 1975, he has been serving here for more than 40 years. In the meantime, he has changed FIVE different horses ...

"How, how could I bear to leave the lives of my brothers and sisters on the desolate mountains and sands?" Wuhaas said. On his first out-call, he encountered a Mongolian woman in difficult labor. She had been struggling for five or six hours. When he arrived, the mother was already in a semi-comatose state. If not handled in time, it may cost two lives!

"Doctor, I'm begging you! I'm begging you to save them ..." Her husband was a stalwart man, but he knelt to plead with Wuhaas — for the sake of his wife and child.

Before that, Wuhaas was a veterinarian on the grassland pastures, and responsible for helping herdsmen cure the disease of livestock such as cattle and sheep. But now he suddenly had to treat illnesses of mankind, and his patient was a pregnant woman, who was in difficult labor!

"I, I don't know what to do! I have never delivered a baby before ..." Wuhaas didn't lie.

"But you're a doctor ... please, I'm begging you to save her, to save my family!" Her husband even started to give a kowtow to him.

"I ..." Wuhaas had to help her. He opened the medical box in a trembling move, took out a pair of medical scissors, and then got started ...

Nervously!

"Waa ..." The baby cried as if the entire mountain hollow and grassland were shaken.

Wuhaas's fame as a doctor who once was a vet spread across the grassland ...

Since then, a vet has become the "omnipotent doctor" in herdsmen's eyes.

"I compelled myself to treat human disease ..." Wuhaas spoke to me with a bitter smile, he continued his job as a vet but gradually was prone to becoming a doctor.

"In these decades, do you still remember how many newborn babies you've delivered?" I thought Wuhaas was truly remarkable. Delivering a child meant that another descendant of the herder came to the vast grassland and our big family of the Chinese nation also has one more member.

"It's probably more than 2,000!" Wuhaas replied casually.

An official from the Publicity Department of Yumin County, who accompanied me to interview Wuhaas at his home, discreetly told me that Wuhaas had delivered over 2,800 children in the pasturing area.

"Golly! That's a lot!" I exclaimed in surprise.

You can imagine that if these newborns are put together in a line, how magnificent it would be!And all of them were delivered by this ordinary doctor who was a vet before.

No wonder people call him the "Angel of the Grassland".

"It's very common to give birth to children on the pastures. Herdsmen usually go out for months with their whole family. Therefore, whenever I go to the pastures, I would record the pregnancy dates of women there. In that way, I would have a rough estimate of when they will give birth so that I can make preparations." Wuhaas spoke calmly, but I couldn't help but think that when he delivered those 2,800 newborns, how many unimaginable difficulties and challenges had he encountered?

He dedicated himself to the herdsmen on the grassland ...

Sharapati, who lived in the area near Mt. Balluk, can still remember how her child was born. It was on the afternoon of March 29, 2002, when she was in labor in her yurt, and she felt that the pain might kill her. Her water had broken for three days, but the baby's head still didn't protrude. Her home was more than 60 kilometers away from the county town. As they didn't know what to do, Dr. Wuhaas appeared.

"The life of the mother matters the most!" After basic observation and diagnosis, Wuhaas, who rushed into the house braving snow, immediately took emergency measures for Sharapati ... After over an hour of emergency assistance, the baby was finally delivered, but with no breath.

"I want my child alive, please ..." The faint plea of the mother deeply touched Dr. Wuhaas. With no equipment available, he started performing mouth-to-mouth artificial respiration on the baby for 10 minutes, 20 minutes ... "Waa!" The baby cried, with this sound echoing through Mt. Balluk.

Sharapati smiled. And her entire family laughed.

Today, 20 years later, the whole family stood in front of Dr. Wuhaas, laughing happily.

"umbilical cord father!" Wuhaas was thus addressed intimately by Sharapati's child, who was tall and at the age of 20.

Over 180 children from more than 10 ethnic groups, including Han, Uyghur, Kazakh, Mongolian, and Hui, in the grassland, all called Dr. Wuhaas "umbilical cord father". Their mothers all went through difficult births. And it was Wuhaas who gave these children their lives to be the new generation of Tacheng.

"The story of Dr. Wuhaas is never-ending!" The herdsmen in the pastoral areas told me so.

It was a pitch-black night, snow had already buried all the rugged mountain roads ... Suddenly, an urgent knocking on the door startled Wuhaas, who had just laid down. "Doctor! Doctor! We have a patient at home, please come and take a look ..."

It was like a "command"! Wuhaas grabbed his medical box and rushed out.

"My father's got stomachache ... which is excruciating, please save his life!" The patient's family, stamping their feet in the snow, begged Wuhaas to go into the mountain.

It was impossible to see the mountain road, obscured by heavy snow, so they could only find their way relying on man's senses and estimate through the movements of the horses ... "In the first couple of miles, I fell off the horse three or four times ..." Wuhaas said.

"Later, when we couldn't ride any further, I had to temporarily leave the horse at a herder's home and continued to go on foot in the snow ... It took us over an hour to reach the patient's home. The patient had acute appendicitis. Based on his condition, I provided conservative treatment, and then together with his family and neighbors in the pasture, we carried him out and rushed him to the county hospital. Finally, he received timely surgical treatment and recovered soon." Wuhaas said he encountered cases like this several times every year.

"If there's an urgent case, do you have to handle it on site by yourself?" I thought that some disease couldn't wait.

Wuhaas nodded. "Yes, that's right. People are more prone to getting sick in the wild, such as food poisoning, acute illness, women giving birth, as well as more cases like broken limbs from falls ..."

"Is your small medical box enough for that?" I asked with a smile.

Wuhaas shook his head and said, "Not only my medical box is not sufficient, but also my medical skills ..."

"Then, what can you do about it?"

"I learn. First, I learned from the teachers who became doctors earlier than me. Then, I became a teacher for younger people, and I have to learn better through practice so that my skills have been improved. I have almost become an expert after delivering dozens or even hundreds of babies, and I am not afraid of such cases anymore ..."

"Have there been any problems?"

"No, for some cases that I can't handle, I would promptly send my patients to the hospital, and ultimately, everything turned out well, which brought me great comfort. And I sincerely bless the new births. So, I have many friends in Tacheng and Kulustai grassland. Some of them are young people I helped deliver, even including their children. Maybe in a family, I helped deliver two generations, so they call me 'adoptive father' or 'grandfather' affectionately, which makes me very happy. I am responsible for about 5,000 people on the ranch, and I stay with them for almost half year every year. Wherever they go, I follow them, just like family. In the meantime, I also take care of their livestock. That's why they treat me like a family member. Even if they have any quarrels, they would ask me to mediate. As a doctor, since I've cured their ailments, I hope they can live a more fulfilling life. It wouldn't be good if they quarreled with each other, then, I have become a 'doctor' handling disputes as well ..." Wuhaas laughed as he spoke.

So he is really an "omnipotent doctor", whose work varies from that of a vet to a doctor, then to a "psychologist".

Wuhaas lived in downtown Yumin County, but for several decades, he spent less than a third of his time at home. "Once the spring snow melts, cattle and sheep begin to run in the ranch. And that's the time I have to set off. I will stay there until snow falls in the winter and herders can't graze anymore. So, I almost have no time to take care of my family and I feel incredibly sorry for them ..." Wuhaas lowered his head with remorse.

The local officials told me that Wuhaas didn't attend his father's funeral, even his brother's. "It was not that I didn't want to come back. There are thousands of people on the ranch spreading out in different places, and I have to go around like a patrolman, constantly moving and visiting patients. If I went back home, it would have taken at least three to four days to return to the ranch. During those days, there might be eight to ten patients who need medical care. I can't delay the treatment of patients for my own affairs!"

With more and more regretful circumstances, Wuhaas became the person who was the most indebted to his family. On one occasion, his wife was seriously ill, but he couldn't take care of her, let alone accompanying her in the hospital. After his wife was discharged, she said to him, "You have been working on the ranch for decades, and you have done what you have to do. We are not young anymore, how about you transfer back to the county town. I have been sick for a few years, and I want you to be by my side." Wuhaas didn't know what to do ...

"My dear, I know you care for the people in the pastures ... You have served them for your whole life, and we have been honored by it. Go ahead, they need you more. We'll manage all the things at home!" In the end, his wife told him generously.

Wuhaas said that he had done what a doctor should do on the ranch his whole life. But without the support of his family, he couldn't have done it for such a long time. He was grateful for his family's support and understanding, especially his wife's.

In fact, the good deeds that Wuhaas did on the ranch over the decades were far more than the "few things" he mentioned. One could say that what he did was as numerous and beautiful as the flowers in the Kulustai grassland.

Once, on Wuhaas's medical tour, he saw a Han herder named Yang Zhanlin collapse on the ground. After rescuing the man's life, Wuhaas learned that because Yang's family was very poor, he had gone out to find a job, but unfortunately, he didn't find one. Eventually, he fainted because he didn't have money to buy food.

"Take this money, and then we'll figure out how to find you a job ..." Wuhaas handed Yang Zhanlin a few hundred yuan from his pocket and then helped him move to a safe place. Afterward, he has helped him out with problems in life as well as work many times.

"Dr. Wuhaas is a good man. He is truly an angel on our grassland because he cured our disease selflessly and even gave us advice for our happiness!" Such praises for Wuhaas were most common among the herders in the pastoral areas. He was reserved when talking about his own affairs during the interview at his own home. But once he was with the herders, Wuhaas was like a patriarch of a big family, who was escorted by big crowds, being invited to drink and dance. Just like a fish diving into the water, he joyfully and freely blended into the lives of the herders. It was truly an enviable sight.

I even wondered who would have the most cohesive force. It is amazing to see that a doctor could possess such tremendous power of cohesion.

Isn't it?

Meilian is the second angelic doctor and model for ethnic unity that I met in the pastoral area.

Meilian is well-known in Tacheng, even in Xinjiang, and she has a beautiful name that makes people think of the snow lotus on Mt. Tianshan, which only blooms in the season when the winter plums bloom. Does her name "Meilian" have such metaphoric meaning? Meilian smiled and said that her father might think of the metaphor when he gave her that name.

When she was young, her fate was indeed closely related to the meaning of her name. Meilian's mother was originally from Sichuan Province. In the early 1960s, incited by the Soviet Union, some residents in border areas such as Ili and Tacheng forcefully crossed the border and fled to the Soviet Union. At that time, to stabilize the border areas, the Chinese government assembled soldiers from many places across the country to carry out the missions of acclaiming farmland and guarding the border near Tacheng. Meilian's mother arrived in Xinjiang from Sichuan that year and was assigned to the 161st Regiment, the 9th Agricultural Division, Xinjiang Production and Construction Corps, stationed adjacent to the border. As a high school graduate, Meilian's mother, with her beautiful appearance and the advantage of being an "intellectual", was soon married to a young man in the Corps, who was Meilian's father ...

Meilian was the second child among 5 siblings in her family, who loved reading from a young age, which perhaps inherited from her mother. Life in the Corps was tough, and apart from conducting military training, the soldiers were actually farmers. Meilian had to take on the household chores without complaint, as her parents worked tirelessly in the fields. She was very young at that time, but the hard work shaped her strong-willed character.

When Meilian was five years old, it snowed heavily in the winter, and the area around Mt. Balluk where she lived turned into a world of ice and snow. The transportation was already inconvenient, but the blizzard in the severe winter completely blocked all the roads to the outside ...

"Mom, I want to ... drink some water ..." Meilian's younger brother, who had a high fever, desperately asking for water in his mother's arms. His mother hastened to give him a bowl of water while Meilian was scared by the look as he drank.

One hour passing by, his fever was not gone but became even worse. Meilian didn't dare to touch his fevered body ...

"This won't do! Our son can't bear it anymore!" His father, who had been sitting by the door smoking with his head down, patted his legs, suddenly stood up, and said, "Let's take him to the hospital in the regiment headquarters. The company medic said what he has is measles, which is very serious! Let's go right away, and don't waste any more time!"

"But it snows so heavily outside, and the roads are all blocked ... Can he withstand it?" His mother cried.

"We have to take him to the hospital despite the weather!" He waved his hand and made the final decision.

"Little brother ..." Five-year-old Meilian watched her father drive the cart while her mother holding her brother, disappearing in heavy snow. She was extremely scared and cried out "Little brother", hoping that he would come back safely, as well as her mom and dad ...

A few days later, her mom and dad came back with her little brother, a small lifeless cold body without breath ...

"If there were a doctor here in the company, my son couldn't have passed away ..." Meilian's mother kept repeating these words in the following years as if she were speaking to the heavens and the earth, and it was deeply engraved in Meilian's heart.

When I grow up, I want to be a doctor. And I want to save my little brother!

I want to be a doctor to save the younger brothers and sisters of other families in the company, as well as those uncles and aunts ...

This pledge was etched in Meilian's young heart.

"I remember, when I was a child, every year, there had been one or two children about the age of my little brother who would die from sudden illness in the company. Some of them might die of a common cold or a regular gastrointestinal infection, owing to lack of timely treatment ...” Such incidents kept happening in Meilian's childhood.

The inarticulate Meilian grew older year by year, and people noticed that this quiet girl would always go to the company clinic, and sit there silently, listening to the conversations between the medic and the patients, or observing how the medic prescribed. She also liked to borrow books there and ask various questions.

“So, you want to be a doctor, right?”

“Yes, I want to treat the illness of my brothers, sisters, and other people's siblings ...” Meilian replied innocently.

“Well, then why don't you want to treat the illness of your parents and others' parents?” The medic asked in curiosity.

“Treating the illness of adults is your responsibility!” Meilian replied earnestly.

“Haha ... I see!” The adults laughed.

In 1984, because her family was very poor — in fact, many of the regiment's families were not rich back then. Besides, she had so many siblings. Therefore, after graduating from junior high school, Meilian became a farm worker in the 14th company, the 161st regiment. Farm workers were farmers who received a salary. But what they did and ate as well as living conditions was no different from farmers in other places. However, Meilian's dream of becoming a doctor remained unchanged. Compared to her peers, she was indeed someone with a strong determination. Without attending medical school, Meilian chose the path of becoming a doctor through self-study. Nowadays, we may find such a choice a bit “unconventional,” but at that time, in the Xinjiang Production and Construction Corps, in the border areas of China, it was entirely reasonable.

In fact, it was Meilian and millions of other people striving from the most basic and primitive starting point, working tirelessly to make progress in modernization of the country. China is great and prosperous today, attributed to ordinary people like Meilian, who have taken the simplest, most diligent, and hardest-working path of entrepreneurship.

Meilian chose to study Traditional Chinese Medicine(TCM) by herself. And the essence of TCM lies in practice and summing-up.

Meilian was not a genius, but she ingeniously chose the right path.

There were no modern instruments or equipment in the wilderness, nor mentors guiding and teaching her. However, there were grass, flowers, water, soil, sand, and livestock ... With slight changes in quality and quantity, there would be new substances and looks. Meilian embarked on her journey of learning medicine in such an environment.

She had books as references and a vast world to support her quest ...

The path she had taken was like an extremely rugged mountain road, with innumerable thorns and vines, and if she went through without much attention, she would get hurt ...

It was like a desert, with frequent windstorms blowing sand and stones off the ground, and if she weren't attentive, her body would be smashed into pieces ...

It was like an unreachable mountain, with its peak as the essence of human knowledge and experience. Even a professional doctor needed a lifetime hard work to enable him to enjoy the scenery and beauty there ...

Meilian was one of the hardworking pursuer, facing winds and sandstorms with her delicate body, and climbing steep cliffs with small yet steady paces. Traditional Chinese Medicine was extensive and profound, as a junior high school graduate, her every step forward was like climbing a mountain. It was naturally challenging, but exertion didn't necessarily lead to gains. To achieve something, she must cross numerous high mountains.

The book *Treatise on Febrile Diseases* contained much classic knowledge and experience in treating febrile diseases in cold regions, but it was a profound and mysterious medical text written in classical Chinese. In the beginning, Meilian found the book too difficult to read, so she had to learn classical Chinese first, which was a difficult task even for students majored in liberal arts. However, she must overcome such obstacles one by one before she could cross the threshold of reading and comprehension.

She even specifically consulted a high school student who came to visit his family in the company.

"How ... how did you come? Why don't you knock on the door and come into the house? It's so cold outside and you are a girl ..." One morning, when the "temporary teacher" opened the door, which was about to be covered in snow, he suddenly saw Meilian waiting outside, with snow all over her body. He was deeply moved and said to the people in the company, "Meilian is amazing. There's nothing she can't accomplish. In the future, she will definitely be a good doctor, a great one!"

"I didn't dare to imagine becoming a great doctor in my lifetime. To be able to treat daily and acute diseases of families in the company and the people in neighboring villages, and ensuring that they can live peacefully and safely, are my greatest satisfaction!" Meilian said.

After acquiring some basic knowledge, Meilian began to collect Chinese herbal medicine. The places where the regiment was stationed were not developed, but the natural environment there was great, with lush vegetation. During the slack season, Meilian would climb mountains and cross hills to search for herbs on various mountain tops and grasslands ... Countless times, she returned home with herbs, but her family was scared out of wits, for she had to personally taste those herbs, whether she could name them or not. Naturally, not all plants are medicinal, and even non-toxic herbs recorded in books may carry toxicity in grasslands and deserts.

Even if it was the same herb, its medicinal or toxicity can vary greatly in grasslands and snowy regions. Therefore, what Meilian was doing was apparently risky.

"No matter what happens, I must taste it myself before giving it to my patients, as it may cause harm if consumed." This was a rule Meilian set for herself, which was not mentioned in any medical books.

"I had nowhere to learn medical skills. Besides knowing some Chinese herbal medicine, I mainly relied on acupuncture to treat illness of my patients ..." Meilian sitting in front of me was already a renowned doctor. However, she said that in the first few years, she mainly used acupuncture for volunteer medical care. "Because all I need to do was to follow the diagrams and prick myself ..."

She simply began to practice acupuncture on herself. You can imagine a delicate girl being pricked by countless needles, how painful it would be!

When her father saw it, he shouted, "Are you crazy?"

When her mother saw it, she cried and said, "Do you still want to get married?"

Meilian didn't say anything, but she thought, "If I can trade my life for the health of everyone else, what's not worth it?"

Everyone in the Corps knew that Miss Meilian was studying medicine, and she already looked like a doctor! But initially, most people laughed that treating illnesses was not a frivolous matter. If it went wrong, people could die, which was no a joke.

However, if people were ill but didn't see a doctor, they might also die. Illnesses could cause unbearable pain, and even if it wouldn't kill the patients, it was still very distressing.

"Call Meilian, now! Let her have a look at whether she can cure it or not!" There was really someone who got a sudden illness! It was a summer afternoon in 1987. Meilian was reading at home as usual when she suddenly heard someone shouting outside the door. It was the political instructor who ran to her, panting heavily and said to her, "Jiang Shiren and his wife have food poisoning. The medic is not here. Meilian, you'd better go and have a look ... it is a matter of life or death!"

The instructor said that it was a serious matter. Of course, he meant to save the lives of the poisoned couple in the Jiangs. But he probably didn't consider that if Meilian's medical skills were insufficient and someone died, it would be another case concerning life or death.

Meilian said she didn't think that much, and saving lives was her first priority. Food poisoning could also be fatal if not treated in time. So when she heard the instructor "requesting" her, without saying a word, she dropped her books, grabbed her medical box, and followed him to the medical room.

Jiang's family was in chaos. The patients had already been brought to the medical room, which was crowded with people inside and out. The ill couple was lying on a bench, with pale faces, covering their stomachs with their hands in unbearable pain.

"Meilian, what should we do?" Everyone looked at her. It was the first time Meilian encountered such a situation. Although she had used acupuncture to treat people's shoulder pain and toothaches before, rescuing someone in critical condition like the couple, she had never done it before!

"You must save them! Now that I'm here, what you should do is just to save their lives with the skills you've learned ..." The instructor encouraged her.

Meilian became determined as if she was supported by a powerful force.

She gritted her teeth and got started. First, she examined their vomits and then observed where their abdominal pain was. She tentatively concluded that they were poisoned by residual pesticide in vegetables.

Meilian immediately put them on a drip ...

"Ouch! It hurts ..." It seemed that the intravenous therapy was not so effective, and the couple continued to wail in agony.

Meilian was already sweating on her forehead. She observed again and then opened Mr. Jiang's mouth, using her two fingers to press down on his tongue to let him vomit ...

Mr. Jiang immediately vomited several times, even splashing on Meilian's clothes.

She didn't have time to mind that and opened Mrs. Jiang's mouth, using her fingers to press down on her tongue ...

Mrs. Jiang also vomited all over the floor.

"Bring me some boiled water!" Meilian looked for pills such as atropine and pralidoxime in her medical box while asking others to fetch water.

After all these had done, the couple got better and gradually recovered.

"Meilian is incredible!"

"Meilian really knows how to treat illnesses!"

"Meilian can cure diseases with ease ..."

The news of Meilian treating illnesses and saving lives spread throughout the regiment and even appeared in the *Tacheng Military Reclamation Newspaper* of the Corps.

The entire regiment headquarters and residents in the region of Mt. Balluk knew that there was a girl named "Meilian" in the 14th company who was a "highly skilled doctor" and could cure diseases!

Meilian was also particularly excited, as it was the first time she had experienced a sense of success in "saving lives and healing the wounded". From then on, more and more people came to her for medical treatment.

In the winter of 1987, an old neighbor, Mr. Wang Jinfu, suffered a cerebral thrombosis and was in critical condition. When Meilian was called to see him, she saw the old man clenching his teeth and already falling into a semi-comatose.

"Oh my, I've never seen such a serious illness, let alone treating it ... what should I do?" Meilian was quite scared then, but she couldn't decline or avoid it because people's eyes were fixed on her, with pleading and hope.

"It's snowing heavily, and it wouldn't work if we send him to the hospital down the mountain just like that water from afar wouldn't help quench a fire nearby. Meilian, you should check him out, we trust you!" The patient's family and the officers of the company all said so.

Meilian nodded, and her originally timid mood was adjusted quickly.

She gently took out a thin silver needle, determinedly found the acupuncture points, took a deep breath, and calmly inserted ... starting with one, then two and three; first on the patient's hands, then on his head and feet ... with a total of 16 needles.

Meilian was sweating on her face, forehead, and neck, while everyone in the room held their breath ...

After inserting the needles, she needed to twiddle them continuously, one by one. Meilian's delicate and soft fingers twiddled them rhythmically and ceaselessly ... for one minute, two, five, six ...

"Does it work, Meilian?" Someone nearby couldn't help but ask.

Meilian was also asking herself the same question.

Sweat had dripped from her neck, but the patient didn't seem to get better at all ...

Ten minutes, thirteen, fifteen…

"He moved and made a sound!" Someone exclaimed as he noticed the patient murmuring and moving his lips slightly ...

"Well — he will be fine!" Meilian took a deep breath and said.

"Meilian! Meilian!" Meilian suddenly collapsed to the ground, causing everyone to gasp in shock.

She opened her eyes and smiled, saying, "I'm fine, just a little exhausted ..."

An officer bantered with her, "You were just too nervous earlier!"

Meilian nodded in agreement. She had indeed been extremely nervous. It was her first time to save a man's life with acupuncture treatment on the spot .

"Hurry please, Dr. Meilian, come to my home!" At that moment, another worker from the company, Zhang Xianggui, ran to see Meilian in haste.

"What's the matter, Zhang Xianggui? Why are you in such a rush?" An officer stopped Zhang Xianggui and asked.

"My, my wife is in labor ..." Zhang Xianggui stammered anxiously.

"Then why are you coming here?"

"I'm here to ask Meilian for help ..."

"How could you think up such an idea? Meilian is just a 20-year-old girl, she has never delivered a baby before! Go home and find a midwife!"

Meilian stood up and said, "I'll go to help her."

"Great!Meilian is a doctor now. I'll rest assured if she comes." Zhang Xianggui said joyfully.

"Meilian, can you really do it?"

Meilian said with a forced smile, "I don't know either. But it was you who pushed me to treat Uncle Jinfu's illness."

"That's true. Then please hurry ..."

Meilian really went to Zhang Xianggui's house. "It was my first time to deliver a baby, and I had never seen a woman giving birth before, even though I was a woman." Meilian recalled during her interview.

"When I arrived at Zhang's house and saw his wife in labor, I was trembling with fear. Especially when I lifted the blanket to examine her body and witnessed that the baby's head was already partially exposed ... I hurried to follow the procedures for assisting in childbirth as stated in the textbooks. Fortunately, it was a normal delivery. However, when it came to cutting the umbilical cord, I was confused: How should I cut? Should it be left longer or shorter? But I couldn't hesitate at that time! So, I picked up the scissors and cut it unwittingly ..."

"For over a week after that, every time I closed my eyes, I would dream of the inflamed wound on the baby's umbilical cord with pus spraying on my face ... and wake up in a startle at midnight," Meilian said. "It wasn't until about ten days later when Zhang's family told me that the cut on the baby's umbilical cord had healed, that I burst into tears of joy with a runny nose ..."

I know that Meilian has helped deliver over 5,000 newborns on the grasslands afterwards.

What a battle and labor it has been to welcome new lives! Thrilling, heart-pounding, overwhelmingly joyful, emotionally stirring, greatly touching ... all of these adjectives are fit. Meilian said that she couldn't recall the joy she felt when lifting each newborn with her hands for there have been just too many times!

"But at that moment, I truly felt that my life was meaningful, and with the baby's first cry, I realized my own value. Nothing can better demonstrate the deep friendship and affection between me and my fellow compatriots of different ethnic groups than this!" Meilian said.

At my request, Meilian shared with me one particular case out of the 5,000 births:

In a summer over 20 years ago, when a worker named Zou Renhui from the 9th company of the 161st Regiment was about to give birth, she was too weak and unable to deliver the baby herself. The baby was stuck in the birth canal, with a risk of suffocation. Helpless, Meilian quickly came up with a solution and forcefully pulled the baby out of the birth canal.

However, what happened next surprised her even more. The baby didn't cry or move, and its entire body turned purple.

The mother and her family were in a panic and crying out loud. "Don't worry ... I'll have a try!" Although Meilian said so, she was even more anxious than anyone else.

She wiped the sweat from her forehead with her arm, then leaned down and held the baby who was covered in amniotic fluid, meconium, and the amniotic membrane, and performed mouth-to-mouth resuscitation ...

One minute, two, five, seven ... ten minutes passed, but the baby still did not react!

Keep going! Meilian encouraged herself: Don't give up!

"Waa —" Finally, the baby cried. Zou Renhui's family couldn't contain their joy, tears streaming down their faces as they cheered.

Meilian once again collapsed onto the ground, and there was a smile on her face, a smile that couldn't be hidden ...

The 14th company which Meilian worked for was stationed in a remote area, a newly formed unit consisting of the second-generation of the soldiers in the Corps before. There had been constantly changing of medics, some of them often deserted their posts. The members of the company complained a lot about it.

"Meilian, could you consider taking the post of medic here?" One day, a leader of the company asked her.

"As long as you trust me, I would love to." Meilian said. In fact, she had already prepared for this because her purpose of studying medicine was to provide medical care to people. Once she accepted the job, it would mean that she could become a doctor officially.

Exams were required if she wanted to be an official medic, and Meilian smoothly passed it. From then on, she started to take care of the people in Mt. Balluk, which lasted for decades ...

"After practicing medicine for decades, how many patients have you helped?" I asked Meilian. She smiled and shook her head, saying, "It was a lot, and I can't remember at all! I don't bother keeping records ..."

However, the relevant authorities provided me with the number — 70,000 patient visits.

What a staggering figure! The problem faced by Meilian was that most of her patients were in the grasslands and wilderness. Whenever she visited them, she had to cross mountains and often stay to care the patients for one day and a half. One time, an elderly herder fell seriously ill while grazing. His family traveled down the mountains overnight to request her assistance. She packed her medical box, mounted a horse, and rushed to the place dozens of miles away. The herder suffered from high blood pressure and fainted a few times. After emergency treatment, his physical condition became stable. But to ensure his safety, Meilian stayed by his side for dozens of hours until he was completely out of danger.

A worker in the company suffered from liver cirrhosis and cirrhotic ascites, who could no longer take care of himself. Meilia traveled for dozens of miles on the mountain roads every day to administer intravenous therapy and deliver medicine to him. Later, she also patiently taught his wife how to administer injections.

"You are like my daughter ... even closer than my own." For numerous times, the elderly man, with tears in his eyes, held Meilian's hand and spoke affectionately.

Years later, he passed away. Before his death, he repeatedly asked, "Where is my daughter Meilian? I want to see her ... I will be at peace if she is by my side ..." Meilian went to see him and stayed by his bedside until he peacefully passed away.

It was easy for the people who lived in the mountainous and grassland areas to get diseases, which might be sudden and severe. One female employee of the company suffered a sudden stroke, which made her hemiplegic. "Meilian! Meilian ..." Echoes of calls for help reverberated through the mountains.

"I'm coming! I'm coming!" Meilian rode her horse hastily to the woman's bedside and provided treatment.

"Can you not go but stay?" The patient held Meilian's hand trembly but tightly as if grasping a lifeline.

"Don't worry. I won't leave ..." Meilian nodded repeatedly.

In this way, for half a month, she visited her every day, performing acupuncture until her physical condition became stable and improved.

When she was young, Meilian, like all young girls, cherished her beauty. Her two long braids were thick and black, and when she rode on horseback, with her braids swinging, she looked so beautiful and vibrant. However, in order to stop a patient's nosebleed, Meilian didn't hesitate to cut off her beloved braids and turn them into a traditional Chinese medicine called "Xue Yu Tan(carbonized hair)," which would help stop bleeding and promote blood circulation. While the patient's nosebleed was cured, Meilian lost her two beautiful braids.

She felt heartbroken, but also content, with a smile on her face, because she believed that being able to cure a patient's illness was more important than anything else.

Meilian couldn't remember how many precious years of her youth she had missed as a young girl who should have exquisite. While others took care of their faces and skin, at least she could put on some skincare cream. But she couldn't. In order to ensure that she administered injections accurately, she repeatedly experimented on her own face, leaving bruises and purple marks. Not to mention her skin all over her body — she didn't even dare to expose her arms easily, because they were covered in pinholes she had inflicted on herself.

"At that time, the company in my hometown had 259 households for grazing and farming, neighboring more than 20 Kazakh herder families from Chatantohai Pasture and Five Star Pasture in Yumin County, who grazed cattle in the depth of Mt. Balluk all year round, and settled in designated living areas only in winter. Due to the inconvenient transportation and communications, as well as scarce medical resources, it was even more difficult for them to seek medical treatment. So, I prioritized treating their illnesses. It seemed like I rarely considered anything else when I was a young girl," Meilian, now in her fifties with gray hair, reminisced about her youth,with some exclamation.

The herders who lived in the Mt. Balluk area and the staff of the Emin Border Defense Corps praised Meilian in this way, "She is the best 'Dehute'er' (Grassland Doctor in Kazakh) here."

People often say, "It's not until you come to Xinjiang that you realize how vast the world is." Indeed, the Mt. Balluk area where Meilian lived was merely a pasture in Tacheng. But it would take at least several days for Meilian to ride across the mountainous grasslands located on the edge of the Junggar Basin. Yet, Meilian has been the "Dehute'er" here for several decades.

It was necessary for her to learn to ride a horse. But even if you've learned how to ride, falling and getting seriously injured was common among fearless male riders, let alone a weak woman like her.

How many times did she fall? She shook her head, saying that she couldn't remember at all. Those who have endured too much hardship become numb to what "hardship" truly means. Meilian recalled a particularly terrifying incident.

On a day in June 2001, Ayiguli's sister-in-law, Marzan, had a constant high fever from pneumonia. Her family were extremely worried, and

Ayiguli rushed to Meilian since Marzan couldn't ride a horse due to her injured lumbar vertebrae. "I'll go to your place after my medical tour every afternoon!" Meilian said.

Thus, after finishing her daily medical tour, Meilian would take a detour to Marzan's home to give her injections for treatment. The way was around 5 kilometers, while Meilian also needed to climb some mountains. One day, Meilian was late returning from her medical tour, and she didn't set off to Marzan's house until the evening. It was windy heavily, so she unconsciously freed one hand from the reins to grab a cloth from under the saddle, but this startled the horse.

"Neigh!" The startled horse reared its head and neighed, leaping its hooves and suddenly accelerating to run forward ...

Oh no! Meilian clamped the horse's belly with her legs, gripping the reins tightly to try to slow it down. But the startled horse didn't obey her commands, instead, it ran faster and faster. The frail Meilian couldn't withstand such bumps, and without warning, she was thrown off the horse's back. What was even worse was that one of her feet was still trapped in a stirrup!

Being caught in the stirrup was the most dangerous situation while riding a horse. The person being dragged would make the panicked horse even more terrified and crazy. If not released in time, the rider could potentially lose his life by hitting stones, ditches, trees, or sharp objects on the ground. Meilian was helpless; her mind went blank, and she just felt a sharp sting on my body ... At the critical moment, Marzan's son happened to pass by. He quickly rode up and stopped the startled horse, saving her from danger.

When Meilian, covered in dust and mess, came home, her husband pointed to the hearty meals on the table and asked her, "Do you know what is the occasion today?"

Meilian's mind went blank once again.

"It's your birthday! Today is my beloved wife's birthday!" Her husband said, walking over to give her a big hug.

Tears streamed down her face instantly ...

"Don't ride horses anymore, look at your bruised face ..." Her husband said, treating her wound tenderly.

Under Meilian's meticulous care, Marzan fully recovered. Later, she walked more than 60 kilometers to the county town to order a pennant with the words "Saving lives and helping the injured with accomplished medical skills," and presented it to Meilian.

In 1999, Meilian, who had more than ten years of rich experience, passed the Medical Qualification Examination of the Corps system and became a real doctor. In 2000, she was enrolled in the Open University of China and began to move toward a higher peak in medicine.

From being able to provide medical treatment to becoming a doctor, and eventually becoming a renowned local physician, how long was the path that Meilian has taken? Only the tens of thousands of patients could tell. Meilian's working range covered the Mt. Balluk region and later, as her fame grew. it expanded to the vast areas of Junggar Basin where the space was big enough to be inclusive to all the love and resentment, beauty and ugliness ...

Meilian, less than 1.6 meters tall, was just a small shadow like the point of a pin when riding a horse on the grassland. Even if she rode a galloping horse while waving a whip, she would only resemble a blade of grass swaying in the wind. However, in the mind of herders from various ethnic groups, she was a ray of warm sunshine, a beautiful cloud, and a beacon of hope ... Whenever she appeared, people would cheer, rush to lead her horse, carry her medical box, and even give her back massages. She was often exhausted, sometimes spending several hours on a medical visit, not to mention having no time to have a meal or even "relieve herself". But whether she was on the ~~rugged paths of the vast~~ grassland, enduring the cold wind while crossing mountains, or sitting down for consultations, Meilian was always meticulous, enthusiastic, and wholeheartedly dedicated to treating her patients. Herders praised her as an "Angel" on the Balluk grasslands, as the good deeds she had done for herders and workers on the Corps were countless, like bunches of grapes on a vine ...

Ms. Zou was suffering hemorrhea resulting in shock when she gave birth to her two children. It was Meilian who treated timely to save their lives. In addition to helping them pass the most dangerous period in life, Meilian also sent clothes and diapers for the infants and even gave her own 94 sheep to Ms. Zou to help support her family.

A herder suddenly got acute appendicitis and needed to be sent urgently to the hospital. However, due to the late hour and lack of vehicles, Meilian had to stay to care the patient throughout the night. At dawn the next morning, Meilian quickly rode her horse back to the company, took out 1500 yuan for the patient, and escorted him in person to the hospital at the regiment headquarters.

It was another stormy night, with snow and wind swirling outside, and Meilian couldn't sleep but kept tossing and turning in bed all night. Suddenly, she remembered that the retired couple, Guan Qinghe and his wife, already in poor health, had been suffering from a severe cold and she hadn't seen them for several days. Were the elderly couple safe? Thinking about this, Meilian got up in a hurry. Her husband asked, "It's dark outside, where are you going?" Meilian said she wanted to visit the Guans. "It's snowing heavily! Can't you go tomorrow?" Her husband was worried. Meilian shook her head, saying "It's OK", then rushed out. By the time she pushed open the door to Guan's house, she had become a "snowman". When the old couple saw her, tears flowed as they called Meilian "Good girl" with deep gratitude ...

"Guojun! Guojun! What's wrong with you?" One day, Meilian returned home from the medical tour outside. When she hastily washed up and prepared to go to bed, she suddenly noticed her husband, Li Guojun, lying on the bed silently. She trembled as she checked his breath ... There was no sign of life! "Guojun! Guojun —" She was terrified, desperately calling his name, but she couldn't wake up her beloved husband anymore.

Her husband passed away from sleep apnea syndrome(SAS). Meilian, whose mind was completely occupied by her patients, was overwhelmed with regret. She had treated patients outside every day but neglected the health of her loved one. They had just married for a dozen years, and Meilian lost her husband which left deep sorrow to her.

On the day of her husband's funeral, people from the company and herders from the vast Balluk grassland all came to bid farewell to the beloved of their "Angel". The line was very long ... In everyone's eyes with concern, Meilian could feel emotions deep as the sea and warm as the clouds.

A few days later, Meilian, riding a horse, appeared on the grassland once again, in front of the herders ...

> I love my motherland
> I love the borderland
> Under the fertile Mt. Balluk
> It is where I graze
> The vast Tasti River
> Is the place to fight
> For the sake of my motherland
> We are willing to shed blood and sacrifice
>
> ...

This song has been passed down in the Mt. Balluk region for half a century, praising the "borderland heroine" who dedicated herself to defending the border and maintaining national unity. Her name was Sun Longzhen, a woman with a poor family background in southern China. In 1959, shortly after getting married, Sun Longzhen responded to the call of the state and went to Turpan, Xinjiang. In 1962, she voluntarily signed up to work on the front line of the border. On June 10, 1969, around 9 pm, Sun Longzhen suddenly heard someone shouting, "Foreign soldiers are provoking and abducting our people again!" Despite be pregnant for six months, she picked up a shovel and rushed out of her home, running towards the incident location with other militia ...

"No trespassing! No sabotage in our country's territory!" Sun Longzhen fearlessly stood on her own country's territory, sternly reprimanding the crazed aggressors.

"Bang! Bang ..." At that moment, a series of evil bullets were fired at her, hitting the young Chinese female militia member. She fell in a pool of blood alongside with two other militia members.

"Longzhen! Longzhen!" Meilian's mother, Wu Zhixian, was a comrade-in-arms to Sun Longzhen in the same battalion, and she was also a witness to Sun's death. "At that time, I was right beside her, and I could touch her feet with my hand." When Meilian was a child, her mother often told her stories of heroes and heroines as well as the significance of guarding the border.

Sun Longzhen was a heroine whose name and spirit were engraved on the Balluk grasslands, where Meilian lived. During my interview, people often mentioned Sun and took me to visit the place where she sacrificed her life ... "I was born and raised on the land defended by martyr Sun Longzhen. I won't leave the company, the Mt. Balluk, and the honest and kind herders. As a doctor, the needs of patients are my greatest value, and my life motto is: Be good-hearted and sincere; dedicate myself to medicine, strive for excellence; serve the people, forever and ever." That was something Meilian often said.

The Mt. Balluk is a passionate mountain range, and the vast grasslands here know how to be grateful. After several years, this god-like mountain and beautiful grassland are moved by Meilian's selfless actions. She was elected as a delegate to the 18th National Congress of the Communist Party of China(CPC) and received honors such as the "Bethune Medal". Her name, like martyr Sun Longzhen, was praised by the people of all ethnic groups here. Then, some people began to ask her if she would like to work in Urumqi or other big cities. "With your reputation and medical ethics, you will definitely receive higher rewards ..." they said to her like this.

Meilian smiled and shook her head, saying, "I belong to Mt. Balluk and the herders here. I will never leave this land!"

Another spring arrives, and the flowers in the grassland near Mt. Balluk bloomed as abundant as the clouds in the sky, presenting a rainbow-like beautiful scenery. In the midst of the winding hills and grasslands, we can see a horse slowly approaching, with the familiar figure of Dr. Meilian on its back. Although her hair has turned white, she remains vigorous and valiant ...

A little poplar
Grows beside the outpost
Deep rooted with strong trunk
Guarding the northern Xinjiang
The gentle breeze blows
Making the green leaves rustle

The sun shines, making the green leaves shimmer
Come on, come on
Little poplar, little poplar
It grows as I do
Together, we guard the border

…

Meilian loves singing this song called "Little Poplar." That day, when I went to visit her workplace, I immediately noticed a flag flying high on the hill, and beneath the flag was an outpost, which was the famous "Little Poplar Outpost."

That day, I made a special trip to visit my border defense comrades, touching the white poplar tree that held a revered position in the hearts of the entire army and the people of the country. I felt that every soldier and border resident here silently guarded the border and protected the peace of our homeland, just like the white poplar tree. Meilian shaped her own "little poplar" with her accomplished medical skills and noble medical ethics. There have been many doctors like Wuhaas and Meilian who are riding on horseback while singing touching songs for the vast and beautiful borderland …

Chapter 9

Keep singing, and I become an artist of singing

Martin Luther once said: Music is the source of embryos of all virtues.

Beethoven also said something similar.

He believed that music was a higher revelation than all wisdom and philosophy,

Permeating the sorrow and joy of a nation.

Whether an ethnic group cherishes its culture, patriotism, and harmony of living together

Depends largely on the number and joyfulness of its traditional songs.

Ayiguli, inspired by her love for her hometown with its beauty and blissful life there,

"Keep singing and then becomes an artist of singing" owing to her deep love and flair.

People like her can be found all over Xinjiang.

Their melodious voice adds to the magic and charm of this land.

Undoubtedly, she must be one of prettiest women I have ever seen in Tacheng and Xinjiang, and even the prettiest one.

It was a pity that I didn't get to see this beauty when she was young. However, even though she has a son who is about to graduate from university, she still looks attractive. This is true beauty, no flattery. Beauties from Xinjiang, with their ethnic features, temperament, expressive eyes and charming dance style, are often captivating to men and the envy of women. That is the impression left by her and other women in Xinjiang to us.

Another personal charisma of Ayiguli is that she never flatters or ingratiates herself with others. Although she looks sweet, she is inherently upright and has a sharp tongue. Perhaps this is why she becomes an artist of singing in Tacheng.

She humbly said that she was recognized as an artist of singing only by the locals, without any official recognition or promotion. However, all the people in Tacheng acknowledge that she is the pride and glory of their city and that her singing is a representation of the art level of Tacheng, even no less than that of the professionals in a song and dance troupe.

"We love to listen to Ayiguli's songs and invite her to perform."

"She never puts on airs and will sing with all her heart anywhere and anytime if she can manage."

All the people in the city think highly of her.

She is well-known among the older generation and children alike in Tacheng, for she has been singing here for decades. Sometimes, she performs in various locations throughout a day, including ranches, communities, parks, factories, mines, military camps, even at daycare centers, weddings, groundbreaking ceremonies, and dinner parties of friends. All the people here consider her to be the true artist of singing, a lark in their hearts.

Her song is an expression of her deep love for the land that nurtures her.

She puts all her energy and emotions into singing, which in turn gives her life meaning.

What she sings perfectly echoes the words in heart and emotions to express by Tacheng locals.

It was at my interview with a local family that I first met her. That day, a group of "lovely flowers" brought life to the room, making other people excited and delighted.

When Ayiguli appeared, everyone cheered and shouted, "Here is our artist of singing!"

"My pleasure, but I'm just an ordinary woman singing for you," the humble Ayiguli stated. Despite her modesty, everyone continued to commend her, "She is an artist of singing!" "She is the pride of our Tacheng!"

The praises didn't make Ayiguli blush or show any affectation — she was so accustomed to such scenes.

"In Tacheng, everybody will cheer enthusiastically as soon as she appears and then all of us will enjoy her singing. Emotionally stirred,we will all dance together to her songs," said the women present.

I often heard people there talking about a play named "Loving at Home," a large-scale song and dance drama arranged by the locals based on the golden wedding ceremony of a couple who have been married for decades.

It is said that this Tacheng-style play is a favorite in Tacheng and gained widespread recognition after being staged throughout Xinjiang. It is surprising and valuable that the creators and cast members of this show are all amateurs.

As the lead singer, Ayiguli has enhanced this highly acclaimed play with her voice and stage presence, making her the most admired by the people of Tacheng.

Beautiful Tarbahatai (namely Tacheng)
How beautiful!My hometown, Tarbahatai
The lush green meadows are where I graze my sheep
Fatty cattle, sheep, horses, and camels, thousands upon thousands
Look! grains and cotton pile like mountains during the harvest
Tarbahatai, my picturesque hometown
Happiness and joy, boiling in my chest
How beautiful!My hometown, Tarbahatai
How beautiful!My hometown Tarbahatai
How Lovely!My hometown Tarbahatai
Surrounded by mountains, rich in resources
All ethnic groups live together in harmony and enjoy life
The oil flows, converging into a sea
Tarbahatai, a beautiful hometown
Happiness and joy, boiling in my chest
How beautiful!My hometown, Tarbahatai
How beautiful!My hometown Tarbahatai

The song "Beautiful Tarbahatai" was written and composed by a local artist. As Ayiguli sang it in a gentle and melodious voice during the performance of "Loving at Home," the audience was deeply moved.

The place name of Tacheng City originated from the Tarbahatai Mountain, which is 300 kilometers long and 3000 meters high. The north slope is gentle yet magnificent in winter, with a sense of masculine strength due to the freezing weather, while the south slope is steep and covered by extremely lush vegetation.

The area surrounding these magnificent mountains boasts vast and picturesque grasslands, home to over 2000 species of plants. Botanists refer to this area as the "flora gene bank" as it contains the vast majority of wild plant species in the world.

The Tarbahatai Mountain, along with the surrounding grasslands, constitute the backbones and bloodline of Tacheng. They are the "parents", representing the history, present, and future of the people who live there. Ayiguli, a native of Tacheng, has a better understanding of the lyrics and melodies than anyone else.

She told me that when she performs, she is not actually "singing the notes" but telling her stories and expressing her love and feelings for her hometown, the nation, as well as Tacheng.

Where there is Ayiguli, there is her singing voice. When I first met her at a family gathering, she sang like a lark, captivating everyone's attention and earning warm applause. She presented one song after another until the audience felt embarrassed to ask her to go on. Finally, it was Ayiguli who was reluctant to put an end to her show. She sang with great passion, despite the absence of spotlights, music, stage, fellow dancers, and makeup on her face.

"I was born with a natural gift for singing. I haven't learned any music theory or scores, but I can sing a new song just by listening to it twice." That's what she told me at the party, amidst the cheerful atmosphere.

It's unbelievable that an artist of singing who never received any formal training in music can deliver such a miraculous performance. She is truly a miraculous singer in the Tarbahatai!

Undoubtedly, Ayiguli is miraculous.

"That's what I am," she said humbly and authentically without any pretense, exuding perfect confidence on and off the stage.

"In Xinjiang, raising livestock can lead to wealth for men, and marriage to the influential can bring a prosperous life to women. Ordinary people can enjoy a modest living through hard work. My parents were teachers who instilled in me a love for others since childhood. With such affection, I can better love my hometown, Xinjiang, and the motherland. But when I was a kid, I was too young to understand what love is, and all I cared about was singing.

I am the fifth one among eight children in my family. My elder and younger siblings always protected me, which made me courageous enough to speak and sing in public. Whenever we had guests at home, and they joked that I could earn a dime as a tip for my performance, I would sing to them with all my heart.

When I turned eleven, I was invited by the county's art troupe to participate in a show. It was there that I witnessed firsthand how much people enjoyed my singing. This experience helped me understand the true meaning of the word "love," which my parents had always emphasized to me. My family is ethnically diverse, with my Grandpa being Uyghur, Grandma Tatar, and Mom Kazakh. We have always lived happily and harmoniously together without any concern for each other's ethnic backgrounds.

Since childhood, I have noticed that if I sing well, the audience will be kind and applaud me, regardless of their ethnicity or background. As a result, I have come to realize that my genuine love for others stems from my wholehearted efforts to bring happiness and joy to them through my singing. I believe my singing can bring people from different ethnic groups closer together, just like a family."

That's how Ayiguli blazed a trail of "singing," and the way became broader and more stable as time passed.

"When I was 12 years old, I had a memorable performance. I had prepared two songs, one of which was a backup. After finishing my first song, the audience applauded so warmly that I returned to the stage to sing my second song. However, after finishing the last note, as the audience became more enthusiastic and wanted another piece, I quickly went on stage to sing the third song. Finally, I sang four songs in total until they were all satisfied! This experience made me feel extremely excited for several days.

My parents told me, 'This was because they love you and your songs. You must do your best in every show. Your wonderful singing may prove that you have love for everyone. With such love, everyone will naturally love you, too. Harmonious and delightful relationships among people arise from mutual respect and love.' Although I didn't fully comprehend what my parents meant at that time, I kept in mind that I had to devote myself to singing so that I could gain the support of others and serve them and the society better. This has been my motivation and original aspiration, and why I keep singing till now."

Ayiguli, aged 50 this year, still appears youthful and energetic. She attributes her good health to singing. "It brings me immense joy and makes me reluctant to stop," she said, "Despite occasional bouts of cold and sore throat, I can alleviate these minor ailments by singing!"

Xinjiang people are known for their proficiency in singing and dancing. However, Ayiguli stands out as a rare talent and can be considered a master among nonprofessional singers.

"Her enchanting voice always excites and moves us the most!" The local people acknowledge her as "the artist of singing in our Tacheng."

After Ayiguli became famous, she was invited by various working units, departments, communities, schools, industrial and mining enterprises, and families to sing for celebrations. It was during that time that she realized her performances were closely related to many activities of the country, the government, and the society, playing an irreplaceable role. She understood that she was not only singing or performing, but also doing her part in creating a harmonious and better life for the people of all ethnic groups around her in her beloved hometown, Tacheng. This understanding prompted Ayiguli to sing more attentively and passionately.

Tacheng is a multi-ethnic community where people of different ethnic groups reside and speak various languages even in the same area, street, working unit, and ranch. To cater to their need to understand her charming singing and give perfect performances, Ayiguli learned different languages. She can now sing popular and ethnic songs, and even Peking Opera, in more than ten languages, including Chinese, Kazakh, Uygur, Mongolian, Russian, Kyrgyz, and even Mexican and Japanese.

Versatile, beautiful and generous, Ayiguli is highly regarded by the people of Tacheng, who is always enthusiastic about her performances.

She also has a sense of humor and often boasts, "Keep singing, and I become an artist of singing!"

She is such an exceptional grassroots artist of singing. The phrase "keep singing" truly embodies Ayiguli's perseverance, continuous efforts, and dedication, year after year. As a singer's singing resembles the sweat on a worker's back, the more sweaty it is, the more joyful the song becomes.

Ayiguli often says, "Keep singing, and I became an artist of singing." After learning about Ayiguli's experience, I understood the meaning of her words. She was born with an affection for singing and a natural talent. Later, she realized that her singing could also serve the people and contribute to the development of Xinjiang and the whole country concerning social progress and national unity. With this understanding, she no longer regarded singing as fun, but a sublime need, a way to express her love for her hometown as well as a sense of responsibility and mission.

She thought she must "keep singing" and "even sing forever."

In 2005, Ayiguli formed a group called "Lilac" in collaboration with folk artists from other ethnic groups, which gained popularity and earned rave reviews in Tacheng. As a result, the invitation for their performance grew several times more than before, and they were also invited to various important celebrations in the district and the city with their performance as a repertoire, which greatly inspired Ayiguli. She felt more responsible for using her singing talent to serve others.

> Too much sadness in your eyes
> When you play Mandolin
> Singing melancholic ballads
> Do you still remember the girl in your hometown
> Herding cattle on the banks of the Nenjiang River
> The outposts in Tarbahatai
> Defending the faraway border areas of Xinjiang
> You have been stationed at the frontier for a long time
> I'll always be here, waiting for you
> The warrior of the Daur ethnic group
> My face remains the same as when I was in my youth
> I'm playing my lute
> Singing the song of Uqin, seeing you off
> I still remember the horses to the west
> Your smile was enchanting when you glanced back

The outposts in Tarbahatai
You have been stationed at the frontier for a long time
I'll always be here, waiting for you
The warrior of the Daur ethnic group

Ayiguli's song *Love in Tacheng* deeply touched the people of Tacheng. Her gentle voice not only inspires the audience to unite and strive for a satisfactory life, but also encourages herself to shine bright in her life.

Whenever Ayiguli sings, she exudes youthfulness, beauty, and energy. In recent years, her son Sharayddin Shatar has often been spotted accompanying her - a handsome young man.

Sharayddin is a 25-year-old professional dancer who graduated from the Xinjiang Academy of Arts with a major in dancing. Prior to graduation, he sought advice from his mother Ayiguli regarding his future plans. She suggested, "You were born in Tacheng, a multi-ethnic community where you could continue to develop your artistic skills and live with us. Moreover, the people in Tacheng would support you with great affection."

"My boy, come back!" With his mother's encouragement, Sharayddin returned to Tacheng after completing his studies.

"Whether an artist is successful or not depends on his audience. You should experience the process by yourself!" Although Ayiguli used to take her son on stage to play during his childhood, as he grew older, she wanted him to figure out what success, career, mission, and responsibility meant for a man.

After numerous performances, Sharayddin started to comprehend what his mother had told him earlier. Although he has gained widespread recognition in recent years, he refused offers from big cities like Beijing and Urumqi. He explained, "I regard dancing as his life and profession, but if I can make significant contributions to the society and national unity, just like my mother, I think that is the life and career I am pursuing. I believe that Tacheng is the place with the best stage and ground for me to achieve my goal."

Sharayddin has been performing in Tacheng for seven or eight years, with his personal qualities of arts, like his mother Ayiguli, widely praised by people. His performance of "Loving at Home" with his mother has drawn enormous admiration from the audience. Gulinazi, a renowned dancer of Xinjiang, commented on him as follows, "The progress of arts in Xinjiang plays a vital role in its social development and the national unity. Younger dancers, like Sharayddin, can take root among the general public, which is a valuable contribution."

"Here they come, Ayiguli and her son are ready again." The audience cheered up on another performance, expecting these two artists to come out onto the stage.

Ayiguli sang while Sharayddin was dancing, offering a spirited and energetic show.

"Look! The man and his son with their Donbula are also here!" The audience burst into cheers again.

A father and son stepped onto the stage: Duman Hazati and his handsome son. They both played Dongbula, producing a mix of passionate and melodious tunes.

Duman Hazati is also a well-known figure in Tacheng, coming from a family of Dongbula players. His father, Hazati Saitihan, was a renowned local Kazakh Dongbula player acknowledged as the "father of Dongbula"in Tacheng. Hazati Saitihan was a self-taught player who made his own instrument, composed music sheets, and sang pastoral songs during his nomadic life in the grasslands. He was considered as "an irreplaceable

Dongbula player" in Tacheng and northern Xinjiang.

When old Hazati was alive, people form many universities and theater troupes visited him in Tacheng to learn and record the Dongbula repertoire of this renowned folk artist. He had traveled across the vast expanse of Tacheng and even Northern Xinjiang, playing his Dongbula and singing his original compositions for people of various ethnic groups. Through the beautiful, melodious and passionate music, he expressed his love for the country and nation.

That was the "past" Hazati. Now, Duman Hazati, standing in front of me, is about my age. Before his retirement, he worked for the song and dance troupe in Tacheng as a Dongbula player. As a pure Dongbula musician, he does not care about worldly matters. On the walls of his house display various types of Dongbula, most of which he made himself.

"Those made by my father are the most precious." He picked one of them and played for me.

I was pleasantly surprised by the beautiful sound of Dongbula. It was my first time hearing this famous Xinjiang musical instrument played live. At times, it sounded like the clip-clop of galloping horses, while at other times, it resembled the mournful cries of a woman perched on a cliff. In short, musicians could turn this seemingly simple musical instrument into both a rallying flag for a vast host of army and a flashing saber making the enemy tremble with fear.

"Whoever can play musical instruments is extraordinary, and it is so amazing that you can even make the musical instruments yourselves!" As a layman, I was shocked by the musical talent of the three generations of the Duman family and said.

Duman's imperturbable exterior hides an energetic soul. He said, "Although there are many horses running on the grassland, only those trained by skilled riders are truly exceptional. Dongbula is the most popular and favorite musical instrument among the Kazakh people, producing a variety of fascinating sounds, such as the gurgling of a spring, the chirping of birds, and the joyful sound of sheep and horse hooves. All these lifelike effects rely on the players' performing skills, influenced by their inner feelings about the beautiful scenery of the majestic grasslands.

Various personal perceptions of the world may result in different musical effects of one Dongbula. My dad had been the most famous Dongbula player in the Tacheng area. When I was five, Dad would take me along to herd the livestock. As we were on the road or waiting for the cows and sheep to graze or resting in a tent, he would always play his Dongbula and sing. I often saw him lean his ear on the strings during playing.

Back then, I was too young to understand his behavior. But as I grew older, he explained, 'strings are the soul and the world you come to know. If you fail to understand the world, try to ask the strings for a solution. The flat box of Dongbula resembles a human brain, and whenever you are confused, you should 'pluck it.' Every person may have a different understanding of the outside, a skilled player must create their own Dongbula so that it would reflect their perception of the world.' Growing up, I came to realize that my father's words made sense."

"So all the Dongbula you use now are made by yourself?"

He nodded.

"Have you ever tried your father's Dongbula? What does it feel like?" I asked.

Without hesitation, Duman took an old Dongbula on the wall, which was frequently used by his father during his lifetime, and began playing it.

"What's the difference between it and the one you made yourself?" I asked.

"I can't perform so well with it as my father." said Duman.

"Why? His Dongbula should be the best one!"

"It is. But I still fail to grasp father's feelings and his perception of the world, so I can't get control of it as perfectly as my father did!" He said, "players now are inferior to my father's generation in terms of the comprehension of the grasslands and even the world."

"Do you still have his classic music scores?"

Duman pointed to the photos on the wall, saying, "after the founding of New China in 1949, the national and Xinjiang cultural departments have sent experts several times to help father convert his songs into written music scores, among which there are several classics, such as 'Galloping Horses' and 'A hundred Birds Singing'. These songs have since become exemplary models for regular study in university music courses."

"He never composed and wrote down any of his songs?"

"Yes. He just followed his heart to play."

"Does it mean that he didn't use any music scores to play 'Galloping Horses'?" I was amazed.

"That's right. we all play in such way!" said Duman.

"So do you?"

"Yes, all the time," he nodded again.

"Oh, that's amazing!" I was really shocked.

"Could you play one of your father's famous song?" I made a request.

He immediately took his own Dongbula and played his father's famous song for me. I enjoyed and listened, quietly.

A really marvelous performance.

After the playing, I made another request to him, "Could you play your own song like 'Galloping Horses'?"

"Sure."

Another wonderful song began.

I listened attentively, attempting to discern any distinctions between the two songs. Here it was — the tune of the first song was like a river that rushes ahead at first and then flows gently, while that of the second one was like a river that surges forward endlessly.

"Exactly. You have a great sense of music." Duman smiled for the first time. He went on to explain that having experienced turbulent times, his father would like to leave room for unforeseen circumstances, and that's how he described nature. But Duman, who grew up at the happy times of New China, has a different perspective. He prefers swinging a whip on the prairie and walking to the ends of the earth.

Well, this is an important difference among artists. Literature is similar in this regard: Different genres may produce diverse effects on the same topic, and even articles in the same genre may have different effects. This is especially true of music.

"What do you think of your father's songs?" What did the son think about his father and other seniors? This question might be a little awkward, but I was curious.

Thinking about it for a moment, he said, "I am much less accomplished than my father, who stood atop the towering Dongbula peak, while I am merely at one of its hilltops.."

An objective remark. I was deeply shocked by his following words, "When my father taught me to play Dongbula, he always told me that whether a player was excellent didn't depend on his self-assessment but the audience. That was why he particularly took the reaction of his companions seriously. If those who were not musically inclined could still be moved by your music, it is because your performance touched them and evoked deep feelings within. And that was what made a good work!"

People who knew Duman's father said that he considered it the most successful performance to reconcile two quarreling herders or a couple whose relations were in tension, after they listened to his Dongbula playing. Duman said that the most important things he had learned from his father was that he could make a positive impact on the society with Dongbula.

The sound of Saitihan's Dongbula had spread to every corner of the Tacheng Basin. Local inhabitants are singing his songs and sharing his stories about how he helped others live in harmony.

Since childhood, Duman followed his father all the time, and later joined the song and dance troupe. Being a little introverted, he only enjoyed the time with his Dongbula, pursuing his artistic dream by plucking the strings. Decades later, when Duman was about to retire, his son, who also learned Dongbula from him since childhood, left Tacheng for Beijing and Shanghai after graduation, carrying the Dongbula passed down by his grandfather and father.

One day, his son returned with long hair and full of artistic personality traits. With excitement, he told Duman, "The world outside is wonderful with touching stories. Thanks to the Dongbula passed down by Grandpa and you, I have made many friends, making those who haven't been to Xinjiang in love with my hometown." He asked his father seriously, "Dad, don't you also think I am doing well for Xinjiang?"

Duman nodded and said, "Yes. Well done! Excellent! You use a Dongbula to make people love Xinjiang, which is a great contribution by a Dongbula player!" At that moment, Duman suddenly understood why his father had been with the herders in the pasture all day long tirelessly, sharing the most melodious songs with them.

In 1986, Duman had an acquaintance with a Han young man named Zhang Zhi. At that time, Zhang studied in Karamay city. He had two "treasures": a guitar and a Dongbula, which made his classmates mistook him for a Kazakh boy! Then, a Kazakh classmate from Tori County in Tacheng suggested that Zhang should learn playing Dongbula from

Duman.

"Who is Duman?" the proud Zhang asked curiously.

"He is an extraordinary Dongbula musician in the northern Xinjiang region," said the classmate.

Then Zhang learned that Douman was the "father of Dongbula" in Xinjiang, especially in the northern region!

Finally, Zhang found Duman Heizati, son of Heizati Saitihan.

At the very sight of him, Zhang was attracted by his large black eyes, "He must be my Dongbula teacher!"

From then on, Zhang became Duman's good friend and called him "elder brother" .

After learning from Duman, Zhang has made significant progress in his skills and obtained a completely different understanding of Dongbula. Hereafter he devoted himself to music and earned the title of "King of Dongbula" in the entertainment circle. He always emphasizes that "Duman is my teacher," making Duman well-known as a Dongbula master among Dongbula players nationwide.

People across the country came one after another to visit Duman out of admiration, and many wonderful stories began.

"Master Duman, may I be your student?" A young man from Yunnan province came from afar to Tacheng, wishing to be an apprentice to Duman.

Douman asked him, "Do you love Xinjiang?"

"Well, I can't say I love it, but I like Xinjiang's Dongbula," the young man replied.

Duman said, "it might be impossible for you to learn playing Dongbula well."

"Why?" The man was puzzled.

"Because Dongbula is unique to the Kazakh ethnic group," said

Duman.

"Yeah, I know that!" the young man interrupted.

Duman gently halted his words with a gesture and said kindly, "but you don't understand Xinjiang yet."

It appeared that the man had encountered a temporary setback.

A few months later, the young man came back with tanned skin. When Duman asked him where he had gone and what he had done, the man said cheerfully, "I took a trip around the Junggar Basin and around the grasslands in Tacheng." Then he said seriously to Duman, "Teacher, I have got what you said last time, and also realized what Dongbula meant for Xinjiang."

Duman smiled this time.

"Teacher, please accept my bow to be your student!" Saying that, the young man knelt on one knee.

"Oh, Stand up! Please!"

Then, Duman agreed his request, making him an extraordinary Dongbula player with careful cultivation. Later, the young man brought the pure "Xinjiang stuff" he had learned from Douman to make it shinning brightly in the national music circle. As he said, as long as the tunes of Dongbula resounded, there would be singing and melody of the song *Xinjiang is a good place*, and the audience could conjure up the scene that people of all ethnic groups lived harmoniously together.

"My life became more fulfilling after I learned from Duman. I used to play musical instruments just for fun, but now, being a Dongbula musician, I become a volunteer advocate for national unity, intentionally or unintentionally, which makes me proud and honored," the young man said.

A bunch of grapes sweetens one's heart while grapes in vineyards sweeten the hearts of all. After retirement, Duman had hundreds of apprentices from all over the country and gave numerous lectures nationwide on the musicianship of Dongbula. He said, "the audience could feel as if they were in Xinjiang, visiting yurts set on the grasslands while listening to the sound of Dongbula, which sublimates the atmosphere and emotion of national unity."

Now, Duman considers passing on Dongbula's playing techniques to his apprentices as a way to contribute to national unity and social development.

"After retirement, he became more active and looked younger," his wife whispered with a smile. I looked at him, engrossed in his singing and the melody played by Dongbula —

> Dongbula Dongbula
> Oh Dongbula
> Dongbula Dongbula
> Oh Dongbula
> ……
> What place,what place
> What place is so beautiful
> Rosy clouds drift on high mountains
> What is the most gorgeous on the streets there
> The girls there are so enchanting
> ……
> The enthusiasm of the people there is like the tide
> Who smiles like a rose
> Boys play Dongbula
> Girls smile like a rose
> The enthusiasm of the people there is like the tide
> Who smiles like a rose

Boys play Dongbula
Girls smile like a rose

……

As I was listening to the beautiful melody, I found myself humming along and thinking about Ayiguli's words, "Keep singing, and I become an artist of singing." It's true that in Xinjiang, everyone has the potential to be an artist of singing or dancing, which is a beautiful way of life that people all over the world aspire for.

Chapter 10

There is A "Life Guardrail" at Laofengkou Area

Every frontier is the "wind gap" of the country,

The hurricanes there can be bitterly cold or scorching hot, sometimes even gloomy and perilous ...

That is why those who guard "Laofengkou Area" (a well-known intense wind gap) are always awe-inspiring.

It is their fearlessness, selflessness, sincerity, and loyalty that make our country's territory as solid as a rock.

"Laofengkou" has existed since ancient times, and it still remains today.

However, it has become a lifeline that protects lives amid the wind and snow.

Where people no longer feel dread,

Because it gives life a solid "Guardrail"—

When I first came to Xinjiang, what impressed me most were the grand but rather terrifying Gobi deserts on its vast land, the immense prairies and glaciers, and the perpetually snow-covered Mt. Tianshan. Of course, there were also countless picturesque landscapes, flowers and fruits with fragrant scents, as well as Uyghur girls and their singing and dancing.

However, before going to Tacheng, I already knew that there was a remarkably famous "Laofengkou" there. You may have a rough idea about how strong the wind is there from the CCTV program *Weather Forecast* every winter — The wind power and accumulated snow are beyond imagination for outsiders, yet the people of Tacheng have been accustomed to it.

Today, as we travel around Tacheng, we are on the highways most of the time. However, during our journey, we often came across some peculiar landmarks on certain sections of the roads: tall poles standing on either side of the highway, each with a horizontal arrow sign hanging sideways, pointing towards the ground ... At first, I didn't know what they were for, then the locals explained to me that these were the directional signs for drivers to follow in case of heavy snow covering the roads.

"The wind at Laofengkou usually reaches magnitude 7 to 8, and it is considered normal when it's in magnitude 10. There are several occasions every year when it exceeds magnitude 12 ... When it snows, it is common to have a depth of 2 or 3 meters of snow cover, and if we meet heavy snow, the snow cover may be higher than the height of two stacked cars!"

"In the past, Laofengkou was akin to the Gate of Hell for the people here. Only a negligible few could get through it. And it is like a sharp sword that cuts down from above, almost dividing the central part of Tacheng Prefecture. It's hard for you to avoid it."

"When the roads were not yet built, it was extremely challenging for people and horses to traverse 'Laofengkou' on foot. Now even though we have highways, it is still very perilous on a snow stormy day for the drivers if they were trapped in the snow. Without timely rescue, they would likely be frozen to death ..."

Here is Laofengkou, the Old Wind Gap that Tacheng people refer to.

The special geographical and topographic feature in Tacheng made this gap, which is an immutable "open wound" of the land. The local elders describe it as such: As long as the wound persists, it will bleed and inflict pain. Tacheng is located in the west of the Junggar Basin, surrounded by mountains on three sides with an opening to the west. Its terrain is high in the north and low in the south, inclining from northeast to southwest, allowing cold wind and snow from Siberia go all the way to be rampant in Tacheng, causing unrest to both people and animals ...

Tacheng area is a region primarily affected by drought, with a unique climate due to the influence of cold air from the west. Its weather is highly unpredictable throughout the four seasons. In spring, the temperature rises rapidly but remains unstable, while summer is short and scorching. Autumn always brings a sudden drop in temperature, and winter is long and extremely cold. Therefore, the winter and summer in Laofengkou area are both like hell. In winter, temperature could drop to minus 39 degrees Celsius in an extreme case, while in summer, temperature could rise to over 40. Actually in Gobi Desert, summer temperatures generally range from 40 to 50 degrees Celsius — It's really scorching.

The winds in Tacheng are particularly fierce. According to the *Chorography in Tacheng Prefecture,* "It's windy in the city with the wind speeds varying significantly depending on the seasons". "The annual average wind speed ranges from 2.23 to 2.30 meters per second, and its maximum wind speed reached 40 meters per second." You can imagine how intimidating it was!

There are some words describing Laofengkou, Toli County in the *Chorography*, "Laofengkou in Toli County is the largest wind source in Tacheng Prefecture, which is located on the saddle-shaped pass between two mountains and is a narrow channel. Due to the unique combination of specific underlying terrain and atmospheric circulation patterns with the obvious funnel effect in the narrow passage, whenever there is air pressure gradient of high in the east and low in the west, cold air would flow back through Laofengkou, resulting in strong eastward winds. These winds typically occur from late August to early May, with an average speed of about 10 meters per second and a maximum speed of 40 meters per second ..."

Laofengkou has long been a place of terror viewed by the locals since ancient times. According to folklore, during Genghis Khan's Westward Expedition, one of his concubines and her 300 guards escorting her happened to encounter a strong wind at Laofengkou. When the wind subsided, they were never seen again.

During the reign of Emperor Guangxu(1875-1908) in the Qing Dynasty, the Minister Counsellor stationed in Tacheng petitioned the Emperor to build a Wind God Temple at Laofengkou to seek divine protection. The Emperor agreed and awarded him a tablet with the writing "Blessing the Frontier". However, the winds persisted, causing havoc year after year. In an attempt to combat the winds, an official there came up with a plan. He noticed the abundance of cattle and sheep in the area and instructed local inhabitants to prepare thousands of cowhides, which were sewn together to create a "Leather Wall" several kilometers long to block the winds. Unfortunately, as soon as the "Leather Wall" was built, the wind mercilessly blew it away.

After the founding of the People's Republic of China, there have been several unfortunate incidents in which guards stationed at Laofengkou were blown away by the strong winds, resulting in their loss of life.

On December 7, 1987, a rare snowstorm lasted for 17 hours in Hoboksar Mongolian Autonomous County, Toli County, and Emin County in Tacheng Prefecture. Locals described it to me, "On that day, we were like being trapped a cave of wind and snow. All we could hear was the howling wind and mournful cries of the injured and dying." According to reports from the meteorological department, the average wind force reached magnitude 11. Tragically, 23 people lost their lives, 188 people were injured, 12,396 livestock perished, 117,859 livestock were lost, and countless yurts were blown away.

"In fact, the damage to lives and property caused by the blizzard in 1987 was far from being the worst or the most severe ..." A historian from Tacheng said so, telling us that when he was young, he experienced a major windstorm on May 3, 1954. "Many large trees in Tacheng urban area were uprooted, and the iron sheets on the roofs were lifted up to tens of meters high and thrown out two or three hundred meters away!"

Laofengkou is still there, and it will always be there. It induced my ambition, "when I go to Tacheng, I must visit Laofengkou to feel it". But when I did pass by there when our car ran on the highway, I felt like sitting on a boat in the waves — the wind force at Laofengkou had an impact even on a whizzing car.

"It's better not to go down there." My friends advised me not to get out of the car at the last moment. I guess the unspoken words were probably,"we will regret it if you got blown away."

Is it really that powerful?

When I interviewed at Laofengkou, the official there told me a frightening story. One year, two of his colleagues went to Laofengkou to tow a car trapped in heavy snow. After completing the task, they opened the car doors to get out and were ready to return. "We kept waiting, but they never came back. Later, we got anxious and sent someone to look for them but we failed. Finally, people from the army and public security departments were sent to search the area within several miles of the place, but still couldn't find them. It wasn't until a week later that local villagers several miles away reported that they found two bodies."

Laofengkou, with the opening stretching for more than 70 kilometers, is a place where people in several counties of Tacheng area cannot bypass, let alone the fact that Tacheng itself is a transportation hub for the western regions of China to the outside world. Therefore, ensuring the safety of vehicles, people, and livestock traveling to and from this area has always been a major concern of the local government. For this reason, after the founding of New China, relevant departments have specially set up teams of highway management, public security, and emergency disaster relief there, who were thus known as the "Wind Chasing Life Guardians" by the locals.

The words "Chasing the Winds" are of great significance. You can't accurately grasp their meaning and essence if you don't follow up at the scene and interview the teams.

When we came to one of the "key junctions" in a wind gap at the intersection between the Tacheng Basin and the Junggar Basin, we visited the Mayitas Wind and Snow Emergency Relief Base of the Tacheng Highway Administration Bureau. We immediately felt that the wind brought a painful feeling to our faces as we got out of the car, however, as I knew, over 20 team members in this base needed to stay here for more than seven months every year, steadfastly guarding this place, and ready to confront death at any time. The base stood alone like a small piece of dried bean curd on the Gobi Desert, appearing to be fragile against the wind. However, the heroic relief worker, Batusan, who was the leader of the base, told me that it was because of their presence that the risky areas of Laofengkou in Emin County had seen a reduction of at least several thousand casualties and tens of thousands of vehicle accidents over the past decade, not to mention the countless risks of livestock movement during grazing. Looking at the exceptionally rich pictures in their small exhibition room, I couldn't help but pay my respect to this group of "Wind Chasing Life Guardians".

Batusan is a Mongolian, who has been working at the Mayitas Emergency Relief Base since 1998. "Our work is like that of special forces in a war, which requires physical strength, experience, and a relatively young age. Generally, those who worked in Laofengkou emergency relief team will have to change positions after serving for eight or ten years …" Batusan's words made me understand that being a "Wind Chaser" guarding Laofengkou might sound romantic, but it was actually a special job which was both hard and tiring, and could be life-threatening at any time.

"'Chasing the Winds' is the name we gave to our job. Previously, we often used the words 'Guardians of Death' to describe our profession, but the young team members in the base face psychological pressure. In fact, with the increase in research and investment from the government and the country in disaster response and protection at Laofengkou, both the technical and hardware aspects of the relief work have been greatly improved. Moreover, the quality of our team members has also been enhanced, many of whom are university graduates. Changing from 'the Guardians of Death' to 'Wind Chasing Life Guardians' reflected the progress of the times and the improvement of our understanding of our work." When Batusan first joined the team, he had a low level of education. Over the past twenty years, through the trials and tribulations at Laofengkou, not only has his level of education greatly improved, but his understanding of lives and the meaning of human life has also undergone qualitative growth.

"Without the willingness to sacrifice, you might face the danger of death at any time if you work here; without complete technical skills, one mistake could lead to the loss of everything, including your own and others' lives; without being culturally influenced, you would feel that working here is even harder than reform through labor, as there is hardly anything relaxing apart from dealing with the wind; and if you are lack of experience, each time you go out on duty, you could probably embrace death ... Therefore, it's more important for us to treasure the spirit of teamwork, sacrifice, and 'passing on knowledge' here." Batusan said that their work of disaster response seemed very simple, but actually there were high demands on faith, psychology, experience, and willpower.

"Laofengkou in Emin County is 53 kilometers long, which is the main arteries of traffic and transportation in the western region and a large area for the livelihood and survival of the nomadic people in Tacheng. The wind blows from here all the way to Karamay, so whoever protects the safety of this area reflects an issue of faith as for whom you work. From time to time, members of our team have learned from the predecessors of wind guardians about the unchanging loyalty and faith in loving the country, our homeland, and our fellow compatriots of all ethnic groups, who have been selflessly dedicated themselves for decades ... I was so happy to be able to stay at home for 7 days for the first time this Spring Festival, because I have always been on duty during Spring Festival before. Generally, the wind and snow during Chinese New Year are particularly heavy, so usually I can't go home. This year, the reason why I was able to spend 7 days at home was that, on one hand, our windproof facilities have been greatly improved, especially with the installation of snow barriers in the area of the wind gap; on the other hand, the head and other officials from the Highway Administration Bureau took over our shift at the base, which touched us deeply. Two years ago, we wrote a letter to General Secretary Xi Jinping, reporting our work as 'Chasing the Winds'. He personally wrote back, giving us great spiritual encouragement and motivation, making the spirit of 'Chasing the Winds' our spiritual support and lofty belief for all relief workers here."

Who would have thought that a small disaster relief base would have so many fascinating stories?

However, when you delved into the specific work of Batusan and his colleagues, you would realize how hair-raising the life and work of these "Wind Chasers" were.

The wind at Laofengkou is like a wild horse, so you never know when it will become crazy and reckless. Once it goes wild, it will ruthlessly ravage and devastate the land. At that moment, all living creatures in the wind zone, including humans and animals, have no chance to resist, and all their struggles will be futile. What is the strength of humans and animals compared with that of running stones on the ground? In a gust, wind speeds can reach 20 to 40 meters per second, and the storm can last for several hours, or even more than ten hours, destroying everything in its path. A tiny moan may already be your greatest form of resistance.

"Oh no, Captain, we're in trouble. We only have 5 to 8 minutes to retreat, or we could be stuck in the eye of the storm for three to four hours …" This often happened all of a sudden. While Batusan and his team were on patrol, the storm was approaching. At this point, evacuation was the only possibility for survival. But Batusan told his team, "Even if there's only one minute left, we must give it to all the vehicles, herders, and passers-by who haven't escaped from the wind zone ..."

At this moment, his words became a command that the team members should carry out without any hesitation while they never considered their own life.

So the "Wind Chasers" have to move as fast as possible ahead of the blizzard, to inspect and search for the vehicles, people, and livestock trapped in the wind zone. By doing so, it would mean that Batusan and his team might leave the fate of death to themselves ...

There were too many occasions like this, sometimes similar, sometimes completely different. On a winter day, just as the storm alarm was triggered, the blizzard had already arrived at Laofengkou.

"According to the report, there are currently at least 30 vehicles on the wind gap section of the road, they would be trapped midway by the forecast of the coming blizzard. We must send rescue vehicles immediately!"

"Rescue vehicles and guides, depart now! We must guide the vehicles to sections with lower wind speeds as quickly as possible and ensure that all people in the vehicles are out of the storm's path!"

"Yes, sir!" Four vehicles carrying rescue team members raced out of the base. They drove against the wind, with the storm carrying hurling bullets of flying stones at the windshields, bringing a terrifying feeling as if a sword was hanging overhead.

"Oh no, a van has been overturned by the strong gusts. Some people might be trapped in the van ..."

"Leave vehicle No.1 behind to rescue them immediately, the rest vehicles continue to accelerate forward!"

"Yes, sir!"

The snowstorm intensified, and the oncoming vehicles were all trembling and swaying. Some drivers were panicking and pulled their vehicles over, and people who got off clung to nearby power poles for survival ...

"Rescuers from vehicle No.2, immediately go to rescue those who get off. They must get inside rescue vehicles at once, or they'll be carried away by the blizzard ..."

"Roger!"

"Watch out for your own safety!"

"Copy that —"

Vehicles No.3 and No.4 continued charging forward. Vehicle No.2, like a tug-of-war, pulled the terrified people in distress to get on their vehicle from the Death of Hurricane.

"Hold on tight, don't let go ..."

"Keep your head down, step by step, grip the rope and follow it to come over here —"

The rescuers on vehicle No.2 shouted and gestured to the trapped people. But perhaps due to excessive nervousness, a woman held a rescuer's neck and refused to let go.

"Ah — can you loose your arms a little bit? I, I can barely breathe!" The rescuer was pulling another person in distress with his hand, so he was dragged by the hurricane, the blizzard, and the two people in distress ... which was the most dangerous situation. If he slackened even slightly, all of them could be swept away by the storm.

"Come on!" "Don't let up!" The rescuer's face was distorted, but he had to hold on until he could grab the door handle of the vehicle ... He made it! Subsequently, along with the rescued people, he collapsed on the vehicle, gasping for a long time.

"That was too close!" he said.

"You saved my life!" One of the rescued cried, unable to stop crying. Later, all of the rescued shed tears and they were all grateful for the rescuers' great kindness.

As vehicles No.3 and No.4 continued moving forward, they encountered a bigger problem. The road was blocked by numerous stranded vehicles, making it difficult for them to rescue more trapped people and minimize property damage. The more urgent situation was that some ignorant drivers were still attempting to rush through Laofengkou, unaware that it was a trap rather than just a challenge by luck.

"Vehicle No.3, keep going and block the vehicles behind heading to the wind gap ..." It was Batusan commanding, who was on vehicle No.4.

"Sir, let us stay behind and you go ahead —" No.3 asked.

"Obey the order!" Batusan commanded sternly.

"All right, sir, stay safe —" Vehicle No.3 vanished into the blizzard in an instant.

At that time, only Batusan and his assistant remained on vehicle No.4. It was too difficult for them to rescue and direct a dozen of other vehicles to a safer place.

"I'll get off. You turn the vehicle around and lead them to our base ..." The moment Batusan opened the door, he had jumped into the snow.

"Captain —" His assistant was driving the vehicle and suddenly saw his master walking in the opposite direction of the vehicle through the snow. He knew his master was very experienced, but the storm was like a tiger, with a mouth widely open! Thinking of this, instantly he broke out in a cold sweat, not only out of nervousness but also for fear that his master would suddenly disappear ...

"Captain, Captain! Where are you now?" He was really anxious because he had no idea where Batusan was at that moment. The snowstorm completely blocked his vision so he could see nothing beyond three meters.

Batusan, after getting off, laboriously made his way toward the stranded vehicles …

He was crawling rather than walking in the snow, inch by inch …

As he passed by a vehicle, he would grab its handle, searching if there were any injured or trapped individuals inside. If there were people in need, he helped them open the doors and carefully get off on the sheltered side. Then, he organized a group of people hand in hand or using a rope to walk together toward the direction of the rescue vehicle. If there were no people left in the vehicle, he would check if the doors and brakes were secure to prevent them from being overturned by the wind and snow … It didn't seem to be complicated by saying so, but it was actually as dangerous as pulling a tooth from a tiger's mouth. In this way, Batusan made every effort to check the trapped vehicles one by one, so as to minimize casualties and losses.

This kind of "battle" usually lasted for several hours, or even more than ten. The rescued individuals were extremely grateful, but Batusan and his team were exhausted and even injured. When they returned to the base, they enthusiastically shared their personal supplies with the rescued. Sometimes, they might look after them for weeks because of the ongoing snowstorms, so the rescued have to eat and live there.

"For the sake of our brothers and sisters from different ethnic groups, it doesn't matter for us to bear hardship and tiredness," Batusan and his team members have become accustomed to this kind of life and work. They do not care about themselves, what they mind is to reduce accidents and minimize the loss of lives and national assets amid blizzards.

That's why they deserve people's admiration. "Every award the higher authorities granted to us was won by our team members at the risk of life, so we especially cherish these honors." I knew that Batusan himself had received numerous personal commendations and awards at the national, regional,and municipal levels dozens of times, and his team was also recognized as an outstanding representative of the national transportation system. In Tacheng, they have long been the "heroes" in the eyes of the locals.

The average age of these heroes at the Mayitas Emergency Relief Base is around 35. Some of them have just graduated from university, some are newlyweds, some have families to support, and some have just fallen in love. However, whenever the wind and snow start, they will become fearless warriors. As long as there is a person on the road section at the wind gap, they will spare no effort to rescue them ...

Rescuing lives in the snow and hurricanes is not as simple as it seems. It requires knowledge, courage, and experience, which is why the master-apprentice relationship is highly valued among the members at the base. Batusan's master was Li Jiancheng, who retired a few years ago, then Batusan became the captain of the base. Shortly after, Li Jiancheng's son, Li Changqing, joined the base and became Batusan's apprentice.

"Like his father, he is courageous, tough and clever. He will surely have a promising future," Batusan appreciated his apprentice and introduced Li Changqing to me.

"The lessons taught by my master out of his experience are priceless, which I can't learn from any book. They have been ingrained in his bones, spirit, and beliefs. They were derived from countless tests of life or death, which are indeed invaluable," Li Changqing praised his master in this way.

"I didn't speak Mandarin well, and he also taught me ... which is very useful for our rescue operation," Batusan said that he had experienced situations in the past where their rescues were delayed due to his inadequate Mandarin proficiency. "During emergency operations, if the rescued misunderstood a single word or gesture, it could cost a life!" Batusan said.

Li Changqing has been on the frontline with Batusan for 5 years now, who grows into a manly guy. Every member of the rescue team at Laofengkou is a hero, a true hero! Each one of them at the Mayitas Emergency Relief Base has saved numerous lives and millions of properties ...

They have fulfilled the mission of "Chasing the Winds with Their Lives", dedicating their youth and passion to the great unity of the nation.

On the line of Laofengkou which stretches for dozens of kilometers long, stationed is another heroic group, the police officers of public security and traffic police brigade. One of them I knew is Ding Yonggang. During his 20 years on duty, he has participated in over one hundred rescue operations, saving more than ten thousand trapped people. As a result, he earned himself a title — "Wind Chasing Man of Iron".

Becoming a "Man of Iron" at Laofengkou is not easy at all. Who knows the hardships and difficulties it takes to turn one's body into iron and steel?

Ding Yonggang is the first person who goes to the road section whenever a blizzard approaches. He must be in the forefront of the most difficult place whenever it is most dangerous during the snowstorm.And he is always the last one to leave whenever a blizzard subsides ...

It seems that his name has already determined his destiny and the nature of his job.

The blizzard in February 2014 was still clearly remembered by the people in Tacheng. The strong wind reached a force of magnitude 11 instantly, and it was impossible to measure the wind force at the eye of Laofengkou. "It was rare to see a blizzard like that. The strong wind threw the accumulated snow on the ground into the air for dozens of meters. The whole Wind Gap area was covered in white snow, and nothing else could be seen. Visibility is almost zero on all sections of the road, resulting in a surprisingly large number of vehicles and people trapped."

"Captain Ding, go to support the rescue team immediately! Ensure the safety of personnel and vehicles on the road ..."

Ding Yonggang and his colleagues moved instantly according to the order of the Bureau, and at almost the same moment, numerous distress signals were sent to them.

It was a race against time between life and death.

But the wind and snow were like numerous sharp knives obstructing the steps of Ding and his teammates. Their shoes and clothes were pierced by the fierce wind, inflicting bone-chilling coldness and excruciating pain ... They had to hold their breath, turning around to catch some air, and then moved forward one or two steps, thus they moved towards the trapped with great difficulties.

"It was extremely chaotic at the scene, with vehicles strewn across the snow, and some have already been buried ..." Ding Yonggang described the scene to me, "Our first task was to rescue people, especially the elderly and children. Three team members formed a group, and we had to make sure that each rescued person stayed close to us. We stayed among those rescued, anchoring them, and slowly leading them to safe areas."

That rescue operation lasted for 20 hours, during which Ding Yonggang and his colleagues rescued a total of 957 trapped people.

In the next five days, they dug out hundreds of vehicles out of the snow one by one to ensure smooth traffic after the snow ...

That week, they rested for less than 6 hours. Ding jokingly called it the "Battle of Shangganling" in Tacheng.

On one evening in November 2019, just as Ding Yonggang and his colleagues began to have dinner, the alarm suddenly rang. They immediately put down their bowls and rushed to the police vehicles.

The most terrifying aspect of the snowy nights at Laofengkou was that the road covered with ice debris was slippery and wet. It would be easy for vehicles to lose control, and combined with the strong wind, the moving vehicles could be easily overturned, which would be more perilous. Ding Yonggang and his colleagues encountered such a difficult situation during that night shift.

"Watch out! Pay attention to the speed and the wheels of the vehicles ..." Ding Yonggang searched for trapped vehicles on the road while commanding his comrades on the rescue mission.

"It was very difficult to rescue in a dark night. The sound of car horns, cries for help, and the sound of wind and snow mixed together, and with the intertwining of car headlights and flashlight beams, it flickered, which made it easy to have unexpected accidents — That night impressed us a lot. We spent nearly 5 hours rescuing 28 vehicles and 58 trapped individuals. By the end of the battle, each of us carried at least 10 kilograms of ice and snow on our bodies!"

"What happened?" I was curious.

"It was too cold outside, and we spent too much time in the snow. Luckily, no one was injured. But every time we continuously fight in such heavy snow and strong wind at the temperature of minus 10 or 20 degrees Celsius, or even minus 30 or 40, it would be like being soaked in icy water for hours. Over time, it is hard for us to avoid being frostbitten ..." Ding Yonggang told me that a considerable number of his team members have to be replaced every three to five years working on the road section of Laofengkou.

I knew he had been working at Laofengkou for 20 years. Why was that? He smiled and said, "My name is Yonggang (forever staunch)after all!"

Ah, the eternal steel warrior. It is with the "Wind Chasing Men of Iron" like him and the "Wind Chasing Life Guardians" like Batusan, that a "Life Guardrail" has been built to protect the people, firmly guarding the lives of people of all ethnic groups.

Such a song of chasing the winds is that of life.

Chapter 11

Home, the Warmest Place

"Homes make a country. No country, no home." "Home is the smallest country, while the country is the biggest home …"

These lyrics were created by 1.4 billion Chinese people with more than 5,000 years of vicissitudes.

Five thousand years of Chinese civilization have taught us an unshakable truth:

If we want to guarantee and ensure the integrity and beauty of our country, we must begin with building each and every family well,

Because home is a warm haven of life and living of each and every one of us …

Then, what is Xinjiang like today?

When you step into the homes of the locals, you will naturally come to the conclusion that

The moon may be bright or dim, wax or wane. People have sorrows, joys, separations, and reunions.

But if each family is built into a warm haven, then no matter how hard the outside trials and hardships are,

They will embrace tightly like pomegranate seeds, love each other, and can not be torn apart.

In today's Xinjiang, there are warm havens like this everywhere.

There is no warmer and more comforting place than a home in the world, because it is the place where our lives are nurtured. It is also the foundation of the survival and thriving of a country and a nation, which are composed of countless families where no one can leave. Those who have no home are lonely and unfortunate, while home is synonymous with happiness and fulfillment.

In Tacheng, Wureken, a Kazakh uncle, was very famous because of his family rather than himself with something special. His wife, Bayirehe, was a Mongolian, and there were 23 members in his family who were from four different ethnic groups — Kazakh, Mongolian, Uyghur, and Han. In fact, it was quite common in Tacheng to have families composed of members from multiple ethnic groups like Wureken's family, who usually lived in harmony. This could be seen as a valuable "Tacheng Phenomenon."

What made Wureken unusual was that he had set up a multi-ethnic family museum at home. There were numerous artifacts and photographs that made us truly feel the warmth and sunshine of a united and harmonious multi-ethnic family —

Wureken said, "Setting up a family museum like this, we aim to let the younger generation see what life was like in the past and understand that the happy life today has been hard-won so that they could unite closely like our generation, be grateful to the Party and the country, follow the Party as always, and be the defenders of the stability and prosperity of our motherland."

What he had done has gained the admiration of many locals in

Tacheng. During my days of interviewing there, I could see vivid "family museums" of ethnic unity among the ordinary people everywhere ...

One day, I visited an ordinary family on the outskirts of Emin County. As I stepped into the courtyard, I saw a middle-aged woman chatting with an elderly man about family matters.

"Dad, try on this new coat ..." the woman said.

The old man replied with some displeasure, "I've told you before, don't buy any more clothes. I don't even have the chance to wear all the ones I have!"

"But we need to change clothes properly for the season!"

He laughed and tried on the clothes, saying, "It's my daughter who treats me best!"

"That's it. You're my dearest dad!"

From their conversation and expressions, you can never imagine that these closely bonded two people are not actually biologically related father and daughter, nor are they in-laws. One of them is a Hui and the other a Han, who were complete strangers 20 years ago, but now they have lived together as family for 18 years ...

Now, let's talk about the story of this special family.

The woman, Ma Xinhua, is the mistress of the household and a police officer at the Vehicle Administration Office of the County Public Security Bureau. Her husband, Mijiti Abduresiti, is a Uyghur and demobilized soldier. Their son, Jiawulan, also once served in the army. Mijiti's mother-in-law, Hanipa, is a Kazakh. What's more interesting is that there is another elder member who joined them less than 20 years ago but now is the oldest member in their family — Jiawulan's "grandfather," Ma Xinhua and Mijiti's "father": Yang Jichun.

From his name, it is evident that Yang Jichun is a Han. So why has he become a member of Ma Xinhua's family and respected as the "father" and "grandfather" ?

The story began from the time before Yang Jichun came to this family.

Yang Jichun used to be a translator for the 9th Division in Xinjiang Production and Construction Corps near Ma Xinhua's house but later moved to Emin County due to his job transfer. He had been married once but had no offspring. After his wife passed away in 2003, Yang wandered to Taserhai Village on the outskirts of Emin County because of his impoverished life. Over 80% of the residents in this village were from ethnic minority groups. Since Yang could speak multiple ethnic languages, he decided to rent a house there and make a living by doing odd jobs and collecting recycled materials.

However, as he grew older, his life became more and more difficult.

On a summer day in 2003, amid scorching heat, the elderly Yang was still laboring at a construction site. Mijiti who was passing by happened to see him, sweating and staggering. The scene of an elderly man in such distress made this former soldier deeply sad. He returned home and mentioned it to his wife, Ma Xinhua, expressing his thoughts, "This lonely old man should have a home and family to take care of him. Could we take him home to live with us, at least we can look after him."

When Ma Xinhua heard her husband's words, she was initially stunned, but then tears welled up in her eyes, and her lips trembled. She said, "If you truly think so, I wholeheartedly agree." Ma Xinhua was deeply moved and excited, as she had lost her father at a young age.

"Then let's talk to him first and ask about what he thinks," Mijiti said.

"OK, I have to go to work tomorrow, so you go to visit him first and ask his opinions," Ma Xinhua replied.

The next day, Mijiti paid a visit to Yang Jichun. "This is not like a place for a human to live!" Mijiti found Yang Jichun for the first time and saw his living conditions, with his tears almost welling up in his eyes. "His house was cramped,with the roof leaking, and there was no glimmer of light ... I was so sad to see this!" Mijiti would sigh whenever he mentioned it.

"No! No! This won't do!" After seeing the terrible living conditions of the elderly man, Mijiti proposed to bring Yang to his home, but Yang repeatedly refused him.

The reason why Yang refused was that he didn't want to trouble Mijiti's family. "I am an old man of Han nationality. I am not sure when I would get ill and become a burden. How much trouble would that cause?" Later, he spoke his mind.

"If you come to live with us, you will become a member of our family, and in terms of age and seniority, you could be my father. It won't be any trouble if anything happens. It's our duty and filial piety ..." Mijiti repeatedly visited Yang with these words, but he never agreed. Even when Mijiti brought his wife to give their "assurances," Yang was touched but remained adamant, only silently wiping away his tears.

"So after a few months, on a day in early 2004, I passed by a place on my way home from work and saw the old man squatting alone in the snow, trembling from the coldness. I asked why he hadn't gone home yet, but he was so frozen that he couldn't even say a word. I quickly helped him up and brought him home ..." Ma Xinhua said.

After arriving at Mijiti's house, Yang Jichun was moved by a hot meal and the sincerity of the whole family.

"Stay here. Our home will also be yours. Mijiti and I will be your son and daughter-in-law, and Jiawulan, your grandson ..." Mijiti once again proposed his longstanding idea to Yang Jichun.

"Grandpa, come and live with me! You can teach me, I want to go to university or join the army in the future ..." Jiawulan, Mijiti's son who was still in high school, called him warmly. His sweet addressing of "grandpa" made Yang Jichun burst into tears.

"I'll stay, but won't ...won't it cause any trouble to you?" Yang Jichun stuttered.

"No, you won't! Your presence is a blessing for our whole family ..." Mijiti said while pouring a glass of wine for the old man, and Ma Xinhua brought out a new cotton-padded jacket she had prepared for Yang Jichun to try on.

"It fits me perfectly!"

"Grandpa looks much better in the new clothes!"

On that night, Mijiti's family officially welcomed Yang Jichun's coming in a simple and warm way, and with a sumptuous family dinner, they held a family recognition ceremony — Actually, it was very simple. Mijiti and Ma Xinhua called Yang Jichun "Dad," and Jiawulan called him "Grandpa" formally. But for Yang Jichun, it was a new beginning and a new chapter of his life.

On the first night in his new home, sleeping on a warm kang (heated brick bed in North China) with a thick quilt, Yang Jichun couldn't sleep at all. He told me that it was the happiest and most unforgettable day in his life.

"I never thought that I would have a warm home after my 60s ... I could never imagine, and I didn't even dare to think!" 18 years later, the old man said so while he wiped tears.

It was easy to cross the threshold, but difficult to integrate into a new family, especially for an elderly person who has been living alone for so long. However, the biggest challenge was the one faced by the woman in charge of the household — Ma Xinhua, Yang's daughter-in-law.

When I visited Mijiti's house, Ma Xinhua received me because Mijiti and his son Jiawulan were out working. As soon as I arrived, I saw Ma

Xinhua bustling around, preparing meal for Yang Jichun.

If I hadn't known the story before, I could never tell that this family was newly formed. Yang Jichun was already 78 years old. Because he had suffered so much in his youth, he looked older than his actual age, but he was still hale and hearty, calling Ma Xinhua "daughter", which sounded natural and affectionate, and Ma Xinhua's replied with a simple "yes", which showed that they were at ease as family members.

In Ma Xinhua's house, they lived their lives in a Uighur manner. In the center of the main room, there was a large kang where people could also dine there. The kang was neatly stacked with brand new quilts, and a table on it spread with unique foods and fruits in Xinjiang, which aroused a strong appetite ...

Ma Xinhua invited Yang Jichun to sit beside her in the middle of the kang, and they were truly close like father and daughter, quietly waiting for my interview. The happiness shown was really moving.

Yang kept smiling, saying that his daughter bought him another two bottles of wine and a new suit of clothes that day. "I want to give her the money I earned this year, but she refused, saying that I should keep it myself. What's the use of my keeping it?" The old man muttered to me.

"You keep it safe, and it will come in handy later. Next time pay for a bottle of good wine with your own money." She teased him.

"All the food I eat is bought by you, so what else can I spend my money for?" The old man said.

Ma Xinhua whispered to me, "The reason why I ask him to keep his money is that it could be used for his funeral one day! He doesn't think too much, but I have to consider it for him!"

I understood. She was indeed a good daughter-in-law.

Aged 78, Yang Jichun had some hearing loss, and his body was not as agile as before, so most of the time he needed someone to take care of him.

Just imagine what if such an elderly person was living alone in poverty, perhaps he would have already passed away ...

"Me? If I were living alone, I would have met the King of Hell a long time ago!" I'm not sure which part of our conversation Yang Jichun had overheard, but he suddenly interjected.

What he said moved us all.

"Don't worry, Dad. You are fit as a fiddle. Didn't you recently have a medical checkup? The doctor said you're fine ..." Ma Xinhua added immediately.

"I'm fine! You guys go ahead, but I have to go to work!" He suddenly got up and headed towards the door.

"Be careful, and come back early!" Ma Xinhua hurriedly escorted him outside.

"I know, I know ... I'll be back after work." He disappeared from our sight after saying these words.

Ma Xinhua turned back, smiling at me, and said, "My dad is now working as a security guard in a small factory in a village with great enthusiasm! He thinks that he can still earn some money for the family ... And he has a wish that when the day comes that he can't move around anymore, he wants to reduce the burden on our family as much as possible. How kind-hearted he is!"

When kind-hearted people get together, they may create a warm social atmosphere of kindness, so what we see is something noble.

In this special family composed of different ethnic groups, there is no doubt that Ma Xinhua's role is particularly important. She is a woman of Hui nationality and the homemaker of this family. Without her understanding, tolerance, and genuine heart, Yang Jichun would not have been able to integrate into this family.

That day, I witnessed firsthand that the relationship between Ma

Xinhua and Yang Jichun was truly that of a "father and daughter", and I could feel from their conversation that there was no trace of affectation. At that moment, I really felt that the old man was truly happy, as he had found a real family.

The second year after Yang Jichun came to Mijiti's family, he had a sudden illness — hypertension. "At that time, his condition was very severe. He was hospitalized for first aid, and the medical expenses amounted to over 5,000 yuan for only one night. The hospital said that we had to pay before they could provide treatment. What could we do? We didn't have any savings, so I had to hurry around to borrow money. It took me three or four hours running around to get enough money. Later, I stayed in the hospital to help the old man relieve himself ... After he was discharged, he always told people everywhere that he truly had a good daughter. As for me, I'm especially grateful, as I have another father since then!"

What Ma Xinhua said had no trace of grievance, but rather there was happiness and pride on her face.

For an old man of Han nationality, it was not easy to adapt to the habits of a minority ethnic family. For example, Yang Jichun used to eat pork, but when he came to Ma Xinhua's house, he willingly changed his dietary habits. Thus, during the Spring Festival, Ma Xinhua said to him, "Dad, why don't you go to a friend's house in the village for a meal?"

The old man immediately shook his head, "No, I won't. I'll stay at home and eat the same as you."

Ma Xinhua smiled, understanding what he meant, so she prepared a table of delicious food and wine specially.

"Is it tasty?" She asked.

"Yes, it is." The old man raised his glass happily and said to his daughter-in-law, "The food in our family is the best."

"Grandpa, since today is New Year, we wish you a long life and good health all year round …" Mijiti's son, Jiawulan, filled up a glass of wine and toasted him affectionately.

At that moment, Yang Jichun hugged his grandson with tears streaming down his face.

This family has become closer and more harmonious day by day … Now, 18 years have passed, and there will be countless years to come.

When Jiawulan grew up, he joined the army. After his service, he returned home and his parents decided to renovate the old house for his wedding. But building a house requires money. "Take this passbook, I have 63,000 yuan in deposit … take it to build a new house for my grandson!" That day, Yang Jichun handed over a savings passbook to his daughter-in-law excitedly.

"No, no, this is the money saved for your old age. You have to keep it, Dad. Don't worry about the fund to build the new house!" Ma Xinhua refused to take his money.

Yang Jichun asked his son and daughter-in-law at a loss, "Then what can I do for my grandson's wedding?"

Mijiti and Ma Xinhua laughed and said, "Your grandson is a naughty boy. You keep an eye on him and make sure he doesn't cause trouble."

"Alright, alright, he listens to me, and I will not allow him to cause trouble!" Yang Jichun hummed a little tune happily and found Jiawulan, who was feeling a bit down on the side.

"Grandpa, my mom is so stingy. Other people picked up their bride with a great convoy on their wedding day, but we only rented six cars. It's so embarrassing!" Jiawulan whispered to Yang Jichun.

Unexpectedly, his grandpa raised his fist "mercilessly" towards him and said, "How difficult it is for your mom to take care of us! She was bustled in and out to hold this wedding for you and spent a lot of money.

How could you say your wedding is not decent enough? She is the pillar of our family and did everything so well. What more could you ask for? My grandson, you must listen to your mom.Never complain. Do you understand?"

Jiawulan, who had always listened to his grandpa, understood his mom after this stern talking-to.

Ma Xinhua said that the happiest thing for him was to play with his little great-granddaughter in the yard when she came home ...

For a once forlorn old man, it was his luck and happiness to spend his remaining years in comfort in a new family. In fact, since the old man came to Mijiti's home, he has also brought warmth to this ordinary family.

Ma Xinhua worked in the traffic police department so she was often busy at work, leaving home early but returning late. "My father worries about me all the time, waiting for me at the door every day. Sometimes when it's raining or I have urgent work to deal with, as he doesn't see me at the time for me to go home, he will go to my workplace to pick me up ..." Ma Xinhua told me happily that sometimes she worked late in the office, while her husband was already fast asleep, the old man was always waiting for her at the door.

"You are my daughter, so I can't rest until you come home!" Yang Jichun said so.

"With such a loving old man in the family," Ma Xinhua said, "What bliss it is!"

Yes, in such a family, there is no distinction of who you are or where you are from, let alone which ethnic group you belong to — they eat from the same pot, live in the same courtyard, striving for a happy and better future together ... This is the deepest impression that Tacheng gives me.

It is said that Xinjiang has beautiful landscapes, but in my opinion, the most beautiful thing in Xinjiang is families like Ma Xinhua's. In such families, the colors are diverse, languages are varied, and habits differ. However, after they form a new family, life becomes colorful, vibrant, and full of joy. These talented family members gather together, singing, dancing, laughing, and loving each other.

Maybe such a sight can only be seen in Xinjiang ... These families make us enviable and even intoxicating.

One day, a friend took me to Ma Lianhua's house. As soon as we entered, we were surrounded by all the people in the room, who dressed in beautiful but different ethnic costumes that were all different, which made me dazzled. I didn't know who took the lead, but everyone in the room started singing and dancing ... Although I couldn't sing or dance, I was extremely happy watching them, as the women and men in the room were singing Russian songs, and dancing in Xinjiang style, with accordion accompaniment, creating an especially lively atmosphere.

"Are you all of the same family?" I asked the host, Ma Lianhua. She nodded and said, "Everyone here today is from Tacheng, but less than a half of our family members came ..."

I smiled. How many people should there be in this happy big family?

Ma Jinhua, Ma Lianhua's older sister, was the director of the local neighborhood committee, so she became the "spokesperson" for this big family. She told me that Ma's family had a total of 62 members, and currently over 50 of them live in Tacheng. "Our parents had 12 children — 9 boys and 3 girls. The oldest is now 71 years old, and the youngest is 42. I'm the oldest of the girls, so after our parents passed away, we usually gather at my house ..." She said.

The three girls of Ma's family were all present that day, who were Jinhua, Yinhua, and Lianhua.

It was evident that Ma Lianhua was the most active one in this family.

She was not only a good talker but also a good singer and dancer. She was especially active on the day of the gathering at her house, so, she had a "strong voice".

"We have formed such a big family thanks to our parents." Ma Lianhua introduced their "family history" to me —

The head of Ma's family back then was naturally Ma Zhiqiang, father of Ma Lianhua and her siblings. "Our father was from Guyuan City, Ningxia Hui Autonomous Region. Life had been hard there, so my family migrated to Tacheng. Our father was an educated man and participated in the revolutionary struggles in Tacheng before the establishment of New China. He liked to paint oil paintings and was an excellent dancer, who was especially good at tap dancing, which charmed many girls ..." Ma Lianhua burst into laughter after saying these words.

"Our mom must have been attracted by dad's dancing back then ..." Even though both of their parents had passed away many years ago, the younger sisters in Ma's family still joked about them, with a sense of pride in the atmosphere.

Ma Zhiqiang and his wife Bai Xiuzhen were an especially kind-hearted couple. "This is a photo of our family taken in 1980 ..." Ma Lianhua took out a black-and-white photo, showing her father Ma Zhiqiang was in a dark coat, sitting next to her mother Bai Xiuzhen, while their children stood around them.

"At that time, our family was very poor, and we lived an extremely difficult life. Look at our house back then, it was made of adobe walls. But I remember very clearly, despite the hardships, our parents were always optimistic. During festivals, they would always cook extra dishes to entertain people no matter acquainted or not. And our door was always open ... Thus the name 'Ma Zhiqiang' was known far and wide, and anyone could come to our house at any time. Once they arrived, as long as we had food and clothes, we would always receive them. This is the family tradition of the Mas." Ma Lianhua and her siblings were rushing to introduce. In fact, from the moment I stepped into their house, I had been immersed in a relaxing, joyful, and pleasant atmosphere, which was actually a sense of peace and happiness.

"In our family, what we appreciated the most was that our parents never interfere in our marriages and love," Ma Lianhua said, "In 1975, my second elder brother was the first to find a date, who was a Kazakh girl. Initially, he was very nervous, afraid that our parents would not agree. But later on, when my father found out, he said to him, 'If you truly have the ability to marry a Kazakh girl, I will organize a proper wedding for you.' At that time, our family was poor, so my father went around borrowing money,who then bought a sheep and organized a simple but lively wedding for my brother. We are especially happy that his wife can make authentic Kazakh-style Naren(hand-grabbed mutton noodles). All of us love the food ..."

As Ma Lianhua spoke, her second elder sister-in-law was busy in the kitchen. She peeked her head out and said with a smile, "Since we have guests from Beijing today, I have to make the Naren even better!" Her words filled us with joy.

"My eldest sister Jinhua's husband Valodia is a Russian, my second brother Ma Jinyong's wife Fu Hong is a Han, while my fourth brother Ma Jinfeng's wife Guli is a Uyghur ... Our parents didn't oppose any of their marriages and always found ways to arrange weddings according to different ethnic customs. Each wedding left a deep impression on us." Ma Lianhua's words suddenly sparked a discussion among the siblings, and they immediately told me about their memories of each wedding, which was enchanting.

There have been four generations in Ma's family, adding to their deceased parents. Ma Jinhua's siblings have all gotten married and most of them have grandchildren. Over 60 relatives come from ethnic groups like Han, Uyghur, Kazakh, Mongolian, Hui, Russian, and Daur. When they gather together, they speak different but mutually understandable languages, dance in joyful ethnic style, and enjoy food that everyone loves. "For decades, we have never quarreled. Several couples got married out of free love. And there have never been any quarrels between spouses or in-laws. It is something we are most proud of!" Ma Jinhua said that it was the good family tradition that made her become the director of the neighborhood committee.

You can imagine that a multi-ethnic family of more than 60 people get together to be a tremendously joyful and lively group. Especially as members of the same family, they are connected by blood and close kinship. When their voices come together, it becomes a cheerful chorus; when they dance together, it becomes a romantic sleepless party at night ... If members of such a large family are dispersed among different work units in normal times, they would bring the same joy, beauty, and romance to the people around them, would there still be disputes, distress, poverty, and sadness in the world? Would there still be so many inexplicable divisions and conflicts?

The officials in Tacheng told me that there were a total of 270,000 households in Tacheng Prefecture, of which 7.5% were composed of families with more than two ethnic groups. In its central urban area, this proportion reached 20%, which meant that at least 2 out of 10 households were composed of people from multiple ethnic groups.

The larger the family is, the more diverse it is in its ethnic composition, and the more diverse the cultures and traditions are in the family. Therefore, in such a large family, there are frequent festive occasions when people from each ethnic group have the opportunity to showcase their own culture and virtues. This display of cultural charm enhances the blending and understanding among different ethnic groups, strengthening the bonds of affection, so they ultimately form an inseparable extended family.

> Warm and affectionate are the brothers and sisters,
> And all relatives are connected by blood.
> Treating each other sincerely with deep affection,
> We face the trials and tribulations together.
>
> ...

This popular song, *Relatives*, is widely circulated on the grasslands of Hoboksar Mongolian Autonomous County, which was composed by Tseva Monkebayer, an outstanding local musician.

Tseva Monkebayer was born in Bustunger Ranch, which was a multi-ethnic gathering place with a harmonious environment of mutual dependence among different ethnic groups. More than a dozen ethnic groups there respected and supported each other, forging unbreakable friendships akin to a large family. After graduating from the Music Class of Xinjiang Mongolian Normal School in 1996, Tseva Monkebayer returned to his hometown and has been working in the local Dzhangar Art Troupe. He appreciated the beautiful scenery of his homeland and the harmonious multi-ethnic family, so his compositions focused on these themes. That is why herders also enjoyed singing his songs.

"There are no sorrows but only sweet laughter on the faces of the people in Hoboksar." Tseva Monkebayer often said. His smiling face could always prove his words. Since a young age, he had visited friends from house to house with his siblings, enjoying hand-grabbed meat at one house and then drinking butter tea at another. Just after leaving the yurt of his Kazakh friends, he would sit on the warm kang at his Han friends' home ... With such kind of atmosphere, the flower of ethnic friendliness and harmony was planted in Tseva Monkebayer's heart, which blossomed alongside his natural talent for music.

After graduating from school, Tseva Monkebayer flew back to his hometown like a bird in the sky. Thus, he composed his debut song *Grassland Birds*.

> The birds on the grasslands are beautiful and affectionate, only soaring over their familiar land, and sharing their beautiful songs with every herder. Because that is their home, and they love it, they would never be tired or weary ...

Tseva Monkebayer worshiped the heroic epic *Dzhangar*.

This Mongolian heroic epic is widely circulated in Tacheng and Altay Prefectures of Xinjiang, a pride of the local Mongolian people. The epic tells the story of twelve lion-like generals headed by Dzhangar and thousands of warriors fighting arduously against evil forces to defend their hometown Baomuba, reflecting profoundly the ideals and aesthetic pursuits of the Mongolian people, which is one of China's national intangible cultural heritages. It is considered one of the "Three Great Heroic Epics of China's Ethnic Minorities", along with *King Gesar* and *Manas*. The entire *Dzhangar* is so extensive that almost no one knows the exact wordage of it. To this day, no one has been able to sing the entirety of *Dzhangar*. The most fundamental of all is the artistic ideology with the magnanimous temperament and valiant qualities of the Mongolian people. "There is no decay or death, everything remains fresh forever, and the people there are always as strong as 25-year-old youth. In Baomuba, winter is as warm as spring, and summer is as cool as autumn. A lonely man comes here, he would have more children; a poor man comes here, he would become prosperous. In Baomuba, the wealth of people is balanced, and the boundaries between the rich and the poor disappear ...” Such a beautiful place is the blissful homeland that Tseva Monkebayer and all the ethnic groups living with him on that land are yearning for.

“That is the reason why I have always stayed here. It is a place that I can’t leave emotionally and mentally,” said Tseva Monkebayer. It is precisely this sentiment that has inspired this great musical talent of the prairie, who was like a hard-working bee picking pollen, to transform the stories full of love from his homeland into songs and music, resonating among his fellow villagers as well as in this era. At the same time, it also made the new stories here become more affectionate and enchanting.

Tonnur, a lively and beautiful Kazakh girl, expressed her yearning for a good life and a happy family through her dancing and singing. Then her wish was fulfilled. In the first few years of her marriage, her small family was blissful and happy. When her daughter, who was as beautiful as a flower, was born, their life became even more enviable. Perhaps it was due to Tonnur’s love and excessive indulgence, her husband would physically abuse her and their daughter with no reason after getting drunk. Although she had tolerated him many times, what she got was just more severe beatings. For her own happiness and her daughter’s future, Tonnur made a firm decision to divorce him, who showed no signs of changing his abusive behavior.

“We need to go far away, so he won’t be able to see us anymore ...” Faced with a relentless ex-husband who continued to harass and threaten her even after divorce, Tonnur decided to leave her hometown, taking her daughter with her to settle in Emin County, Tacheng, where love and flowers bloomed, and began to lead a life of wandering and laboring.

For a vulnerable woman taking a little girl who had left their hometown, we could imagine how hard their life would be. "Since you're still young, I can offer you a sum of money, as long as you show some coquetries ..." There were inevitably someone despicable in the streets, and Tonnur was not spared from insults. But she remained diligent and down-to-earth, enduring countless hardships to earn every meal for her daughter with her sweat.

Life was never fair. But for Tonnur, who had lost her home, true hardships were still to come ...

One year, her daughter fell seriously ill. Tonnur was on the brink of collapse, as she had no means to afford the exorbitant medical expenses for her daughter. With no other choice, she had to exhaust all efforts to save her little girl. After borrowing money from all her relatives and using up her own hard-earned wages, she had to borrow 20,000 yuan from a moneylender, who required that she had to repay 1,000 yuan every month, plus interest. Tonnur earned a salary of only 2,000 yuan, after deducting the debt repayment and rent for their dwelling, there were only around 500 yuan left per month for their living.

How could they get by in such circumstances? Despite everything, they had to persevere ... The mother's life was hard, but that of her sick daughter was even more pitiable.

The working mother had no strength left, surviving on just cold water to stave off hunger. As her sick child couldn't have any meat to eat, she grew weaker and weaker ...

A woman and a child without home were truly pitiable.

However, the mother and daughter caught the attention of a kind-hearted person, who was also a mother and a teacher at the Fourth Primary School in Emin County. "What's wrong with your child? She's so emaciated. How could she survive without anything nutritious to eat? Just wait a moment, I'll bring you something delicious ..." From the very first moment she saw Tonnur and her daughter, she showered them with unconditional love, despite being strangers, and from then on, she gave them the warmth of home once again ...

"This is my husband, and this is my daughter. We came here today to see you. I already know your situation, so from now on, as long as you don't mind, we will be your family and you will be mine!" Later, Zhang Li, the teacher at Fourth Primary School in Emin County, with her husband and daughter, found Tonnur and her little girl, who was living in a rented room and said those words as soon as they entered.

"Yes, that's right. What my wife said represents the thoughts of our entire family. My little girl, come here, let's divide the tasks. I'll be responsible for tidying up the house, your mom will chat with Auntie, and you, play with your elder sister or read textbooks with her ..." Zhang Li's husband assumed the role of a host, as if he were at his own home, commanding " thousands of horses and soldiers"!

"Hey, I will listen to Daddy! I like my elder sister!" The two little sisters became a pair of joyful butterflies in less than a few minutes, flying around everywhere.

Soon, the dark and dirty little room was tidied up and filled with a sense of warmth and coziness.

"Here, take this 5000 yuan for now, and we'll figure out a way to pay off that high-interest loan together!" Zhang Li handed over a stack of money to Tonnur and said.

"How can I accept it!" Tonnur was so moved that she almost knelt down, but Zhang Li lifted her up immediately.

"We are now family, don't consider yourself as an outsider! From now on, your affairs will be ours. Please rise! Let's take the children to the restaurant to have a good meal so that our daughter can supplement nutrition!" Zhang Li let Tonnur put on a new outfit she had specially brought, holding the hands of the girls, and then the "whole family" walked out to the street together ...

In this way, two more family members were added to Zhang Li's home. Tonnur and her daughter got a home again.

Home is so warm, which allows a once-wounded heart to start healing. Tonnur's daughter was enrolled at the Fourth Primary School where Zhang Li worked. Although Zhang was not her class teacher, she cared deeply about her. Besides her daily life, she also supervised and helped her study. Not to mention teaching her extra lessons, even when she wanted to play, Zhang Li always took time to take her out for fun. The well-behaved child often walked arm in arm with Zhang Li, showing their close bond. "Ms. Zhang, you have another good daughter now!" Zhang Li replied with a smile, "Yes, I have another daughter. Do you think she is beautiful?"

"Yes, she is! With big twinkling eyes, how lovely she is!" Zhang's acquaintances praised Tonnur's daughter.

Zhang Li's own daughter also adored her little elder sister, who was good at singing and dancing. The two little girls played together joyfully, especially at school. And they also flew around like happy birds at home, leaving behind waves of laughter ... Whenever Tonnur returned home from work and saw this, tears would well up in her eyes.

"Sister, call the children inside for dinner!" Zhang Li called.

"Okay, sister!" Tonnur wiped away her tears quickly and took the children inside to sit at the dining table with savoury meals ...

As the days passed, bathed in richness and happiness, Tonnur was no longer worried, and her daughter's face became even rosier and healthier. When another festival was approaching, Tonnur start embroidering after work. A few days later, she solemnly presented Zhang Li with a beautifully embroidered piece of work.

"It's amazing! Thank you, my dear sister!" Zhang Li was incredibly excited as she looked at the embroidery of Kazakh ethnic customs that Tonnur had crafted stitch by stitch.

"Come on, let's take a family photo!" Another Chinese New Year came, and Zhang Li's eldest daughter, who was studying at a university in Wuhan, returned home. She asked Tonnur and her two little sisters to take a family photo with her parents.

Year after year, they are living in harmony. Now, if you ask where Tonnur's home is, she will confidently point to Zhang Li and say, "I live in my sister's house. Where she lives is my home!"

Mengke and Narenhua are siblings, but they are not from the same ethnic group. Mengke is a Han, while his sister Narenhua is a Kazakh. However, they are truly a family. When Mengke opened his eyes for the first time, he saw the same parents as Narenhua did when she was born ... But why are they from different ethnic groups?

These kinds of things happen all the time on the grasslands. Mengke and Narenhua are lucky children because they have loving and kind-hearted parents.

In fact, Mengke had no blood relation with his father, Bartel Batejulong, who was a forestry worker in Hogeert Mongolian Township, Emin County, Tacheng Prefecture. More than ten years ago, on November 22, 2007, while riding his motorcycle on his way to work, Batejulong noticed a rolled-up cotton quilt laid near the roots of a tree. He walked closer and was shocked when he saw that inside was a newborn baby.

"Waa, waa ..." The baby cried when Batejulong touched him lightly.

What should he do?

He was at a loss, so he called his wife immediately.

"Bring the baby back immediately. It's so cold outside. The baby will freeze!" His kind wife said.

"Good boy, don't cry, we are going home now …" Batejulong scrupulously picked the baby up and went back apace.

"There's a note!" When he came home, his wife took the quilt and opened it. Inside, there was a note next to the baby, saying, "To the kind-hearted person who brings this unfortunate child home, he is a Han, born on November 22, 2007. I will always appreciate your kind behavior."

Batejulong's wife was breastfeeding their own baby, so she wanted to feed the baby they had just found but suddenly noticed that there was something wrong with the baby's lips.

"What's wrong?" Batejulong saw his wife worried, while the baby, who couldn't feed, continued to cry. He said, "Maybe we should take him to the hospital to see if there's anything wrong with him …"

"Take him to the hospital now to avoid delay of medical treatment." His wife agreed.

After an examination at the county hospital, the doctor said, "This boy suffers from a congenital cleft lip."

"What can we do now?" Batejulong and his wife became anxious.

"Early surgery might cure." the doctor said, "But Batejulong, you already have a daughter at home, and you can barely make ends meet with your salary. Now, by taking in this baby, you have to pay for his treatment while supporting your family. Can you handle it?"

It was a very realistic problem. Batejulong did hesitate, but when he looked at the baby's face and saw those bright and lovable eyes, he became decisive. He said to the doctor, "Please do everything you can to treat my child …"

Although the surgery did not achieve the desired result, Batejulong and his wife brought the baby securely back home with peace of mind.

"From now on, he is our son, and I'll go to register him at the police station later," Batejulong said to his wife.

His wife nodded, "I'll prepare some milk for him ..."

"Mengke. We'll call you Mengke." Batejulong gazed at the poor little one in his arms for a while and uttered spontaneously.

A Han baby now had a Mongolian name, and an abandoned baby now had parents.

Little Mongke grew up healthily in Batejulong's family, just like any other child, until it was time for school.

"Mengke, you're going to school soon. Mom and Dad are planning to take you to a large hospital for another surgery so that you can play and learn happily with your classmates ..." One day, Batejulong said to little Mengke.

Little Mengke understood what his parents thought. Although he was the most loved at home, whenever he went outside, there were always someone who taunted and bullied him because of his congenital cleft lip.

For Mengke's surgery, Batejulong and his wife worked tirelessly and saved every penny for four to five years. They took Mengke to the People's Hospital in Xinjiang Uyghur Autonomous Region for the surgery, which was very successful. "Thank you, thank you so much!" When Mengke was discharged, although Batejulong encountered "financial deficit", he still carried Mengke on his back, hand in hand with his wife, joyfully setting foot on the journey back home. The words of the doctor kept echoing in his ears: When the child becomes 10 years old, come back for another surgery. By then, his lips will hardly show any signs of abnormality ...

"It's just four more years! We'll tough it out!" Batejulong and his wife started their new struggles once they returned home.

The first year of their new struggle passed, followed by another challenging year ... It wasn't easy for an ordinary family of four, relying on Batejulong's salary while his wife worked hard to manage the household industriously and thriftily. But despite it all, Batejulong and his wife remained optimistic, and their son Mengke grew up healthily and performed well in school.

"It's cold and windy today, be careful on the road ..." Just like every other day, Batejulong would first see his children off to school before heading to work. On one morning in January 2018, after dropping off the kids, he noticed a group of neighbors gathered around a trash can, discussing something. Batejulong went over to have a look and discovered a newborn baby girl with freezing purple cheeks who was abandoned next to the trash can ...

"Waa! Waa!" The baby's cries scared off many onlookers. "Oh no, the baby will freeze if left like this!" Without hesitation, Batejulong reached out and scooped up the baby girl, and then hurried home.

"Hurry, put this baby on the warm kang ..." He told his wife.

"Why, why did you bring another child home? Whose child is she?" His wife exclaimed in astonishment.

"I have no idea whose child she is! They abandoned her next to the trash can! If I had arrived any later, her life would be in danger ..." Batejulong said as he searched for a small blanket to cover her.

"Do, do you think bringing her home will save her life?" His wife didn't speak aloud, but what she said indeed hurt Batejulong's heart.

Batejulong stood up straight, with his eyes fixed on the baby who had stopped crying, and gently said to his wife, "With a good mother like you, I believe this baby will grow up healthily just like our son Mengke ..."

Tears filled his wife's eyes right away. She picked up the baby, holding her tightly against her chest.

"We found out! The baby's parents are very young. She was just born

a few days ago, and may have congenital hydrocephalus and epilepsy …
That's why they abandoned her." A neighbor came over at noon to inform
Batejulong. It was clear that if they raised this baby, she would be their
lifelong burden.

Like struck by a bolt from the blue, Batejulong and his wife stood still
for a long time …

"Waa! Waa!" Suddenly, the baby, who hadn't even been in their home
for half a day, as if knowing something, opened her mouth and cried
loudly.It was so heart-wrenching.

"It's up to you. I will listen to you this time …" Batejulong looked at
his wife and asked seriously.

"Alas, what else can we do? You have brought her home, so she is
meant to be our child …" His wife shook her head helplessly, embracing
the crying baby in her arms gently.

"Waa …" The baby stopped crying. She fell asleep peacefully, enjoying
the feeling of lying in her mother's embrace.

When Batugulong and his wife looked at each other, they smiled
bitterly.

Batugulong went to the police station to register the child and gave
her a resounding name — Narenhua, which meant the "bright sun" in
Mongolian.

Batejulong had a strong desire to cultivate this little girl into a
beautiful and radiant flower, like the sun.

Narenhua's arrival added more burden to this already financially
strained family, but Batejulong and his wife's faces were filled with
happiness and joy. Even if their sweat kept dripping down or the wind
and rain made them suffer, they still stood straight, providing warmth and
strength to their children.

Their son Mengke's second surgery was perfect, and he was growing taller, becoming a handsome and intelligent young man!

Accompanied by her Mongolian father and mother, Narenhua, a Kazakh girl, received medical treatments in hospitals in Sichuan Province and Urumqi City successively, which cost nearly 100,000 yuan. Her congenital epilepsy was also completely cured, and she gradually grew up as an adorable little angel who was skilled in singing and dancing, loved by everyone ...

"Come on, this year we'll go to the photo studio in Tacheng to take a family photo. The photographer there is very skilled."

"Dad, wait, Mom wants to give me a new dress!" When Batejulong was about to get in the car with his two sons, his daughter Narenhua's sweet voice, like a bird's song, came from behind.

"Alright!" Batejulong signaled to Mengke, saying, "Go, bring your sister and Mom ..."

"Okay!" Mengke walked into the house swiftly.

After a while, Mengke led his sister Narenhua out, and Batejulong's wife, dressed in new clothes, followed their children, walking towards him ... At that moment, Batejulong's face sparkled with happiness.

Now, a family photo of the five, composed of three ethnic groups, hangs prominently in the center of Batejulong's principal room. Whenever the guests visit, Batejulong would always point to the family photo proudly and say, "We are a happy family."

Indeed, the flower of ethnic unity, nurtured by Batejulong and his wife, continues to bloom more brightly, vibrant and enviable.

This is the happiness and warmth of home.

Kind-hearted people have nourished it with their painstaking efforts and love, healing the wounds and restoring hope for countless individuals who had once lost faith in life, giving warmth and beauty to previously hopeless lives, and bringing together innumerable people who were once strangers, allowing them to love and support each other throughout their lives.

On the land of Tacheng, stories about "home" are as numerous and brilliant as the stars in the sky, and they can be found everywhere.

One day while passing through Shanghu Township in Emin County, the locals insisted on sharing a story with us about "home" in No.3 Kumak Village.

The person, who had lost the love from home, was Zhu Guangwu, an elderly Han man who was born in 1934. He was the poorest in the village, enjoying the five guarantees, i.e. childless and infirm rural residents who are guaranteed food, clothing, medical care, housing, and burial expenses. Especially after 2008, Zhu Guangwu's health deteriorated rapidly. "He is a lonely old man with poor health. What can we do for him?" The villagers discussed.

"Don't worry, I will be responsible for looking after Uncle Zhu for the rest of his life," said Zesbek jiangnumujiang, a Kazakh man.

"You? Why would you look after an elderly Han man devotedly with whom you have no connection?" The fellow villagers who were puzzled asked Zesbek.

Zesbek calmly replied, "All of us will grow old someday, and people all hope to have children by their side when they are in their old age. Now, Uncle Zhu is old and in poor health, in need of a home and someone to accompany him. So, I want to give him a home, a warm one that can make him happy and content until the very end of his life ..."

His words touched the villagers, especially when he mentioned that "I will look after him for the rest of his life." Definitely, some doubted whether Zesbek could actually act as he said all the way.

It was indeed quite a test. The village where Zesbek and Zhu Guangwu resided was 35 kilometers away from the county town, which consisted of 130 households with 585 people from four ethnic groups — Han, Zang (Tibetan), Manchu, and Kazakh. Although the minority ethnic groups made up 86% of the total population, harmony and close relationships had always been maintained among the villagers, so when Zesbek proposed to give a warm home to the single and elderly Zhu Guangwu, who was enjoying the five guarantees, it seemed like a natural course of action. However, the problem was that Zesbek's own family was not wealthy. His family of four barely made a living from their 50-acre arable land and more than 50 head of cattle and sheep. Furthermore, Zesbek often went to work outside the village, and his wife, Jianati, was in a poor health. The couple couldn't provide the best care for the elderly man. Therefore, after bringing Zhu Guangwu to his home, Zesbek decided to send him to the well-equipped Elderly Care Home in Emin County at his own expense, where Zhu could spend the rest of his life comfortably. In the meantime, he would regularly bring the old man home for reunion.

"Good! Good! This is even better!" Zhu Guangwu expressed his gratitude for this arrangement. He was also aware that it was a huge burden for Zesbek's family to send him to the Elderly Care Home. But Zesbek said, "Since Uncle Zhu is now in my family, he is now my senior, just like my father. When it comes to taking care of the elderly, how could we think of the cost?"

Zesbek worked hard to care for old-aged Zhu. Despite their own hardships and financial constraints, Zesbek never hesitated to spend money on him.

In the summer of 2013, Zhu Guangwu suddenly had a recurrence of a cerebral hemorrhage and had to be admitted to the hospital. It happened during the wheat harvesting season, and Zesbek was busy with farming and household chores during the day, while at night, he insisted on staying at the hospital to take care of Zhu. When he was away, he would ask others to help look after his "father" — The hospital staff all considered Zhu Guangwu as Zesbek's father.

Zesbek often helped the old man walk in the courtyard to bask in the sun, wash his hair, change his clothes, and feed him medicine and meals like his son. The sick old man urinated a lot at night, waking up four or five times, so Zesbek would support him with his hand to the bathroom, help him go back to bed, and then rest in a tent bed next to the sickbed.

"My sweet son! He is my sweet son!" The old man praised him in front of everyone he met, with a happy expression on his face.

The old man loved listening to Pingshu (a kind of storytelling program in China), so Zesbek bought him a radio. He loved eating meat and fish, so Zesbek would buy such food at home and his wife would carefully cook it and bring it to the old man's bedside.

Zhu Guangwu suffered a lot when he was young. As he grew older, the ailments on his body multiplied. Another spring came, he fell ill again. It was the time of spring plowing, Zesbek was busy with farming, also with an empty pocket. With no choice, he sold a few sheep to provide medical treatment and better nutrition for the old man. Later, with no money to pay the medical expenses, he had to sell a cow.

"Zesbek is as stupid as a goose. The old man isn't even his real father, but he treats him even better than his own father ..." Some people commented.

Zesbek smiled and responded, "Since Uncle Zhu has become a member of our family, I should take care of him just like my own father!" In the end, Zesbek added a weighty statement, "I really want to celebrate his 80th birthday!"

What a promise it was!

Zhu Guangwu, who was lying on his sickbed, shed tears after hearing it and said, "I have a son of my own now!"

Year after year, Zhu Guangwu enjoyed a happy and blissful old age.

In early April of that year, the disease-ridden old man was finally taken away by the merciless illness. During his last days, Zesbek stayed by his side, feeding him medicine and food, looking after him in every detail ...

"To have a home and a sweet son like you, I am already content ..." At the moment when the old man was gone, he was in peace and satisfaction.

For six years, Zesbek kept his initial promise and, with the warmest love, gave a sick old man his final precious moments. During that time, another villager Borbek was also inspired by Zesbek and frequently helped look after Zhu Guangwu.

People, like Zesbek, Batejulong, Zhang Li, Tseva Monkebayer, and Ma Lianhua, reshaping warm and happy homes with love, whose stories are so touching. I know that there are many stories like theirs in Tacheng.

In Tacheng, a musical drama *The Love for Home* performed by a group of artists has captivated countless people from Tacheng and other places. The secret lies in people's longing for love and home.

> A warm home is the source of happiness
> And a happy one is filled with heartwarming scenes
> It is inevitable to stumble when you go out
> But just the thought of home may bring infinite warmth
>
> ...
>
> ...

Everyone desires to have a warm and happy home because only with it can our hearts and spirits be at peace, and we gain the courage and strength to soar; only with it can our nation achieve prosperity, and our homeland become more beautiful.

Isn't it true?

Chapter 12

Sweet Days After Forging a Bond of Kinship

During the making of the Chinese nation with a time-honoured history,

the unique family bond culture of "kinship and brotherhood among different ethnic groups" has played a crucial role,

intertwining their hearts and minds for generations.

It is precisely the cohesion and affinity of such culture that have enabled the Chinese nation,

no matter how cruel the aggression might be,

to stay inseparable like a family over the past five thousand years,

and the Great Wall has always stood tall in the eastern world.

The "National Unity, One Family" initiative is widely spread in Xinjiang today, becoming a voluntary social trend among people.

It is not only the continuation of Chinese civilization,

but also a naturally indestructible force like pomegranate seeds, which tightly embrace each other.

In Chinese, the word "qin"(kinship) has the same meaning as that in foreign languages, which implicates close relationship and deep affection while it also refers to family or marital relationships. In ancient Chinese, the character "qin" was adapted from another Chinese character "zhi"(dearest).

In our daily lives, we tend to refer to people with whom we share special relationships as "my dear" or "family". On the internet, Chinese people often use "qin" to address those with ordinary relationships. This word is frequently used in communities, such as using the phrase"as close as one family" to describe ethnic unity which means there are no barriers among ethnic groups, and they live together under the same roof, share the same food, and sleep on the same kang(a heatable bed widely used in northern China).

"Family" is more reliable than anyone else in the world. "Qin" stabilizes the basic form of human society, country, and nation,energizing humanity to prosper and develop stronger than any animal kingdom.

"Qin" is love, and there is no better way to explain the relationship better between people than the word"dear."

In Xinjiang and Tacheng, there have been significant changes and achievements in national unity over the years, which can be largely attributed to the "National Unity, One Family" initiative that was launched by the Xinjiang's government in 2016. This initiative encourages all regional cadres and workers to build a bond of kinship with local people from different ethnic groups through extensive communication and exchange. By doing so, they can support each other and create a better future, painting family photos of numerous multi-ethnic families in this vast land north and south of Mt. Tianshan.

Although literature often excludes numbers and some objective reasons, certain numbers themselves carry fascinating and irreplaceable stories.

Local people who are involved in the initiative often say that they are intertwined for life once they built kinship with other cadres. It's true. As a bird flies high, it becomes the closest "companion" to the sky. As the cows and sheep walk into the grassland, they never leave the land under their feet. Once a river flows, the sea becomes its destination. This law of "qin" is the source of eternal emotions that cannot be changed. All we can do is to follow it.

It is how human society has evolved. Those who follow would prosper, while those who oppose would decline.

Tacheng is a place where visitors would find the locals to be hospitable, cordial, sincere, and closely united, like a family. In fact, Tacheng people often refer to themselves as a family. It's rare to find such a strong sense of family among over twenty ethnic groups, thousands of villages, and millions of people in one place.

It was not recently that the social mood of Tacheng, characterized with the unity of all ethnic groups, was formed. Instead, it has been a historical trend that developed over time, with traditions in the bone. With the introduction of the "National Unity, One Family" initiative, this long-standing public trend has become even more prominent, deep-rooted, and meaningful in its contents.

"One family, one city. One city, one family." Building "kinship" among different ethnic groups on this beautiful land in Northern Xinjiang is like the warmest flame, representing people's deep passion for the family, nation and motherland, which could not be ignored.

Just like in spring, the blossoms of ethnic unity and friendliness dot the whole of Xinjiang and Tacheng, brought about by "National Unity, One Family."

Let's gather them together.

Those passionate and flavorful nangs (a type of bread)

More often than not, when life is improving, some people may become idle and indulge in fantasies. On the other hand, when life becomes difficult, someone tends to fan up the flames of trouble and induce people to lose their way. For some time, there were also such people in Tacheng who constantly complained about everything, as if the world owed them something. They even expected to gain without making efforts.

Yakefu Itahong, a Uyghur, used to work as an electric welder in a small factory. Despite being on and off duty on time, he could hardly make ends meet with his low wages for supporting a family of three. Yakefu often complained, unwilling to abandon himself to despair. He felt extremely depressed for some time, having no idea what kind of life he should pursue.

At one point, he even cried out of frustration.

"Brother, look at yourself. You are strong, skillful, and having many friends in Tacheng, and I admire you for that. However, have you ever considered why many people live a better life than you?" One day, Sun Xiaodong visited Yakefu, and the two sat on the kang, chatting for a long time.

Sun, being about the same age as Yakefu, works for the Housing and Urban Rural Development Bureau in Shawan County. Despite being from different ethnicities (Sun is Han and Yakefu is Uyghur), they consider each other as "brothers".

"I don't know why," Yakefu said to Sun, shaking his head.

Sun helped him analyze, "It is because you haven't realized your full potential yet. Once you do, you will become a prominent figure, and the life of your family will be no worse than anyone else."

Yakefu looked at Sun seriously and asked, "Do you really believe that?" He was afraid that Sun might be deceiving him.

With a smile, Sun continued to explain, "Working in a small factory might provide you with stable fixed wages, but you may not be able to fully utilize your abilities there. Moreover, due to the limited resources of the factory, your wages may not be sufficient to support your family's basic needs, let alone provide a comfortable life."

Sun's words struck a chord with Yakefu, prompting him to urgently ask, "So, what should I do?"

"Are you complaining? Are you going to listen to the people who don't really want you to take the right path and live a better life?" Sun asked Yakefu.

"I don't want to do that at heart." Yakefu replied, feeling a bit upset.

"I understand," Sun said, patting Yakefu's shoulder. "Do you really want to take practical steps to make your family's life prosperous?"

"Yes! I've always dreamed of it!" Yakefu stood tall and proud like a warrior ready for the expedition.

"Great! That's what I want to hear!" Sun grinned warmly.

"Please tell me quickly, brother. What will I do, and how should I do it?" Yakefu couldn't wait any longer.

"Since you have quit your job at the small factory, you should consider starting your own business from the ground up," suggested Sun.

"But I don't know what to do. I don't have any special skills," Yakefu suddenly lost his confidence and began to stutter, lowering his head like a frostbitten eggplant.

Sun smiled and patted Yakefu's shoulder, "Do you consider me your brother?"

Yakefu looked at Sun confusedly and nodded, "Of course!"

"Then show me something. Make some nangs for me, and I'll tell you what to do after I eat them."

"That's too easy!" Yakefu exclaimed as he started making dough and building a fire for baking. After a while, he placed a few flavorful nangs in front of Sun.

"These are the most delicious nangs I've ever tasted in Shawan!" Sun said while savoring the food.

Yakefu beamed with pride and said, "I dare say few people could challenge me when it comes to making nangs."

"Why don't you take it as your business?" Sun asked seriously.

"Did you mean that I could sell Nangs?" Yakefu asked confusedly.

"Yes. That's what you just said: No one can beat you in making nangs! Isn't this to make the best out of you?"

Yakefu was taken aback for a moment and asked Sun seriously, "You just said to give me a tip on starting my own business, is it selling nangs to get rich?"

"Sure, why not!" exclaimed Sun, "I want you to showcase your special skill of making nangs, which are the best in Shawan and even in Tacheng."

Yakefu replied shyly, "You flatter me. I don't think I would be the best, but I'm definitely not inferior to others when it comes to making nangs."

Sun was extremely delighted and exclaimed, "That's it!"

"Business requires a good speaking skill to promote products. However, I even struggle to speak Mandarin fluently," Yakefu felt a bit embarrassed once again.

"Look, look at me," Sun asked, "What do you see?"

Yakefu looked straight at him and replied, "I can only see you, my brother."

"That's right, don't worry. With my help, everything will be fine," Sun said. "I'll teach you Mandarin for free. But if you don't learn seriously and end up losing money, maybe I'll have to charge you tuition!"

Sun's joke made himself laugh out loud first.

Soon Yakefu followed, laughing heartily.

Most people in Xinjiang are skilled in making nangs, but there are variations in the methods used. Creating the perfect nang depends on various factors, such as the quality of ingredients, personal expertise, and state of mind. However, the most important factors are having conscience and empathy towards others.

Yakefu wasted no time in starting his business. With the help of Sun and other relatives, he built a pit for baking nangs, created panels, and contacted designated stores for flour, oil and other ingredients. He paid careful attention to every detail in the process.

"A brand is especially needed for business," Sun thought about it after selling several batches of nangs.

"You said that you can compete with everyone in making nangs, you should build your big reputation," Sun encouraged.

"So ... how about calling it 'Ana Nang' ('Ana' means 'mother' in the Uyghur language)?" Yakefu said.

A wonderful name! "Ana" sounds so loving and palatable! Sun was overjoyed upon hearing Yakefu's suggestion.

After "Ana Nang" became popular, its scent started spreading throughout Shawan and Tacheng.

Initially, the villagers always got hungry due to the fragrance of nangs.

Gradually, the people from nearby towns and counties also got attracted to this scent.

Eventually, people from Shihezi City came from far away to buy "Ana Nang" made by Yakefu.

"We have been reported on the 'Xinjiang Headlines' !" Although Yakefu was very busy, he looked cheerful with a smile on his face. His wife and children helped him with delivering the products and receiving payment. His "relative" Sun Xiaodong acted as a "volunteer press agent" to help promote the business.

"Your nangs are large and tasty. I'd like another 30 pieces!"

"Please do me a favor. I came afar for your nangs. I'd like to take 50 pieces !"

"Me too!"

"Line up! Line up!"

Nowadays, Yakefu's shop often sees crowds of buyers, which also greatly benefits the villagers. The villagers said that with the delicious scent of Yakefu's nangs, the reputation of their village has spread far and wide.

That thoughtful "little warm cotton-padded jacket"

In Chinese culture, a daughter is often referred to as a "little warm cotton-padded jacket". This is because daughters are believed to be a source of comfort, thoughtfulness, and warmth for their parents, especially as they grow older.

To Ding Shenxing and his wife, Yu Fa'e was like such a "little warm cotton-padded jacket" that they had "picked up", bringing them happiness and comfort.

What does "picking up" mean?

Six years ago, Yu Fa'e was on a rural work trip with her colleagues from the Transportation Bureau of Tacheng City. When she reached a market in Axier Township, a suburb of the city, she found herself getting separated from the group and losing contact with them. Yu, holding many things in both hands, was at a loss for a moment. "What should I do?" She was extremely anxious.

"Excuse me, lady. Is there something wrong? Or take our electric bike back?" Suddenly,an old man and his wife parked their electric bike and asked Yu.

Yu felt a bit embarrassed and blushed, replying, "Yes, yes, but I lost my way."

The old man then kindly offered, "Would you mind us taking you home?"

As Yu accepted the offer and hopped on the electric bike, a warm sensation filled her heart.

"Now that you're here in our home, you may wash your face and have a rest, then you can savor some delicious food I make for you." After bringing Yu back to their home, the old couple warmly received her.

"It is so kind of you. I'm a little embarrassed!" Yu was too overwhelmed to know how to react and express her gratitude.

"It is not a big deal. We are destined to meet. Now that you come to our home, we will regard you as our own daughter!" said the old man.

"Really? Will you truly regard me as your daughter?" The old man, who is as old as Yu's father, with his sincere and enthusiastic words, extremely touched Yu, who lost her father in childhood, making her shed tears.

"Do you think we are kidding?" The old man shrugged and spread his hands.

Yu shook her head and said, "I trust you."

At this moment, the old lady had already served the tasty dishes and asked her to take a seat.

"Daughter, what's your surname?" the old man asked affectionately.

"'Yu" the girl replied.

"Oh, what a coincidence! My surname is Ding, and these two Chinese characters look almost identical. If you add a stroke to Ding, it becomes Yu. We are family!" The elderly man was Ding Shenxing, a Daur. He had five children, all of whom were very successful, except that they all worked far away from Tacheng, especially the three daughters, who work in Urumqi and Karamay. When the old couple learned that Yu's father had passed away early, they kindly offered to take her in as their own daughter, "Would you agree?" Ding asked as he served Yu some food.

"Yes, I do," Yu replied.

"Ha-ha, great! Come on, let's toast for our new daughter!" The old man happily took out a bottle of liquor that had been stored for many years.

"We have found a good girl!" From that day on, Ding and his wife, Dai Zhao'ai, would often share this good news with others. Yu would also frequently visit the old couple's house to help them with some chores.

In 2016, the "National Unity, One Family" initiative was launched in different townships in Tacheng. Upon hearing the news, Yu was the first person to sign up at her workplace, and she proudly declared, "I already have relatives in Axier, and today I will visit them."

That day, Yu went to Ding's house to reveal the news. She declared to Ding and his wife, "Mom, Dad, I am officially your daughter forever!" After hearing the news, Ding was elated, and his wife showed Yu a new bed they had prepared for her in the inner room, saying, "We have made this bed for you, and you are always welcome to stay with us."

Then Yu immediately threw herself into the old lady's arms, with tears streaming down her eyes.

After becoming a member of the Ding's family as a "little warm cotton-padded jacket," Yu took the responsibility of taking care of the old couple very seriously. "Oh,yes. I'll go shopping after work today." Why?It was her Dad Ding's 75th birthday. How could a daughter forget about this?

On that day, Yu dressed herself in new clothes, grabbed two large bags of presents, and went to her Dad Ding's house in Axier, over 20 kilometers away.

"We are happy enough that you come here. Why do you bring so many things?" Ding said as he saw his "daughter" running around with sweat on her forehead.

"It's your 75th birthday! I bought you a set of warm pajamas to protect your waist. Have a try, Dad." Yu excitedly took a brand new set of pajamas for the elderly from her bag and gave them to her "Dad."

"They fit well!" Yu exclaimed as she looked at her "Dad" up and down, clapping her hands happily.

As it was the first time Ding had worn pajamas, he stood there feeling a bit lost and soon showed off to his wife, saying, "Look! Our girl dresses me up like ten years younger!"

To which his wife playfully replied, "Huh! Are you still in your daydream?"

"Ha-ha. Don't worry, Mom, I'll buy you an even more stunning one later!" Yu interjected.

"Did you hear that? My girl is going to buy me something even more attractive!" The old lady exclaimed.

"Yes, our daughter is absolutely a 'little warm cotton-padded jacket'!" The old man quickly changed his tone and said.

"Oh, I would like to have Dad's longevity noodles!" Yu said coyly.

"We have already prepared, just waiting for your arrival, then we'll cook!" The old couple looked at each other happily.

"Great! I can't wait to taste them!" Yu's cheerful voice warmed the hearts of the old couple, with their faces full of happiness.

The feeling of being a family was so wonderful.

Yu worked in the city, but whenever she had free time, she would visit Axier to bring food and clothes suitable for the elderly, helping the old couple clean up, tidy the house, or cook delicious meals. Her kind and helpful nature had created a joyful and harmonious atmosphere in the family, making the neighbors envious.

Another "National Unity, One Family" event was organized by the locals, the old couple arrived at the venue before everyone else to wait for their "daughter". However, as the other villagers' relatives arrived, their "daughter" was still nowhere to be seen.

What was the matter with the girl? When the couple asked about her whereabouts, they were informed that she had been hospitalized due to heart disease!

"Why didn't send a message to me? We are so worried about you," Ding called the girl, anxiously stamping his foot.

The girl on the other end reassured her parents, saying, "Dad, Mom, I'm okay. I've been discharged, and I feel good. Please don't worry about me. How have you been? Is everything going well?"

"Good to hear that you're feeling better. We're doing alright, too," Ding replied, relieved.

"That's good! I'll go to the village to see you in a few days," said Yu.

"Take good care of yourself, my daughter. We'll go to see you soon," Ding said, hanging up the phone. Then he turned to his wife and said, "Please gather all the eggs in the house. I'll bring them to our daughter!"

"Are you leaving now?" his wife asked.

"Yes, I am!" Ding replied, appearing as anxious as if he were the one who had fallen ill.

After undergoing some conditioning, Yu quickly regained her strength. As she realized she had not visited her "Dad" over the past few days, she took a few days off to stay with the elderly couple and help with household chores.

In April, most families in Tacheng no longer needed to make a fire for heating. But Upon her arrival, she discovered that the old couple had already prepared a fire to keep her warm and even laid out an electric blanket on the bed.

"I am so grateful for your kindness. How can I repay you?" Yu was deeply moved and couldn't hold back her tears.

"My daughter, we are family. Your return fills our hearts with warmth and joy. It is us that should be grateful to you!" replied Ding.

This "little warm cotton-padded jacket" has brought hope and joy to the once lonely elderly couple. In return, the couple has shown love and care towards Yu, who has a sense of belonging.

Yu has become a beloved member of the Axier village, affectionately known as the daughter of the Ding's Family. Also, Yu feels proud to be recognized in this way.

Carried in the arms of a younger policeman like a princess

Tangnuer Tohetasen, a young Kazakh woman, once considered herself the most unfortunate person in the world. At the age of 19, she could have enjoyed her youth life at college, but unfortunately, she was diagnosed with necrosis of the femoral head, which paralyzed her lower body. This sudden and severe blow left her devastated and miserable, causing her to become withdrawn and even hesitant to go outside her home.

"I just want to finish my life and end the trouble!" She has been thinking of suicide many times, and she might have left this world for good if her elder sister hadn't find out in time.

Year after year, she has lived in great grief, and even at the age of 30, she still has to rely on her sister to move around, who acts like a pair of crutches for her. Occasionally, Tangnuer's sister would ask their neighbors to help carry her downstairs so that she could feel the earth's smell. Tangnuer, sitting in a wheelchair, would sometimes tiptoe to touch the ground, being so excited to shed tears.

But she didn't get many chances to do that. Only with her brother-in-law's help could she go downstairs to get the happiness of touching the earth without guilt. Unfortunately, her brother-in-law worked in an oil field hundreds of miles away and thus could not return frequently. While her sister was unable to carry her, it wouldn't be easy to ask for neighbors' help. As a result, she lost the desire to feel the earth, and loneliness and other negative emotions started to torment her.

But all changed on April 8, 2018. Whenever Tangnuer recalls what happened that day, she will laugh happily.

On that morning, her sister had just helped her up and let her lean against the wall to watch TV when a tall and handsome young man presented in front of Tangnuer and said heartily and kindly, "Tangnuer, Sister. I am Shao Qi, a police officer from the Hoboksar County Public Security Bureau. I am two years younger than you, so I am your younger brother."

"Brother Shao?!" After Tangnuer had to leave school at the age of 19 due to paralysis, to tell the truth, there hadn't been any young man taking the initiative to talk to her. So she felt pleased and a bit shy when she saw Shao.

"Take a seat, Brother," she blushed with excitement, inviting him to sit down.

"Thank you, sister," replied the young man, bright and straightforward, coming to sit beside her and asking about her health and living conditions.

After enduring many hardships and suffering over the years, she has accepted her tragic life as her fate without any emotional outbursts. "I have grown accustomed to being alone and spend the rest of my days watching TV as a way to learn about the world," she said.

"That's too boring! I'll take you out. There is nothing interesting staying at home!" Shao stood up, reached out his hands, carried Tangnuer in his arms, and walked around the room a few times. Tangnuer was both surprised and ecstatic, laughing heartily.

"Let's go downstairs!" The young police officer easily carried her downstairs, like carrying a princess. The several floors were nothing to him, he seemed like walking on the flat ground and they arrived at the community square just in a while.

Tangnuer, who hadn't been downstairs for a long time, sat on the chair Shao had brought her. She threw back her long hair over her shoulders and looked up at the azure sky, enjoying the sunshine on her face. "It's so beautiful! This place has changed a lot!" she exclaimed.

She closed her eyes for a moment and then turned her gaze toward the small community square. The vibrant scene of blooming flowers, fresh green lawn, and children frolicking made her crack a large smile.

"Open your arms and take a few deep breaths in this fresh air," said the "younger brother" as he demonstrated while gesturing for Tangnuer to follow suit.

Tangnuer then stretched out her arms, took a deep breath, and gently exhaled. After completing several sets of actions, she closed her eyes.

"What's your feeling now, sister?" asked the "younger brother".

In silence, two lines of tears streamed down her cheeks. She cried.

It's tears for pain and injustice.

It's tears of satisfaction and happiness.

"Let's go to a place further away," said the "younger brother". Without Tangnuer's agreement, he carried her to a place further away from her house for sightseeing.

"No, No! Put me down!" Tangnuer suddenly shouted.

"What's wrong, sister?" the "younger brother" asked in a hurry.

"I ... I feel embarrassed if others see you holding me like this," she said, feeling ashamed.

"Hey, I don't care! You're my sister, and there's nothing to be ashamed of. Let's go!" Shao stood up straight, carried Tangnuer in his arms again, and walked towards the bustling crowd.

How excited was Tangnuer that day? Her constant cheerful singing by the bed at that night could tell.

"Sister, what do you think of this young police officer?" Her older sister asked with joy.

"He is nice for sure! Tomorrow is Sunday, He said he would come to carry me downstairs so that I could bask in the sunshine," Tangnuer said, unable to contain her excitement.

"Tomorrow?Will he really come?" Tangnuer's sister expressed her disbelief.

"Yes, he said he would," Tangnuer responded promptly.

Her sister's face lit up with joy, "Alright then! If he comes tomorrow, I'll cook a delicious meal for you two."

"Thank you, sister!" Tangnuer replied, humming the tune of "Happy Flowers" again, a song she had always loved to sing but couldn't for over a decade due to her illness.

Tangnuer had a pleasant dream that night.

"Sister ... let's go downstairs!" At some point, Tangnuer felt her head resting on a thick and strong chest, and it was such a delightful sensation that she didn't want to open her eyes.

"Go ahead and come back for dinner later," her sister smiled as she watched Shao carry Tangnuer out of the door with his strong arms.

Shao took Tangnuer, sitting in a wheelchair, to visit the streets she had not been to for over ten years. They strolled around her favorite shops while Shao occasionally pointed out the changes and the newly built buildings in the county. Tangnuer was moved and shocked by the new scenery before her and often asked Shao to tell her more details about what they saw.

In some places where the wheelchair was not accessible, Shao would carry her with his arms, which would attract much attention from pedestrians, making Tangnuer blush with embarrassment. But after several times, Tangnuer became accustomed to that. Her feeling of shame were replaced by that of happiness and joy.

"Sister, whenever I have free time, I will take you out so that you can enjoy the outdoors. And whenever you wish to go out, just give me a call. I'll come to you as soon as possible. What do you think?" Shao asked.

"Okay. But for now, you must be tired after the day, so go home and rest! My sister will take care of me!" Tangnuer replied when Shao dropped her off at home.

Late at night, looking at Tangnuer, who was even smiling while sleeping, her sister was immensely grateful to the younger police officer, who had chosen Tangnuer as his "relative" in the initiative of "National Unity, One Family."

Whenever Shao had time off, he would take Tangnuer outside to enjoy the sunshine. These excursions rejuvenated Tangnuer and filled her with happiness.

After Shao moved 50 kilometers away for work, he and his pregnant wife took turns to accompany Tangnuer. Kind and skilled, Shao's wife often prepared presents for Tangnuer and taught her all kinds of craft, which made Tangnuer feel that she could gain happiness and a sense of belonging not only just by breathing in the fresh air or hanging out. Her life became more colorful and meaningful.

Shao still makes full use of time to carry Tangnuer out to bask in the sunshine. Moreover, he has persuaded his two colleagues to look after Tangnuer every day.

Almost every day, Tangnuer will be carried outside in the arms of "sisters" and "brothers".

Tangnuer, once lost hope in life, is now brimming with joy and cheerfulness, singing lively and growing self-reliant.

She always tells people, "I don't feel lonely, for I have already enjoyed the warmest tenderness in the world."

The Spring in the Bahati Courtyard

In Tacheng, you will be amazed by the stunning scenery surrounding you. The abundance of captivating landscapes may leave you overwhelmed by beauty. Personally, I find the small private courtyards where locals live to be particularly appealing. Whether in towns or rural areas, these courtyards provide a glimpse into the living conditions of the families inside. In rural areas, the courtyard's size and arrangement might indicate the family's wealth, quality of life, and aesthetic values.

In the Harabula Township of Yumin County, there is a Kazakh herdsman named Bahati Hasen who lives in Hoshabak Village. When other villagers recalled Bahati's family courtyard from the past, they shook their heads in ridicule, saying that the house was so shabby that even livestock were reluctant to walk in.

Bahati's family was known as a poverty-stricken household in the village, consisting of four members, including two daughters, and a wife who had breast cancer. As the only breadwinner for the family, Bahati had to bear the weighty financial burden, including daily expenses, tuition fees for his daughters, and high medical expenses for his wife. These challenges have taken a toll on Bahati's health, though aged only 40, he has already stooped prematurely. Although he is not an idle man and wants to tidy up a spacious yard, the difficulties in life have caused him to lose interests and enthusiasm.

Jiang Xinliang, the Party secretary of the township who can speak Kazakh, kept in mind the hardships faced by the Bahati's family. As a result, he decided to make Bahati his new "relative" under the "National Unity, One Family" initiative.

"They are in desperate need! I would like to help them out," Jiang said during the meeting.

As soon as Jiang stepped into Bahati's house, the sight of the sick wife lying on the kang weighed heavily on his mind. In that moment, he made a decision: he must help the family get rid of poverty and become rich!

But it was not easy for such an impoverished family like Bahati's to cast off poverty. Lack of able-bodied workers but heavy burden, let alone fund to start a business. Within several minutes, Jiang took glances around the house and then thoroughly knew the condition of this family.

"Do you want to improve your life?" Jiang had a serious conversation with Bahati.

"I'd dream it, but my dreams are always nightmares. I hardly ever have sweet ones," Bahati said in a dejected tone.

Jiang shook his head and spoke seriously, "Since you are a few years older than me, from now on, I consider you as my elder brother. You can take me as your own relative. Family members don't harm each other, right?"

Bahati suddenly became excited and said, "I'd be blessed to have you as my brother!"

Jiang happily grabbed Bahati's hands and said, "Let's pursue our happiness together, Brother Bahati." Then he pointed to the yard and suggested, "This courtyard is very spacious. I think we can rebuild this old, dilapidated house into a new one and renovate the yard together. We can raise some sheep as a source of income. What do you think, Brother?"

"Me? Build a new house? No way, I can barely afford my pants, let alone a new house!" Bahati was taken aback by Jiang's suggestion.

"Don't worry, Brother. The Party has introduced many new preferential policies. For instance, we have housing projects subsidized by the government, and poverty-stricken families can even apply for subsidies for raising sheep. In this way, you can build a new house and get rich through raising livestock!" said Jiang.

"Really? It sounds too good to be true!" Bahati exclaimed, feeling like it was just a fantasy.

"Absolutely! If you are confident and determined, I will assist you in applying for those subsidies," Jiang nodded and assured.

"Brother, you are so kind to me!" Bahati couldn't even find the words to express his gratitude.

As each problem was resolved, the old mud house was replaced with a new brick and tile house covering over 80 square meters. Bahati and his wife were overwhelmed with excitement and shed tears as they looked at the clean white walls, flat cement ground, and spacious new rooms.

"Brother, how can we ever repay you?" The couple held Jiang's hand and expressed their gratitude repeatedly.

Jiang humbly replied, "I don't deserve your thanks. You should be grateful to the Party and the government for adopting favorable policies.

As for us, we are just intermediaries to help improve your living conditions in accordance with these policies."

Soon, with the help of Jiang, Bahati received ten sheep subsidized by the government, which made him even smile while sleeping. For Bahati and his small courtyard, the changes have just started. Later, they bartered those sheep for several cows — a crucial way to get rich: raising cows and selling milk.

When Bahati sold his first bucket of milk, he hoped it would afford his child's tuition and his wife's medical expenses.

In order to ensure that his customers can taste the fresh milk, Bahati bought a motorcycle. As he delivered the milk, he has been imagining his bright future.

"Fresh milk produced by fat and healthy cows fed with fine hay!Good for your health!Very nutritious!The milk and cows are the best!" Bahati proudly called out to passers-by.

"It's true, I can vouch for it. The milk tastes amazing!" Those who have tried the milk commented.

However, since Tacheng is located at the wind gap, people often get lost in snowy weather. Just as Bhati's life was improving, a frigid winter hindered his progress.

Bahati, who had been busy milking all morning, was preparing to deliver fresh milk on his motorcycle. But heavy snow had blocked the road and made it even difficult to open the door. What should he do?

If he was unable to leave the house, he wouldn't be able to sell fresh milk and earn money. To make matters worse, it looked like the snowy weather would last for several days. Thinking of this, Bahati fell into despair.

While Bahati was feeling helpless, a sudden string of car horns sounded outside the yard.

"Brother, is the fresh milk ready?" It was Jiang who drove his car here.

"Yes, are you coming to give me a hand?" Bahati replied while helping Jiang pat the snow off his body.

"Yes, I came to help you. I guess you can't go out due to the heavy snow," said Jiang.

"Will it delay your work?" Bahati asked, feeling grateful.

"No, don't worry. It happens to be on my way," Jiang replied.

Soon they delivered the fresh milk to the milk purchasing station. Watching Jiang's figure disappear into the snow, Bahati was so moved with his lips trembling.

Bahati expressed his appreciation with exclamation when he realized how lucky he was to have such a good brother.

The snowy weather persisted for three days, but to Bahati's surprise, his brother Jiang helped him deliver fresh milk every day, ensuring that Bahati earned thousands of yuan by selling milk. Whenever talking about this, Bahati couldn't stop praising his good "brother" Jiang for his help.

Like sesame flowers blossom one by one, Bahati's life has gradually thrived. He has been able to raise more and more cows and sheep in his courtyard which has become brighter, cleaner, and more arranged. "To earn more money, you need to expand the number and variety of livestock. Additionally, you need to learn how to settle some general problems as well as how to treat common diseases of the livestock." Jiang was pleased with Bahati's successful start of the business, so he took him to a professional breeding farm to learn some expertise.

Bahati has a wit and interest in learning about new breeds of cattle and sheep. "Excellent breed cattle and sheep are the keys to wealth, and the professional knowledge is a guarantee of sustained prosperity." With the recommendation of his "brother" Jiang, Bahati often visited livestock breeding bases to learn artificial breeding technology of cattle and sheep from technical personnel.

In the past, Bahati needed to pay for the fees of sanitary examination of the fresh milk. However, he has learned the testing technology himself now and registered health certificates for each cow with the help of Jiang, which made him feel very proud and would show off to everyone, saying "My cows have health certificates!"

Each year, Bahati surprises everyone by achieving the impossible. The newly built house has been tidied up more and more beautifully, and the orchard has been yielding better harvests year by year. Then a vegetable garden has been built. Eventually, Bahati has opened a courtyard style farm stay to receive tourists.

What made Bahati most satisfied was that he could afford his wife's medical expenses and his two daughters' tuition fees. Additionally, he has got extra money to expand his family's side businesses and invest in other promising industries.

"Everything I enjoy now is out of the question without my brother's help," Bahati said as tears filled his eyes. He explained that his entire family enjoyed a promising future, thanks to his "kinship" with the Party's cadre.

Today, Bahati's courtyard is a lively and inviting place, with constantly bustling guests. Even the neighboring courtyards have become more beautiful with his help and influence.

Chapter 13

Brooks Converge to Rushing Rivers

"A cluster of thousands of pomegranate flowers press against the railing,

Like cutting the red silk into small pieces but forming a ball."

Bai Juyi depicted the unique and overwhelming beauty of pomegranate flowers vividly.

And that is the truth. When people talk about the natural beauty of Xinjiang, they always praise it unceasingly.

Perhaps because it has extraordinary and transcendent beauty,

Some malicious countries and forces try to distort it or even slander it.

The real Xinjiang is like the people in Kuertobe Village,

Who use their diligence and wisdom to transform the barren deserts and Gobi into oases and granaries,

Building modern socialist new countryside.

Even the children who studied far away start to return home,

Because their hometown is no longer poor or lonely,

Life there is becoming prosperous, and people would regret getting there late ...

In fact, there are many rivers in Tacheng, and the water in those rivers is particularly clear. Where the rivers flow, the grassland is exceptionally lush, and countless forests grow on hills and valleys. There are 13 well-known rivers with records in Tacheng, including 2 boundary ones. These rivers receive water not only from melting snow but also from the melting glaciers, forming their perpetual and rushing currents.

Tacheng belongs to the sub-alpine zone, with more than 1,360 glaciers of various sizes, covering an area of 1,160 square kilometers and having an ice storage capacity of 82 cubic kilometers. Among them, the longest one is the No. 52 glacier on the Harart River, which is located upstream of Bayingou River, with a length of 9 kilometers and an area of 39.6 square kilometers. Plentiful glaciers are making the Bayingou River, Gurtu River, Moto River, Manas River, Jingou River, Kuitun River, and Emin River in Tacheng abundant in water all year round, which also give green wings to the land along them, flying and dancing over the land in the western region of the motherland for dozens of centuries ...

The vicissitudes of history and nature tell us that where there are water and rivers, lives there will become affectionate and sentimental.

After I walked along the Jingou River, Emin River, and Kuitun River ... and explored every grassland, yurt, courtyard, and town in every county of Tacheng, I couldn't contain my excited mood and surging emotions anymore because I have discovered a remarkable "Tacheng Phenomenon": In those beautiful and peaceful villages, there have always been a well-respected "Bellwether" — just like why the vast and strong sheep herds on the grasslands never get lost, or the strongest winds at Laofengkou cannot separate the passing herds of cattle and horses.

I have long wanted to explore. I couldn't wait.

That day, after leaving Tacheng, the comrades from the Federation of Literary and Art Circles said they would take me to a beautiful village. Along the way, they didn't talk much about the village but rather the snow they experienced every winter —

"The snow has been terribly heavy. People in every house had to sweep the snow off their roofs, otherwise they might collapse ..."

"Every winter, whether at home or at work, as soon as it snowed, it was the first priority to sweep the snow. Usually, we started by sweeping it from our own rooftops, then we stepped out of the house and shoveled it on the way to work ... It was common for the snow on the road to be waist-deep, and you couldn't walk if you didn't clear it."

"Is it still like that now?" I asked.

"Well, people still have to sweep the snow on the roads, but they don't need to go on the roofs anymore ..." they answered.

Why?

"Well, you see, we don't have to go on the roofs every time it snows because we have the red roofs. Its triangular shape allows the snow to fall off naturally ...a major feature of the houses after the new rural development and renovations." They pointed to the red roofs both near and far, saying to me.

I noticed the red roofs after I arrived here, but didn't realize their purpose!

"The old mud houses with flat roofs were prone to collapse, while the new red-roofed ones can not only withstand wind and snow but also be attractive, so everyone likes them. Additionally, Tacheng is surrounded by vast grasslands, and the red houses look especially beautiful scattered in the green world ..."

Hey, it is truly beautiful. When people look far into the distance, such"Tacheng's scenery" brings a uniquely comfortable visual enjoyment. As we immersed ourselves in the beauty of the red and green combination in the fields and nature, the car suddenly stopped on an exceptionally wide asphalt road.

"Here is Kuertobe Village in the Asir Daur Ethnic Township, where Zhong Ping is serving as the village secretary, which is a model village of ethnic unity known in Xinjiang and nationwide ..." My companions from Tacheng told me proudly. I was amazed in heart: How could there be such a beautiful village like those in coastal areas in a place like Tacheng with a relatively backward economy in Northwest China?

Look, the straight and spacious main road in the village is a four-lane one, with lush and tall green trees shading both sides, like two rows of guards of honor welcoming guests. The road is clean and tidy, and the flowers naturally growing on both sides wave to the guests in the gentle breeze ... The most eye-catching sights are the buildings along the road with completely different yet harmonious styles, which are the red-roofed houses where the villagers live and the cooperative's pasture processing plants ...

The impressive administrative building of the village committee and the village square as big as several basketball courts all show that this village is "wealthy."

"The village is indeed wealthy, but more importantly, it has a good atmosphere of ethnic unity. Under the leadership of Secretary Zhong Ping, its development is getting better each year ... It has become an advanced model village in Tacheng and even in Xinjiang." As we continued walking, there was no shortage of stories about Zhong Ping and this village.

I was becoming more and more interested in interviewing them.

Zhong Ping appeared in front of us, who was a sturdy man. He said that most of the villagers including him were Daur.

"In the past, when we were poor, we often quarreled and fought to determine our status. If someone instigated a fight, it would be chaos. As living a better life, people now compare with each other about the sense of happiness and achievements, as well as contributions to the construction of the new village ..." Zhong Ping illustrated the spiritual realm of the Daur people in two different eras vividly.

Without unity, it's easy for people with ulterior motives to take advantages. When people are poor, it's even easier for bad people to manipulate the villagers. Zhong Ping may have a deeper and more painful understanding of it. When he was a teenager, every household in the village was poor. So when someone came and incited them, saying that life in another place was as good as being an emperor, many villagers would follow them and head north, only to end up with broken families and ruined lives. Later, someone else came to make trouble, saying that the Asir Township was a place where even cows and sheep wouldn't stay, while their Kuertobe Village was a "dry and dead land" where not even a mouthful of water could be dug out.

"Those people wanted the villagers to sell off their cropland at low prices, so they could forever control the villagers. That was why people in the past couldn't live a decent life. When life became unbearable, grievances and dissatisfaction would build up, and eventually, it would erupt like a volcano ..." Zhong Ping is a clear-headed Communist Party member. When he realized that his village was about to be buried in poverty, he resolutely returned to take on the role of village committee director.

It was in 1998.

From that year on, Zhong Ping put all his efforts into the development and construction of the village, right up until today ...

Though the journey was long, the rewards were abundant.

"In the past, we were poor because we didn't have water." Since becoming the director of the village committee, Zhong Ping's first priority was to address problems of drinking water and irrigation for the villagers.

According to ancient legends, there were "three springs" in Asir Township. Zhong Ping had heard it from his grandfather, but no one in the village, including his grandfather, had actually seen where the water was. In the past, villagers had to walk several miles to fetch water or carry water on horses. Even then, the water they used was other people's downstream water, and it was difficult to get clean water. During winter, the so-called water was just blocks of ice that needed to be melted in advance ... In days of water shortage, people's lives were unreliable, like trees uprooted.

In order to unite the villagers, the water problem had to be resolved first. But where was water in Kuertobe Village? Zhong Ping remembered that when he grazed cattle with his grandfather, he once told him where there would be water and where there definitely wouldn't be. Based on this memory, he boldly declared to all the villagers that he would hire a drilling team to dig a well.

"It will cost 300,000 yuan. The well will be worth drilling if we can get water!" Zhong Ping's words were immediately refuted with opposition, "The village still owes 500,000 yuan in debt. If the money were spent, but we still wouldn't find water, would you compensate for it yourself or let us repay it together with you?"

All the villagers stared at him, waiting for his response.

Zhong Ping gritted his teeth and said, "If the well drilling failed, I would repay the debt myself!"

"Did you hear that? Quickly bring a pen and paper to write it down ..." someone shouted.

For a farmer in a mountainous area, a debt of 300,000 yuan was equivalent to a death sentence. But Zhong Ping knew that his own life wasn't worth as much as water was to the entire village. So he made this choice without hesitation.

"When you have nothing, sometimes you have to take a gamble." This was Zhong Ping's life philosophy, in fact a helpless choice.

The drilling team arrived. Zhong Ping proposed a condition: if the team couldn't find water, they would only pay half the price; but if the team did find water, the price would increase by 50%.

"That's fair enough." The head of the drilling team accepted.

But where exactly would they dig the well? The drilling team said that they needed extra money to hire experts for exploration and positioning. Zhong Ping disagreed, saying that he didn't have extra money!

So what should they do? They were embarrassed.

Zhong Ping said, "I'll determine the location."

Everyone of the drilling team was surprised, "you? Have you studied water conservancy exploration?"

He shook his head. "No, I haven't."

"Then you're just kidding!"

"Who's kidding? When I herded cattle with my grandfather, I knew roughly where there was water in the village ..."

"Haha ... Is that so? Well, in that case, we have to make clear that if we can't find water, it can't be blamed on us, and the agreed-upon amount of project price should still be paid in full!"

"I understand that. I will take responsibility for the location I determined." Zhong Ping replied firmly.

Once the words are spoken, a man of noble character cannot change them at will. As the director of the village committee, Zhong Ping was naturally facing immense pressure. He began retracing the paths he took with his grandfather at young age and inspected every hill and piece of land. After he believed "there is water here", he invited experienced villagers to join him in assessing and discussing.

They concluded that there was a great hope to find water.

But it was just hope. Zhong Ping was still facing great pressure. "That's it! If we dig in the wrong place, I'll take all the blame!" Zhong Ping made up his mind. He was willing to exchange his own life for 300,000 yuan of debt in order to change the village's condition of no water supply.

"Let's start working!" On the open field, the opening ceremony for the drilling was quite solemn because it carried the hopes of the entire village and Zhong Ping's life.

Drilling ten meters a day, which was the speed for the first two days. Then it slowed down to five or six meters a day. As they encountered rocky terrain, the speed decreased, which made Zhong Ping's mind weighed down ...

It was already100 meters underground, but there was still no water. The drilling team was getting impatient and suggested stopping the work.

"No way! Keep drilling!" Zhong Ping got angry and the veins on his neck bulged.

"It'll incur higher costs if we keep drilling ... I think we should stop here and save some money."

"We don't need to save money now! If we give up, wouldn't the cost of drilling over 100 meters be wasted?" Zhong Ping said.

"That's true, but if we keep drilling and still don't find water, wouldn't the losses be even greater?"

"I'll bear the losses, to the end, with my own life!" Zhong Ping shouted at the top of his voice.

"Th-then ... let's keep drilling." The constructors were stunned by Zhong Ping's determination and frenzy.

The drilling machine continued to drill deeper ... 110 meters, 120 meters ...

"Look! Look! There is water coming out!" Suddenly, someone at the well platform shouted.

"Where is water? Where is it?" Zhong Ping was the most excited one. He rushed to the well, his body falling onto the edge of the well ...

"It's water! Water ..." Zhong Ping, in his 30s, cried like a child, unable to stop his tears.

Crystal-clear spring water gushed out of the barren hill, saving Zhong Ping's life, because if they dug a dry well, the debt of several hundred thousand yuan would have weighed Zhong Ping down in the future.

In fact, the water truly saved the entire village. "Zhong Ping, from now on, wherever you point, everyone in the village will follow your command. With your abilities, the village will surely prosper just like sesame blossoming!" Several "wise old men" in the village praised Zhong Ping. The young people, both boys and girls, followed Zhong Ping eagerly to inquire about when the water would reach each household.

"Before the New Year's Day, I promise that every family will have clean spring water and be able to take a proper bath ..." Zhong Ping assured everyone with a smile.

"Great — we'll be able to drink sweet water in the New Year!" On New Year's Day in 1999, Kuertobe Village ushered in an unprecedented festive atmosphere, because when this New Year came, thanks to Zhong Ping, every household would get sweet well water through pipes.

The Daur people pay more attention on cleanliness. But the Daur people in Kuertobe Village, for generations, had never truly enjoyed the clean and refreshing days they longed for. On the day the fresh water was supplied, several elderly men in their 80s held bottles of wine to drink with Zhong Ping heartily. It was on that day that they finally understood the true meaning of cleanliness — someone broke the news that a villager was unwilling to get out of the bathtub after spending a whole day in it.

After Kuertobe Village had water, many "folktales" and "legends" appeared, which made Zhong Ping convulsed with laughter. But he told people that the good days for the village were just beginning.

Indeed, water acted as a cohesive force, bringing together the previously scattered villagers. However, Zhong Ping noticed that although water had changed many of the villagers' habits and increased their enthusiasm for farming, the good days they envisioned seemed far from them. The reason was that while each family had plenty of farmland, their income was not much. Meeting basic needs was not a problem, but the journey to prosperity was still long.

"Besides the Daur, Kuertobe Village is also home to 8 more ethnic groups, including Russian and Kazakh. In the past, due to our poverty, conflicts among villagers were easy to occur. Because of different ethnic customs, there were significant differences in the understanding of labor and farming among the different ethnic groups. At that time, I noticed a problem: due to our small population and remote location in the entire township, coupled with the lack of water, the hilly and mountainous areas were abandoned. Although each villager had more allocated land, most of them couldn't fully utilize and cultivate their responsible fields, resulting in a significant amount of land wasted."

What should they do?

First, Zhong Ping approached a few prestigious elders and discussed his idea with them to see if it was feasible.

"This is a good thing! We sign up first!" The elders expressed their support for Zhong Ping's idea.

His idea was as follows: the village committee would borrow 3 acres of responsible land from each household and operate with them collectively.

The first lease period would be 10 years. The village committee would subcontract the farmland to neighboring large-scale farming households and entrepreneurs in the towns. After making a profit, the main portion would be distributed as dividends to the villagers who lent their land, while the remaining portion would be used for collective development, including paying off past debts.

"Before the first lease period was not even halfway through, not only did the villagers benefit greatly, but the collective economy of the village also started to recover," Zhong Ping pointed to their office building while mentioned how village meetings used to be held at his dining table in the past. "This office building was newly built a few years ago ..." Zhong Ping took me on a tour upstairs and downstairs, and I felt that even in villages along the eastern coastal areas, it would be difficult to find such impressive premises for villagers' affairs. It had everything needed, including a small bank, clinic, activity room for the elderly, study room for party and league members, and legal consultation room.

Kuertobe Village, on its way to achieving moderate prosperity, has already gathered people together, with desire for wealth and a better life stronger than ever, which encourage Zhong Ping, who has become the village secretary and committee director, to have ideas which are beneficial for the interests of the villagers and the development of the village.

"In Tacheng Prefecture, many of the people were nomadic, who were used to living separately. Even after joining collectives and production units after the establishment of New China, they would still build their houses wherever appropriate. As a result, villages were generally scattered and disorganized. Even if the village became rich, the cost of improving and installing public facilities would be high. Therefore, after accumulating a certain amount of fund, we started planning for the construction of a new rural area. In brief, we would build a main road that would connect every household, and the village would unify the planning, renovation, and refurbishment of everyone's living conditions and courtyards ... This project was unprecedented for our village. We hoped for its implementation, but we also faced some obstruction. For example, the expansion of the central road we see now encountered some specific problems, it was mainly that the homestead and yards of some villagers had to be removed to make room for the road."

The plan was good, but when it involved each specific household, the situation became somewhat complicated. So everyone stared at Zhong Ping, waiting to see how he would proceed this time. According to the posted planning map, a newly built house of Zhong Ping's father had to be demolished ...

"Who dares to demolish my new house?" Zhong Ping's father openly declared to the villagers.

"If he won't demolish his own house, how could he be able to demolish ours!" Someone followed to say.

Zhong Ping encountered a dilemma. He knew he had to convince his father first, as it was extremely important. Thus, a "contest" between father and son began —

"Dad, you know, the village is planning to construct a main road. It's not just about improving the appearance of the village, but also about allowing our village to move forward and attract investment, so as to make people live a better life. That's why we need everyone's support ..." the son said.

"This is a good thing, so I fully support it," the father responded.

"Dad, you've always been the biggest supporter of my work, so this time, you have to keep supporting me!"

"Of course," the father replied cheerfully.

"So, do you agree to demolish that house?" The son was getting to the point.

"Which one?" The father pretended to be confused.

"The one within the planned area ..."

"It's a new house, how can we demolish it?" The father's voice rose suddenly, and he stared at his son as if to say: What are you going to do? Do you want to demolish my new house?

"I know it's a new house. But it's in the planned area of road building, so it's in the way," the son explained.

"Can't it make a turn? Besides, can't the road be adjusted to fit the circumstances? Can't it be narrower?" the father suggested.

"That's not acceptable! How can it still be called a road like that!" the son retorted, speaking with the tone of the village secretary.

"Well, then, spare your chatter! Demolish my new house? No way!" The father stood up in anger and was about to leave.

"Dad —" The son also became anxious and stood up, grabbing onto his father's sleeve, coaxed him in a spoiled manner, "You've always been proud of me as the village secretary. Now, if you don't support me, does it mean you want me to step down and quit?"

Upon hearing that, the father stopped in his tracks, turned around, and scolded, "who said you should quit?"

"If you don't support me in doing such a thing that benefits the village and the villagers, then I might as well step down!" the son said pitifully.

"Is it that serious?"

"Of course! If the villagers see that I can't keep my word and even can't handle my own family affairs, how can I expect them to follow me in the future?" the son explained while observing his father's reaction.

The father thought for a moment and said, "That's the truth ..."

The son took the opportunity to flatter the father, "In the past when everyone praised my leadership, I always said that I couldn't have led the villagers in the right direction without the joint effort of everyone as well as the guidance and support from my dad."

The father's expression had changed significantly, showing a hint of pride, and then said, "So, are you saying we must demolish our new house?"

It seemed promising! The son's heartbeat quickened with excitement, and he added quickly, "Yes. Just think about it, if we don't demolish our house, how can I demolish others'?"

"Then we demolish it?"

"Yes, let's do it!"

After a moment of hesitation, the father swung his right hand and said, "Demolish it! Just ...do it!" Then, he walked away with a bit painful expression on his face.

"Dad ...thank you!" The son's eyes became a bit teary as he said these words.

At the end of the village, there was a lively scene: the villagers gathered around Zhong Ping's new house, watching him operating a bulldozer to demolish and clear away the newly built house and its foundation quickly ... What he did only took about an hour, but it left a tremendous impact on the villagers. "The village secretary himself demolished his own new house for the sake of building the road. What reason do we have not to cooperate and support the village's development?"

"That's right, being a decent person means considering the public good. We can't let our own selfish desires disrupt the pursuit of a better life for everyone!"

"Exactly, we should keep up with Secretary Zhong Ping ..."

As people expressed their thoughts, Zhong Ping became excited, and as a result, the road construction and the improvement of the house foundations proceeded smoothly. Especially after the completion of the road and the proper arrangement of the house foundation of each household, in accordance with the requirements of building a new rural area, the villagers could not help but admire the changes.

"It was in 2008. There was a heavy snowstorm in winter. We put in a lot of effort to build the road and tidy up the house foundations, but little did we know that the village, which was already in a wind-prone area, would be further tormented by natural disasters ... The rare heavy snow ended up with many villagers' houses collapsing. It was a great blow to everyone, and I felt heartbroken to see the new homes we had worked so hard on being destroyed by a single snowstorm," Zhong Ping said.

But what good did feeling heartbroken do? There were even rumors in the village, "It is because Zhong Ping disturbed the geomancy of the village that God got angry and punished us."

Sayings of superstitions should not be believed, but what people saw were real. In the past, houses being crushed by heavy snow happened frequently, but at that time, each household took care of its own affairs, and there wasn't much complaining. After the houses were crushed, they would simply say that they had bad luck and that was the end of it. Things were different now. After Zhong Ping proposed the idea of common prosperity, every major action in the village was carried out under the unified call of the village branch. Hence, some people started making such kind of comments.

"The fundamental solution is to prevent the villagers from getting hurt and losing their interests. So, after careful and arduous research, I decided to solve this problem from the root through collective efforts ..." Zhong Ping said.

"You mean replacing the roof, using red-colored roofing?"

"Yes. That year, I happened to visit my friends and relatives who were Daur in Northeast China. I saw that they used colored steel plates for their roofs, keeping warm while withstanding the weight of snow, and they looked really nice. These types of houses are already very popular there. So, after returning home, I discussed it with the village cadres and decided to fundamentally solve the problem of villagers suffering from snowstorms in the winter by initiating a renovation project for old houses in the whole village. When this idea was proposed, everyone was ecstatic, and there were hardly any objections ..." Zhong Ping explained to me.

In rural areas, whether in the relatively underdeveloped western regions or the more affluent eastern ones, houses are the most important assets for Chinese farmers. The number and quality of houses even affect matters of family succession and marriage prospects for boys, as in most rural areas, the bride's side primarily considers the condition of the bridegroom's house.

At that time, Zhong Ping wanted to renovate and rebuild all the houses in the village, with the new ones being both warm-keeping and aesthetically pleasing. Who would oppose that?

However, the absence of opposition didn't mean there weren't any difficulties. In Zhong Ping's words, he and the village cadres had exerted great effort to advance this project.

It was definitely about money, but opportunities were also crucial. Zhong Ping said he encountered "good luck" in this regard: there was a kiln factory in the village, and coincidentally, a businessman came to contract it for 10 years. "I was worried that there might be changes midway, so I proposed a condition that he could temporarily delay payment, but provide us with bricks. The contractor agreed. With these bricks, I started the renovation project for all the new houses here. Each household received a subsidy of 30,000 bricks. If it wasn't enough, they could buy more affordable bricks from the factory with their own money. But bricks alone wasn't enough to build houses, so we still need money for other materials and labor costs. Fortunately, the aid funds from

Liaoning Province were allocated at that time, providing 28,000 yuan per household. With the money and bricks, the renovation project went smoothly," when Zhong Ping talked about it, he was so happy and excited.

He mentioned that he had never seen the villagers so joyful and dedicated before ... "Everyone was working hard and sweating for their own new houses. It was so joyous and unforgettable," Zhong Ping said.

Actually, one thing Zhong Ping didn't mention was that during the first winter and the first Spring Festival in the new houses, the villagers sang and danced several days and nights in gratitude to the village cadres and to celebrate their new lives.

"Secretary Zhong got drunk several times during those days!" Some villagers whispered to me happily.

Zhong Ping's words left a deep impression on us. He said, "For ethnic minority areas on the border, if you make people live a better life, then there would be the greatest unity; when you make this land prosperous and affluent, it would undoubtedly be the most stable area." As a village secretary, he may not have a high level of theoretical knowledge, but these words contained profound and universal truth. Working in Kuertobe Village for decades, Zhong Ping has been tirelessly striving according to what he believes, advancing step by step towards the direction which is better and more in line with the interests of the villagers.

From 2009 to 2010, he successfully solved all the housing problems in the village, and the farmers' new homes with red-colored steel roofs in Kuertobe Village shone brightly across Tacheng and even Xinjiang — Especially these warm, solid, and beautiful houses with color steel roofs have become a model for other villages to learn from.

However, for Zhong Ping, there were still many things to do to achieve "unity" and "stability" in his mind.

After completing the new houses, Zhong Ping decided to build another brick factory in the village immediately. Half of the bricks would be sold to customers from neighboring villages who were enthusiastically learning to rebuild new houses, while the other half would be distributed to every household in the village to build fences around their own yards. After everything was done, the look of the village was greatly improved. Subsequently, the income of cattle and sheep-raising for each household also doubled.

Life kept getting better day by day. The young people who used to work outside gradually returned to their hometown. After returning, they started new businesses in the village, leading to rapid growth in animal husbandry and agriculture while the contact between Kuertobe Village and the outside world increased, with a continuous influx of merchants who came to contract cropland or purchase goods from the village ...

The economic returns have continuously brought benefits to all villagers. All expenses of medical care, social security, water and electricity usage, even garbage cleaning, health and fitness, learning and entertainment can be paid by the village!

What would villagers do with their increased income?

"They would buy houses and send their children to study in town ..." Zhong Ping said, "Now, at least one-third of the villagers have bought houses in town."

"In the past few years, more than 20 children from the village have gone to university and pursued postgraduate studies!" This number was what Zhong Ping and the whole village were most proud of, for there never had been a college graduate in the village before the year 2000.

There was another thing that made Zhong Ping and all the villagers proud: there were more and more brides from other places, and the intermarriage between different ethnic groups was also increasing.

"In the past, outsiders had a common perception of our Daurs, thinking that the people of Kuertobe Village were lazy and poor, so no girl wanted to get married here." Speaking of this, Zhong Ping, who was now over fifty, recalled when he was looking for a wife, feeling quite emotional. "My wife is from Sichuan Province. She came to our village because her hometown was also very poor. When we fell in love, her family disagreed for they heard that our village was mostly Daurs who were very poor and lazy. It wasn't until my wife took me to Sichuan and let her parents see for themselves if I was really poor and lazy that they finally agreed ..."

People in the village told me that Zhong Ping's three brothers also married Han girls, two of them from Sichuan Province and another from Hebei Province. "Later, people find out that we Daurs are not lazy at all, but very wealthy. So, the girls are willing to marry our villagers now!" Zhong Ping was very proud of it, even showing a bit smug.

He has a little sister who married a Hui man. Intermarriage between different ethnic groups is an important symbol and manifestation of ethnic unity and harmony. As a prosperous village, the intermarriage rate between different ethnic groups in Kuertobe Village increases every year.

"I am particularly pleased about this ..."

"Why?"

"Because our next generation will be smarter than us, and they will be able to accomplish even better than our generation."

These were Zhong Ping's last words to me during the interview.

As we left Kuertobe Village and traveled along the rural roads, we discovered that in the villages of Asir Township and its surrounding areas there were now clear water channels running alongside the roads. They were flowing with a gurgling sound, heading towards the places in need ...

This is actually the most thrilling sight of the desert and hills in Tacheng and even in Xinjiang. Because people here told me that Xinjiang

"Indeed, when I was a child, my grandfather always told us to follow the directions of the Party and Chairman Mao, because it was the leadership of the Communist Party that brought us happiness and peaceful lives and gave us a beautiful homeland. So, we should love the Party and our country ... We have grown up under the effect of such thought. Now that we have taken over the baton of building our hometown from our parents, we understand the profound meaning of what our elders said: Without the Communist Party and PRC, there wouldn't be beautiful Xinjiang or our happy homeland!" Amaguli said.

An eagle is flying over the grassland, while a flower gives out fragrance in the garden. The villagers said that they were fortunate to have Amaguli as their "bellwether", who was a beautiful and ideologically progressive girl leading their way to achieve their ethnic unity and construct their new village.

"Today's Xinjiang is different from that in the time of Captain Ashan and my grandfather. People's aspirations for a better life have become more specific and enriched. Our work standards and requirements should keep up with the country's development and the pace of the times rather than only focus on people's basic needs. We hope everyone to have not only a more prosperous life but also an enriched and healthy spiritual world. As a cadre of the village committee, I always take Captain Ashan's spirit of hardworking and my grandfather's deeds of uniting various ethnic brothers and sisters as my work standards and requirements. I hope to let everyone from various ethnic groups enjoy the kindness of the Party and government like bathing in sunshine and dew, while the Party branch will play its core role as solid as a 'hitching post,' providing a foundation for the people to live and work in peace, create a better life, and embrace future hopes ..." Amaguli, since taking office a few years ago, has always remembered her sacred duty as a Communist Party member. Despite her young age, she has great determination and a sense of direction when it comes to work. She has focused on Party building work and planning, coming up with new ideas every year that has benefited the villagers.

"Just like her name, Amaguli is bringing a breath of fresh air to the whole village. When she took office, she proposed the development goal of 'clearing debts in two years, having surpluses in three years, and surpassing the advanced villages and teams in five years.' Look, now only three years passed, but the goals she set have already been achieved ahead of time!" The villagers gave her compliments generously in front of me.

Several indicators are milestones for a village like Upper Jal Agash: All the impoverished households there has been lifted out of poverty ahead of schedule, and the per capita annual income of the villagers has increased from 8,000 yuan to over 17,500. In 2019, 7-kilometer long courtyard walls and over 20 dilapidated houses between villages were completely renovated. The kitchens, toilets, and yards in every house have taken an entirely new look, up to preliminary urban standards ... Don't underestimate these changes; they are truly earth-shattering for the border residents living far away from cities.

> Dare to turn the wasteland into a fertile field,
> Swear to turn the deserts into an oasis.
> Sunlight sprinkles on people's hearts,
> Soft songs and graceful dances bring eternal springs.

This is a poem written by the villagers exhibited in the "Folk Culture Industrial Park" of Narencha Khan Kule Village, reflecting the joyous mood of the villagers in their happy lives.

"Mr. He came from Beijing and has broad knowledge and experience. Now, please give us valuable suggestions for our village's 'Folk Culture

Industrial Park' ..." At the end of the interview, the publicity officer of the Town led me to the entrance of the Park, hoping that I would tour and give them some advice.

At first, I didn't take it seriously, but when I entered the Park, I couldn't help but exclaim inwardly: I almost overlooked this "treasured place".

In the developed coastal areas and my hometown of Suzhou, Jiangsu Province, there have been many "featured industrial parks" and "village-themed parks"during the construction of beautiful countryside and rural revitalization in recent years. But I never expected to see similar "cultural scenic areas" and "featured industrial parks" in remote western border villages. This may be more exciting than hearing a few abstract data concepts like "poverty alleviation" because "cultural richness is true wealth" and "industrial prosperity is the real flourishing of life." After visiting the "Folk Culture Industrial Park" in the village, I could feel its abundant natural resources, foreseeing the prospects of industrial and cultural development throughout Emin County that I passed through on my journey.

The beauty of the red rose is cultivated by the sunshine and rain.
Its fragrance can't be controlled, which makes the poet intoxicated.

This was from a poem written by Yang Wanli, a poet of the Song Dynasty, in praise of roses.

There is a place called Bayimuzha Grassland, located 100 kilometers east of Emin County on the China-Kazakhstan border, which is as beautiful as a paradise. If we compare it to West Lake in Hangzhou City, the former is like a noble and beautiful princess, while the latter, a pretty girl from the countryside. If you don't believe me, then you can observe it in my words:

Naturally, the most dazzling is definitely the Bayimuzha Grassland itself, which is more like a vibrant garden with countless flowers than simply a meadow land. There is a mesmerizing valley of wild roses, nestling deep in a gorge. In the middle of it, a narrow passage allows vehicles to reach the area known as the "Rose Valley." In June and July, when wildflowers are in full bloom, people sitting in a car and traveling through it would feel like wandering in a heavenly realm. The roses extending for dozens of miles give us a sudden feeling of being in a romantic and passionate Eden. There is scent of flowers everywhere, and even your breath feels fragrant ... The roses in the valley exude elegance and beauty, enveloped in infinite love, easily evoking dream-like imaginations. As it is a primitive valley, besides various types of roses, there are also countless unknown wildflowers, displaying their unique charm and vitality. Since it is a valley, it is accompanied by mountains, forests, meadows, and streams, giving the Rose Valley a transcendent and natural atmosphere, attracting guests from afar with its unique charm.

Therefore, I believe that when you come to Tacheng, to Emin County, if you miss it, you will lack a real understanding of this land. To talk about ethnic unity and explore the simplicity and kindness of the folk customs here, you must experience the Rose Valley to understand why the people of different ethnic groups here can naturally be friendly and united. Since ancient times, they have integrated their lives into nature and become a part of it. This is so important, and it is the essence of life!

What I must mention is the Bottomless Lake in Bayimuzha. In a mountain pass between Mt. Tarbagatai and Mt. Urcashal, there hides an oval-shaped lake. Although its area is less than 10,000 square meters with no water flowing in or out, it is unfathomably deep, so the local people call it the "Bottomless Lake." In the summer, it appears with a deep blue color, but strangely, there are no signs of any living creatures, no fish or shrimp can be seen. It is more puzzling that the nearby Bayimuzha River is fresh water, while the water in the lake is salty. Another interesting feature is that the water level of the lake remains constant throughout the year, maintaining its "eternal" state. There is a legend saying that during the westward expedition led by Fan Lihua(a fictional female general in the Tang Dynasty), she set up camps here, who accidentally dropped her comb and mirror, which turned into this expanse of a clear and deep lake. Many tourists try to see their own reflection in the lake, for the clarity is several times higher than that of a SLR camera. If you don't believe it, you can try it yourself.

The most remarkable things in Emin County, in Tacheng, and even in northwest China, are the well-known "One Grassland at Waterside" and "One Spring". The "one Grassland at Waterside" refers to the Kulustai Grassland located in the Tacheng Basin. Located in the southern part of Tacheng city, it is called the "Nanhu(Southern Lake) Grassland" by the locals. "Kulustai" means "reed shoal" in Mongolian, so it is proudly referred to as their "One Grassland at Waterside".

The Nanhu Grassland is vast, surrounded by Yumin County, Emin County, Toli County, and Tacheng City, spanning 76 kilometers from east to west and 36 kilometers from north to south, with a total area of 3.89 million mu. The available grassland covers 3.15 million mu, making it the second largest contiguous plain grassland and the largest high-quality grassland in Xinjiang.

Kulustai is a low-lying area.Compared to other parts of Tacheng, it is the "bottom" of the Tacheng Basin, hence earning the name "Tacheng Treasure Bowl".

Where there is water, there is vegetation. With abundant vegetation, livestock thrives, and the people here who dominate all of these are especially proud and outstanding. Especially during springtime in Kulustai, the grass grows lush, wildflowers bloom, clear water flows, and fragrant scents fill the air, truly creating a refreshing and pleasant atmosphere.

In the heartland of the Kulustai Grassland, there is a place inhabited by the Kazakh people called "Moyinta," which means "big forest" in Kazakh. There, ancient willow trees stretch for over 10 kilometers, towering and dense, each with its unique shape. It is said that these ancient willows have a lifespan of three to four hundred years, making them extremely precious and rare. In such a vast forest, this multi-ethnic village thrives with generations after generations living harmoniously, leading a life akin to an idyllic paradise.

"Do you want to go to New York? To live in houses with gardens and high-rise buildings?" A Western journalist once tempted the villagers with these words. The villagers smiled and shook their heads, saying, "We have heard of New York and seen it on TV. A place like New York is similar to Shanghai or Shenzhen, but there is only one Kulustai in Emin County, in Tacheng, and in the world. That's why we love it and won't leave it. Our lives naturally flourish here, healthily and happily ..." Later, the journalist published their words in European newspapers, as a result, Kulustai and the people there became famous instantly ...

Emin County has another "Pearl" growing high in the center of Mt. Urcashal. As there are many springs, the locals call it "Quan Yan(mouth of a spring)" or "Menblac" in Kazakh.

The Grassland is located on the top of a mountain, so it is also known as the "Grassland in the Air". Menblac is an alpine grassland with an average altitude of over 2,300 meters, and an annual average temperature of only about 5 degrees Celsius. In winter here, it is extremely cold, with the average snow cover of over 1 meter. In summer, influenced by the southeast monsoon and warm airflow from the south slope, there is abundant rainfall and unusual weather changes. Even during the hot summer days, it remains cool and pleasant here. The grassland on the high mountain boasts lush and diverse vegetation, it is no exaggeration to say that the cattle and sheep here "drink natural mineral water and eat golden grass". There are over 300 springs on the grassy plateau spanning over 300 square kilometers. Therefore, every summer, more than 20,000 herders from 12 townships in Emin County gather here from different directions to let over 500,000 head of cattle and sheep enjoy the tasty grass as well as the fresh air of the "natural oxygen bar"for the whole summer time.

The "Grassland in the Air" is not only a place for cattle and sheep to enjoy but also a scenic spot for travelers. The roads from Tacheng and Emin County to Menblac are rugged and perilous, especially the winding and precipitous gorge where the path sometimes seems impassable and sometimes reveals hidden beauty. The mountain tops are covered in colorful wildflowers, swaying in the wind like charming young girls, which are really enticing.

There are two pastures in the "Grassland in the Air", mainly inhabited by Kazakh and Mongolian herders, who live harmoniously and treat each other like family. They herd, cook, sing and dance together, and share happy occasions and responsibilities together ...

These are the scenery and customs of the valleys and grasslands in Tacheng and Emin County, reflecting mutual respect and love between nature and all living things that are coexisting, just like what I have seen in the villages and towns I visited.

Chapter 15

The Couple, the frontier

Every time I go to the border,

I will have a strong respect for the boundary markers standing there.

They are a symbol of national dignity, a sign of national territorial integrity,

They also represent the concept of "motherland" in the eyes of every citizen.

The boundary markers survive with the country; the more powerful the country is, the more imposing the boundary markers are.

We often refer to a nation as a "warm land" because people sacrifice their warm blood on it.

They cast the border as sturdy as steel with their ordinary life.

With such enthusiastic people, is the great land of the country still worried about not being energetic?

With such ordinary people, is the country still worried about not being robust and united?

Upon my arrival in Tacheng, I was told constantly about two individuals: Bashibai Qiaolake Baping and Wei Deyou. Bashibai Qiaolake Baping was a Kazakh who had passed away, while Wei Deyou, a Han, is a prominent figure of Touching China.

Unexpectedly, while I was on my way to interview Wei Deyou, I happened to "meet" Bashibai, a landmark he built that always stands on the land of Tacheng, a bridge on the Emin River connecting Tacheng and Yumin symbolizing national unity. People named it "Bashibai Bridge" after Bashibai to commemorate his remarkable achievements.

Bashibai Bridge, surrounded by lush greenery, began to be constructed in 1941. Before that, there had been no bridge across the Emin River, making it inconvenient for traveling.

One day in 1940, Bashibai was passing by when he came across a poor herder who was being brutally beaten by a wealthy man for not being able to pay the ferry fee. Bashibai was extremely angry and warned the bully, "You won't prey on the poor anymore next year !"

Next year, Bashibai invited Soviet bridge design experts and Zhao Jianfeng, then the chief executive of Tacheng, to supervise the project.

The bridge was completed on July 31, 1942. The main body of the bridge was made of wood, 87 meters long and 6 meters wide, 25 tons in load capacity, with a total cost of 55,000 yuan. The bridge is a convenience for people of all ethnic groups living on both sides. In honor of Bashibai, the locals named it after him, and it is now known as "Bashibai Bridge."

Bashibai passed away in 1953, leaving an indelible mark on the land and in the hearts of the people. He was a patriotic and enlightened Kazakh who served as the first administrative commissioner of the Tacheng District after the founding of New China.

In Tacheng, "Bashibai" is ubiquitous. some people say that he warmed every person who grows up here like sunshine.

If you take the time to observe the pasture of Tacheng, you will notice a special breed of sheep known as the "Bashibai Sheep". These sheep are physically robust, with a thick and clear coat, and are known for their delicious meat. They are a renowned breed in Tacheng, as well as in western China. It's believed that Bashibai himself developed this breed.

According to the locals, Bashibai started animal husbandry as an adult in 1919 after he lived apart from his parents. He began with a herd of 150 sheep and some horses. To develop fine varieties of sheep, he studied breeding techniques from various experts. With his intelligence, hard work, and persistence, he succeeded in breeding a type of big-tailed sheep with a red-brown coat color. These sheep have good quality meat and thick wool and also mature earlier than ordinary sheep. They can endure extreme cold or dry weather conditions and digest coarse fodder, making them suitable for breeding in the Gobi desert region of Xinjiang.

Naturally, these sheep are known as a fine breed for their quick growth period of about 120 days, high net meat percentage of up to 56%, and a one-fourth bone-to-flesh ratio. With these desirable characteristics, they have become popular among herders in Tacheng. Since the founding of New China, the government has supported the breeding of Bashibai sheep, which has helped it become a well-known brand in Yumin County and has played a significant role in the local animal husbandry industry.

Bashibai's shepherd business peaked in the 1940s and 1950s, with more than 25,000 sheep, besides which he had countless horses, cattle, and camels.

Bashabai, a local of Tacheng, had achieved great wealth through is super huge with many deserts, Gobi, and barren lands. If there is water, those places will become the most fertile land and the most hopeful home with the most beautiful scenery.

In fact, there are already many places like this in Tacheng and Xinjiang. A clear and warm stream flows quietly there, continuously nurturing people's hearts. It is the love of Communist Party members and people with love in their hearts, who use the sacred spring of their noble souls to shower love upon the villagers. And it has made countless once barren and desolate places grow flowers and fruits with herds of cattle, sheep and horses running freely, and clusters of "red-roofed houses" ...

Compared to Zhong Ping's Kuertobe Village, the Kuerblack No.3 Village in Shanghu Townhad truly made the Village Secretary Jiang Xiaoming so worried that his hair turned white overnight.

It was the story when Jiang Xiaoming first took office.

Kuerblack No.3 Village was also a village lack of water. Among the 162 households, 97% were Kazakhs, and out of 538 villagers, there were 206 registered impoverished individuals, with nearly half of them being elderly, weak, sick, or disabled. Just like the people in other pastoral areas of Tacheng, they lived in severe coldness throughout the year with wind and snow, and due to lack of water, the yield of their farmlands couldn't meet their basic survival needs. As a result, they could only survive on herding in harsh, humid, or arid fields. With such conditions, the number of sick and disabled individuals naturally remained high. On average, each family has one disabled member. Thus, the words "happiness" and "contentment" were far from the village.

Jiang Xiaoming was previously the branch secretary of the Wubale No.4 Village who was so capable that he changed the appearance of the village in less than 3 years. That was why he was transferred to his current position as the secretary of Kuerblack No.3 Village in 2019. The intention of the government was very clear: Kuerblack No.3 Village, a poor and dispute-ridden village, urgently needed to be changed.

With such a poor condition but numerous disputes, where exactly did the problems lie? This was the most important thing Jiang wanted to figure out when he first arrived there.

According to his interviews and investigations, he found out that the most prominent problem was that the 162 households had been leasing their 11,500 mu of farmland at low prices to others, thus keeping the label of poverty firmly on their heads.

Land is the lifeline of farmers. At the beginning of the reform and opening up, in order to help farmers across the country get rid of poverty and stimulate the enthusiasm of hundreds of millions of them, the great revolution of "distributing lands to households" and "household responsibility system" was carried out. Later, with the development of society, it was allowed for farmers to transfer their land through various forms to large-scale farmers or collectives. However, the premise was that the transfer of land must allow the original owners - the farmers - to obtain the most basic living benefits and development possibilities. If these two points were not met, then transferring the land would be equivalent to depriving the farmers' original right to survival.

Kuerblack No.3 Village was facing such kind of problem. The powerful contractors had placed the original owners of the land in a weak position.

"The practice that does not bring more and better benefits to the owners of the land must be corrected. No matter how much resistance there is, the village committee must take a firm stand!" After Jiang Xiaoming understood the critical issue which made villagers poor, he made a firm statement during the village branch and village committee meetings. Ultimately, a plan was formulated to reclaim their lands.

"Who is he? He's only been here for a few days and he already tries to break the rules of the past?"

"Let's smash his damned head!"

As soon as the land reclamation plan was announced, several individuals who had been benefiting from contracting the villagers' lands became arrogant and made threatening remarks.

"Since I'm here, you can talk to me directly. The plan to reclaim the land is made to rectify the unreasonable practices in previous land transfers that have adversely affected the interests of all the villagers. The decision aligns with the policies of the country and the Party. You can voice your opinions, but you cannot refuse to implement the plan of the village." Jiang Xiaoming fearlessly approached the contractors who were clamoring to smash his head.

"We have an agreement with the village. If now you want to tear it up, then you must compensate us!" Since they dared to shout aloud, they certainly weren't weaklings. They presented their "ironclad evidence" to Jiang Xiaoming.

Jiang was well prepared for this and smiled as he said, "The village committee always operates within the bounds of law and order, so we won't act recklessly. The new land reclamation plan is not meant to tear up the original agreement but rather adjust its unreasonable parts. You can take a closer look, the original agreement clearly stated that the village-level organization has the authority to adjust the terms of the contract based on situations that are detrimental to the original land owners ... I kindly urge you all to study the agreement carefully!"

Is that so? Is there such a term? The contractors panicked. After they finished reading the terms of the agreement, one of them shouted angrily, "Fine, you can take back the land, but you must compensate us double for our investment in the land over the years! If you don't, we will sue!" Their arrogance still prevailed.

"Is it ? If we have to compensate you for your investment, then shouldn't you also compensate for the damage you have caused to the land? Which is greater, the annual income you have gained from the land or the investment you have made in the land?"

"Well ..."

Jiang Xiaoming's well-founded work had successfully advanced the plan to reclaim contracted land, and the whole village has reissued contracts for ten thousand acres of land. Each household benefits more than before, which has also reassured the large-scale land contractors.

Land is the lifeline of farmers. As the land vitalizes, the rural areas thrive.

The adjustment of land contracting practice by Jiang Xiaoming immediately brought about a change in the spirit of the entire village. Subsequently, the village also paid for cooperative medical care expenses and endowment insurance for all villagers, addressing the long-standing burden of healthcare and retirement. According to the villagers, these two measures were getting rid of the "two ice cubes pressing on their heads", and they "felt like the sun shining upon them" ...

However, just like our ten fingers, there are bound to be differences in different people, such as personality, customs, habits and hobbies. If not careful, disputes can easily arise. Grassland herders are forthright by nature, but they can also easily become fiery when provoked. If not dealt with in a timely and meticulous manner, it can ignite fierce troubles.

Kuerblack No.3 Village used to be known as the "village of troublesome people" due to these reasons.

"From now on, we must ensure that small disputes are resolved within the households while major disputes are resolved within the village. The party branch and village committee should bear primary responsibility for this goal." Jiang stated during the village cadres meeting. He also set responsibility target for himself.

The disputes of the villagers were primarily related to their interests and mood. In order to address the issues, corresponding approaches were needed, i.e. timely and effective ideological work and relevant economic services. Therefore, Jiang Xiaoming, with the support of entrepreneurs he knew in Emin County, established a "Pomegranate Seeds Charity Team" and invested a certain fund. The charity team was led by respected individuals in the village, along with village cadres and enthusiastic people with expertise in various fields. In addition to the support from entrepreneurs, all funds for the charity were voluntarily donated by village cadres and residents. Jiang Xiaoming's efforts yielded impressive results. Within a couple of weeks, the charity fund raised over 100,000 yuan. With the sum of money, the "Pomegranate Seeds Charity Team" solved the problems of providing heating equipment and coal supply for 16 impoverished households like Beshan Ati's, and provided living supplies in urgent need to 10 households with congenital disabilities like Hasenlikhan Samat's.

"Why should I go to village cadres' homes to cause troubles? I won't do it anymore! Secretary Jiang and the village have relieved my from winter hardships, providing me with meat, and even sent me consolation money. What else should I complain about? Tomorrow, I will apply for work in the village!" This is what the former "Lao Lai (deadbeat)" in the village now tells people. What's even more interesting is that some people used to cause trouble during festive occasions in the past, hoping for gaining benefits, but now, having been educated by this "Lao Lai",they would blush with embarrassment, giving up such bad practice.

"It is crucial and fundamental to improve people's livelihoods in order to solve the problem concerning ethnic unity." Jiang believed that almost all disputes in rural areas stemmed from specific livelihood issues. Only by solving and handling these problems in a meticulous manner can other disputes naturally be resolved.

In the past, there was a high number of elderly, weak, sick, and disabled individuals in the village. In winter, when heavy snow blocked the ways, villagers had more time for idle chatter. When spring arrived and the snow melted, able-bodied laborers would go out to work on farming or grazing, so no one in the village was willing to put in extra effort to take care of the sanitation of the village. As a result, it looked dirty and messy, becoming a typical example of poor village cleanliness in the town.

"We can establish a cleaning team with the elderly as the main members. In this way, we can provide jobs for the elderly and disabled who can still work so that they can earn some money too! The village will pay them, and everyone can work together to maintain the cleanliness of our own village!" After proposing this idea, Jiang Xiaoming immediately received a positive response from the villagers. Afterward, according to the actual situation, the village arranged for elderly or disabled individuals from 24 impoverished families to join the cleaning team. Each cleaning worker may receive a salary of 1000 yuan per month.

"In the past 30 years, I complained because no one thought of giving disabled people a means to earn a living. Now that I have food to eat, even get a good meal, and don't starve anymore, why should I keep complaining?" The former "troublemaker" in the village later became a key member of the cleaning team, who worked diligently every day, eager to make some contributions. Under his influence, all the cleaning workers performed their tasks with great responsibility. As a result, Kuerblack No.3 Village is now clean and tidy every day, transforming into a civilized new village of the town and the county.

The differences between villages are like those between fields, it is clearly inevitable. From the perspective of economic strength, Kuerblack No.3 Village, where Jiang Xiaoming currently serves as the village secretary, is indeed not comparable to Kuertobe Village led by Zhong Ping. The difference is that Zhong Ping started serving as the village leader in the mid-1990s and has been leading the villagers on the path to prosperity. Jiang Xiaoming did not have such an opportunity before. It was only in 2019 that he was transferred to Kuerblack No.3 Village, a poverty-stricken village with more problems. However, the changes that Jiang Xiaoming has brought to the village after being there for one year have deeply touched the villagers.

"Compared to affluent villages, we are a bit poorer, but the hearts of the village cadres are close to ours, and we feel extremely warm. How can we worry about barren land not growing grass?" What the villagers said also greatly encouraged Jiang Xiaoming and other village cadres. On the one hand, they fully tap into the existing resources and focus on the development of agriculture and animal husbandry production. On the other hand, through continuous and thoughtful ideological work, they help families or villagers with practical difficulties, providing warmth and assistance when needed ...

Domestic affairs are trivial and complicated, and some may suddenly arise which cannot be anticipated in advance. Jiang Xiaoming, through targeted assistance between each cadre and the registered impoverished households as well as comprehensive assistance measures with the "Pomegranate Seeds" fund, has promptly solved any potential problems or disputes that the villagers might face. At the same time, he would personally take on the difficulties, so that they could be solved quickly and effectively.

Yerkenbek Altan is raising his grandson who is still attending school as his son died of illness, and what's even worse is that he had a car accident, resulting in physical disabilities, which added insults to injury. With only 20,000 Yuan of grazing fee for 30 sheep as their main source of income, it is clear that they are living on a tight budget.

"Big brother, just treat me as your younger brother, and let me shoulder any difficulties in the family together with you!" Jiang Xiaoming thought about it and decided to personally take on the difficulties faced by Yerkenbek's family.

"My good brother! You, you take on things that shouldn't be your responsibility. What can I say?" Yerkenbek tearfully looked at Jiang Xiaoming as Jiang repeatedly helped solve his problems.

Just a few days after Jiang took his role as a "younger brother," a "younger sister" Tsilykha Carcass, a widow from previous years, suddenly collapsed in the field. It turned out that her husband had left a debt of 40,000 yuan before his death, and now she has to bear the living expenses and tuition fees for her two school-age children on her own. Tsilykha lives a frugal life and her health has been deteriorating. That day, she finally collapsed in the field due to exhaustion.

"Save her life first!" Jiang Xiaoming rushed to the scene and took her to the hospital with other villagers without hesitation.

"Who is the patient's family? Sign here quickly." The doctor asked.

"I'll sign, I'll sign!" Jiang Xiaoming picked up the pen and was about to sign his name on the admission form.

"Are you her husband?"

"Me? No, no ... I'm her brother," Jiang Xiaoming said on the spur of the moment.

"Then sign and pay the expenses."

"Alright, alright."

The position of being her "big brother" had been settled. Jiang paid 1000 yuan on the spot, and then spent over 2000 yuan buying various things before and after her discharge.

"Secretary, how can I repay you?" Tsilykha's eyes were red on the day of her discharge, murmuring.

"Ah, don't worry about it. Go home now, the children are waiting for you!" Jiang Xiaoming said.

"But I'm sick. I don't want to burden you, Secretary ..." Tsilykha still felt apologetic.

"Dear sister, didn't you hear the hospital staff calling me your brother all these days? Since I am your brother now, stop talking about repaying me! Just go home!"

"Brother ..." Tsilykha suddenly shouted at him in a loud and affectionate way.

Jiang Xiaoming was momentarily stunned, but then a happy and cheerful smile bloomed on his face. "Ah! Sister, let's go home!"

Go home.

Go home.

How great it is to go home!

How nice it is to have a good and beautiful home!

How great it is to live in a united, peaceful, tidy and beautiful home every day!

The villagers of Kuerblack No.3 Village rejoice and feel fortunate from the bottom of their hearts that they now have a homeland that makes them proud and happy.

"We want to go home!" This is the heartfelt and passionate exclaiming of 27 college students who have left Kuerblack No.3 Village to study outside with the village's subsidies every year. Their youthful, resounding, and powerful voices resonate around Mt.Tianshan, like a clear stream traversing Gobi and grasslands, converging into rivers and flowing ceaselessly forward ...

Chapter 14

The Pomegranate Seeds in Narencha Khan Kule Village ...

Indeed, the pomegranate seeds in Narencha Khan Kule Village are truly beautiful.

Its beauty lies in the presence of the village head, Ashan, who had the honor of meeting Chairman Mao, and in the flag

Fluttering with the "Ashan Spirit" that shines bright in the village today.

There are many legendary and dazzling villages like Narencha Khan Kule in Tacheng and throughout Xinjiang.

Their common feature is that after getting rid of poverty and becoming prosperous,

They have achieved continuous enrichment in culture and spirit.

There, you can not only enjoy the picturesque scenery of the vast grasslands, the abundant flowers in the depths of the pastures,

The modern and well-equipped homes, and the brand-new tents of the herdsmen,

But also find surprisingly the cafes and amusement parks at the foot of snow-capped mountains along the flowing streams ...

Here is the home of the people in Xinjiang after getting rich.

And here is today's Xinjiang, which has entered a modern and happy life in sync with the eastern coastal cities!

After leaving Cao Zhenxin's house, the people of Jal Agash Town in Emin County warmly invited me to visit a village called "Ashan", saying that since I was there, I must visit their new village. To be frank, at that time, I had some "doubts":I am from Suzhou, Jiangsu Province, and I have traveled extensively throughout the country, especially in the Jiangsu and Zhejiang regions. What kind of modern new villages that I haven't ever visited? Is there any new village worth seeing in Xinjiang?

However, what I thought was completely wrong. This village, which is called "Ashan," although "hidden" in the hills, is no less beautiful and prosperous than the new villages in Jiangsu and Zhejiang regions. The beauty of its natural scenery goes without saying — you can see the famous Mt. Tarbagatai in Tacheng, surrounded by the picturesque Jal Agash Pasture. More importantly, the road leading to Ashan Village and the beauty of the greenery and flowers on its sides are even more captivating than those in the south of the Yangtze River. Furthermore, the pastures and the houses are well organized, which are neat and beautiful, with appearances that can even rival starred hotels. Inside the village, there are high-end tourist attractions called "Mujiale" (ranch stay)and dining stations sponsored by the assistance project of Liaoning Province, which are on par with those similar tourist reception facilities in Jiangsu, Zhejiang, and Shanghai ...

Ashan Village is a famous "Typical Case" in Xinjiang, which gained its fame in the 1950s. When the cadres of Emin County showed me around, they introduced it to me all the way, especially when we visited the showroom in the village cultural activity center. Only then did I know that when the village was just established in the 1950s, a poor Kazakh farmer named Ashankake Yiman was elected as the captain of the Narencha Khan Kule Production Team because the villagers' trusted him. Ashan was a kind-hearted Kazakh man who had always been able to unite and care for others since he reached adulthood. It was said that on a stormy night, several herders from different ethnic groups were stranded by the heavy snow together with Ashan on their way. For the snowstorm was strong, they were blocked for quite some time, if they went out individually, anyone could have been in danger at any moment. At that moment, Ashan extended his arms and said, "If we stand apart, we may be blown away by the stronger winds and snow. But if we hold hands and stand together like pomegranate seeds, even if we get blown down and roll out tens or even hundreds of meters, as long as we stay together, our lives won't be in danger." In this way, the herders caught Ashan's hands, holding arms with each other, sticking it out until the snow storm no longer raged ...

After becoming the captain of the production team, Ashan had always emphasized the unity among the villagers, propelling the village forward on the socialist path and making it one of the advanced villages in Xinjiang in the early years of the People's Republic of China(PRC).

In 1964, Captain Ashan went to Beijing as one of the representatives for the advanced ethnic villages,who was warmly received by Chairman Mao Zedong. It was a grand gathering of national unity, a great honor for Ashan personally, and a source of pride for the entire village. So, after Captain Ashan returned to his hometown, the photo of him and Chairman Mao was hung in the center of the village committee house as a symbol of their unwavering faith and commitment to following the Communist Party of China. Once, when some ethnic separatists had came to the village to plot something, Ashan and the villagers pointed to the photo and told them, "We are Chinese, and here is Narencha Khan

Kule Village in socialist China. Nothing can change it, no matter what happens." The separatists had no choice but to leave dejectedly.

During the three-year famine, some people died of starvation, including those who ran to the village from other places and those who left the village, which left an indelible impression on Ashan. As the time of difficulties ended, he led the villagers to carry out a battle to reclaim agricultural land from the deserts in order to let the villagers from different ethnic groups live a happy life of peace and contentment forever ...

"At that time, under the leadership of our captain, we worked from dawn till dusk, cultivating farmland in the deserts, digging channels to bring water from the mountains. We successfully transformed the low-yield fields of the Gobi desert into a grain depot renowned around Mt.Tianshan." Several elderly villagers told me that it was because of this, their village came to be known as "Ashan Village", namely "the Village of Captain Ashan".

"Ashan was our captain, but he was more like our patriarch, a symbol of unity among different ethnic groups. When he was alive, everyone in the village listened to him and voluntarily engaged in the socialist construction with him. After he passed away, the villagers have inherited and developed his hard-working entrepreneurship and friendliness of unity as the spiritual wealth of the village year by year, so that's why we are enjoying a prosperous and happy life today." At the village cultural square, villagers dressed in colorful traditional costumes approached me when they heard that I was from Beijing, pouring out their commemoration and gratitude for Captain Ashan.

"Ashan's son, Kabian Ashankake, is also a remarkable young man, who is also kind-hearted and caring like his father." The villagers told me a story emotively. There was an elderly Han man named Zhu Yufeng in the village who had no one to look after. Since 2016, due to his old age and frailty, he was unable to take care of himself.

"Uncle, it's inconvenient for you to live alone. I'll take you to my home ..." Kabian Ashankake came over and said to him.

"No, no! With my ailments, I would drag you down ..." The old man pointed to his dirty and untidy small house, feeling excited but embarrassed.

Kabian, who didn't mind it at all, smiled and said, "It doesn't matter. When we get old, we would all have difficulties. Now you are sick and in need of care ... I want to take you to my home so that I can look after you well." Afraid that the old man would hesitate, Kabian continued, "Don't worry, as long as I have food, I promise you will eat well. I will treat you as my father!"

"Kabian ..." Upon hearing this, the old man instantly burst into tears, repeatedly saying, "Your father was a great man. Without him, I would not be alive ..." It turned out that when Zhu Yufeng arrived at this village at a young age, he was unfamiliar with the place and its people, and there were few Han people, making it difficult for him to integrate into the local society. But Zhu Yufeng was fortunate because as soon as he arrived there, he received special care and protection from Captain Ashan, who treated every villager in the same way, even those unrelated but in need of help from their village. "Why shouldn't we help them? We are all Chinese and members of the big socialist family. If I have something to eat, I would share it with others ..." These were the words Captain Ashan often said.

Kabian took Uncle Zhu into his own home to support him. As the elderly man's health deteriorated later, it made Kabian's family very busy. Additionally, it cost money whenever he saw a doctor, but none of the family members ever complained.

"What good things have I done? Look, Kabian treats me just like his own father ..." Zhu Yufeng tearfully said to his old friends in the village several times.

In 2018, Zhu Yufeng, who had been suffering from a long-term illness, passed away in Kabian's home.

"Perhaps it's inappropriate to hold his funeral in a Kazakh house like yours!" Someone from the village came to Kabian and said.

"Indeed, Uncle Zhu is not my relative, but he was already a member of my family, so his funeral should be held in my house, and according to the Han customs …" Kabian replied very clearly.

On the day of the funeral, many villagers attended. Following the Han customs completely, Kabian bought a wooden coffin for Uncle Zhu and then invited a local master of funeral ceremonies to give the old man a dignified farewell …

This event sparked a discussion among the different ethnic groups in the area, and everyone agreed that Kabian did the right thing with reason and compassion. "If Captain Ashan were still alive, he would also approve of it!" the villagers said.

Bathing in the village's mountain breeze, walking on its paths, and interacting with villagers from different ethnic backgrounds, one can deeply feel the "village spirit" that permeates every inch of its land and every breath of its air, which is embodied by the presence of Captain Ashan's image and soul.

"Yes, from Captain Ashan back then to the present 'Ashan Spirit,' the revolutionary heritage of Narencha Khan Kule Village has been promoting different ethnic groups to unite as close as one family and to pursue continuous development. And it radiates and influences the entire Jal Agash Town and even the broader border areas …" These were the words of the officer from the Publicity Department in the town.

She took me to the "Ashan Spirit" Village History Museum, where she showed me something extraordinary, which is said to be the "Treasure of the Town" — a huge and magical tree root, a "sacred object". It was said that the tree root used to be the horse-hitching post of Hazyi Kuonsac, a villager from Upper Jal Agash Village near Narencha Khan Kule. In the past, where the Jal Agash Town was used to be a sand beach with few residents, but many travelers and caravans passed by, making it sort of a courier station. Hazyi Kuonsac was a mild-tempered, kind-hearted, and generous man, who was always ready to help those people in need, regardless of their ethnic background. Whenever he saw tired travelers with horses passing through, especially when they were in need of rest, a hitching post could solve many problems. Hazyi Kuonsac noticed it and promptly placed a hitching post not far from his door. Soon, the passing caravans would stop here to rest, tying their horses to the post and taking a break for a while, or even setting up camp for the night ... Over time, the "hitching post of Upper Jal Agash Village" became a well-known resting spot for anyone traveling within dozens of miles around. As a result, the reputation of the village grew. After the establishment of the PRC, when townships were set up, not only did the name of "Upper Jal Agash" Village remain, but it also became the name of the township. It was not surprising, but the astonishing part was that the hitching post gradually took root, sprouted, flourished, blossomed, bore fruits, and even grew into a towering tree!

The villagers said it was a "miracle"! They believed it was the manifestation of the "Ashan Spirit" as well as promulgation of Hazyi's virtuous deeds ... At first, I smiled as I listened, but when I saw the tree root, I exclaimed on the spot, "Is this for real? You didn't deliberately 'sculpt' it, did you?"

The villagers got serious, "Take a closer look. It is definitely not artificially carved, and it grew like this naturally ..."

I had to look closely and attentively. Indeed, the tree stump was huge, resembling the body of a big yellow ox! That's why the locals here said it symbolized their inheritance of Captain Ashan's spirit of arduous struggle on their path to achieve socialist prosperity.

"Then look at it from this side, it resembles a saber-toothed tiger, symbolizing the vigorous, invincible, and thriving construction of our new village ..."

That was true. I looked at the "hitching post" from that side, it looked like a tiger coming down the hill, majestic and imposing — How astonishing!

"Come over here and look at this side," the host said with a smile as he led me to see another side of the "hitching post." "What does this shape look like?"

"It looks like ...an elephant!" I exclaimed in awe.

"Yes, it's very much like an elephant!" the host continued, "This is an elephant of peace, representing the people of all ethnic groups here, always being inclusive, caring, harmonious, friendly, and united, just like Captain Ashan and Grandpa Hazyi ... strong like an elephant, shaped like a pomegranate, always tightly embracing each other, bravely marching forward under the banner of the Party and socialism!"

What he said was great!

Sometimes things in the world cannot be simply explained through materialism or idealism because the objective existence itself has the power to "transform decay into magic." Moreover, when it is right in front of you, how can you easily deny it?

Amaguli Halle, a beautiful and captivating girl as a blooming flower, who stood in front of me, was the current party branch secretary of Upper Jal Agash Village. When someone told me that Hazyi Kuonsac was her grandfather, I was even more surprised and delighted. It was also the inheritance of the revolutionary spirit!

Upper left / Healthy Mongolian teenagers from Hoboksar Mongolian Autonomous County

Lower left / The world's first Dzhangar Palace

Right / Populus euphratica forest in Hoboksar Mongolian Autonomous County

How beautiful is it in Tacheng, Xinjiang?
Its beauty runs through nature,
In the lives of millions of people on earth,
Hiding in the wonderful moments life has brought.
The natural scenery of Anjihai Grand Canyon

Here is Xinjiang.

A land so vast that if you throw a whip away, you could hardly get it back ...

Getting off the horse,

You find your campsite, a new beginning of your life,

Or maybe it's the birthplace of another life.

Left / Traditional horse racing event

Right / Beautiful Menblac Grassland

Tarbagatai Mountains and its surrounding pastures,
Constitute the skeleton and blood of Tacheng,
Being the "father and mother" of Tacheng people,
Being "you and me" in Tacheng with their past, present,
and future ...

Doctor Wuhaas in a winter pasture in Yumin County

Every beautiful land,
Always has beautiful stories and legends.
Because of them,
Such a land is becoming more and more
beautiful and abundant ...
This is true in Tacheng as well as in Xinjiang.

Haxilegen Bingdaban

Plentiful glaciers,

Are making the Bayingou River, Gurtu River,

Moto River, Manas River, Jingou River,

Kuitun River, and Emin River in Tacheng Basin abundant in water all year round,

Which also give green wings to the land along these rivers,

Flying and dancing over the land in the western region of the motherland for dozens of centuries ...

In Xinjiang, there is a very famous highway called Duku Highway, also called "Tianshan Highway".

It is self-evident that the Highway brings great convenience to the north-south transportation in Xinjiang.

Before this highway was built, people in northern Xinjiang had to ride horses to graze and travel.

Even after the opening of the Duku Highway,

In the grasslands and pastures of most areas, people still ride horses as main means of transportation.

Left / Duoku Highway amidst the sea of clouds

Upper right / A view of Mt. Tianshan from Usu

Lower right / Herders grazing in Yumin County

Foggy Bayingou River

Anjihai Grand Canyon

You are the embodiment of beauty,

The grassland extends thousands of miles away, which can link the sky and earth.

Where horses, cattle, and sheep can roam uninhibitedly;

You are a symbol of strength,

The wind and snow in the air are the carving knives waved by Heaven to shape the earth,

Each of whose impassioned roaring is a note of strength.

Antler Bay of Shawan City in the depths of Mt. Tianshan

Rivers and mountains, human
beings and plants, love and gratitude,
In Tacheng, in Xinjiang, in this land
full of love,
Extend freely, being thriving and
prosperous, in the history so long ...

In the spring of Tacheng, flowers
on the grassland bloom as abundantly
as clouds in the sky, creating beautiful
rainbow-like scenes on the curvy hills
and vast grasslands ...

CONTENTS

The Origin of Love

The People's Republic of China has gone through more than seventy years of development,

No matter how our nation suffered from the tribulation, the great unity of the Chinese nation

Has always been upheld highly by people of all ethnic groups

"We have bathed in sunshine all our lives. We must hold love in our heart.

With love, we have everything," a 97-year-old Uighur aunt, Manreyamu often said.

In Tacheng City, what impressed visitors the most at first might be the houses painted in red here.

The color of the houses here differs from that of the Forbidden City in Beijing. It is more brilliant and blazing, just like a flame, making people feel an upsurge of emotion. It is more seductive, like the desire and impulse of the youth.

Once you calm down to touch and feel the red, it will give you another feeling that flows gently through your body. That is love, the most indispensable and universal emotion in human nature.

Bing Xin once said: With love, everything is possible.

Yes, my understanding of Tacheng City first came from its appearance, *i.e.* the natural environment. When we say Xinjiang is a wonderful place, we refer to its natural beauty.

Its beauty has attracted numerous people, many of them became jealous and avaricious, which caused repeated pillage and invasion, leaving untold tragic memories in history ...

Nevertheless, all those people who settled down have transformed these memories into impetus and volition to reproduce the next generation, and gradually nurtured another beauty on this land — love, the noblest beauty in human nature.

Love makes Xinjiang more beautiful, and its beauty converges into certain torrents, powerful and unstoppable. The nature and history of Xinjiang is actually an epic of love and being loved.

The red houses under the green shades characterize with Russian architectural style and charm, which is also the main tone of Tacheng's beauty, as well as of the dwellers' character and emotional world. *The Three-Character Classic* says that man on earth, good at birth. In modern society, there goes another similar saying, kindhearted people are beautiful.

In an ancient border town which locates in the fortress and connects all directions, how can it sustain prolonged tranquility, social stability and prosperous life of people? This is a question that all the visitors are thinking about — Everyone has his own conclusion.

I came to find the answer to the same question.

Fortunately, on my first day, I met a pure local family with a tender old mother who lived in a house in Tacheng City.

The walls of the house were made of a mixture of grass and mud, which was a traditional type of construction form here last century. Situated on the northwest border of China, Tacheng was subjected to political ups and downs. At that time only a rich family could afford to build houses with walls made of a mixture of grass and mud.

A local inhabitant told me that the old house built by Tatar people had a history of over a hundred years, and now it was inherited by the constructor's grandson who was in my age. Accordingly, it was one of the oldest houses existing in Tacheng.

I was amazed by the intact preservation of the house: A featured building with such a flavour survived the repeated turbulence in history. What a miracle indeed! From the architecture, we can perceive how steady, tranquil, satisfying, and lovely the city is.

Towering oak trees stood in the yard, which made me feel that the old owners of the house were still living here. The T-shaped house was similar to the old-fashioned ones in South China. Two separate rooms connected to the main building, serving as kitchens: one for baking bread, and the other for cooking.

The principal building appeared to consist of three large rooms, but in fact, apart from the larger one in the middle, the other two on both sides were small and medium-sized. Here, severely cold weather has made people design the house with only one door to the main building, surrounded by a wing room, which is different from that in South China.

But I found that the function of the main room was also different from that in South China. The host told me that the bed leaning against the rear wall in the room was for wedding, first for his grandfather, then his father, and now for him. "I spent my wedding night in this bed as well ..." he said.

"Our first child was delivered in this bed," the hostess said, pointing to the bed.

What they said astonished me and made me curious. It turned out that the nomads in Xinjiang had followed such a marvelous custom of reproduction. Although they drifted from place to place, their children still started their earthly life in the same tender bed. Hasn't it been the most magnificent heritage of love in the world!

With this everlasting love, shall we be scared of the uncertain and dreadful world? No! How splendid and marvellous it is!

The host's tough exterior covered a very kind soul. He barely talked, but he would even considerately give me a hand when I stepped across the threshold. He told me that it was their tradition to usher the honored guest into the room.

He first showed me around several rooms where various ancestral tools for living and farming were displayed, including the saddle used by his grandfather 100 years ago when he came to Tacheng and all kinds of production tools, some of them could be identified at one look as tools invented during the Industrial Revolution era in Europe, such as a lathe used for a century.

Other tools, big or small, covered all aspects of daily life, such as hammers, saws, axes, chisels, planers, etc., which were more abundant than what a Han family had. Generally speaking, Han families have many tools for farming but few for daily life.

Such complete preservation of numerous utensils in such a small room impressed me, with a understanding of how the people of Tacheng have evolved their lives over the past century.

Undoubtedly, if they did not cherish this land, they would not make such a rich variety of utensils with which they drew such an eye-catching painting on this primitive soil — The earth is our mother and she needs dressing up to be resplendent and gorgeous too.

Love makes the soil fertile.

A fecund land nurtures more inhabitants to make a better living ...

"Come and taste the speciality of our Tatars!" During my visit, as I was accompanied by the host to see the displayed 'antiques' in this traditional house, the hospitable hostess invited me to sample her cooking.

On the table, there were assorted pastries and other foods, dozens of unknown delicacies which were mostly made of flour and local fruits. Although I hesitated to eat desserts, their aroma were so enticing that I could not resist them. Indeed, they were delicious and fresh for me.

"For you came here for the first time, it is only natural you haven't tried our delicacies of 'Yiman Tree Manor', the food made by my wife, which is unparalleled in not only Tacheng but also Xinjiang province!" the inarticulate host suddenly spoke highly of his beautiful wife in public, which surprised me.

Hearing what he said, everyone couldn't help laughing.

"Oh, really?" I asked the cadres of the local Publicity Department accompanying me. "Absolutely, with the unique culinary skills, Zaitunna is recognized as the only inheritor of the national intangible cultural heritage of Tatar in Tacheng and Xinjiang" they all agreed.

So that's it! I couldn't help but admire her.

Before I came here, I had never met Tatar people and therefore I barely know them. This feast was a great occasion for me to expand my understanding of this ethnic group.

"The name of Tatar comes from 'Ta' of Tacheng. That's why we are called Tatars!" By saying this, the hostess was giggling. "Due to our strong affection for this city, we hardly divide the residents into other ethnic groups but call ourselves 'Tacheng ethnic people'. For this reason, Tatars are people of 'Ta' in Tacheng!"

As she explained, all of us bantered with her, "Since we all love Tacheng, we are 'Tatars' as well!"

The joke made us laugh again.

"These are my grandpa Kalimu Qianixuefu and grandma Hadixai ..." Among a row of old photos on the wall, the host pointed at the most eye-catching one to us. An elderly couple were in the photo, who were apparently his grand parents.

Then he continued, "The little boy was my father named Abushamaiti Qianixuefu. He was a younger child among my grand parents' children."

"I guess the photo was taken in the 1920s or 1930s," I said.

"Pretty much. Might be 1920s."

"My father-in-law and his ancestors were craftsmen who mastered farming and other skills for living. They almost made everything in the house, such as tables, chairs, benches, and wooden beds, as well as barrels, pots, stoves, plates, bowls, knives, forks, etc. These furniture and utensils are all serviceable for us till now.

My mother-in-law was an excellent cook in making bread and other delicacies. She taught me how to cook after I married my husband. Finally, I have acquired all the skills for cooking food of Tatar. Now it has been listed as one of the valuable intangible cultural heritage in Tacheng!"

With great pride, Zaitunna told me.

No wonder she is an excellent cook!

She introduced, the most distinctive Tatar foods were "Gubaidiei" and "Etberisi". "Gubaidiei" is a kind of sweet cake mainly made of rice. First, wash the rice and dry it in the air, then mould it into a round shape and cover it with cream, dried apricots, and raisins. After that, bake it in an oven. "Etberisi" follows the same recipe but the ingredients are different. It is made of pumpkin combined with rice and meat.

"Apart from traditional family museum of Tatar, our manor is famous for my cooking as well as Tatar song and dance." Immediately, she immersed herself in the beautiful melody and danced in a joyous spirit ...

Take a Dombra with your confidante
Don't forget the dried beef and Russian whole meal bread
Come and dance Khara Jorha
Let your guard down
White snow mountains still keep silent
The wild purple pea flowers bloom for it down the hill
Let us booze the Wusu beer
Sober buddies will never leave until they are drunk

On the foot of the Mount Tarbahtai
Why not booze up tonight
Our boys and girls should get married at the right time

On the foot of the Mount Tarbahtai
Why not booze up tonight

Keep those precious memories in mind
Shake off whatever bothers you

On the foot of the Mount Tarbahtai
Why not booze up tonight
To this happy moment!
To our brighter future!

"Great! Encore!" Zaitunna hadn't stopped dancing yet, the crowd around the table shouted out loud again — Here is Xinjiang, everyone is good at dancing and singing. Someone takes the lead; all will follow to dance and sing without ending!

Then Zaitunna sang a *Love in Tacheng* in Kazakh written by a local singer. I have found residents of Tacheng, like Zaitunna the Tatar, all could speak several principal local languages.

"Tacheng is an ethnically diverse community where we communicate in the language of each group. As time goes by, we have forged a family-like close relationship and each of us is able to speak several languages," Zaitunna explained.

Among the cadres of the local Publicity Department, two are Han people. Both of them nodded, "Exactly."

How enviable it is! I said in my heart.

"My first night in Tacheng" was so cheerful. We stayed up late to savour innumerable delicious foods offered by the hospitable host while enjoying songs and dances by the local friends.

Among them, only the host and I were not capable of singing and dancing. What we could do was to applaud the performers. During the feast, he silently guided me to his "treasure house". I was amazed by the treasure displayed — textbooks and exercise books in school days, national flags and promotional materials in different periods, all collected by him and his father, Abu Shamaiti.

"Our ancestors were nomads who were illiterate and homeless. But things have changed after my grandparents' generation. Grandpa always told his children that the Tatars had wandered from place to place for living till they settled in Tacheng, Xinjiang. Tacheng enabled them to be free from worries of searching for somewhere to live. They truly owned a home.

My grandparents walled up every room of this house with their own hands, including a bakery. They made every table, chair, and bed and planted every tree in the courtyard.

Grandpa has always taught Papa that this is our first home and our descendants must cherish it and make our family survive and thrive like the oak trees.

Papa had suffered from tribulations in the old society and then he threw himself into building New China. He could tell the advantages of the socialist system. As grandpa told him, he has drummed it into my mind that since grandpa had settled here, this house has been our root and we can never forget our blood ...

Accordingly, our whole family has been living here till today. To meet the needs of development in the new age, we upgraded the house from a household to a museum for people to get to know the history of our family, to appreciate the intangible cultural heritage of Tatar and to taste traditional foods ..." the host told me.

He continued, "Our achievements should be attributed to the efforts made by my mother and my wife, who have done their parts in the construction of Xinjiang and the border area. As common people, they seldom say proud words but they pass on the culture of Tatar through our family cooking skills and share with other ethnic groups in Xinjiang."

Though his introduction, I realized how this Tatar family could have inherited its history till now. And what he said before I left made me stay up the first night in Tacheng.

He said, his mother had told him all the time until she passed away, which went like this, "If you share your love with the world, you will be rewarded with a more prosperous world!"

She was only a common people in Xinjiang, however, her words were so philosophical and considerate to humanity!

"This is what our family has always pursued in the long run ..." His words had an overwhelming effect on me as a sudden thunder in the silent sky with its echoes lingering in my mind, evoking my enduring admiration for the towering oak trees standing firmly in the courtyard of the Tatar family ...

The next day, a cadre of the Federation of Literary and Artistic Circles guided me to visit an elder Uygur. Numerous visitors might have come to Xinjiang for sightseeing, but few of them could get an opportunity to walk into local houses.

I was rather excited.

When we arrived at the house, I came to know that she was called Manreyamu Turdeva, aged 97. As one of the most prestigious elders, she was called "Mama" by local people.

Tough she was nearly one hundred years old, she looked robust physically. She could understand a little Mandarin, but I couldn't understand her language. Verbal conversation was unattainable, but we can communicate through gestures and facial expressions —

When she heard that I came from Beijing, there was a gleam in her eyes. She stepped forward to hold my hands, greeting me warmly with her big eyes typical of Uygurs, and talked to me in Uygur. Her son translated diligent work and wisdom. Despite his success, he remained kind-hearted and always willing to help those experiencing poverty. Additionally, he never held prejudices against people from other ethnic groups. Due to these qualities, he had earned the title of "a kindly Kazakh uncle".

"Every year after the autumn harvest, poor people from near and far always gathered at his doorstep, expecting his financial assistance. Whoever had reasonable grounds could receive generous donation from Bashibai," a little older man in Tacheng told me.

Due to the popularity of Tacheng's border trade, many Han business people with their family members came to Xinjiang. As time passed, some of them accumulated wealth while others lost everything they had. As a result, many impoverished people sought assistance from Bashibai, a local man of fortune, which brought various troubles and difficulties to him.

The housekeeper said to Bashibai, "Sir, we can't care for everyone! If we do, we will end up like them, insolvent."

Bashibai smiled and replied, "We are not poor yet. And if we became poor, then nobody would ask us for help!"

In 1945, Bashibai, who had high prestige, was elected as the first commissioner of the Administrative Office in Tacheng, an absolute "high official" in the local area.

One day, as Bashibai's sheep wandered into an old Uyghur's vegetable garden, the old man quickly drove it away. However, a servant at Bashibai's house saw what happened and shouted angrily, "How dare you beat the sheep of the Commissioner?" Upon hearing this, the old man knelt and kowtowed for mercy. Later, when Bashibai found out about the incident, he was outraged. He personally took the servant to the old man's house to apologize and left compensation for that man.

"He was loved and respected by us." Tacheng people always say that when talking about Bashibai. In Tacheng, the good deeds by Bashibai were as countless as the stars in the sky.

I learned that he donated to the first nine-year school in Yumin County and even paid the faculty and staff when he was alive.

I learned that he donated to build the People's Club in Tacheng.

In 1941, he invested in the construction of Bashibai Bridge.

In 1949, when Tacheng was liberated, Bashibai delightedly presented 2 tons of wheat and 40 cows to the PLA soldiers.

In 1951, he donated a plane for the war to resist U.S. aggression and aid Korea.

> Your heart is as pure as the white clouds,
> Your eyes are as clear as water in the lake,
> You're our benefactor,
> You are the pride of Tacheng.
>
> …

Bashibai, who built up his fortune through hard work, was an honest and upright official and regarded ordinary people as his family. This is why people of all ethnic groups in Tacheng sing praise of him in different languages and dance in the place where he showed his kindness.

In 1953, when Bashibai visited the mainland with a delegation of progressives and democrats from all walks of life and different ethnic groups organized by the United Front Work Department of the Central Committee, he died of a sudden heart attack in Hangzhou at the age of 64.

The central government attached great importance to Bashibai's funeral, sending a special plane to transport his body back to Xinjiang and buried him at the foot of Mt. Balluk, where he was born.

During the past 70 years, people of all ethnic groups in Tacheng have gone to the cemetery of Bashibai at different memorial times to pay homage to this "kindly Kazakh Uncle".

The legend of Bashibai as well as the material and spiritual heritage he left for this beautiful land of Tacheng make me think about a question that is easy to understand but difficult to answer: Every beautiful land has its own stories and legends that add to its charm and prosperity. This is true for Tacheng and the entire region of Xinjiang.

Then, I would see Wei Deyou, a well-liked and respected "kindly uncle" in the Tacheng community, whose story has become well-known throughout China. In 2017, at the age of 76, he was celebrated as a Touching China figure and was received and commended by General Secretary Xi Jinping in the Great Hall of the People.

He was 82 years old at the year when I planned to meet him. So, the thought of visiting him made my heart soar like a cloud over Mt. Tianshan.

"We are almost there!" said a comrade of the Federation of Literary and Art Circles after crossing the Bashibai Bridge over the Emin River, a cross-border river, "That is the border, and Kazakhstan is on the other side."

The off-road vehicle was bumping in high speed toward the border located in the Gobi desert. Occasionally, a few trees could be spotted along the Emin River, apart from them, what we could see were only iron grey land, rocks, and some patches of sand grass. The strong winds were so powerful that if you were wearing a hat, it would be blown far away.

As we traveled along the road, we came across a series of tightly secured barbed wire fences and signs bearing messages like "It is the greatest honor to defend the border and the country" and "Border Areas. Do not Approach." These constant reminders indicated, "You have reached the border!" Our destination is the No.173 boundary marker at the Sino-Kazakh boundary line, the place Wei Deyou has been defending for the past 58 years.

Oh, what kind of territory is that? My eyes went far with the bumpy vehicle, but I couldn't see the end of the land.

"We have arrived at the Salbulak grassland, where the surrounding area for miles is uninhabited," said Guo Tiancheng, a member of the Tacheng Writers Association. He used to work as a Political Department cadre in the military sub-district stationed here, and thus was familiar with every nook and cranny of the border. Ten minutes later, he pointed to a solitary mud-built house on a hill and declared, "That's his home."

As I looked afar, I noticed a red flag waving on the roof of Wei Deyou's mud-built shack, with certain sacredness. However, I was still puzzled as to why there was only Wei Deyou's shack present along the long border, aside from the military's border posts.

"The borderline is too long, the border guards may not always be able to complete the second and third-line patrols during times of strategic tension. To help with this, some military companies are allowed to raise livestock, such as cattle and sheep. Veterans were hired to herd the livestock as well as assist with patrols. Wei Deyou is one of these border guard assistants." Thanks to Guo's introduction, I gained knowledge about the situation at the border.

Wei Deyou was born in Linyi, Shandong Province, which was an old revolutionary base in 1940. He vividly remembers the revolutionary events that took place in his hometown. He often says, "When I was a child, I witnessed PLA soldiers led by General Chen Yi to our village. At that time, a telegram machine was placed in my house, some soldiers responsible for sending telegrams lived with us."

In 1960, Wei Deyou was drafted into the army and worked with the army in Tangshan, Hebei Province for four years. After leaving the army in 1964, he was quickly transferred to the front line of border defense in Xinjiang. At that time, the Sino-Soviet border area fell into strategic tension in an all-round way. Wei Deyou, as a reserve border combatant, was assigned to the Second Company of the 161st Regiment of the 9th Agricultural Division of Xinjiang Production and Construction Corps. His task was to herd animals and patrol the control area of the No.173 boundary marker. He also needed to cultivate crops on a wide land by the river, which served as a "lifeblood" for his survival at first and later for his whole family. For border guards, defending the frontier is a sacred duty. For Wei Deyou, guarding this area is not only a holy duty given to him by the motherland; here is also a place he has depended on.

Upon his arrival, the Second Company of the 161st Regiment of the 9th Agricultural Division of his Corps was stationed in the uninhabited Salbulak Grassland. Armed with only sickles and hoes, they have cultivated the land and protected the borders for 58 years, never leaving their duty even once. Even today, at the age of 82, Wei Deyou is still there, faithfully carrying out his duty.

From a distance, one can see the outposts and mountains of neighboring countries in front, and the beautiful Tacheng City behind. However, in the 1960s, the now peaceful area was once the site of severe border riots, causing it to fall into a state of "a border without defense." It was during that time that Wei Deyou and his comrades came here to set up posts and patrols. In those days, they all lived a hard life, relying totally on farming and herding. They had to be physically and mentally strong to defend the border areas.

"There were occasionally accidental fires and even serious armed conflicts, which were often fueled by the scramble for land and pasture. At that time, it was their physical strength and mental will that supported

Wei Deyou and other officers of the Corps to defend the motherland's territory and fight against invading enemies," the border guards said. Those imaginable past events are vivid in their minds. Back then, Wei Deyou was assigned as the leader of Salbulak "cattle group." Later, he recalled, "In 1969, border conflicts frequently occurred. I participated in Operation 'Iron Bull Team' organized by the 161st Regiment, which lasted three days and nights. Armed with a steel gun, we confronted the enemies on the south bank of the Tasti River. We were facing accidental shootings everyday at that time. That was how we maintained the dignity of our motherland's borderlines."

One day in winter, it snowed heavily. Wei Deyou, carrying a 79-style rifle, was riding along the unmarked disputed area to herd cattle when he heard the roar of a helicopter hovering high in the sky. He immediately hid in the snow, at minus 30 degrees Celsius, staring motionlessly at that invading air vehicle. Just as he was about to attack the helicopter, it hurriedly flew away after making a big circle. But Wei Deyou remained on guard and searched for any suspicious clues in the place where the helicopter had circled. He found several trails of big footprints and galloped to report to the headquarters of the border defense company stationed along the Emin River. Upon learning the facts, the border defense company quickly conducted a thorough search until dawn, finally forcing the suspicious people back outside the border.

"His family came later and followed him until now," Guo told me, "This is his house," he pointed to a low hut with the national flag flying high on the roof.

On the vast expanse of sand that stretches out to the horizon, stands a small and lonely hut belonging to Wei Deyou. It looks like a plain and unremarkable brick structure, without any indication of the fact that its owner is a July 1st Medal winner. However, this is the very house where

Wei Deyou and his family live. It has been renovated three times — the latest being its transformation into an educational center for "patriotic border defense" by the local government after Wei Deyou was recognized as a Touching China figure and personally awarded the "July 1st Medal" by General Secretary Xi Jinping.

Wei Deyou is 82 years old who likes to be called a "veteran". He lived in his first home for almost 40 years — a mud-built, cellar-style shack with an area of over 40 square meters. He dug out the dwelling with a pickaxe all by himself, then "lured" his newly married wife to move from their hometown in Shandong to the Gobi Desert, where they raised four children together.

Then, he rebuilt his house using bricks and concrete, instead of mud walls and floor, which was the only difference with the previous house. In his early 60s, the head of the border guards persuaded him to officially retire as he could have returned to his hometown with a state-subsidized "settling-in allowance." However, despite his third daughter crying and begging him to go, he refused to leave at all. He said, "From the first day I came here, I was determined to work here until I couldn't walk. Even after my legs failed to support my body, I still have my eyes to defend the border. Even if my eyes were closed forever, no breath, no heartbeat, I would bury my soul here to guard the frontier for my motherland forever. My home is here!"

After winning the "July 1st Medal" in 2021, Wei Deyou's house was renovated by the local military sub-district, Tacheng Prefecture, and several schools to serve as an education base for patriotism. The new house has three rooms, with two rooms respectively allotted for Wei Deyou, his wife and his daughter, and the middle one serves as a living room for visitors, each of which is about 15 square meters. Outside the house, two circles are surrounded by wooden fences, which serve as areas for raising livestock and poultry such as cattle, sheep, and chickens. These are all of Wei Deyou's belongings. They seem to be worth only one or two thousand yuan!

"Here you are! Welcome,chiefs." As the vehicle arrived at Wei's doorway, a hunch-backed elderly woman stepped out. She was wearing a thin floral shirt that made her look even more delicate. What made me most painful was to see her long gray hair and shrunken mouth, which must be a result of losing most of her teeth. One could not help but feel sad seeing her dry, rough, and weathered face ...

Hearing that I was from Beijing, her eyes brightened and said, "I have been to Beijing and met General Secretary Xi. How has he been these years? Does he send you to visit us?" What could I say to such a simple elderly lady? I could only repeatedly answer, "Yes, yes! General Secretary Xi sends his greetings to you!"

Hearing this, she took my hand enthusiastically to the door and said, "Could you wait a minute, Chief? And would you mind if I changed my clothes and took a picture with you?" She quickly went into the room and returned shortly wearing a camouflage suit and an army cap.

"She is wearing the overalls sent by the military sub-district to the elderly," said Guo Tiancheng, who accompanied me.

While taking pictures, I felt a bit embarrassed as I was much taller than the elderly woman standing by me. The elderly woman, who was around 80 years old, suffered from severe rickets, appeared even shorter and frail. Seeing her physical condition made me upset. Although Shandong girls are usually tall in figure, the years of burden on this elderly woman had taken a toll on her body when she followed her husband to defend the border area for 58 years and raised four children in this arid land.

I couldn't help but feel my eyes welling up with tears as I looked at her wrinkled yet smiling face.

Guarding the frontier areas was originally a task assigned to men, and it was her husband who made the personal decision to move from Shandong to Xinjiang for this purpose. In 1960, she was delighted when he successfully joined the army in their hometown. After waiting for a few years, she was even happier to welcome him back home, hoping to live a happy life together from then on. However, upon his return, he revealed that there was tension in the western border areas, as a veteran, he couldn't think selfishly about his own life, he should go there to help his comrades-in- arms defend the border.

"I won't go alone. Lao Chen and hundreds of other good comrades-in-arms will go with me!" the man confidently told her. He added a tempting offer that would be appealing to rural girls, "We can receive a monthly salary there, thus life will not be so tough!"

She believed what he said, as she always trusted that his broad chest could give her warmth like the sun.

At the time, she was unaware of where the "Western Border" was and had no idea how far it was. It was not until he took her out of her hometown did she realize they were heading to Xinjiang. Their journey began by walking from home to the county, then taking a ride to Linyi, and getting to Xuzhou by train. After transferring numerous trains, they finally arrived in Urumqi after more than half a month. Later, they traveled for five days by coach from Urumqi to Tacheng, followed by two additional days in a carriage until they arrived at their current residence.

"At that time, I felt honored to see many friendly PLA comrades around me. They were so kind to me." She didn't understand the hardships of life back then, but to be with PLA meant happiness and glory to her.

Later she realized that they couldn't live with the PLA and had to dig their dwelling and live in a semi-underground shack.

"It took us a whole winter and spring to realize that if our house had been built on the ground level, it would have been destroyed by the strong winds and heavy snowfall. Even though the shack was dug more than two meters deep underground, the roof had still been lifted by the strong wind and collapsed under the weight of the snow several times. It was so cold, extremely freezing!"

I listened to her silently, the difficulties were unable to describe.

"Once, our whole family was covered in snow for several hours. Fortunately, border guards came to rescue us, or we might have all frozen to death," she murmured as if it were an everyday occurrence.

Among many unexpected occurrences, she just told me one of them: One night, Wei Deyou's shepherd dog started barking wildly, waking him up and alerting him that something was wrong. When he looked outside, he saw that 36 of his sheep were missing. He shouted angrily, "Who stole my sheep?!" but no one responded. On another foggy morning, someone intentionally scattered his sheep while he was unprepared. Feeling anxious as the sheep were one of his weapons to guard the border, Wei Deyou called for help. The moment his wife heard his cries, she locked her children inside and went out with flashlights with him to search for the lost sheep in the wild, braving the howling wolves. After a long search, they found the bodies of 80 lost sheep on a mountain, all of them dead miserably.

Witnessing the scene, Wei shed tears, and his wife cried even more sadly. However, for decades, such deliberate theft of chickens and sheep has been a "common occurrence" for them. There were also countless other difficulties in their life.

"Shortly after our arrival here, my comrade Lao Chen was bitten by a wolf while patrolling. He later died of rabies. What a pity!" Recalling that, the elderly woman wiped away tears

In fact, she bore numerous sufferings in her heart.

When she first arrived here, she was a Shandong girl who loved dressing up. However, within three months, she was completely different. One day, she went with Wei to the military barracks to collect cattle and sheep.When she caught a glimpse of herself in the mirror that soldiers used to groom themselves, she suddenly burst into tears, exclaiming, "How did I end up looking like this?"

"How did I end up looking like this?" She repeatedly asked him on their way home and even kept questioning herself all night. Eventually, after her tears dried up and her voice became hoarse, she had to accept the fact that this was how she looked.

Afterward, she got pregnant. During that period, tensions over the border areas had risen. As life became more difficult, more individuals sought to cross the borders. While her husband and other soldiers were guarding the last defense line on the border, she rode on horseback with a big belly every day, warily watching any suspicious "moving object" around the No.173 boundary marker.

"Who's there? Do not go any further!" She spotted some "object" moving in the grass around a dune. The shocked "object" fled away even more quickly, apparently trying to get rid of her.

"Stop!" she urged her horse to chase the man trying to illegally cross the borders, but as she was about to catch him, the horse suddenly stepped out of balance, throwing her off.

"Ouch!" She was in unbearable pain, but a voice in her mind urged her not to let that man get away. She struggled to her feet, aimed her gun at the man, and shouted, "Freeze! Or I shoot!"

The man stopped, quivering and kneeling in front of her for mercy, "Good sister, please spare me and let me go." Then he told her his "misfortunes" with tears.

"Brother, I believe what you're saying. You must have gone through a lot of difficulties. But think about it: Are you sure you would get a better life over there? We're all Chinese, and no matter how poor we are, we are the owners of our country. Look at me. I live so close to the border, but I've never left our country. Do you know why?"

"Why?" The man goggled at her for an answer.

"Because people in every country won't like those who do not love their own country! Whoever loves his own country holds a promising future," she said.

The man stared at her for a moment, then nodded in understanding and said, "Reasonable! I will listen to you and go back home," after a while, he added, "Sister, you must keep it a secret for me. Please do not report it to the police!"

She replied affirmatively, "Sure, I won't. As long as you go back, there is nothing serious. Don't worry and go home. Good time will come someday."

The man bowed three times in gratitude before going away. Then she smiled and patted her stomach, whispering to her unborn child, "Your mother has made another contribution."

In those years when there were tension in border areas, she would meet such opportunities of doing meritorious service every day.

After becoming a mother, she came to have a complete concept of family: she had to prepare food and water for her husband to take with him on the way out every day. She had to be busy with daily routines for the children, feeding poultry, cattle and sheep, and preparing for the attack of wind and snow.

It was a woman's fate to endure such life experiences, no matter how tough they were. She was expected to face all the challenges, fatigue, risks, and dangers as a frontier defender — things that were rare for other women in the world, but daily occurrences for her.

She couldn't remember how many times she held her children tightly in arms, suffering from hunger and coldness, waiting for her husband to return in midnight. "Why didn't Dad come back? Was he eaten up by wolves?" Her daughter asked.

"How can you say such words?" She slapped her daughter in anger.

"Wah ...Mom is bad! Mam is bad!" Her daughter's cry penetrated the wind and snow in the border areas, but her husband still didn't return.

After soothing the child to sleep, she stood alone at the door for hours ... She even thought in horror: What if he couldn't return?

Thinking of this, she cried, with tears wetting the front of her clothes.

For many times, she has endured such intense suffering and torture.

But she has withstood it every time.

Someone asked her, How did you make it?

She replied, "I just thought about my children's father, my children's future and the fact that someone was in need to guard this land."

This is a mother who can't be more ordinary and greater.

That's how she went through the difficult time. Then I know that she has a nice name: Liu Jinghao.

"Why did your parents give you such a nice name?" I asked her.

She smiled, "You come from Beijing, so you must know what 'Jinghao' means."

I smiled and replied with my own interpretation: When you were born, your parents named you "Jinghao", which means "Beijing is good", because they believed that Beijing would offer Chinese people with a prosperous life.

She giggled incessantly. "I have been to Beijing and . It is really a wonderful city, really!"

It is in this simple, proud, and satisfied manner that she understood her name.

This woman, who grew strong from bitterness, is like the Gobi desert and able to withstand anything with unwavering faith and willpower.

"I would listen to and follow my husband's decision and action." The woman had lost half of all her teeth before she turned 60. "The doctor said that the water here has a high salinity level, so it is unhealthy whether we drink more or less. In the past, we would drink snow-broth in winter, while in summer, we would carry water home from the Emin River, one bucket for three-day drinking.

Unlike here, Linyi, my hometown, has sweet mountain spring water!" Having difficulty speaking due to loss of teeth, Liu still has a sharp memory, especially that of her hometown.

"Aunt, how often have you been back to your hometown since you arrived in Xinjiang?" This was what I was curious about.

She initially stretched out five fingers, but after some contemplation, she added another finger from the other hand. Then she shook her head and retracted the other hand, telling me with certainty that the total was five.

"Five times?!"

She nodded, stretching three fingers again, "I went back respectively when I gave birth to the first and second babies. After my husband retired, it was the last time we returned to our hometown. There were two more times, but I can't remember the occasion ..." She smiled with some embarrassment. At that moment, I noticed a trace of beauty still left from her youth on her wrinkled face with messy gray hair.

"Don't you want to go home?" I asked again.

"At first, I did, but now I don't!" Her voice suddenly cleared up, "My hometown is here. This place is my home!"

After spending 58 years here, the impression of their distant hometown must have faded, leaving only the grass and trees here to accompany them day and night with sincere feelings.

"Please come inside and take a rest. The wind is strong outside," said the elderly woman. As she ushered us into the house, she would occasionally look back at the national flag on a wooden pole in front of their house and expressed her concern, "Will it fall down?"

"No, Aunt, please come in with us!" After being confirmed by Guo Tiancheng, who is experienced with life in the border areas, the elderly woman took us into the house with relief.

"Uncle Wei Deyou was blown down by the wind when raising the flag a few days ago, and his leg was broken. He just came home from the hospital yesterday." Guo Tiancheng said before we entered the house.

It was my first time entering a residential house closest to the border. The house comprised of three low, narrow, and dark mud brick rooms. Apart from the entrance door, there were only one window in each of rooms on the left and right, which made the entire space look dimly lit. If there weren't a few light bulbs hanging above, the house would be in total darkness.

"Electricity was not available until recent years. In the past, even our troops had to rely on small diesel engines to generate electricity!" Guo explained. The elderly woman has spent decades living in a lonely hut with no neighbors within dozens of miles. As a woman from Linyi, Shandong Province, how has she managed to run this "home" all by herself?

As I gazed around the residence of these two border guards, a strong sense of admiration overcame me. How has this couple from Shandong managed to settle down and raise their children while protecting our border at the times without electricity or water supply, facing intense storms, heavy snowfalls, scorching sun, and sandstorm?

The answer lies right in the faces and bodies of Liu Jinghao and Wei

Deyou, who were leaning against the bed.

Upon seeing Wei Deyou, a veteran, I understood that he was the backbone of his family. Despite being confined to a kang(a kind of traditional Chinese heated bed) with a leg wrapped in splints and gauze, the 82-year-old still showed the toughness of a Shandong stalwart man. He wore a vest, his head bare and his bright, eagle-like eyes shining fiercely. I could imagine that it was with these eyes that he has guarded the border line for millions of people.

"None of the offenders have escaped from under your nose?" I started our conversation directly, with the smell of "gunpowder" traditional in the border areas.

"No, no one could escape!" The old man shook his head, very confidently.

"I heard that you have arrested and stopped more than 1,000 people trying to illegally cross the border in decades?"

He smiled but didn't answer, as if to say: The figure should be more, yet I couldn't remember clearly anyway.

"Now, almost no one flees!" He said.

"Hmm? Why?"

"Unless he is stupid. He can't have a better life in the other countries," he said contemptuously.

It suddenly dawned on me: Now that our country has grown powerful and prosperous, how would people want to go to the less developed places?

Wei Deyou sat there like a mountain, quiet yet resolute like steel. Seated on the kang, he held a radio of unknown time and place of production. Before visiting him, we had learned that he always carried a radio, along with other items he considered his "five treasures" — a horse, a whip, a pair of binoculars, and a kettle.

The horse is his means of transportation to patrol the border, without which he couldn't make an inspection tour all over the border around the No.173 boundary marker. Walking on foot will be ineffective in safeguarding the security of the border area.

However, Wei mentioned that there were occasional exceptions. "When the horse got sick, I must go on duty as if mounting a horse, for there was no 'leave' on the border line," Wei said.

"How many miles did you have to walk in such a day? You must be worn out!"

The old man looked out of the window and didn't answer my question, but his eyes, which were full of determination, told me that this was how he came through in those tough days.

"If the horse was ill, he would run to patrol the border line. He could run more vigorously than the horse when he was young," Liu joked, and Wei just smiled in agreement without saying anything.

"All the young men would strive hard." Wei smiled and told us a story like opening an old calendar, "During the 1960s famine, not a few people tried to flee to neighboring countries. Sometimes, we caught dozens of them a day; some were family. Once my horse was frightened and ran away, several people took the opportunity to flee from the back of the hill I guarded. As soon as I noticed, I immediately chased after them and managed to stop them until the public security border guards arrived."

"What if someone made up his mind to flee?"

Wei snorted and said firmly, "No way! Illegal activities must be punished!" Although he didn't mention the use of force, I guess that must be inevitable.

"I didn't carry a gun very often. I convinced those people by my mouth, and this, too." He held out his powerful hands.

"With a mouth and arms, did they listen to you?"

"They had to." There was dignity in his eyes.

Of course, crossing the border is illegal and can result in punishment by border guards and law enforcement officials.

"When I have difficulty stopping them by myself, I could send a signal, and the border guards would come and help," said Wei.

I see that he is a "wall" guarding the motherland's border. Behind him stands a more substantial Great Wall of Steel.

"He has many ways! No one dares to challenge him." His wife said while tying a tight belt for him.

"The People's Liberation Army has guns and grenades, and we have cattle and sheep!" She said.

I was a little puzzled, "Can cattle and sheep be weapons?"

"Anything can be weapons," Wei jerked in.

She smiled at her man with admiration as if she hadn't admired him enough over the past. Then she recalled, "Sometimes people fled in a group, thinking we couldn't catch up with them simultaneously. But he (Wei) had many tricks up his sleeve. With one whistle, he was able to gather hundreds of cattle and sheep and commanded them to encircle the fleeing group. Finally, they had no choice but to surrender. Do you remember, dear? Once, dozens of sheep tripped three men, causing them to faint to the ground. Then, the cattle crapped on the men's faces and bodies. Finally, they surrendered dejectedly."

Whenever Aunt Liu talked about this experience, she would laugh as if they had won a battle wonderfully.

While looking at Uncle Wei's expression, you would find calmness in his face. It seemed that he was used to these incidents.

There were also difficulties. Aunt Liu added, "During winter, heavy snow prevented the cattle and sheep from going out. Despite this, he continued his duty by riding a horse. On that day, he found a suspicious man at dusk. However, as night fell, it was too dark to follow him, so he hid in the snow until midnight. The suspicious man ran toward the border, while Wei chased him in the snow for three or four hours. Finally, the man was desperately exhausted and stopped, with his feet suffering from frostbite. Then Wei carried him back to our house and saved him!"

"Most of those violators are good in nature, bad ones are very few," said Uncle Wei.

"Yes, that's true. Few of them really mean to steal out. Life for them is hard!" Aunt Liu sighed and said, "They did everything to flee, but that's not so easy. It's said that several people who actually fled away were either put in jail or forced into hard labor over there. Even if they survived, their lives were more miserable!"

She sighed again.

"After these people were caught, should they be handed over to the troops or border police?" This was what I was more concerned about. Back then, those who violated the law to cross the border would have a tragic future if they were caught. Even if they were not in jail, they were very likely to be convicted of treason, incriminating their families.

"They would be seriously punished," he said grimly.

"Although he is able to catch people, his ability to release them is also great!" Aunt Liu really admired her husband from her heart. She took a look at him sitting at the kang and continued proudly, "'Catching' or 'persuading' made great difference here. If a bad man were caught, he would be sent to jail, while people who were not bad would be persuaded to return home. If they obeyed, leaving far from the border line, they may go without any punishment."

Oh, I see! I finally made clear an important "matter" concerning the border area.

The old couple smiled at me affirmatively.

"Your work is really not that simple!"

"Yes!" she said, "We don't have many guests now, but in the past, we used to take people back home almost every day, with our home as a hotel. Just after this one left, the other one would come. Sometimes, several people would stay here, some of them would even stay for a few days. We often help them keep secrets, or they could be reported to the border police, which would result in severe consequences. You can confirm this with him."

I turned to look at Uncle Wei, who was fiddling with the old radio but didn't answer. Obviously, he has many secrets that he was reluctant to reveal. Perhaps these secrets were considered taboo at that time.

Needless to say, Wei Deyou, who has been guarding the border for nearly 60 years, must have knowledge of many sensational and tragic stories that ordinary people may not know. From his eyes, I could tell that anything you could imagine would have happened on the border. After all, there is another country situated at the upper reaches of the Emin River, it is just there. Some people with delusions in mind might have the impulse to try at any cost, even their lives.

Tragedy might happen at any moment, especially in a multi-ethnic community with over 20 ethnic groups, such as Uyghur, Kazakh, and Russian. Certain anti-China separatist groups outside the border have been continuously trying to cause discord. From the moment Wei arrived from his hometown in 1964, he knew what was his responsibility. After taking the oath under the national flag, he was determined to defend and protect every inch of our border land with his life.

As the saying goes, one ant hole may cause the collapse of a thousand-mile dam. Wei and his wife Liu were very serious about their job, inspecting every corner around the border line of the No.173 boundary marker, which is under their patrol and control, making sure that no one would cross the border illegally, even wild animals like cats and dogs. "If we let the animals roam freely, then the bad guys might do the same too," Wei often said.

In his lifetime, Wei dedicated himself to guarding every inch of the land around No.173 boundary marker to prevent any "ant holes" along thousands of miles of the border line.

Here is the Gobi desert, where snowstorms and harsh sun rays prevail, and also a ranch that Wei never has reached its ends ... But he has to walk by every dune, inspecting every plant and rock, with his sweat dropping wherever he has been. Thus Wei has done for nearly 60 years, from a Shandong lad to a humpbacked man aged 80. We can hardly imagine what kind of historical vicissitudes he has gone through.

According to the local border cadres, Wei and his wife have been patrolling the No.173 boundary marker border line for almost 60 years, covering a distance of up to 200,000 kilometers, which is equivalent to five laps around the Earth. As ordinary people, it is impossible for us to imagine such a distance. When I stood at the door of Wei's house and looked at the seemingly endless border line, I realized that here was only a tiny part of the motherland's frontier. Compared to the Earth, the land is only the size of a human hair. However, these two ordinary heroes, who rode horses, drove sheep and even trekked on foot, have covered a total distance of five laps around the Earth in nearly 60 years. Who else would have the willpower, perseverance, and belief to achieve such a feat?

It is the couple of Chinese border guards who have created such miracles.

When Wei was young, he would whip and gallop the horse away in a handsome and mighty manner every day, which made his wife watching him at the door proud of him. When he returned at dusk, he would bring countless "stories" and "adventures" to his wife, which would amaze and entertain her, making her both surprised and delighted, laugh and sometimes even cry.

When middle-aged, he would look back at his wife and the children every day before going out, with a little sense of reluctance to leave. However, he would turn away with determination, leaving a word to his wife and children, "Wait for me!" They would wait. Sometimes, they would have to stay up late until midnight or even dawn. Whenever he got back home, the whole family would cheer and then go to bed quickly, leaving the room in darkness and silence, for he would set out on another journey the next day. "Let your father have a good rest," his wife softly told their children in the dark.

As he became old, his wife would remind him before he left, "Don't only search for bad guys. Watch out for the uneven roads! Do you hear me?" He would obediently nod like a schoolchild, "Yes, I do." In the morning light, these two curved figures cast long shadows, like two giant towering trees growing in the Gobi desert. When he returned at night, a lantern would guide him home until he dismounted from the horse and took off his cloth shoes.

As he became even older, aged 70 and 80, he still insisted on patrolling the border line of the No.173 boundary marker every day. His wife would talk much more, reminding him to cover the kettle after drinking water, not to expose himself to the heat of the sun, and to tie his hat tightly since he was now bald. Then he would raise the whip in his hand high and keep responding, "Uh-huh. My old lady! I see!"

"What did you see? Did you forget that last time you had suffered from diarrhoea for several days because you forgot to cover the kettle and drank cold water?"

"What did you see? Did you forget that you had your head sunburned because your hat was blown off in the wind?"

She began to complain.

"Come on, am I so delicate? I've come through for decades, and I can walk out and back even though I close my eyes."

He responded with firmness and perseverance.

"Yes, proud of you! You can go out and back with closed eyes!" She glared at him, bringing the hot soup to his mouth and wiping his face with a clean towel.

"Why did the hair on the back of your head turn white?" He exclaimed sentimentally, looking at her hair.

She patted her own head and said, "We are grandparents now. If our hair doesn't turn white, aren't we immortals?" Saying that, she smiled with some happiness and pity.

Later, the wife discussed with her husband: Since their children have grown up and get their own work, the couple might as well go on patrols together as when they were young instead of staying home lonely and waiting for the other's return.

"OK, as long as you can walk, I will patrol and herd with you." Wei nodded and carefully helped his wife onto the horse while he followed behind.

"Can you still remember how to sing our Linyi ditties?" She asked.

He replied, "Yes."

"Then — we sing a short piece of it?!"

She started to sing an unaccompanied folk song that echoed through the vast Gobi desert.

> Everyone praises that Mt. Yimeng is attractive
> Mt. Yimeng, nice scenery ...
> Nice scenery —

He sang his part loudly:

Verdant mountain and limpid water, what a picturesque scenery
The wind blows through the grass, revealing cattle and sheep

They sang together:

Sorghum turns red, soybean flowers are fragrant
Ten thousand buckets of millet, filling the whole barns
…

"Why don't you sing? Are you crying?!"

He asked her, pulling the rein in surprise.

She did cry and couldn't stop.

"I'm thinking, what if one of us can't walk anymore? Is there anyone else guarding the border?"

He smiled and said, "You must be senile! Do you think the earth would stop turning when you're gone? Maybe it will turn even faster and more stable."

She stared at him with anger and disbelief. "I don't believe it. Since you arrived here, even the leaders of the border guard said that there have always been safe here. They have also admitted that with my assistance, we have set their mind more at rest about the border line of the No.173 boundary marker. So tell me, haven't I contributed half of your meritorious deeds?" She fixed her gaze on him, waiting for his answer.

He smiled brightly, as bright as the flowers in full bloom in Salbulak grassland in May, and said, "More than a half! You have contributed most of them!"

"You said it!" She said with utmost seriousness, "I have been following you for decades, ever since I was a young lady, from Linyi to the western end of the country; from being free from worries about delicious meals to managing family affairs for you and worrying you all the time. But look at me now: humpbacked, toothless, grizzled, tottering and useless. It's making me think ..."

She cried once more, her skinny shoulders were shaking violently, then her whole body was shivering, even the old horse she mounted knelt down on the ground, letting her vent her "resentment" against her husband to her heart's content.

He dismounted from his horse, put away his whip, and sat beside her, letting her lean on his muscular body and sighed, "Alas! Think about it. You have surely suffered so much all the time."

She suddenly lifted her head, wiped her tears, looked at him strangely, and said, "You have never said that before. Previously, whenever I cried and complained, you would turn to me and scold me maliciously, warning that if I was reluctant to stay here, I could go back to my hometown! When I replied how could you stay here if I left, you would be even heartless to suggest divorce! You are cruel enough, especially for me! Tell me now, did you really want to divorce me? Ah? Have you ever thought about that?"

Now it was his turn to laugh again and say, "I don't want to divorce you from the bottom of my heart. But if you were really eager to leave, I thought I should let you go!"

She shouted angrily, "How can I leave? I have married you and gave birth to four children. How can I leave? where can I go?"

He got serious, "Wasn't that what you had said? If you broke up with me, leaving me here alone, then how can I hurt you again?"

Then, in a soft voice, she said, "You have caused trouble for me and our children all our lives." She cried again and continued, "But I believe that my life is worth it because I spend it with the man I love, and we have never been separated, never!"

He nodded, "Indeed, except for occasional meetings outside and a few unexpected confrontations with the enemies, we have enjoyed the meals and slept together." He laughed and reveled as when he was a young man.

She immediately, like a young lady, gave his arm a hard twist with her fingers and said in a playful way, "You wish!"

On that day, the moonlight over the border of the No.173 boundary marker was exceptionally bright. Wei and Liu, the "old couple guarding the Gobi desert", did not go home after sunset as usual but sat together on the sentry tower in front of their home for a long time, chatting a lot about their future.

Liu started with suggesting that they should return to visit their hometown after years of absence. However, Wei initially disapproved, saying that despite relatively fewer tasks assigned by the troops due to his age and relative peaceful situation on the border than before, he did not want to shirk his responsibility, patrolling the border and raising the national flag on time every day. In short, he has not changed from the early days, so he disagreed with the unexpected proposal from his wife to visit the hometown.

"If you don't go back, I will go myself," she was a little stubborn this time.

"Why do you insist on that? Apart from spending money, you would be exhausted along the long journey, as you are of old age, is it necessary?" said Wei.

"It's none of your business. I will go back on my own. I want to honor the memory of my parents at the grave and burn some incense for them," said she.

He shook his head and said, "It's all superstition. What's the use of that? It's the same to show filial piety by burning more incense and doing more kowtows here!"

"It's different!"

"What's the difference?"

"Quite different!"

"What's the matter with you?"

"I want to go back this time. I am already over 70 years old, and you are even older than me.How many more times are we able to visit the hometown again?" She cried again.

He seemed to understand, "Well, then go back for once? You mean ..."

She finally confided in him, saying, "We should go to visit our hometown while we can still walk and then come back here to stay until the end of our days. If I passed away before you, I want you to bury me behind the house so that I could accompany you.Otherwise how could you live alone?"

He didn't say a word for a long time, but his eyes were wet.

"In fact, I have considered it many times, but I didn't want to bother you. Ever since I came here, I have never considered going back, and I have decided to stay here until I die. I wish to have my bones buried here after my death. Since I have been here, I will guard the border for my motherland as long as I am living. I have no other abilities, only such a bit ability. So, I live to do such a deed. After my death, my soul would be buried here to make as many contributions for the motherland as possible. However, it is my personal decision, and it wouldn't be fair to ask you and our children to suffer with me, is it?"

She gazed lovingly at this tough man with great admiration, just like she did when they were young, saying, "You didn't get rid of me when you were alive. Do you really think you could do that after you die? No way!"

She put her head on his lap and said contentedly.

He stroked her rough hair with equal contentedness and said, "Then I won't let you go!"

On this particular night, the couple had made their second most important decision in life. Their first decision was made 58 years ago on their wedding day when they relocated from Linyi, Shandong Province, to the border area of Xinjiang. This time, they had decided to remain steadfast in their current location until their last breath, leaving their loyal bones in the land they cherished deeply. They wanted their souls to stay with the No.173 boundary marker, where they had spent their entire lives.

Oh, can you find other people in the world like this ordinary Chinese couple who have dedicated their whole lives to defend the border of their country?

In fact, they have made such a decision for some time without informing their children. As a result, in 2006, they refused their children's suggestion when their third daughter, Wei Xia, entrusted by her siblings, persuaded them to spend their retired life in the hometown in Shandong Province.

"No, I won't leave here. I am strong enough to do my work. To guard the border is the best way to spend my retired life. And your mom won't leave either!" Hearing her father's reply, Wei Xia, the favorite child of the old couple, began to cry and act like a spoiled child, just trying to persuade their parents.

"My dear daughter, don't waste time on us. Let me tell you the truth," Wei Deyou called his daughter up to him and spoke honestly, "Think about it. Why did mom and dad move here from Shandong, traveling thousands of miles? It was because Xinjiang needed more people, especially on the border where there were few families. If no one is willing to guard the borderline of thousands of miles, do you think our family and other Chinese people could live in peace? Someone must stay here to ensure peace and happiness for the whole country. Your mom and I have chosen this path even before you were born, so how can we give up midway?"

"Dad, you are retiring now, not retreating!" said the daughter.

Wei Deyou shook his head and said categorically, "Leisurely retired life is for others, but not for me. And if I leave, I may not live happily and in good spirit every day. Do you want your parents to live contentedly a few more years or die early?"

"Dad, how can you say that?" The daughter burst into tears.

Wei Deyou gently stroked his daughter's head just as he patiently taught her to walk when she was a baby. He said, "I am telling the truth. If you force me to leave here, you will take away my spirit! How can a person be in good health without spirit? Only when living in this Gobi desert can I keep fit and strong."

Upon hearing this, the daughter stopped trying to persuade him. Looking up at her aged but extremely resolute father, she seemed to understand everything. She said, "Dad, since you and Mom have made up your minds, I can't force you to do what you dislike. When you are too weak to walk, maybe my brothers and sisters and I will take your place to guard this land!"

"That's my good girl!" Wei Deyou exclaimed, "Her mom, could you please bring out the wine from the cupboard for me to have a drink?"

Wei Xia told us that on that night, she could sense an unusual happiness in her parents' hearts, a rare occurrence in the past decades.

Upon hearing Wei Xia's narration, I turned to Wei Deyou and his wife, who were seated on the kang, and asked them if it was true. They smiled, and Aunt Liu replied, "That was wonderful news for us! We used to be concerned about who would take our duty after we passed away. But now that our children are willing to continue our work, we are overjoyed. We may die without any regrets or worries. And our home can be preserved here." Her words were plain yet touching, which made us, strangers from afar, feel profoundly that there is an indestructible great wall of steel on the border of the motherland. Thus, we can better understand the saying, "The country is the people and the people are the country."

On that day, while I was having a conversation with Wei Deyou and his wife while sitting on the kang, their daughter Wei Xia returned home dressed in camouflage. She informed us that she had taken a leave of absence from work to patrol the border in place of her injured father.

"My sister started working early than me. And she plans to retire early so she can take over our father's duty. Thereafter, I can carry on with my sister's work. Regardless of what happens, as long as we are alive, there will always be someone in our family patrolling the border here!" Wei Xia said.

"Uncle, Aunt, you can rest assured completely!" I said to the old couple.

"Yes, we have already done!" They were smiling proudly.

During my conversation with them, I noticed that Uncle Wei was constantly fiddling with his old radio, which Aunt Liu called a "chatterbox". I came to know that the radio is one of the five "buddies" that Uncle Wei always carries with him, the other four being a horse, a whip, a pair of binoculars, and a kettle.

"He treats them better than me!" Aunt Liu glared at her old man, with her eyes full of "jealousy" and much reverence.

"How many radios have you used in decades?" I asked curiously.

"50. You said 50 last time!" Aunt Liu rushed to answer.

Uncle Wei just smiled, acquiescing to her words.

Aunt Liu told me that the first radio was bought in Shandong right before they moved to Xinjiang shortly after their wedding. "At that time, I served in the army at Tangshan, and radios were rare in our company."

Uncle Wei, who was "less communicative", even gushed when he talked about his "chatterbox".

"This 'chatterbox' is very important!" said Uncle Wei with a smile. "Initially, I used it to relieve boredom. Think about it: if you ride a horse and herd sheep alone on the same route, seeing the same Gobi desert every day, won't you be tired of it? Of course you will. It's called "aesthetic fatigue" in a fashionable way. Besides wind, snow, and sandstorms, what else is beautiful on the border? Cattle and sheep can't speak, and if you meet someone there, they're most likely a troublemaker. They won't talk to you but will try to avoid you and flee. So you don't have the chance to relieve your boredom by chatting with someone. In this case, this 'chatterbox' has become my closest partner besides my wife!"

Uncle Wei smiled when he said this.

"Hum, I am not closer to you than it is!" Aunt Liu muttered, "He carries it when he goes out during the day and also listens to it in bed before sleep at night. Who do you think he is closer to?"

"Ha ha ... I'm afraid this is the truth?" I asked Uncle Wei.

He laughed and acquiesced in it.

"If a person doesn't talk to anyone for a long time, he may even forget how to speak," he said.

"Isn't Aunt still by your side?" I said.

But Uncle Wei shook his head and said nothing.

"Am I any good?Only to prepare breakfast and pack food for him when he goes out on duty and make dinner for him when he comes back home in the evening. After dinner, he is usually too exhausted, and just goes to bed with his'chatterbox' ... Initially, we used to talk a lot, with frequent reminders. Over time, It turned to be just the same few words every day. Then we were reluctant to nag any more. A wink was enough for us to understand each other. Finally, we didn't bother to wink. Just a look may let us know what happened."

"That's called tacit understanding," I cut in.

"Yes, tacit understanding. Gradually, we can only say no more than two or three sentences a day to each other, just like a mute ... He is OK, for he has the 'chatterbox'. But me? I nearly became an idiot." Aunt Liu couldn't help shedding tears.

What kind of life is that? No talks. And they may not see anyone else in days, even weeks. Only the couple who don't need to talk has stayed here day after day ...for decades!

Feeling Aunt Liu's grievances and suffering, I was also choked up.

As I glanced over at Uncle Wei, the tough old man also looked a bit sad. I'm afraid that only this elderly couple knew how many difficulties and grievances they had encountered living in such a remote and isolated border area, like "no man's land." It is said that in the past few years, some people living relatively near the boundary marker No.173, guarded by Wei Deyou, had been incited by hostile forces and attempted to cross the border illegally. Wei Deyou, who couldn't speak minority languages, encountered difficulties when dissuading them. On occasion, those with ulterior motives would become hostile, demanding aggressively, "You can't even speak our languages. What gives you the right to stop us?"

After the setback, Wei started to thoroughly learn every word of the local minority languages. Later, when someone asked him a similar question again, he confidently warned them in a language that they could understand, "This is the border of our China, no one is allowed to cross it illegally. Anyone who breaks the law must be punished!"

Then, Wei Deyou would broadcast the national policies on border management to those who have been apprehended or returned after being dissuaded.

"The 'chatterbox' is not only my life 'partner', but also a good assistant for my work."

Now I finally understand why Uncle Wei can't live without the "chatterbox", and I even think that the radio is actually a critical and indispensable "component" of the couple's bodies.

A common couple hailing from an affluent hometown to the desolate deserts have dedicated their entire lives, energy, and passion to defending the country's border land for nearly 60 years. What does this spirit signify? I pondered over this question throughout the interview, but could not arrive at a definite conclusion.

Then I found the answer behind the details of this elderly couple's life narrated by their daughter: When Aunt Liu gave birth to their three children, the border areas was at the tensest situation, and Uncle Wei hardly had a minute to rest in his daily work. He not only had to guard the border all day long but also had to cooperate with other soldiers to patrol at night. At that time, Aunt Liu, who was either about to give birth or nursing the baby, was left alone at home. "No one have ever given me a hand! I was the only one who did all the domestic chores, taking care of our babies as well as feeding the cattle and sheep in the pen. I didn't complain about him, and I couldn't! In those tough times, we would thank heaven if he could return home safe and sound!"

Aunt Liu's words were flavored with appreciation, not complaints.

That day, Uncle Wei, Aunt Liu, and I sat closely together, having a casual conversation. We talked about the stories that had happened over the past fifty years. Uncle Wei was relatively quiet, possibly due to the pain caused by his injury, and only occasionally joined in on the discussions between Aunt Liu and me.

"Aunt, I noticed that there were no other people in this sentry post except for you. How have you managed to live all these years? You must have gone through a lot of hardships, right?" I asked Aunt Liu directly.

However, she looked at her husband, who had gauze tied to his right leg. After seeing that he didn't object, she replied, "Well, we have managed all!" She let out a sigh.

"What have you been living on without more fields to grow grain and vegetables around your house?" Naturally, I was most concerned about their basic living issues.

"The Corps distributes rations on a monthly basis, but the amount of vegetables is very little," she explained. "We need to find additional sources of food ourselves. In summer, we can still get by, but in winter, we sometimes might not have anything to eat."

"What do you do when you run out of food?"

"Find some wild herbs to eat."

"But how could you do that in winter when snow covers the earth everywhere?"

"We would stock up on dried vegetables in summer and autumn, and then consume them in winter," Aunt Liu replied.

Oh, it is so. I tried my best to imagine, but I couldn't conceive how this couple had spent every season in the wilderness of this no man's land.

"There is difficulties in summer, too!" She said, "Upon our arrival, we ran out of the food. At that time, he went out to patrol and herd sheep while I searched wild herbs in nearby hills. However, the food made from the wild herbs caused us much trouble."

"Why? Did it taste bad?"

"No. The herbs were poisonous and almost killed us. We almost didn't survive for half a year here," she looked at her man again with guilty.

But Uncle Wei looked calm as usual, which seemed to give her courage.

She continued, "I once cooked a pot of wild herbs for breakfast. At the time, we both felt nothing special. However, at noon, my stomach started to hurt badly, and I knew that I had made a mistake. I couldn't help but worry about him. What if he also suffered from stomachache while on duty? Covering the stomach with my hands, I wanted to go out and find him. But I didn't have the strength and fainted outside for a long time. When I finally woke up, I found that he still hadn't returned, even though it was already sunset. I was anxious but didn't know what to do. At that time, I was a newcomer, unfamiliar with the area, and there was no phone in our house. The company was also far away, so the only thing I could do was waiting. As hours went by, he still didn't return."

"And what happened at last?" When I saw that Uncle Wei had no expression and was silent, I asked Aunt Liu.

"Later, I was so anxious that I cried and prayed to heaven for mercy and help," saying this, the rims of her eyes were red, tears dripping on her wrinkled cheeks.

My eyes were also wet.

But Uncle Wei still had no expressions, seeming to be utterly indifferent to all this.

"I was scared to death that night, thinking that he died from the poisonous food I cooked."

Suddenly, Wei's facial expression changed a bit, and he said, "Not so serious."

"He didn't come back until midnight," she said. "When I asked him, he told me that he had a terrible stomachache which was so painful that he fainted. After regaining consciousness, he went to patrol again and looked for the scattered sheep. So, he returned that late."

"It scared me to death!" She repeated the words.

"After that accident, I would taste the food my husband was going to eat the next day every night. If I didn't have a stomachache, then I would prepare the same food for him, or I would change the ingredients the next day." She looked at her husband a bit proudly as she spoke.

There were somewhat "soft expressions" on Wei's face, with inadvertent feeling of gratitude in his eyes.

"That was so hard for you, Aunt!" It was my turn to sigh.

"Not at all. It was all over. I survived, and so did he." She smiled, shedding tears, and then smiled again.

I couldn't bear to ask anymore.

However, she went on, "Since I followed him to move here, I could only try to stay healthy so that I can prepare food for him every day. Otherwise, how can he go to work?" She stared at her man.

Then, there was a silence for a moment.

"Uncle, Aunt truly had a tough time for decades here! Has she ever been unable to keep on?" I asked him.

"Yes. There was once a few years ago," said he.

That was the case: Uncle Wei was selected as a Touching China figure in 2016 and flew to Beijing to receive the award. However, upon his return, he noticed that his wife was ill unusually. After medical examination at the hospital, it turned out that she had contracted brucellosis, an illness that can affect both human and animals. Although the doctor recommended hospitalization, she refused it and was determined to treat the disease at home.

"Please let me go home. Without me, my home will be in a mess," she pleaded with the doctor.

"No, it won't," the doctors said.

"It will! My husband can't take care of himself alone," she said as she was about to get up from the bed.

The doctor held her down and said, "Your temperature is 40 degrees Celsius, you have a high fever! You have inflammation." The doctors comforted her by saying, "All you need to do is to receive the treatment here. Uncle Wei has already called to reassure you that he can take good care of himself."

"He? Take care of himself? No way, I don't believe him." Aunt Liu's head shook like a rattle. The doctors smiled and didn't respond, but insisted on treating her for two weeks.

Half a month later, Aunt Liu hurried home to see her man. As soon as she entered the door, she smiled, "Well, it is as good as before."

Uncle Wei proudly said, "Do you think I would starve without you?" He then added, "Just wait! I will cook a meal for you." The almost 80-year-old man then busied himself in the kitchen, and after a while, he served a bowl of boiled tomatoes and a bowl of noodles to his wife, who had just come back from the hospital. Aunt Liu, who had been following her husband for almost 60 years, had never eaten a meal cooked by him. She was moved to tears and praised, saying, "Taste good!"

During an interview on CCTV, Wei Xia shared the story I mentioned above, leaving the young audience in tears despite her relaxed and cheerful narration.

An elderly couple have been guarding the border for more than half a century, sincere and patriotic. They have been living a life so simple and tough, yet remained optimistic and full of love. Seeing them made me realize something that I had never understood before: This is what our people and motherland truly look like. Our country are built by people like them with iron will. The People have built such an iron-made country!

In 2021, when the Communist Party of China celebrated its 100th anniversary of its founding, Wei Deyou and his wife, Liu Jinghao, traveled to Beijing to receive the "July 1st Medal" awarded by Xi Jinping, General Secretary of the CPC Central Committee, President of the nation, and Chairman of the Central Military Commission. This award is a supreme honor, only given to 39 individuals out of more than 90 million members of the Communist Party of China.

"On that day, I sat with the audience and watched General Secretary Xi present my man with a certificate of merit, take a group photo with him, and congratulate him. I was so overjoyed that tears streamed down my face. He didn't receive this honor for nothing; he truly deserved it!" Liu Jinghao shared in an interview with reporters at that time.

During my visit to the border on June 28, 2022, I interviewed them. Uncle Wei was unable to walk due to a leg injury, so Aunt Liu, who was humpbacked, served us drinks and food. She mentioned that during those days, she had a lot of daily tasks to complete, including raising the national flag each morning, taking care of the livestock, and looking after Uncle Wei.

"My daughter has taken over her father's work!" Aunt Liu added before sending me to the vehicle. She haven't changed a bit, still the "good Aunt from Shandong".

When I departed from them, I felt a little sad: it was too distant, secluded, primitive, and challenging to live there. Even though they had recently renovated their tiny house, they might still face extreme temperatures, either from the freezing wind or the scorching sun. Comfortable living conditions seem to be impossible for the old couple in their seventies and eighties.

"Please take these two watermelons for your children in Beijing, they're very sweet," Aunt Liu said, handing me the fruit before my departure.

"No, no, Aunt, keep them for yourself, and for Uncle." I almost shed tears when I refused to take the fruit.

What simple Chinese people they are!

The vehicle has already gone far away from the borderline, but I kept looking back at the national flag flying high in front of the couple's house for a long time ...

Chapter 16

Love Left on the Land Where Pomegranates Bloom

The world today has been divided into developed and developing countries.

The rise of the former has almost invariably been built upon the plunder and infringement of others.

Some of these countries, despite having begun to decline today,

Still harbor thoughts of hegemony, seizing others' wealth, and even depriving others of their basic rights to survive.

The Chinese people, under the leadership of the Communist Party of China(CPC),

Through hard work, mutual assistance, and many measures like "the poor helping the poor", "relatives helping each other",

And "the East assisting the West", have achieved a comprehensive victory in the tough battle against poverty.

With unity, we are endeavoring to build a modern socialist country with Chinese characteristics.

Its institutional advantages, national features, and the

people's aspirations

Are the crystallization of the indomitable national spirit and traditional culture,

And the key for the Chinese nation to stand tall in the Eastern world, and the foundation for us to move forward to a better future,

Which have already been engraved on the land of Xinjiang like a rainbow ...

Today in Tacheng, there is a special phenomenon: all of the most fashionable, spectacular, beautiful, and inviting buildings, roads, schools, public facilities, and houses for poverty alleviation are invariably accompanied by the label — "Liaoning Aid to Xinjiang."

These are not just a few ordinary words. They represent the radiant glory of the socialist system with Chinese characteristics and signify the inheritance and elevation of the solidarity and mutual assistance of Chinese traditional virtues, through which we have achieved a renewed, richer, and more representative major country consciousness of "putting the people first" and the commitment to defending every inch of our land. This is the unique feature of this era under the leadership of the CPC.

Defending borders and territories is a consciousness shared by every country and nation. However, the extent, duration, and thoroughness of the Chinese government's assistance to border regions is unparalleled, a great achievement beneficial to generations to come, due to new China under the leadership of the CPC and the contemporary China that has become strong and prosperous after reform and opening up ...

    Fifty-six constellations and fifty-six flowers
    Fifty-six ethnic brothers and sisters are one family
    Fifty-six kinds of languages remit a word
    Love China, love China, love China
    Hey, hey,hey

    ...

Almost all Chinese people can sing this song because it expresses the heartfelt wishes for harmonious coexistence and prosperity among the fifty-six ethnic groups in our country.

Since ancient times, the central government had attached importance to Xinjiang. However, it was since the first generation of central leadership, with Comrade Mao Zedong at the core, issued the command and General Wang Zhen led a hundred thousand troops to settle in the Gobi Desert on the border to open up wasteland, that the action to aid Xinjiang has begun. From then on, the action has become a lasting expression of deep national sentiments by brotherly ethnic groups, provinces, and cities toward Xinjiang, spanning over half a century ...

Xinjiang is not only the largest autonomous region of our western border with the longest borderline with neighboring countries but also like a big garden of our motherland. Its "fences" need to be constantly and permanently fortified, and the variety and species of flowers there need to be continuously added and refreshed. The practical and essential purpose of aid to Xinjiang is to make the people of all ethnic groups in this vast and beautiful land live a better and happier life and to make the border more secure.

In the past, aid to Xinjiang was mostly a direct action by the state and the government, and brotherly provinces and cities have always been supporting Xinjiang in various ways. In 1996, the Central Committee of the CPC made a groundbreaking strategic decision to launch aid to Xinjiang. So from the beginning of 1997, the first group of cadres from across the country came to Xinjiang. Thereafter, almost every year, a group of cadres will be sent to Xinjiang, as the "National Aid to Xinjiang Operation" under the unified command of the central government. On March 30, 2010, the National Counterpart Support Work Conference in Xinjiang was concluded in Beijing, the measures of aid to Xinjiang were adjusted, 19 provinces and cities were assigned the task to aid different regions of Xinjiang in a one-to-one basis.

Liaoning Province was the counterpart aid province to Tacheng Prefecture, which was paired with "one City and two Divisions", namely, the relevant cities of Liaoning formed counterpart assistance with the counties and cities in Tacheng Prefecture as well as the relevant units of the Eighth and Ninth Divisions of the Corps. As a result, "Liaoning elements" have appeared in Tacheng rapidly, creating a scene of "pomegranate flowers blooming" that shines even more brightly. National unity, regional development, and people's living standards have been improved rapidly, with "Tacheng Phenomenon" attracting more attention from the world — and this is also the most dazzling glory of this era that I have witnessed while walking on the land of Tacheng ...

"Tacheng College"

For centuries, the people of Tacheng had dreamt of having a college right at their doorstep, for themselves and their children. However, Tacheng had never had one, and this had been a long-held dream in people's hearts. Many years ago, when they saw that their neighboring prefectures established their own local colleges, they finally spoke out about this dream, but it remained unfulfilled for a long, long time.

During my interview, the locals couldn't contain their joy and pride in their hearts any longer and told me, "We now have a college, and you must go and see it."

Is there really a college here? I couldn't believe it, so I wanted to see the campus for myself.

"In 2020, the college was formally registered with the Ministry of Education, and it was built with assistance from Liaoning Province," they said.

That's how it was.

It is a fundamental task crucial for generations to come in aiding the establishment of a college! It was probably the best project among all the aid programs. I thought that besides poverty, the issue of ethnic unity in border regions was mainly the backward education. It is the most important thing for young people in the frontier as well as a fundamental issue to ethnic unity to make the children of all ethnic groups able to go to universities nearby. After learning professional knowledge in the college, they can live independently, have skill to do something, and pursue a brighter future.

"It is an important task given to us by General Secretary Xi Jinping to strengthen Xinjiang in developing education and culture. Assisting Tacheng in establishing this college is a tangible project. Now, over 3,000 young people from various ethnic groups have fulfilled their dreams of attending college in their hometown," the principal of Liaoning Aid to Xinjiang Project said as I stepped into "Tacheng College" i.e. Tacheng Vocational and Technical College. He spoke tirelessly, explaining how they've helped Tacheng over the years, starting with the establishment of a vocational and technical college from scratch, taking into consideration the actual needs of the Tacheng Prefecture.

"Here we are." We came to a vast and beautiful suburban green field. The grand entrance of Tacheng Vocational and Technical College was striking and magnificent, giving us the impression of a newly built college.

"The campus covers an area of 1013 mu ... This is the first phase of the new campus. The construction investment of over 80 million yuan all comes from the funds of our Liaoning aid project. It took two years to build the campus as it stands now," he said.

"In the past, we were one of the few prefectures without a college in the regional education system here. If it weren't for the assistance from our brotherly province, Liaoning, even if we cherished the dream of having a college, it would have remained just a dream," said a leading official from the Tacheng Education Bureau, who accompanied us around the campus. Pointing at the rows of new and orderly buildings, including classrooms and teaching halls, he couldn't help but say, "Now, even many children of cadres from our bureau are studying here ..." As he spoke, I looked at him closely and noticed a glimmer of tears in his eyes.

The people in Tacheng indeed wanted to have a college here!

They are grateful to the people of Liaoning for helping them fulfill a century-old dream!

There's no need for more words to describe it. Just by looking at the faces and clothing of the students coming and going on the school playground, I could tell that most of them were ethnic minority students ... "That's right, nearly 70 percent of our students are ethnic minorities. About 30 to 40 percent of them are from Tacheng Prefecture, while the rest come from various prefectures in Xinjiang, with more from Kashgar," he said.

"Why?" I was very interested.

"Because more such graduates are in need in Kashgar. Their development requires talents in various areas, which gives our newly established vocational college a great advantage in terms of specialization and student recruitment ..."

That's how it was.

"We'll soon celebrate our third anniversary, and a few days later, we'll also have our first graduating class ..." said the principal, who came out of the academic building to greet me, his face filled with a sense of pride and sacredness.

As I asked, I found out that he was an educator from Liaoning. His name is Sun Xiuyan, formerly the vice principal of the Guidao jiaotong Polytechnic Institute.

Although ordinary people know little about this Institute, it was a well-known vocational and technical college in northeast China, an old industrial area in the 1950s and 60s.

"The college where I used to work, the Guidao jiaotong Polytechnic Institute, was established in 1950 and was the first vocational and technical college in China, serving rail transit construction. I worked there for a long time. When I was called to Tacheng to build a new vocational and technical college, I was truly excited, even though I hadn't been to Tacheng before, and it was the same for other teachers who came here. But we all bear this in our mind: to contribute our all to the building of a distinctive new college in the Tacheng Prefecture with our own abilities ..." It is clear that Principal Sun has strong feelings for "Tacheng College" that he established with his own hand.

"How many years have you been here?" I asked.

"It has been almost two years, namely four semesters ..." he answered.

"Compared to your former unit, what is new do you feel?"

"I have a lot to talk about it!" My words ignited his enthusiasm. "In the past few decades, when I worked for the old unit, life was a steady routine. Here, everything is different. Every day is filled with passion ... Look, every stack of bricks, every building, every green patch on the playground, even every classroom, student dormitory, and student ... they are all 'growing' right under our eyes, so we have particularly deeper feelings for them and it makes us energetic!"

"What's the most challenging aspect of establishing a new college?" While communicating with the principal, I was led to an office in the academic building, where more than a dozen teachers were waiting.

"These are the teachers who came with me, and a few of them

are currently in class ..." Principal Sun introduced while answering my question, "Of course, the most difficult part is about how to conduct curriculum offerings and how to teach."

"Tacheng didn't have any college in the past, let alone a vocational and technical college. Although there are some vocational schools in other parts of Xinjiang, most of them are in southern Xinjiang. We are in northern Xinjiang, and the direction of development is primarily determined to be a higher vocational and technical school for nurturing ethnic minority professionals in local areas, which means that we would start from scratch in everything, even in terms of enrollment and curriculum offerings, there are few experiences to draw from ..."

"So you have to figure everything out on your own?"

"You could say that."

"There must be a lot of joys and hardships!"

Principal Sun smiled and said cheerfully, "There are definitely more hardships than joys, but even in the 'hardships' there are still sweetness!"

"How is that?"

"For example, when we establish a new discipline here and successfully incorporate it into our teaching process, proving its feasibility over a semester or more, and after it is gradually improved and completed, we can proudly say that it's an original creation in the country! And through the admissions process, we are able to enroll children who were previously on the pastures or in tents, do you know how happy we are?"

"Why? Weren't you all teachers in colleges before?" I was a bit puzzled.

"It was totally different!" Principal Sun waved his hand repeatedly and explained, "In the mainland, in some long standing vocational colleges like ours in northeast China, although we've been enrolling and cultivating graduates, it's relatively difficult for them to land jobs after leaving college. But it's different here! Our first batch of students hasn't even graduated yet, but there are already requests from many regions in Xinjiang, like Ili and Kashgar, asking for employing our graduates ... which gives us a sense of great accomplishment!"

That's how it was.

"It's more about having a sense of responsibility and mission in our hearts, accompanied by a sense of joy ..." a woman teacher who didn't tell me her name said, "Coming here, we feel the excitement, happiness, openness, rigor, endeavor, and passion every day. From learning the local languages and adapting to the living habits to adjusting to the climate of the four seasons in Northwestern China, especially the freshness of visiting the students' homes, it brings us happiness and vitality, urging us to strive forward. It feels like chasing the sun and time every day, reaping the fragrance of flowers and the fruits of our labor, and filling our hearts with love and joy ..."

"You teach Chinese, right?" The woman teacher spoke with such literary flair.

"No. I teach mathematics ..." Her answer surprised me.

Principal Sun said happily, "Since we arrived here, we have all become poets. Haha ..."

"So I heard most of you are serving overtime?" On the way to the college, the leader of the Liaoning aid delegation had introduced the teachers here.

"Yes, we are. We chose to stay here because here is so attractive and the work here needs us!" Principal Sun explained. According to the rules for aiding Xinjiang, the usual service period for teachers supporting local education is two semesters, "But our college is new, and everyone hopes to see the first batch of students they have brought up can graduate successfully ..." Before he could finish his words, a young woman teacher interjected, "Just like having the first child, it's so exciting and nervous!"

"Haha ..." Her words brought laughter throughout the room.

"You don't go back home during the holidays?" I asked again.

"No, we don't! When the students are having a holiday, it's the perfect time for us to calm down and focus on researching issues related to our disciplines and teaching. Besides, it's particularly important for us to make home visits to students' families, and none of us would want to miss it. Moreover, we really have seen Tacheng as our home ..." She answered.

"Having been here for nearly two years, everyone has made sacrifices, and there were some things happening ..." the principal explained. More than ten teachers who came from Liaoning were the backbone of this new college, undertaking the most important teaching tasks. "Some teachers lost their elderly family members, or their children are preparing for college entrance exams, but they can't go back home. However, no one ever complained ..." He said.

"Is that so?" I asked all the teachers in the room.

They all nodded.

"You've never regretted?" I asked again.

All of them said unanimously, "Never ..."

I was moved, with my eyes a little wet.

At that moment, cheerful voices echoed throughout the campus — it turned out that the students had finished their classes and were taking a break.

I saw so many college students with proud and joyful smiles on their faces, running and playing on the playground like birds about to embark on a distant journey ...

Ah, that was the most vibrant and beautiful scenery in Tacheng!

In fact, I know that in every county, every town, and even in many villages scattered throughout the grasslands and valleys here, there are countless primary and secondary schools built through the Liaoning aid project. They are like stars dotting this beautiful land in the western part of our motherland, bringing warmth and hope to the children.

Landmarks in Tacheng

In Tacheng, there are several landmark buildings, with the most famous being the Tacheng Red Mansion, which is truly aesthetically pleasing. The Mansion was built in 1910 by the Russian Tatar businessman, Jemazan Kanishev, with a pure Russian style, and its red walls were engraved with the year "1911" all around. It is not large, consisting of two floors and 16 rooms of varying sizes. There are delicate designs in its ceilings, floors, tin roofs, door frames, and windows. The walls facing the street are all red, hence it has the name of "Red Mansion". After 1949, it served as the administrative office of Tacheng, and now it is the Tacheng Museum.

The Tacheng Red Mansion is always a landmark in the locals' minds. However, today Tacheng has developed more "landmark complexes," especially in recent years, with one after another appearing in people's sights. Many of these new landmarks are constructed as part of the Liaoning aid project. For instance, the first hotel I stayed in Tacheng was called the "Ningcheng Hotel," which is located in the administrative center. The new administrative buildings, a library, and an art gallery in Tacheng have formed a modern landmark architectural complex, which is spectacular and full of aesthetic feeling, being rare in cities at the prefecture level in Xinjiang. I know that almost all of these buildings were constructed or partially participated in through the Liaoning aid project. They have given a sense of pride and warmth to the people here, especially the younger generation, which perhaps cannot be exchanged for any material wealth ...

Before sunset that day, the afterglow of the sky made the beautiful art palace gleam like gold, as if it were a dreamy world. The deputy commissioner proposed to take me to visit the Accordion Museum.

"Tacheng is the hometown of the accordion and has once set a Guinness World Record with a thousand accordions playing a song for ethnic unity. We are known as the 'Capital of Accordions' ..." He proudly escorted me into the art hall for a visit and then took me to the world's largest Accordion Museum housing thousands of accordions.

Having visited so many art and cultural relics museums, it was my first time to visit a museum with such a rich collection of accordions. Here, you can find the oldest accordions in the world, as well as the most modern and expensive ones. Of course, there are also accordions that bear the imprint of significance of the nation and the times ... In short, the accordion is an important cultural emblem for the local people. When the accordion resounds, they would sing and dance, indulging themselves in the bliss and joy.

The accordion reflects their temperament and character, and likewise, it also keeps their pursuit of a happy and beautiful life. Therefore, when Tacheng wanted to build an art hall and a museum dedicated to accordions, the decision-makers from the Liaoning aid project quickly provided support in terms of manpower and funds.

Just after visiting the Accordion Museum, the next day we came across another museum, the Xibe Ethnic Museum, located in the Karahabak Township on the outskirts of Tacheng City. Although it is not large, the museum boasts a rich collection. The Xibe ethnic group, originally from Liaoning, migrated thousands of miles to the Ili and Tacheng areas due to the need for border defense, thus establishing a bloodline connection between Liaoning and Xinjiang. Complying with the aspirations of the people, the headquarters of Liaoning aid to Xinjiang Operation soon brought the Xibe Ethnic Museum into line with the aid project and brought experts from the Liaoning Xibe Ethnic Museum to fully support and assist in the construction of the museum in Tacheng, symbolizing the "kinship" between the two regions.

"Family matters should be handled properly because we have deep affection so we must help to build this museum well!" It is said that the construction of the Tacheng Xibe Ethnic Museum received high attention from the leaders of Liaoning Province. And it proved to be worthwhile. After it was built, every year during the Westward Migration Festival on the 18th of the fourth lunar month, Xibe people of all ages from various parts of Tacheng will gather in festive attire, play the Dongbuer with the Moke tune, and dance Beile'en heartily with vigorous and rhythmic movements. The girls shake their shoulders gracefully, exuding charm, while the boys perform "duck steps", creating a cheerful and peaceful ambiance.

"Nowadays, not only the Xibe people celebrate the Westward Migration Festival, but people from other ethnic groups also actively participate, creating a more lively and joyful ethnic gathering each time." The locals told me.

There is no need for imagination, for you can experience the joyous scene of people from various ethnic groups dressed in festive attire, singing and dancing in celebration, which is truly delightful and intoxicating ...

Some memories will be etched in one's mind forever just after visiting somewhere once. Outside the town of Emin County, there is a village called Ganquan, where it is said that a clear and warm spring flows all year round. The Liaoning officials had foresight indeed — they, with the support of the local government and residents, invited experts to create a well-thought-out "business plan" in Ganquan Village and built a super stylish and modern food plaza.

The local official took me for a visit in the evening. Although I couldn't see the full view of this food plaza under the moonlight, I was amazed as we walked along the main street towards Ganquan Square, which was such a high-end food plaza that emerged in such a remote wilderness!

Every building has its own unique characteristic, resembling a famous food eatery. Not only are there well-known domestic food brand restaurants from all corners of China but also a few international Western cuisine franchises are found here. Later, I learned that it was also one of the Liaoning aid projects.

"Tacheng is an important gateway for the Belt and Road Initiative and an international border trade city. Since ancient times, it has had a thriving commercial atmosphere and a consumer base, and its future development prospects are limitless. Therefore, together with the local government, we built this food plaza that combines ethnic charm with international standards, aiming to meet the growing consumption needs of the local population and provide services to domestic and international guests. You see, a considerable portion of the famous food shops here have taken advantage of the strengths of our international cities such as Shenyang, Dalian, and Dandong ..." As we strolled, an official from Liaoning assigned in Emin County introduced along the way.

"How's business?" I asked the beautiful duty manager standing at the entrance of a Western cuisine upscale restaurant.

"It's going well. We are busy mainly on weekends when you may see a bustling crowd coming and going in this street of delicacies ..." she replied.

"Are they all local guests?"

"Guests are coming from Karamay and Urumqi, too. And I have also hosted guests from Shandong and Sichuan Provinces!"

I couldn't believe it. But when we sat down in a Chinese restaurant to eat watermelons and drink some tea, I noticed three men at the next table drinking beer and playing amusing finger-guessing games in Henan dialect. It seemed that the woman manager wasn't lying to me.

"When we established this food plaza, we did our research and preparations beforehand. After numerous discussions and evaluations, the project was finalized. The actual results after completion have far exceeded our expectations. The locals call it 'Night Market in Ganquan,' and its reputation has spread far and wide. So, besides the local consumers, now tourists from all over the country often come here ..." The official in charge of the Liaoning Aid Team was quite proud.

Later, I discovered that there were more than one or two popular food landmarks like this in downtown Tacheng as well as in other districts, which was very amazing.

It's hard to imagine that in such a remote border land in northwest China, a prosperous commercial atmosphere would emerge, just like the scene described in a poem, "In the night market, thousands of lights brighten the clouds, visitors can be seen everywhere in and outside the tall buildings." It was indeed remarkable ...

Perhaps because Tacheng's administrative area is much larger than other similar-level cities in other provinces, I couldn't explore every beautiful corner of the entire region. I missed seeing many iconic buildings and public facilities, which was a great regret. But perhaps it was a coincidence that when I passed through Yumin County, a new landmark building caught my curiosity and astonishment. I wondered why the Liaoshen Campaign Memorial had been "moved" to Tacheng.

Look, the front wall with red and white is solemn and grand, with eye-catching big Chinese characters "Liaoshen Campaign Memorial" on it. I could see people streaming in and out continuously ...

"If you look closely, under the name of the Memorial, there are more Chinese characters — 'Yumin Branch'!" A local cadre explained to me.

I chuckled to myself, wondering how I could have missed those big Chinese characters! What surprised me was why the Liaoshen Campaign Memorial had opened a branch in Tacheng.

"In recent years, in accordance with General Secretary Xi Jinping's requirements, we have strengthened our support for cultivating cultural development in Xinjiang. The establishment of the Yumin Branch of the Liaoshen Campaign Memorial is a typical project. By doing so, we can not only ensure that the red culture in Liaoning can be extended to Xinjiang, but also allow people of all ethnic groups here to share the spiritual wealth created by the CPC. Likewise, we will bring the spirit of Populus Euphratica and that of Little Poplar in Xinjiang and Tacheng to various places in Liaoning and strive to transform them into an inexhaustible driving force for the revitalization and development of the old industrial base in Northeast China ..." After listening to the words of the official in charge of Liaoning Aid Team, I couldn't help but feel emotional. The memorial in front of me is more than just a beautiful landmark. It is a spiritual home built together by Liaoning and Xinjiang.

It was warming this land.

And It had already warmed the hearts of people of all ethnic groups here ...

Tacheng Industrial Park

When we talk about "parks" here, we refer to special areas for industrial production and processing. In developed countries and regions, these types of parks can be found everywhere, and usually represent the economic development and driving force of the local economy. You may say, Where such parks are well built and developed, local economy and society will be equally well-developed.

If we put such "parks" at a larger scale, to the national level, then Shenzhen, Pudong and Hainan would be regarded as the nation's "industrial parks", though they are called "special zone" or "new district" at the national level.

A typical industrial park is like the one in my hometown, Suzhou. In the eastern coastal regions, almost every county and city has such "development zones," "industrial parks," or "science and technology parks". Some even have several of them. They are the most vibrant places for local economic development, representing a new form of industry and technology, and cultural expression with Chinese characteristics under the conditions of economic globalization. They have been playing an engine-like role in driving and promoting local economic and social development.

In the past, such kind of industrial parks had developed very slowly in Tacheng. However, since the Liaoning aid team came here, various types of "parks"like miniature special economic zones have developed rapidly, bringing about a strong, vibrant, and colorful new economic wave to Tacheng which once had a relatively single economic structure. The key is that the local inhabitants, especially the young generations are allowed to experience a work and living environment similar to that in "Beijing, Shanghai, and Guangzhou" right in their hometown. It has also allowed ordinary residents here to constantly experience that "life is also wonderful and beautiful at home" ...

"In the past, I was always eager to work in Shenzhen or Shanghai because I thought so many people worked and lived together there. But I couldn't go because my child was still young, and I couldn't bear to leave home. Now I am working in an industrial park less than 10 minutes away from home. Every day, I work in a workshop with familiar girls, laughing and joking. I'm very happy and also earning a good salary. This is the life and work I dreamed of before, and now it has come true right at home!" Ayiguli, a Uighur girl working in an industrial park on the outskirts of Toli County, now has her own motorcycle. Every morning, she rides her brand new motorcycle like a soaring bird, happily zooming along the roads, her face filled with happiness and pride.

Mijiti is a Kazakh truck driver, who used to transport goods over long distances before working in the park. Now he is the captain of a transportation team in a company here, managing around ten drivers. "In the past, I transported bulk cargo from Tacheng to Urumqi, but due to the unstable job, I didn't earn much money although the work was tiring. Having to support a family of four to five, I felt so much financial pressure. Now, I'm working for a large enterprise in the park near my home. My job becomes stable, with a closer transport distance and a salary higher than I earned before.And I can take care of my family. Therefore, I think that building an industrial park at my doorstep is just like ensuring my family's life. I feel reassured, so I can do my work more energetically!"

In Toli County, we met a Hui man in his 30s or 40s, who had just got off work. Because of some disabilities in his legs and feet, he could not work and earn money in Karamay Oilfield, which was not far from his home. In the past, he lived a very difficult life with his family and couldn't afford the tuition fees for his two children. "Relatives from Liaoning have built an industrial park here, giving priority to employ our disabled people to work in the factories. Now I can earn a lot of money myself, and the factory also pays us social insurance, which has greatly improved the living standards of my family. I don't have to worry about the tuition fees for my children anymore!" He said that he worked as a product quality inspector in the factory and the factory's part-time doorman in the evening. The factory director treated him well and gave him an "overtime pay", so he was very satisfied.

How is the industrial park in Tacheng going? Has it really changed the local development pattern and made people of all ethnic groups live a new life? This is a " secret for interview" hidden in my heart.

During my interviews in Yumin, I happened to learn that the Jinyu Ecological Park had officially opened. I was fortunate enough to witness people from various ethnic groups dressed in vibrant traditional costumes gathering here from all directions. According to the locals, the Jinyu Ecological Park is a "must-visit place" in Yumin.

Although it is not an industrial park, it undoubtedly lives up to the name of a "park" that is more suitable for people's lives. It is an ecological park built with a focus on the environment, various plants, and recreational facilities. In fact, it should also be considered a park related to "industry" and "economy," as the builders clearly intend for the park not only to enrich and satisfy the cultural and tourism needs of the local people but also to generate some income.

Just hearing its name, one can tell that it is a product of the joint efforts by Liaoning and Tacheng. "Jin" refers to Jinzhou, Liaoning Province while "Yu" refers to Yumin, Xinjiang.

We soon learned that the Jinyu Ecological Park was one of the important projects in the Liaoning Aid Program. It was established in 2013, covering a total area of 1,500 mu, with a total investment of 120 million yuan, including 92 million yuan from aid funds from Liaoning. Operating for eight to nine years, it has always been the most popular "must-visit place" for the locals. In early 2022, Liaoning Province and Yumin County invested more than 50 million yuan to improve and upgrade its facilities and landscapes, giving this ecological theme park in Yumin a fresh and distinctive touch, increasing its attractiveness to tourists.

"Seeing is believing. Come on, let's go in and take a look," a team member led us into the Jinyu Ecological Park. At that moment, we felt as if we were in a sea of flowers. The colorful blossoms stood out against the blue sky and white clouds. The whole park was filled with a delightful floral scent, which was truly enchanting. The park was bustling with visitors, especially children who were enjoying themselves to the fullest. A resident named Wang Jinhuan told us, "Today, I took my children around, and we think that the scenery here is exceptionally beautiful. The water is clear, the trees are tall, and the grass is green. We have vast grasslands in Yumin County, but we don't have a decent park here. Liaoning relatives helped build this park, allowing us to enjoy nature right at our doorstep. Our life standard has truly been elevated!"

Wang Haman, a tourist from another city, said, "Although it's my first time visiting Yumin County, what I see here is completely different from our perception of a small western county town. It is a beautiful town filled with a modern vibe, which is surprising. Originally, we planned to stay here for just one day, but now we are considering to stay for three days to fully experience the beauty of nature and environment here ..."

"This is exactly what we hope for," said the team members, filled with excitement upon hearing people's heartfelt words.

When I first heard the name "Yemili," I thought it was a mistranslated word and should have been "Yemini" instead. However, I later discovered that I had misunderstood. Yemili is the former name of Emin County and the Emin River. In the early 13th century, Genghis Khan led a victorious westward expedition with his 200,000 soldiers and subsequently divided his empire among his sons. One of these territories belonged to the House of Ogedei, conferred to his third son, Ogodei. The realm included what is now Tacheng Prefecture and the western part of Mongolia. At that time Yemili became the political, economic, and cultural center of the House of

Ogedei. Even today, faint remnants of that era can be found on the barren hills of Emin County in Tacheng. The echoes of galloping steeds can still be sensed in the air ...

Ten years ago, when the Aid Team from Liaoning set foot on this land for the first time, the insightful team leader decided, based on the idea of "concentrating enterprises, gathering investment, and inclining policies towards industrial parks," to build an industrial park in the ancient land of Yemili that could help the local economy "turn the tide." Liaoning Province, an old industrial base in Northeast China, is well experienced in developing industrial and economic parks. In view of the slow industrial development and lower fiscal revenue in the Tacheng Prefecture with agriculture and animal husbandry as main sectors of economy, the Team decided to focus on the construction of an "industrial park" to drive the local economy. Then Liaoyang Aid Team assigned to Emin County prioritized the construction planning of the "Liaoning Aiding Xinjiang Industrial Park" in Yemili.

Later, this park becomes known as the "Emin (Bingdi, Liaoyang) Industrial Park" with a planned area of over 10 square kilometers, divided into recent and long-term development plans. The first phase of construction, covering 4.4 square kilometers, has long been completed. Local residents refer to it as the "New City of Yemili." It rises vigorously on the banks of the ancient Emin River, with wide roads and newly erected buildings, are hope of prosperity and happiness for the locals. Over the past decade, Liaoyang City has made devoted efforts to cater to Emin's industrial needs and continuously improve the development of the industrial park, bringing warmth and blessings to the people of all ethnic groups here. For example, at the initial stage of the construction, Liaoyang invested 5.51 million yuan to build the Mahelesu Reservoir with a total storage capacity of 32.54 million cubic meters, which not only solves the water supply-demand of the industrial park but also provides irrigation for 150,000 mu of farmlands in 18 villages and townships including Emin Town, Mahalesu Town, Huogiert Mongol Ethnic Township, and the regional sheep farms. "Hold a handful of clear springs, grateful of my relatives, the Millennium dream has come true." When the people of Emin, living near the industrial park, drank the sweet spring water from their taps for the first time, they joyfully came to the accommodation of the Liaoning Team with enormous banners, singing and dancing to thank their assistance sincerely. The scene moved the team members to tears.

Perhaps it was local people's deep feelings and high expectations that invigorate the hearts and strengthen the determination of the team members. After successfully establishing the industrial park, they have immediately devoted themselves to promoting investment. With their experience and enthusiasm, renowned enterprises and branded products have been introduced into the park, becoming the driving force of Emin's economy. For example, the project with annual output of 100,000 tons of drip irrigation fertilizer and compound fertilizer invested by Henan Xinye Guanfeng Fertilizer Co., Ltd has successfully settled in the park. The Xinjiang Jiuzhou Agricultural Technology Development Co., Ltd, with a registered capital of 30 million yuan, has also established projects for corn and wheat seed production in the park ...

From enterprises with multi-million-yuan capital to companies with hundred-million yuan capital, the Industrial Park has drawn more and more investment, enjoying a development process of constant change and improvement. Xinjiang Longhuiyuan Pharmaceutical Co., Ltd, established by Xinjiang Longhuiyuan Investment Co., Ltd, is a company primarily focused on the fine processing of licorice extracts. After settling in the Park, the company brought on stream immediately, with an annual industrial output value reaching several hundred million yuan and tax contribution of tens of millions of yuan. It not only became a major taxpayer in the Tacheng Prefecture but also filled the industrial gap in the area. Emin County, known as the "granary, meat storehouse, and edible oil jar", has long been a base for the production and processing of green food in China. In view of such advantage, the Aid Team members proposed the concept and action plan of "green investment" in their efforts to promote investment, they actively formed alliances with Fortune 500 companies and China's top 500 enterprises, bringing in more than 10 environmentally friendly enterprises such as COFCO Sugar, COFCO Tayuan Safflower, COFCO Tunhe Tomato, and China Power Investment Corporation. These have immediately driven the overall economic development of Emin County to a higher level.

"An industrial park is like a clear spring. Its inherent energy and spillover effects have put the economic development of the entire Emin County on a fast track, and the lives of over 200,000 people from various ethnic groups have undergone qualitative changes. We are deeply grateful for the selfless assistance from our brothers and sisters in Liaoning ..." The head of the Emin County government specifically told me to add these words.

I am aware that Liaoning has established no fewer than ten projects like the Emin Industrial Park in Tacheng, especially the Liaota New District in Baketu, covering an area of nearly 90 square kilometers, a super-sized industrial and port park that represents the deep friendship and affection poured in by the entire province of Liaoning for the people of Tacheng of all ethnic groups. Today, these parks, big and small, are brimming with vitality and playing a significant role as engines of economic growth, propelling the comprehensive development of Tacheng's economy ...

Newcomers to Tacheng

In this global village with over 7 billion people, who are your relatives? When you arrive in Tacheng, you'll discover a magical answer. It turns out that all people in the world might be relatives.

Tacheng people and Liaoning people were originally "kin of one family", and this special blood relationship has lasted for nearly a thousand years —

According to historical records, in 1132, Yelü Dashí, who had fought north and south for more than a decade, led tens of thousands of troops from his homeland — the Liao region on a westward expedition and settled near the Emin River. On February 5, with the support of his civil and military officials, Yelü Dashí declared himself emperor in Yemili and, according to local customs, was known as "Chu'er Khan" (meaning Great Khan). His Ministers also gave him an additional honorific title — "Emperor Blessed by Heaven", marking the beginning of the Yanqing era. During his enthronement, Yelü Dashí said to his officials, "After a journey of over 30,000 li (15,000 kilometers), trekking day and night in the deserts, I have dared to ascend the throne thanks to the blessings of our ancestors and the efforts of all of you. It is only right that I take care of your late grandfathers and ensure their honors, so we can all share it." From then on, tens of thousands of Liao people have settled down and procreate in the Emin area. Despite subsequent centuries of war, the bloodline of the Liao people has never been severed.

When I arrived in Tacheng, I asked the locals, especially the Xibe and Tatar ethnic groups, as well as some compatriots in other ethnic minorities, whether their ancestors came from Liaoning, they all nodded without hesitation.

It also makes me understand why the Liaoning Aid Team is so

committed and dedicated to Tacheng. It turned out that they have harbored a secret in their hearts that don't need to be spoken out: Helping Tacheng people means helping their own relatives — those brothers and sisters who have drifted here ...

> This bond of affection is longer than the mighty Liao River.
> This connection is purer than the snow atop Mt. Tianshan.
> We share the same ancestors,
> Our blood flows
> With the same genes
> Therefore, we join hands to build
> A new home
>
> ...

Back then, our people traveled countless miles to defend the border against enemies. Today, we fly across thousands of miles to help our relatives get rid of poverty and become better off, ensuring their everlasting happiness. These are the heartfelt wishes from thousands of Liaoning Aid Team members who come to Tacheng, many of whom have made Tacheng their second home and rooted themselves here. Some cadres from Liaoning, with original three-year term of service for aid to Xinjiang, have asked to extend their service time again and again, staying in Tacheng for as long as five or six years. Technical experts' original term is one and a half years, but the longest time some medical experts from Liaoning served has been more than six years, due to their dedication to the children and patients in need here.

Zhang Chengliang, a cadre of the team, is one of them. He is well-known in the team and Emin County, even to the point of being a household name, for this man from Liaoyang has riveted golden "happiness nails" for relatives in this land with his own heart —

As one of the first members to come here, Zhang Chengliang initially served as the Deputy Secretary of the Emin County Party Committee, in charge of building industrial parks, promoting investment, and upgrading the industrial structure of the county. Each of these duties presented formidable challenges, but Zhang believed that tackling difficult problems was precisely why they were here. Otherwise, what's the use of it? In order to succeed, they must be prepared to endure hardships and exert significant effort.

Everyone knows that Tacheng has a place called "Laofengkou", where the wind and snow are strong enough to lift trucks and cars off the ground. Zhang Chengliang worked in Emin County, where happened to be around that place, with hurricanes and heavy snow being rampant usually more than half a year. "In order to develop, we must find industries which are more suitable for the local condition. Which direction should the local industries go? No doubt, we must promote traditional industries of the past, but we need to adjust, change, and enhance them according to the principles of scientific development. The future of Emin depends on new industries, and we need to seize every opportunity to exert our efforts based on practical considerations ..." At a meeting of the Standing Committee of the County Party Committee, Zhang Chengliang expressed his sincerity to his new hometown.

Eventually, the County Party Committee and the Liaoning Aid Team jointly formulated a blueprint for the development of five major industries in Emin, aiming to break free from the limitations imposed on the traditional industries unchanged for a thousand years influenced by the natural environment of the "Laofengkou".

The blueprint made people excited, but a Beijing-based renowned planning and design institute viewed it as an empty talk, putting it in a state of "freezing coldness." This made the beautiful blueprint face a wave of skepticism from the local People's Congress deputies.

"Chengliang, we need you to persuade the experts from the institute to consider our county's natural environment and conditions and provide us with a feasible guidance," said the County Party Committee leader.

The leader didn't talk much, but Zhang faced great pressure. No explanations, no conditions mentioned, he just simply took on the assignment.

This was truly challenging. Moreover, the advance payment of 2.7 million yuan for the planning and design proposal had already been made, leaving no other choice. In a poor county, paying every penny had been carefully considered. To ensure the blueprint not to be in vain, Zhang Chengliang's only option was to rely on his own perseverance to shoulder the responsibility. In the next three months, he tirelessly visited all 169 villages across 17 townships, gathering comprehensive information about the county. Carrying a large bundle of materials with him, he flew from Tacheng to Beijing, making his way to the renowned planning and design institute.

"This is fantastic! With these on-site materials and data, we won't be stuck with just impractical discussions anymore!" After all, the well-known institute had competent experts who, upon reviewing the firsthand information brought by Zhang Chengliang, grew elated. They said, "You are the living encyclopedia and living map of Emin County. Stay and work with us to complete the planning, so that it may remain in the right direction."

Zhang thought that was a good idea, avoiding the awkward situation that had happened during the first planning process.

After accepting the invitation, Zhang became a key member of the planning and design team. Among the doctoral advisors and researchers with doctor's degree, Zhang was like a "chief consultant," constantly invited to give advice to the experts. As a representative of the Emin County government and a "consultant" for the planning and design project, Zhang wholeheartedly devoted himself. For 59 days straight, he burned the midnight oil in a small room, providing analysis and suggestions to the experts during the day. He even mercilessly rejected their design drafts several times.

"Why do you think my idea is not feasible? On what basis?" At a time, Zhang rejected a proposal that was put forward by a professor-level expert, leaving the expert feeling embarrassed. Zhang was not discouraged because the professor lost his temper. On the contrary, he took the initiative to approach the professor and, drawing from his own experience with the destructive power of hurricanes in "Laofengkou", explained the impact of Emin's climate on agriculture and natural environment. At last, the professor wholeheartedly accepted Zhang's suggestions, presenting a more scientific and practical industrial planning proposal.

Owing to Zhang's three months of field surveys and nearly two months of stay in Beijing, the institute completed the blueprint for the five major industries of Emin County, which successfully passed the review by the Standing Committee of the Emin County People's Congress.

Although the blueprint was in hand, a bigger decisive battle was still to come to achieve the goal, especially during the industrial transformation when some traditional old enterprises and factories must be restructured and reorganized. Then the old and new contradictions of restructuring and reorganizing enterprises would inevitably emerge, forming a reverse trend and force against reform.

"Oh no! Something bad happened!" One morning, as Zhang was

about to enter the office building of the county government, he found that the entrance was blocked by a noisy crowd. As he approached, he found that it was a group of people from the county's Grain and Oil Purchase and Sales Company, which was about to be restructured ...

"If our company is restructured, we'll lose our jobs! Who will be responsible for our livelihoods?"

"That's right! If you want to do it, pay each of us 1 million yuan first!"

"If you don't pay, we will not leave unless a car runs us over!"

The number of petitioners and onlookers outside the main entrance of the office building continued to grow. At that moment, it was like the entire Emin County town had stirred a hornet's nest ... It seemed that no one was willing to be persuaded.

What to do? How can this be resolved? The leaders of the county committee were extremely anxious. "We've encountered various problems regarding the restructuring of traditional enterprises in Liaoning as well as Liaoyang, where I previously worked. Let me handle it!" This time, it was Zhang Chengliang himself who took the difficult task. He was well aware that no one in the Emin County government had dealt with a similar situation before, so he volunteered.

"Zhang? He's an outsider, he'll surely treat us even worse. Don't be deceived by his sweet talks!" As soon as Zhang Chengliang entered the Grain and Oil Purchase and Sales Company for doing some survey, someone dealt him "a head-on blow".

After all, most of the employees in this large collective enterprise were ethnic minorities, so language was a barrier between them. When someone met with Zhang Chengliang, they would start speaking in a language he couldn't understand. When he spoke seriously, they would claim that they didn't understand. When he began to bring out the facts and reasons, they whispered to each other in a language Zhang couldn't comprehend, while smiling mischievously ...

"What did they say to me?" Zhang asked the interpreter.

The interpreter shook his head in haste and said it was nothing, and they were just muttering.

"Well, what did they mutter about?" Zhang grew impatient and continued to press the interpreter for answers.

"Well ...they were actually scolding you," the interpreter had no choice but to tell him.

"Scolding me? For what?" Zhang continued.

"They were scolding you for not being one of them, for not caring about their hardships ..." the interpreter translated.

Zhang fell silent after hearing it. Finally, he said, "We can't blame them. We oversimplified the restructuring process. I need to talk to each employee separately and listen to their demands ... Only when we resolve everyone's problems can we truly achieve the goal of restructuring the company." From that moment on, Zhang changed his approach and patiently addressed each employee's concerns one-on-one. After explaining the policies with great care and patience, all 85 employees of the company eventually agreed to the restructuring plan.

"We trust Secretary Zhang. He understands our concerns like nobody else. What more could we ask for?" These employees who underwent restructuring sincerely voiced their support.

To the surprise of the county committee leaders, out of the 85 employees, 84 raised their hands in agreement with the restructuring. "Chengliang, you've made another contribution to this matter. Make sure to share your experiences with everyone at the Standing Committee meeting." The county committee secretary delightedly praised Zhang Chengliang.

Zhang smiled after hearing his words and said, "Once I resolve the concerns of the last employee, I will report to the Standing Committee members in details ..." The person who had not yet agreed with the restructuring plan was Hailar, a Uyghur middle-level cadre. He intentionally avoided connecting with Zhang Chengliang before to express his dissent towards the restructuring.

"Let's have a proper talk ..." Zhang Chengliang finally found Hailar and said thoughtfully, "It's okay if you don't figure it out for the time being. Take your time to consider it. If you have different opinions, feel free to voice them. No problem cannot be solved. We can discuss it together !"

If Hailar didn't agree on the first day, he would talk to him on the second and third day.

A week later, Hailar joyfully held Zhang's hand and said excitedly, "Seeing how sincere and genuine you are, Secretary Zhang, I believe that the new enterprise after restructuring will surely be better. Our work and lives will also be better. I have now figured everything out and firmly support you. Moreover, I want to be at the forefront of doing a good job after the restructuring!"

In the first year after the restructuring, the new company turned turned from deficits to profit, achieving an increase in revenue of 6.02 million yuan compared to the previous year. The employees who came from the original enterprise praised Zhang for giving them a sense of dignity.

November 2015 was the busiest month for Zhang, who was in charge of promoting investment in the industrial park and the enterprise restructuring in Emin County. But at that moment, Zhang's father, who was far away in his hometown, suffered a cerebral hemorrhage and was in critical condition. Knowing that Zhang had important work to do in

Xinjiang, his family didn't dare to inform him directly. His elder brother only mentioned that if he had time, he should come back home for a visit. Although Zhang promised to go home over the phone in a loud voice, he never left Tacheng.

"Dad has already passed away ... There's nothing you can do by coming back now! Just focus on your work in Xinjiang." The night when his father passed away, his elder brother called and said these words.

"Oh, Dad ... I'm so sorry! Boohoo ..." The grievous news made Zhang collapse in his chair, crying uncontrollably.

"I could never forget that scene. It was around 7:40 pm, with all the lights off in the other offices, only those in Secretary Zhang's office was on. I went to report to him but saw him wiping tears. I asked him what happened and he said, 'I just received the news that my father passed away ...' Secretary Zhang, as he spoke, couldn't hold it back any longer and burst into tears, crying loudly while leaning on the desk. It was the first time I saw such heartbroken crying from a man, not to mention our secretary was so tough at ordinary times. I was deeply shocked and moved!" Wang Hong, the Executive Deputy Director of the Emin Industrial Park Administrative Committee, said.

"Childhood is like pastoral songs, while adulthood is like *Lisao* (one of the works by Qu Yuan). Just like the verses in the poetry, when we grow up, we always travel thousands of miles. We came to Xinjiang to help our brothers and sisters of all ethnic groups get rid of poverty and live a happy life. Although we are far away, unable to show filial piety to our own parents and help our family and children, it is still worth it. It is another form of love and filial piety towards our own family ..." Zhang Chengliang, who could spiel off Tang and Song poetry, often used stories of filial love from history to educate and influence his teammates.

Zhang Chengliang later served as the overall commander of the team in Emin County. He set strict demands on himself and all team members, "Not only should we be like family to the people of Emin, but we should also be the seed of ethnic unity."

Resjiang Kapitan from Sanlizhuang Village, Jiaoqu Township in Emin County, was Zhang's paired "relative". When talking about him, the 80-year-old always said, "Secretary Zhang is as close to me as my own son." The elderly had been bedridden due to illness for a long time and his family faced financial difficulties. Zhang coordinated with Liaoyang medical experts in Xinjiang to provide free consultations and treatment for him, sponsored him medical expenses amounting to 2000 yuan, and later even personally contributed 10,000 yuan to help his family open a family canteen.

Zhang's another "relative" was a Uighur elder Krym Mohammad aged 78 from Sihain Village. His son Asidin Krym had a blocked blood vessel in his thigh, but local hospitals were unable to provide treatment. Upon learning about it, Zhang immediately helped contact a hospital but found out that they didn't have enough money for the surgery. Zhang paid 25,000 yuan himself to cover the expenses of the surgery and comforted Asidin, "Don't worry about the money, I've dealt with it! You just focus on getting better and take care of yourself." Krym and his son held onto Zhang's hand for a long time, saying, "You are even closer than our relatives ..."

Zhang worked in Emin County for 6 years, exceeding the regular service period. Although he has now left Tacheng and returned to his hometown Liaoyang, he continues to make efforts to help with investment promotion and industrial development in Emin County, providing ideas and solutions. He has even quietly paid out of his own pocket to help solve problems for several of his "relatives" in Tacheng.

People around him said that Zhang Chengliang had already become a true Tacheng resident from the bottom of his heart, and Zhang himself said, "The 6 years in Tacheng are the most unforgettable time of my life. How could I bear to let go of this connection? Now when someone asks me where I'm from, I can't help but say, 'I'm from Tacheng ...'"

Like Zhang Chengliang, many team members already consider themselves Tacheng residents. Li Zhaokui, the Deputy Director of the Dandong Women and Children's Hospital in Liaoning, is another " Newcomer to Tacheng."

Li Zhaokui was one of the first group of doctors sent from Liaoning to Xinjiang, and his hospital did not assign him to this mission. The reasons were not complicated. Li Zhaokui was already the head of the Third Obstetrics and Gynecology Department, with a senior professional title, over 50 years old, and could have retired in a few more years. Normally, people in such positions didn't consider going to Xinjiang. Furthermore, Li Zhaokui had health problems at that time, suffering from hypertension and heart disease. Additionally, his daughter was about to get married, and everything was settled, including the wedding date, hotel, and wedding service company. However, unexpectedly, Li Zhaokui proposed to the hospital leaders that he wanted to go to Xinjiang. His colleagues asked him, "Then, what about your daughter's wedding?" He said, "It's all right! My daughter supports me. We saw the situation in Xinjiang on TV. There is really lack of medical care, especially for women in border minority areas. Gynecological diseases are serious there and I have more medical experience, so it is more suitable for me to go."

In this way, Li Zhaokui came to Tacheng with the deep friendship of the people of all ethnic groups in Liaoning Province. "In fact, gynecological diseases here are more serious than we thought, which also forces us to work hard every day, with hardly any time for a rest ..." During his first year in Tacheng, in addition to helping doctors in local hospitals,

Li Zhaokui spent most of his time making house visits in person, even on weekends, and sometimes he even went to the grasslands and the field to see his patients.

"Dad, when will you be free?" His daughter who was to be married called again and again to ask her father when he would go back to attend her wedding. His response was, "Wait a little longer." In fact, he didn't have time to go home.

Day after day. Li Zhaokui calculated. Well, he had been to Tacheng for two years ... How many patients has he seen? Fifty? Eighty? It was more than that. A hundred? A hundred and fifty? It would be more. There must be 200, or more than 200! Later, his colleagues in the department did a rough count for him.

"And he also broke a record. For the first time, a pregnant woman with cancer was treated by him ..." Li Zhaokui smiled a little and then closed his eyes with extreme tiredness.

At this point, his colleagues saw a line of tears streaming from his eyes ...

Later, Li Zhaokui returned home for lung cancer surgery. On the day he left Tacheng, his colleagues from the hospital and many of his patients and their families came to see him off.

"I will come back ... If I can't, I will have my daughter bring a part of my ashes here. Because I'm already a man of Tacheng ..."

As Li Zhaokui waved his hand reluctantly, many people who came to see him off were already shedding tears.

Ah —
In a huge crowd, who am I?
In the surging waves, which one am I?

On the journey to support Xinjiang, I am the one who dedicated quietly;

In the course of glorious undertakings, I am the one that will always surge forward.

I don't need you to know me, neither do I crave for your recognition.

I merge my youth into the rivers of my motherland.

…

On the journey to support Xinjiang, I am the one who is striving selflessly;

In the galaxy of the Republic, I am the one that will shine forever.

I don't need you to eulogize me, neither do I yearn for your gratitude.

I merge the glory into the constellations of our motherland.

…

Zhao Zhen, the leader of the Liaoning Anshan Aiding Xinjiang Team working in Shawan County, accompanied us to interview several well-integrated minority families in the county. As it was lunch time, he had a casual meal with us. While waiting for the waiter to serve the dishes, he, as the Deputy Secretary of Shawan County Party Committee, couldn't help but sing their favorite song — *Song of Liaoning Aid to Xinjiang*, telling us about the difficult journey of their team helping the local people lift themselves out of poverty. Unexpectedly, this seven-foot-tall man started to shed tears while singing …

"Secretary Zhao, what's the matter?" We didn't dare to ask too much. As the saying goes, men only weep when deeply hurt. He must have something that deeply hurt him.

While all of us at the table looked at each other speechlessly, Zhao wiped away his tears and said, "I'm sorry, my son has driven me to the point of helplessness, so …"

"What happened to your son?" we asked cautiously.

But he suddenly raised his head, leaned back, and said, "It's not his fault. It's mine …"

"What do you blame yourself for? People here have been praising you for staying here beyond the scheduled time. They speak highly of you!"

Zhao Zhen smiled bitterly, shaking his head and saying softly. "All is what I should do. We came here to help the locals. That's nothing special. But sometimes, disputes would arise with my family and my child … not really disputes, but more of our helplessness. Being busy with work, I am unable to spare time to look after them, so it's easy to cause misunderstandings. That's why my son is like right now, which is bothering me."

So that was what it was. I hoped this Deputy Secretary of the Shawan County Party Committee in Tacheng and the leader of the Liaoning Aid Team could tell me some of the true stories and emotions hidden in his heart.

Therefore, during that lunch, it basically became Zhao Zhen's storytelling session:

"I have never been to Tacheng before, and I didn't know what the situation was like here. When the government was selecting personnel for aid to Xinjiang, initially, we have the right to choose. We may come and have a look first, and then decide whether to stay or not. I was one of those who hadn't decided yet, so I came here to take a look. After coming here, I found Tacheng was wonderful, but the people here were not rich, particularly with the backward and monotonous industries, so there was great potential for development, and it was worth doing something here. Then, I decided to stay, and later, the government assigned us from Anshan City to aid Shawan County, and I was appointed as the leader ...”

As the leader of an aid team in a poverty-stricken area, Zhao Zhen, delegated by the government, led more than 20 team members to wholeheartedly assist in local industrial adjustment, formulating development strategies and planning, just upon arriving in Shawan. After the planning was ready, they worked tirelessly to promote investment while also carrying out a range of activities, including pairing up and building relationships with local families. As Zhao Zhen put it, “Once you’re in Tacheng, everything is about work and mission. There’s no holidays, and even if we are given a day off, we wouldn’t be able to rest in idleness. So much work is left to be done, each task requires personal attention, and they are all matters that weigh on our hearts. So, we don’t have much time left to take care of our family ... Over time, problems may arise in our own families, which can be distressing.” Zhao revealed genuinely.

He told us that most of the team members had encountered similar problems to some extent. Despite understanding the importance of their work, it is difficult to dilute and resolve specific life issues simply with “awareness”. Zhao Zhen’s problem was quite typical. Shortly after he left home, his wife called to inform him that their son’s academic performance had declined sharply — something that had never happened under Zhao Zhen’s strict discipline. However, after he went to Xinjiang, his son, who was poorly self-disciplined, seemed to have acquired a sense of “freedom.” The result was a rapid drop in his academic performance, and he even failed to enter high school because of his poor grades!

“I do not disapprove of you going to Xinjiang, but you can’t let our son ruin himself like this!” His wife told Zhao Zhen on the phone in tears.

Zhao Zhen had nothing to respond, and that was what he could only do. What else could he do? No one understands a child better than his father. In the past, when he was at home, Zhao had to closely monitor and discipline his son so that he could pass his exams year after year. But now, being in Xinjiang, thousands of miles away from home, his son seemed like a bird suddenly released from a cage, who could stop him?

"I can't leave now ... How about you bring him over to stay for some days? I can talk with him, and you can also relax here." He said to her.

His wife really came to Tacheng with their son. But after they arrived, they saw Zhao who was so busy from morning till night as an aid cadre that he could hardly have time for a proper conversation. "I wake up around 7 a.m. every day, which is equivalent to 5 a.m. in mainland. At that time, my son and wife were still asleep. I usually came back after midnight, and by that time, they were already asleep ... So, we couldn't even have a few words of conversation." Another team member sitting at the same table said that what Zhao said was all true, and every team member was in a similar working state.

After living for a while, his wife said to him, "Xinjiang is such a beautiful place. Can't you spend a day with us?"

He frowned and said to her in apology, "You can see that I really don't have any free time ..."

She forgave him, but their son saw all of it, and he had his own thoughts.

They couldn't stay any longer. His wife and son were going to leave Tacheng. Seeing them off at the train station was necessary. "I've never shed tears. But that day, the three of us hugged together, tears streaming down our faces ... I couldn't help it either."

Zhao took the opportunity of going to Urumqi on a business trip and saw his wife and son off at the airport.

At the ticket checkpoint, his son suddenly walked up to his father, with a serious expression, and said to him, "Dad, if you still do like this next time, I won't come to see you anymore!" After saying that, he turned around and walked away.

He was shocked by his son's words for a moment and stood there for a long time, not knowing what to say.

"What he said truly hurt me ..." Zhao said. Like all the cadres, he owed a lot to his family, and he knew that, including his wife and even his son, they did support his work in Xinjiang. However, the high school entrance examination of his son was a major event that affected his son's life, so his family had to consider it. His son was obviously not a well-behaved student, so he needed to be supervised to keep up with his peer classmates. However when his father went to Tacheng, thousands of kilometers away from home, his academic performance immediately fell off a cliff, which was unacceptable to his mother, even if he did not want to lose face in front of his classmates and teachers. But everything had already happened, and then he grew a rebellious mood. In addition, he and his mother traveled thousands of miles to Xinjiang, hoping to have a family reunion, but Zhao was too busy with work to consider their feelings, so he felt much more dissatisfied. Finally, the misunderstanding between them became more and more serious ...

"Son, Dad owes you. You see, you are a little tired of the school at home anyway. How about coming to the school here? It's also very nice, and you can make some ethnic minority friends of the same age, who treat you sincerely and warmly." After all, even a dispute between a father and son can be reconciled. One day, Zhao, with a very gentle attitude, called his son for more than an hour and patiently talked about his ideas and suggestions.

His son thought for a long time, and finally agreed, "Then I'll tell Mom ..."

"That time, my son was really well-behaved. He transferred to another school in Tacheng as I wished. We had a harmonious relationship when he first arrived here, and he even helped me bathe for I was tired after work. It was touching and made me very happy," Zhao said, then sighed, "But good times didn't last long ..."

"What happened?"

"At that time, he was already in Grade 11, which was a very crucial semester. One day, he came home from school, threw away his backpack, and shouted at me, 'I'm not going to study anymore!' I was taken aback and asked him what happened, but he was so angry that he didn't want to speak to me," Zhao Zhen said. "I realized that there must be something going wrong at school, so the next day I went to his school while on my way to work and spoke to his homeroom teacher. It turned out that my son didn't want to continue studying because of me ..."

What was the reason? The homeroom teacher told Zhao Zhen that while other students went home after school, his son stayed and didn't want to leave. When the teacher asked why he wasn't going home, he said, "My dad is on duty outside 24 hours a day. It is boring for me at home."

Upon hearing these words, Zhao felt guilty. He talked to his son at home, hoping he would understand the significance of his work in Xinjiang.

But the conversation didn't go well. His son initially looked silently at his father, then didn't say a word, showing that he understood the nature of his father's work and sympathized with it but was also unhappy with this living and studying environment.

"If you're not studying, what do you want to do?" Zhao broke the silence and asked him.

"I want to work ..." his son said reluctantly.

"Work? What kind of work can you do at such a young age? Do you think working is easy and fun?" A flame of anger rose in Zhao's heart.

"I want to work! And I don't want to stay with you anymore …" His son swung his hand and left the house.

"You!" Zhao clenched his fist tightly. He wanted to beat him up, but he held back.

They reached an impasse.

His son really left. Zhao was filled with anger, but he was also remorseful and helpless — He continued to work day and night and didn't even have time to think about his family or his son. The projects and tasks in Xinjiang kept going one after another, and he had to give his all, putting in all his efforts for good results.

"In my brief moments of free time, I would think about my son who left in anger …" He said, looking exhausted and frustrated.

As I looked at him sitting at the dinner table, comparing him to the energetic Zhao at work, I couldn't help but feel sympathy not only for him but also for other team members like him, including those doctors and teachers. They all face personal and difficult situations, maybe even harsher than his, but they have endured silently … It was an extremely admirable form of dedication.

"What happened to your son afterward?" I asked cautiously.

"Not bad," Zhao Zhen seemed to regain some strength from his guilt and said, "After about a year, my son bought a ticket from another place and returned home … He spent three days on a bus. Without much money, he could only afford an ordinary long-distance bus ticket. And for the final leg of the journey, he had to walk back home, resulting in swollen feet. When he was back, my father saw him in that pitiful state and angrily called me, scolding me fiercely …"

He smiled bitterly, while we couldn't smile …that was truly bitter for his son and him.

I believe that many of the members also have similarly bitter experiences, but they don't talk about it. They continue to smile every day, dedicating their passion and blood to their posts, pouring their wisdom and sweat into serving the people of Tacheng, watering the arid deserts with clear springs, and planting seeds of prosperity ...

"Thank you, my dear!" A Uighur elder brought a large watermelon and said to Secretary Zhao.

"Come and taste my sweet grapes ..." A Kazakh woman villager pushed a cart to the lodging of the team members, insisting that they accept the freshly cultivated fruits from her own vineyard. "Without your help, my vineyard wouldn't have yielded so well!" She spoke with tears of gratitude in her eyes.

"Uncle, please look at my school report ... I got full marks in three subjects this semester!" A Tartar boy respectfully handed his school report to the teacher from Liaoning, then solemnly saluted as a member of the Young Pioneers.

And then, a Mongolian "Eji" (mother) came to visit her "son" from Liaoning, draping a warm fur shawl over him and saying affectionately, "Minihu (Mongolian: my son), winter is coming. You'll feel warmer wearing it ..."

So we see:

The son was moved.

The loved ones smiled.

The teachers nodded in satisfaction.

Tacheng — the ancient yet rejuvenating land welcomes another warm and blossoming spring. In such spring, the scent of pomegranate flowers becomes even more fragrant with its seeds clasping so tightly.

Lastly, I remember the story of Zhao Zhen and his son.

"My son returned to me to continue his studies. Although his college entrance examination results weren't ideal this year, he was confident and aimed to retake it next year. He has chosen to study broadcasting and hosting. What comforts me the most is that my son has now returned to me and Tacheng, and he has developed the same love for Xinjiang as me ..."

After Zhao's initial three-year assignment in Xinjiang, he applied to stay longer and remained in Shawan.

There are many team members like him, who also choose to stay and make Tacheng their home ...

They, along with the people of various ethnic groups in Xinjiang, are saying the words we often heard, which make us feel fresher and more attractive each time:

Xinjiang is a great place!

Xinjiang really is a great place!

Xinjiang will always be a great place!

That land, the people

In Tacheng, Xinjiang,

Where makes me want to sing and dance,

I want to lift the wings of thoughts and emotions to write about its beauty with deep affection.

Among these kind, brave, beautiful, determined, and loving people,

I want to express my passion and love thoroughly,

And to keep their smiles in mind forever.

Upper / 97-year-old Manreyamu exchanging ideas with young teachers

Lower / Manreyamu and the author

Upper / Zaitunna introducing traditional Tartar pastries to customers

Lower / Street view in Tacheng

Upper / People of various ethnic groups dancing happily in Tacheng Cultural Square

Lower / Dwellings of the Russian ethnic group in Tacheng

Upper / Traditional Kazakh folk dance- Qiaxiu

Lower / Interior decoration of a Kazakh nomad's yurt

Upper / Hayrat taking her daughter to see the rocking bed

Lower / Hayrat (second from the left) and Wang Juzhen (third from the left)

Upper / An elderly Kazakh falconer

Lower / Mongolian herdsmen in Usu performing Mongolian long-tone folk songs

On June 1, 2021, in the National Flag Guard, Shalekjiang Yiming kissed the national flag and then put his face on it with deep affection

Upper / Shalekjiang Yiming raising the national flag in his yard

Lower / On June 1, 2021, in the honor room of the National Flag Guard, Shalekjiang Yiming told the story of raising the national flag in his own yard to the team members

A group photo of the author and a large family composed of 7 ethnic groups
(first from the left in the back row: Han Lian Han Bing)

Upper / Aerial view of Donggui Square in Hoboksar Mongolian Autonomous County

Lower / Daoerbenelut Ancient City Ruins in Hoboksar Mongolian Autonomous County

Upper / Zhang Qiuliang guarding the graves of his comrades

Lower / Zhang Qiuliang accompanying the mother of a martyr during a memorial service

Upper / Cao Zhenxin at his farm

Lower / Cao Zhenxin with local herdsmen

Upper / Dr. Wuhaas from Yumin County in a winter pasture

Lower / Meilian making a house call

Upper / The winter view of Little Poplar Outpost

Lower / Rotational grazing of Kazakh herders in the wind and snow

Upper/ The author and Duman Heizhati's family

Lower/ Scene from the musical drama *Loving at Home*

Upper / The excavator resembling a toy against the tall snow walls

Lower / A Snowplow clearing snow in the "Devil Wind Zone" of Mayitas

Upper / Wureken's multi-ethnic family

Lower / Ma Xinhua (third from the right) with neighbors of various ethnic groups

Upper / Thousands of people dancing folk dances together in Ganhezi Town, Usu City

Lower / "National Unity, One Family" initiative in Usu City

Upper / People of different ethnic groups enjoying a grand
feast together

Lower / Dance performance of *Ethnic Unity, Hand in Hand*

Cadres in Emin Town, Emin County celebrating the Centenary of the founding of CPC at their relatives' house

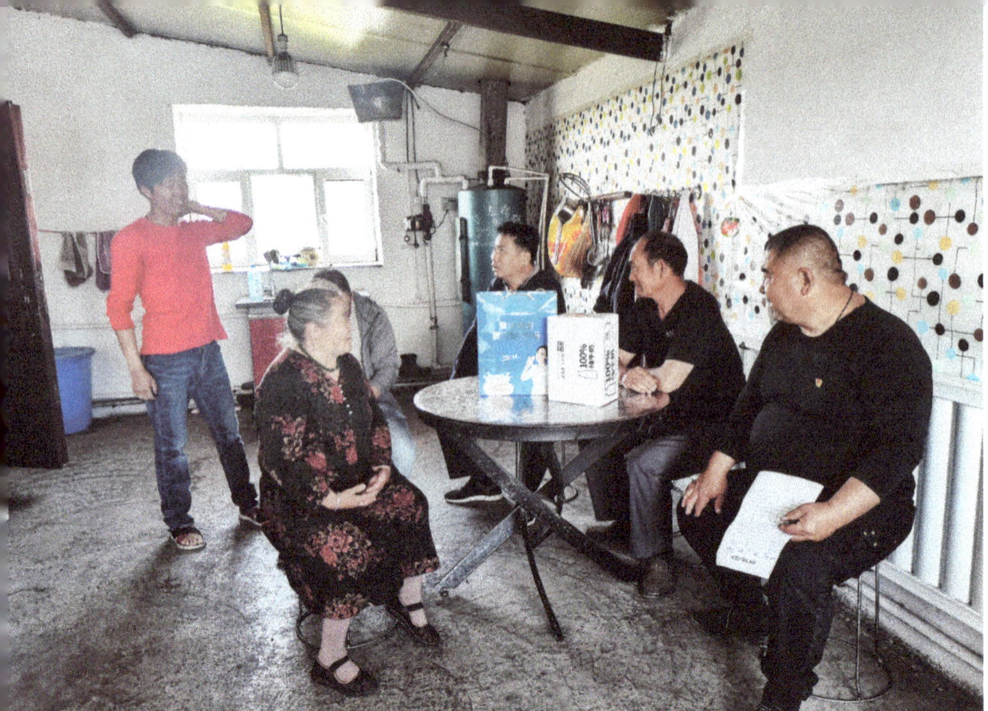

Upper / Courtyard of a villager in Kuertobe Village

Lower / Zhong Ping(first from the right), the Party branch secretary of Kuertobe Village, conducting household surveys

Upper / People in Tacheng who love the Party, the country, and their families

Lower / People of Tacheng from various ethnic groups singing and dancing to celebrate prosperity

Upper / The author with Wei Deyou and his wife

Lower / The Five-Starred Red Flag fluttering high on the roof of a simple mud house

Upper / Wei Deyou shepherding while patrolling the border

Lower / Binoculars and a "chatterbox" are essential tools for Wei Deyou's border patrols

Upper / Building of the People's Hospital in Shawan County, constructed with assistance from Liaoning Province

Lower / Liaoning-assisted project - Little Poplar Middle School in the 9th Division of the Corps

Upper / On April 11, 2009, Bao Zhenping, a teacher from Liaoning at the Third Middle School of Tacheng City, communicated with students during break time

Lower / Xu Xiaoping, a Chinese teacher from Benxi No. 25 Middle School and No. 2 Middle School in Toli County, leading in reading aloud

Postscript

The roots of cedars at Mt. Tianshan are intertwined, and the hearts of people from various ethnic groups are connected. Perhaps because Xinjiang is such a beautiful place, it has aroused the attention of the whole world. Besides its beautiful natural environment, the issue of ethnic unity in Xinjiang has always been a subject of concern. As a writer, I have actually paid close attention to the issue of ethnic unity in Xinjiang for seven or eight years, and I have visited many places in the southern and northern parts of it, witnessing firsthand the touching scenes of harmonious coexistence and family-like bond among the various ethnic groups here. As I was thinking about how to approach and start writing this work of major realistic theme, in 2021, Chen Bing, the Party Committee Secretary and Vice Chairman of the Tacheng Prefecture Literary Federation, extended an invitation for me to "visit and have a look at" Tacheng, showing sincere welcome from leadership of the local government ... This seemingly casual invitation, unexpectedly made me deeply infatuated with the land of Tacheng, henceforth giving rise to this work of reportage literature that primarily focuses on ethnic unity in Xinjiang, with Tacheng as the main narrative subject.

As the pomegranate blossoms, the fragrance permeates the air. I believe that readers will have their own feelings and understanding after reading the contents of this book. Here, I just want to express my most sincere emotions and gratitude to the Party Committee of the Xinjiang Uyghur Autonomous Region, its Publicity Department, and the United Front Work Department, especially to the Tacheng Prefectural Party Committee and Administration leaders for their high level of attention, and to the Tacheng Prefectural Publicity Department and United Front Work Department for their full support. In accordance with the requirements of the Prefectural Party Committee, the Tacheng Prefecture Literary Federation promptly approved the creation of this work, providing me with all-out assistance in interviews, research and creation. The members of the Literary Federation, such as Gurtu and Guo Tiancheng, accompanied me together with Secretary Chen Bing to each interview site all the time, selflessly providing great convenience for my in-depth interviews and research, and I have benefited greatly from their help. In addition, they also did a lot of work behind the scenes during the completion of the manuscript, and I must express my heartfelt thanks to them. Tacheng is the counterpart support area of Liaoning Province, and the Publicity Department of the Liaoning Provincial Party Committee, the Front Command of Liaoning Aid to Xinjiang, and the Liaoning Publishing Group have also provided decisive support and wholehearted assistance in the approval and publication of this book. The careful editing and proofreading by the editors in charge are also touching. Here, I would like to express my deep gratitude to them as well. The four counties and three cities in Tacheng Prefecture, Xinjiang People's Publishing House, and other institutions have also provided great help and support. Naturally, I must thank all the people of Xinjiang from various ethnic groups whom I have interviewed. They are not only the protagonists of this book, but also the true creators of "Xinjiang Stories". I hope readers throughout the country and around the world will get to know them, falling in love with them as well as the beautiful and attractive land they inhabit ...

in the Summer of 2023 in Beijing

Large numbers of exquisite photos appear in this book by courtesy of photographers from Tacheng Prefecture. They are: He Zhenping, Dang Tong, Batu, Chen Wen, Zhang Zongjian, Chen Shuangxi, Xiao Hua, Hu Youming, Wang Gaosheng, Fan Yanshen, Wang Chunlin, Wen Bo, Yao Ming, Zeng Zhaomei, Yan Wenhua, Zhao Hairong, Gao Bo, Zhang Guohui, Dai Jiaomei, and Guan Shujun.